THE

M000198442

Ranjit Desai (1928–1992) was one of the most prolific writers in Marathi. He wrote iconic novels like *Shriman Yogi*, *Radheya*, *Raja Ravi Varma*, *Pavankhind* and *Swami*, among others, and also published twenty collections of short stories and close to twenty plays. He had received many awards including the Maharashtra Rajya Award, the Hari Narayan Apte Award, the Sahitya Akademi Award and the Maharashtra Gaurav Puraskar. The Government of India gave him the Padma Shri in 1973.

Reshma Kulkarni-Pathare is a media professional and an award-winning translator. She has written for several national and international publications including *The Times of India, Bombay Times, The Hindu, Femina, Cosmopolitan, Hello!, DNA India, Maharashtra Times*, among others. She has been syndicated by Celebritext UK, who have published her writing in UAE and Australia. She is a recipient of the Maharashtra Sahitya Parishad Award 2017 for Best Translation. *The Fourth Peshwa* is her seventh work of translation.

THE FOURTH
PESHWA

Ranjit Desai

Translated from the Marathi by
Reshma Kulkarni-Pathare

eka

eka

First published in Marathi as *Swami* in 1962 by Mehta Publishing House

Published in English as *The Fourth Peshwa* in 2019 by Eka, an imprint of Westland Publications Private Limited, by arrangement with Mehta Publishing House

1st Floor, A Block, East Wing, Plot No. 40, SP Infocity, Dr MGR Salai, Perungudi, Kandanchavadi, Chennai 600096

ISBN: 9789388754880

10 9 8 7 6 5 4 3 2 1

Typeset by Jojy Philip, New Delhi 110 015

Printed at Manipal Technologies Limited, Manipal

1

The sultry afternoon was fast giving way to a balmy evening. The sun was in a hurry to dip beyond the horizon. A crimson orange flag, reminiscent of the warm sun, fluttered with immense pride over the Dilli Darwaza of Shaniwarwada. The nail-encrusted gate, which guarded the towers flanking the north face of the grand fort, had been left wide open.

Gangoba Tatya approached Shaniwarwada with quick, furtive steps. A wiry man with hawk-like sharp eyes, Gangoba Tatya began climbing up the huge steps hurriedly. A trusted lieutenant of the Holkars, Gangoba Tatya was known to enjoy the trust and favour of Raghobadada. Seeing Gangoba Tatya, private secretary Dattopant promptly came forward and bowed to greet the man. Accepting the greetings, Tatya asked, 'Has the durbar commenced?'

'Not yet, but all the dignitaries have arrived. We are waiting for Shrimant to begin.'

Gangoba Tatya smiled ruefully and said, 'Dattopant, you are new here. You wouldn't know ...'

'I didn't get you, sir,' said Dattopant.

'You should have been here when Nanasaheb was around. Oh, the glory! The pomp! Well … how the times have changed! We are a mere shadow of our glorious past. It is a sorry state of affairs.'

Seeing Gangoba Tatya in a pensive mood, Dattopant kept quiet. Tatya remarked, changing his tone, 'Anyway, I don't want to reach late and be frowned upon by the other courtiers.'

As Tatya hurried forward, Dattopant coughed meaningfully and called out, 'Tatya!'

'What is it?'

'Tatya, I'm sorry, but I cannot allow you to enter through this door.' Tatya raised a questioning eyebrow in response.

Dattopant squirmed as he relayed, 'It was just yesterday that Shrimant decreed that only those who have the privilege of entering through the Dilli Darwaza may do so. Please do not mind, but you will have to enter through the Ganesha Darwaza.'

Gangoba Tatya's rage flared up in an instant, but he replied, composing himself, 'I see. If Shrimant wishes so, I will enter through the Ganesha Darwaza.' He turned around and started descending the steps as his handcrafted sandals made a distinctively disapproving clicking sound against the stone steps.

Tatya's sandals were covered in dust by the time he had traipsed through half the fort's exterior to reach the Ganesha Darwaza. He dusted his sandals, stepped inside and started walking towards the Ganesha Mahal. The courtroom was up to quorum. All the revered courtiers and lieutenants were already seated at their designated positions.

It was a beautiful courtroom. Intricately carved rosewood pillars held up its stately roof, which narrowed down, leaning towards the Peshwa's throne and canopying the huge idol of Lord Ganesha that loomed over it. The walls of the Ganesha Mahal were beautified with scenes from the Ramayana and the Mahabharata. The entryway from the main door of the Ganesha Mahal right up to the Peshwa's throne was laid with rich red carpets. On both sides of the throne were smaller chairs and seats for the courtiers.

As the curtain towards the left of the throne swished a little, the court instantly fell silent in reverence. The guards announced the arrival of Shrimant Madhavrao Peshwa:

'Ba-adab, baa-mulahija, hoshiyaar!
Nigah rakho!
Shrimant Madhavrao Ballal Pantapradhan
Tashreef laate hain!'

All eyes were on the curtain. A few seconds later, two guards walked out, taking muffled steps.

In a flash, all the courtiers stood to attention as Shrimant Madhavrao Peshwa—the ruler himself, entered the court. Everyone bowed their heads in obeisance.

Madhavrao walked towards the throne, accepting the mujras of his courtiers. Before taking his seat, he prayed to the idol of Lord Ganesha towering over him and then, saluting the throne with respect, sat down.

The courtiers took their seats and looked expectantly at the Peshwa. He was hardly sixteen years old. A heavy moustache was, perhaps, years from making its presence felt over his lips. Fair-skinned with a tall, wiry build that showed his devotion to regular exercise, Madhavrao surveyed the court through his discerning, incisive eyes. The diamonds in the aigrette of his pugree glistened, adding to his allure, as did the square ornament in his ear and a string of beautiful shiny pearls on his neck. The rows of small pearls hanging from one side of his pugree brushed against his ear. The embroidered borders of his smooth muslin undercoat peeked out from under the rich velvet tunic that he wore over his pleated pyjamas.

He said, looking at Tryambakrao Pethe, 'Mama, let the durbar commence now.'

'But ...' Tryambakrao stammered in response.

'What?' queried Madhavrao.

'Well, Dadasaheb has not yet arrived—'

'So what?' interrupted the Peshwa.

'And even Sakharambapu is yet to come ...'

Madhavrao frowned and then gestured Tryambakrao to start the proceedings, saying, 'Never mind. Let us begin.'

'As His Majesty wishes!' Tryambakrao saluted the Peshwa and took three steps back. Suddenly, the whole court got to its feet. Madhavrao glanced at the door to see Raghobadada entering agitatedly, followed by Sakharambapu Bokil, who was trying hard to keep pace with Raghobadada while trying to hold the belt on his waist from slipping past the tunic. Raghobadada accepted the salutations of the courtiers as he whizzed across to his designated seat. Sakharambapu stood to the Peshwa's left and muttered, 'Shrimant ...'

Ignoring his salute, Madhavrao said, 'Bapu, let us start. We have kept everyone waiting for long.'

An ashen Bapu signalled the court proceedings to begin.

The day's work for the durbar was about to close, when suddenly Dinkar Mahadev stood up. He ignored Sakharambapu's frown and saluted the Peshwa, saying, 'With due apologies, I would like to propose retirement. My advanced age is not allowing me to take the onus of such an important task. I request the Peshwa to relieve me of the duty of securing the royal treasury.'

Madhavrao laughed and asked, 'Dinkarrao, exactly how old are you? I certainly do not think you are that old.'

'Shrimant, as I said earlier, I'm finding it increasingly difficult to shoulder this responsibility ... It is burdening me—'

Sakharambapu rudely interrupted, 'Do you think this request is important enough to be presented in the official durbar? Couldn't you wait to tell us? Maybe put in a letter of appeal? We would have definitely thought about it and perhaps released you from the task if we felt it right ...'

'But, Shrimant ...' Dinkarrao tried requesting Madhavrao again, ignoring Bapu in the process.

Bapu butted in, 'Dinkarrao, sit down and keep quiet! This is the durbar of Shrimant Madhavrao Peshwa, not your private parlour to have prolonged discussions on futile topics. An experienced person like you having to be told this is a matter of shame indeed.'

'Indeed!' Madhavrao, who had been listening to this conversation with his head bowed, enjoying the fragrance of a beautiful rose, bellowed all of a sudden.

His voice made Sakharambapu stop short.

The genteel look on Madhavrao's face had been replaced by an aggressive one. His tone went from soft to commanding as he said, 'Sakharambapu! What you are saying is right, but it applies to you as well. When a request is put forth, it is we, the Peshwa, who decide what to do about it, not you. You are there to give us advice if we need it. If you decree decisions in our presence, that will be considered an insult to this durbar.' The deliberate use of 'we' signified the prestige attached to the post of the Peshwa.

Sakharambapu lowered his head in shame. 'Understood, Sarkar.'

Madhavrao then turned to Dinkarrao. 'Dinkarrao, you may speak without fear. Why do you wish to retire from our service?'

Dinkarrao paused for a moment to gather his thoughts. 'Shrimant, the treasury of the Peshwas is a very big responsibility. On various festive or special occasions, many priceless ornaments are sent out to important dignitaries. If we do not get written receipts, it becomes difficult to keep track of them. The Peshwas have been blessed by the Almighty with immense wealth. So a couple of ornaments gone missing will hardly create a dent in the Peshwas' fortune, but a common man like me will go to the gallows for a mistake that I didn't even commit.'

Madhavrao pondered over Dinkarrao's statement for a moment and said, 'The system is very clear. Requests for ornaments are to be submitted in a written form, and their receipts are also to be sent in a written form. At least, that is what I have always believed. So where does the problem lie?'

Dinkarrao answered plaintively, 'The problem lies in the fact that this system is not followed religiously.'

Hearing this, Raghobadada stood up in an instant, his face red with rage. Turning towards Dinkarrao, he yelled,

'Why are you speaking in riddles? Say directly whatever you have to! Say that we do not give you the receipts! Go on, say it!'

Wanting to dispel an unpleasant situation as fast as possible, Sakharambapu raced towards Dinkarrao. 'Take your request back, please. The systems have to be bent a little to accommodate a few people who are privileged to enjoy the trust of the higher powers. It happens everywhere.'

By then, Dinkarrao was trembling in fear. He didn't know what to do.

Madhavrao rose from his throne. 'Bapu! Do not forget that this is the durbar and the throne of the Peshwas! If anybody insults this court and this throne, he will be punished irrespective of his age, position and trust placed in him by us. I hope this is very clear. Dinkarrao, exceptions are to be made but on very rare occasions, and when accompanied by genuine reasons. I want you to manage the treasury with the same discipline with which you have been running it all these years. Not even the Peshwas themselves shall be an exception to those rules. I decree this order to be followed from now and here.'

Madhavrao climbed down from the steps of his throne and, before the courtiers could comprehend what had transpired, left the durbar, with his guards running in tow.

Once Madhavrao was out of sight, the court was abuzz with chatter. A furious Raghobadada walked out with Sakharambapu trailing behind.

The durbar had ended.

Madhavrao was shaking with rage by the time he reached the Ganesha Mahal. His face was red with fury. He turned in the direction of the fountain and walked towards the prayer hall. On his way, he passed several servants who sat chatting idly. No one had expected the durbar to end so soon. They snapped to attention on seeing him, but he ignored them. He looked forward to meeting his mother, Gopikabai.

Maina was standing guard outside the main door to Gopikabai's palace.

The Peshwa asked, 'Maina, is Matoshree in her chambers?'

'Ji, Matoshree just arrived some time back,' replied Maina.

'All right! Tell her I'm here to see her.'

'Ji, Sarkar.'

Maina walked inside to convey the message and soon returned to tell Madhavrao that Matoshree had beckoned him to her chambers. Madhavrao slightly parted the pearl-studded curtain covering the doorway to Gopikabai's private chambers and, bowing low, entered. His mother was sitting with royal elegance on a baithak, a low-seated plush chair. While Gopikabai was not old, early widowhood had added a patina of maturity to her fair-skinned visage and mannerisms. Her face lit up on seeing her beloved son. Madhavrao touched his mother's feet reverently.

'May God bestow his bounties upon you, my child,' she said. Madhavrao took his seat. Gopikabai's personal maid, Vithi, was standing in rapt attention near her mistress, and next to her, an adolescent girl stood hesitantly with her head covered with the pallu of her saree. Madhavrao happened to glance at the girl's feet and saw her nervously scratching the carpet with her toe. Sensing her unease at his presence,

Madhavrao instantly got up and apologised to Gopikabai, saying, 'I'm very sorry, Matoshree. I was not aware that you were hosting a guest. I shall take your leave.'

Hearing this, Gopikabai began to laugh. Vithi covered her mouth with her saree and joined in the laughter surreptitiously. Madhavrao was befuddled.

Seeing her son's predicament, Gopikabai said, 'Quite amazing that the Peshwa does not recognise his own wife!' Then, turning to the girl, she said, 'Ramabai, bring the aarti for Madhavrao.'

Vithi brought out the salver containing everything required for the aarti. Ramabai stood in front of Madhavrao with the salver. Madhavrao glanced down at the face of his wife, which was now free from the folds of her pallu, and was once again struck by her solemn, pure beauty. Ramabai was hardly a stranger to Madhavrao. As a child, he had seen her in a skirt and blouse as they played together. Later, when he had assumed charge as the Peshwa, Madhavrao had noticed Ramabai looking beautiful in her ornate Paithani-shaalu sarees. But today she looked ethereal! Her face glowed with a unique beauty, and it had nothing to do with the stunning ornaments she was wearing. A diamond necklace sparkled on Ramabai's slender neck. An intricately crafted gold amulet made her arm look even more delicate. The precious stones studded in her nose pin shone with glory.

Realising that he had been staring at his wife for quite some time, Madhavrao snapped to attention and accepted the betel leaf held in front of him. The aarti was over.

'Matoshree, I don't understand the reason for today's aarti,' Madhavrao said as they resumed their places. 'Is it a special occasion?'

'Madhava, you may very well say so! Although it has been several days since you were coronated, the ritual was completed in the true sense today,' said Gopikabai mysteriously.

'I don't get you, Matoshree.'

'Today Shaniwarwada got its Peshwa back in the true sense. For the last two months, I had lost hope completely. My only wish was that you carry on the legacy left behind by your respected father, that you prove to be as capable as your brother, Vishwasrao.'

'Are we beyond your wishes, Matoshree?'

'No, you aren't, my son. I know that. But ...'

The conversation was cut short by Vithi running in breathlessly, announcing, 'Dadasaheb Maharaj has come.'

'Please escort him in,' commanded Gopikabai.

Ramabai adjusted her pallu reverentially, and Madhavrao got up from his seat as Raghobadada entered.

'Salutations, Vahinisaheb.'

'God bless you. Come, please sit down.'

Raghobadada threw a sharp glance at Madhavrao and then at the salver. Ramabai touched his feet. Raghobadada muttered something in blessing and said, looking at Gopikabai, 'Vahinisaheb, it seems that you just finished doing the aarti for Madhavrao.'

'Yes, it is an auspicious full-moon day, and the durbar was also held today.'

'I agree. And Madhavrao has also displayed a fantastic feat in today's durbar by insulting us, his uncle!' Raghobadada exclaimed with scorn.

'Kaka! I would never think of insulting you, let alone do it!' exclaimed Madhavrao.

Raghobadada smiled sarcastically. 'Oh, is that so? Then, Madhavrao, what was it that happened in the durbar today if not an insult? Pray, tell us.'

Gopikabai stepped in at that moment. 'I, too, was present in the court. I do not think Madhava insulted you. In fact, looking at the righteous stand he took, you should have been proud of him.'

Hearing his sister-in-law's stern admonishing, Raghobadada adopted a softer approach. 'True, Vahinisaheb. But Madhavrao should not get too big for his boots. The way he spoke to Sakharambapu today ... Who knows, tomorrow he may behave the same with us too.'

Madhavrao interjected. 'Kaka! Don't I understand the difference between you and Bapu?'

'Madhava, I think you are forgetting that when you got adorned with the attire of a Peshwa, Sakharambapu, too, got adorned with the position of your chief manager,' remarked Raghobadada.

'But the manager has to do what the Peshwa decides. If the manager starts taking decisions, then what is the use of a Peshwa sitting on the throne?'

'Oh! So our word holds no significance now, is it?'

'I certainly do not mean that, Kaka,' said Madhavrao in a pained voice. 'There will be no other joy for us than to uphold your command. Would you like us to beg forgiveness from Sakharambapu?'

Raghobadada's visage changed colour in an instant. He chuckled and said, 'No, no, Madhava. How will I ever ask that of you? Oh! How confounded you look, son. I was simply testing you. In fact, if you continue ruling with such righteousness, a big responsibility will be off our shoulders in no time. Our only wish is that the Lord frees us from these huge burdens now.' Saying this, he saluted Gopikabai and said, 'Bapu is waiting for me. Please allow me to take your leave.'

Madhavrao bowed low to offer his obeisance to Raghobadada. Ramabai, too, touched his feet. Raghobadada left the chambers.

Madhavrao touched Gopikabai's feet, when she asked, 'You are going to Theur, aren't you?'

'Yes, we will be leaving on Sunday. On Monday, we will conduct the abhishek ritual in honour of the Lord and then return on Tuesday.'

'Who all are accompanying you?'

'We have not yet decided, but, I think, Tryambakmama, Gopalrao ...' replied Madhavrao.

'Well, then, why don't you take Rama along? She, too, will be able to take the Lord's blessings, and you will get to be in each other's company,' Gopikabai suggested, smiling.

Madhavrao cast a glance at Ramabai and answered, 'Your wish is my command, Matoshree!' Saying this, he walked out of the chambers.

Soon, dusk began to fall. Gopikabai asked Vithi to light the lamps.

Ramabai got up and said, 'I will take your leave now ...'

Hearing this, Gopikabai held her hands lovingly and said, 'Sit with us for a while. Maina ...'

'Yes, Matoshree?'

'Make sure that when your madam goes back to her chambers, you ward off all evil with your ritual. She is looking so radiant today that I'm afraid I myself may have cast an evil eye on her unbeknownst!'

Maina chuckled softly and left Gopikabai's chambers. Outside, Vithi was illuminating the passageway with huge brass lanterns. The lanterns in Gopikabai's chambers had already been lit, and their soft flames were casting a beautiful glow on Ramabai's face. Gopikabai admired the serene beauty, a smile of satisfaction playing upon her lips.

Ramabai caught her mother-in-law's eye and suddenly, without suppressing the giggle that leapt to her lips, hugged Gopikabai lovingly.

'Keep smiling like this always, dear child. May you and Madhava have a wonderful life together, filled with love and laughter.'

⚗

Sakharambapu was standing near a window in Raghobadada's palace. His gaze was fixed on Madhavrao's palace to the west. Slowly, he turned his attention towards the building that stretched from Madhavrao's palace right up to Gopikabai's palace. All the windows and arches were bathed in the glow of the lamps lit within. The hustle-bustle going on inside could be seen from a distance. The courtyard below was lit up with flambeaus, the guards on duty were clearly visible in their bright light.

Twirling his moustache, Bapu observed this silently. A rustling sound behind him made him turn. Sakharambapu straightened himself up to greet Anandibai as she entered, and said, 'Namaskar, Vahinisaheb!'

'Bapu, when did you come?' Anandibai queried.

'Just a few minutes back.'

'And where is he?' she asked, referring to her husband, Raghoba.

'I'm not sure, but I think he has gone to Gopikabai's palace.'

'Oh, I remember now. I heard he was planning to visit her. Please, Bapu, why don't you sit down," Anandibai gestured to a seat nearby.

But Bapu did not sit. He looked pensive. Seeing him so, Anandibai smiled and asked, 'How did the durbar go?'

Without answering her directly, Bapu counter-questioned, 'You were there, Vahinisaheb ... weren't you?'

'Yes, I was, but what do I understand of all those vexing issues?'

'What vexing issues are you talking about exactly?'

Hearing Raghobadada's voice, Anandibai looked up, ashen. She got up from her seat and, wrapping the pallu of her saree around her shoulders, answered, 'No, nothing. I was just asking Bapu how the durbar was today.'

'You were there, Anandibai, weren't you?' Raghobadada asked.

'Oh, yes, I was. And I was really impressed with the way Bapu commanded the situation.'

'Madhavrao is young, a mere child, rather. He does not realise what he is saying,' commented Raghobadada.

'Shrimant should not take this matter so lightly. A child's feet are seen in the cradle itself,' Bapu said pointedly.

Handing over his pugree to Anandibai, Raghobadada turned to Bapu and asked him with a frown, 'What exactly are you trying to say?'

'Nothing, Shrimant. I just hope that the treatment that was meted out to me in court today won't come your way any time soon.'

'It won't matter to me, Bapu. I trust Madhava ... Whatever he decides is going to be for the best,' replied Raghoba.

Hearing this, Bapu leapt up from his seat, exclaiming, 'Did you hear that, Vahinisaheb? I have never seen such a humble soul in my life! Dadasaheb could have become the Peshwa if he had wanted to, but instead, he chose to give it away to his "deserving" nephew. And what does he get in return? Insults!'

Before Anandibai could reply, Raghobadada snapped, 'You are making a mountain out of a molehill, Bapu. It was a simple matter of the treasury ...'

'Simple? I'm sorry, Dadasaheb, but you should not take this matter so lightly. It is best to recognise a snake in the stable before he—'

'Bapu!' Raghobadada roared. 'Watch what you are saying! Who are you trying to call a snake?'

Taken aback by Raghoba's sudden rage, Bapu composed himself and, plastering a fake smile on his face, said, 'See, Vahinisaheb? This is how things get misconstrued. I was only talking about Dinkarrao, but Shrimant here thought something else ...'

'Oh, I didn't realise that,' Raghobadada muttered, still lost in thought. 'What were you saying about Dinkarrao?'

'You thought Dinkarrao was your own man; you trusted him. And see what he did at the last moment? He behaved like the two-faced snake that he is! And this is not the first time that such treachery has taken place.'

'Treachery?' asked Raghobadada incredulously.

'Yes. Last night, Shrimant Peshwa was in the office burning the midnight oil. I'm sure this plan must have been etched out there itself. Otherwise, how would Dinkarrao ever dare to ask a question I was unaware of?' said Bapu, gnashing his teeth.

'You are still being evasive, Bapu. Get to the point, please.'

'The point is simple, Dadasaheb. It was all pre-decided that Dinkarrao would ask the question and Madhavrao would fan the fires of the issue … what else?'

Raghobadada grew thoughtful. After some time, he said, 'It was my idea to engage Madhava in office work.'

'Hmm …' sighed Bapu, cautious not to say more.

'I thought that if Madhava was kept busy with office work, he would not get time to pay attention to the administrative and political machinations.'

'I'm sorry to say this, Dadasaheb, but I think that is where you went wrong. I had forewarned you that this decision of yours would yield adverse results. But you didn't trust me then.'

'What are you talking about?' snapped Raghobadada.

'Time will tell, sir, time will tell. You are as aware as I am about Madhavrao's expertise in official matters. Even the senior-most clerks quake with fear when they realise that Madhavrao is going to inspect their work. And mind you, he always conducts surprise checks. That keeps everyone on their toes.'

'So? How does that matter? How is that going to allow him to interfere in the administrative mechanisms?'

Sakharambapu jumped up, exclaiming, 'How does it matter? Are you really asking me this, Dadasaheb? The Peshwa has got access to all official documents and information. From the weekly household expenses to the annual budget of our army, he is in the know of every tiny detail. In fact, he has the state's balance sheet on the tip of his tongue. Do you think he will allow us to function without interference for long?'

Sakharambapu's tirade had made Raghobadada quite uneasy. He composed himself and said, 'I trust Madhava ...'

Anandibai, who had been listening to this heated exchange silently, now piped in, saying, 'That trust has long withered away in Panipat. What is the use of nurturing a long-dead emotion?'

Raghobadada turned to his wife and exclaimed, 'What are you saying? Do you not trust Madhava?'

'Oh yes, I do trust him,' Anandibai said in a faux sweet tone. 'But do not forget that he is a lion cub. And his claws are getting sharper by the day. It will be beneficial to us all if you opened your eyes and noticed this transformation.'

'Anandibai, I was not aware that you harboured such antagonistic views towards Madhava,' commented Raghobadada.

Anandibai replied in soothing tones, 'I do not harbour any antagonism towards Madhava. He is like a son to me. But I'm not the kind of wife who will not react when her husband is insulted in court. I would have expressed the same rage had it been my own son in place of Madhava.'

Raghobadada was pleased to hear this. He smiled and said, 'And what if I told you that Madhava apologised to me for his behaviour?'

'Really?' Anandibai asked incredulously.

'He did!' continued Dada with an air of pride. 'That is exactly why I had gone to Vahinisaheb's palace immediately after the durbar had ended.'

'And Shrimant was there? You must have found out about Sunday's plans then.'

'What plans?' Raghobadada asked, a little confused.

'Oh, that means you are not going?' Sakharambapu chimed in.

'Going where?'

'Theur.'

'Oh, that! I know about that,' Raghobadada replied curtly.

'So you will be going too?' Anandibai asked eagerly.

'For what? I don't have any work there.'

'That's true ...' Sakharambapu muttered under his breath.

'Bapu!' roared Raghobadada.

'I'm sorry, Shrimant. Please forgive me. But I think you should know that Pethe, Nana, Ghorpade, Moroba, Patwardhan, Ramshastri—all these people will be accompanying Shrimant Peshwa to Theur.'

'Anyone from our side going along?' asked Raghobadada.

Bapu shook his head. 'No. I was told that someone responsible needs to stay back here, hence even I was not asked to go.'

'Oh, is that so? Well, what do we do now?'

Bapu smiled as he answered, 'Do not worry, Shrimant. Even though none of us are going, I have arranged for every little detail from Theur to reach us at lightning speed.'

At that moment, a servant came in and announced, 'Sarkar, Gulabrao has arrived.'

'Send him in,' ordered Raghobadada.

Anandibai got up to go to her chambers. Seeing this, Raghobadada turned to her and asked, 'Why are you going inside? Gulabrao is hardly a stranger to us ...'

'Maybe not to you,' replied Anandibai curtly and swiftly went inside.

Sakharambapu, too, got up in haste; he bowed low to offer salutations to Raghobadada, asking his permission to leave. Raghobadada did not stop him. Sakharambapu exited just as Gulabrao entered through the main door.

'Gulabrao! We have been waiting for you since morning. What took you so long?' asked Raghobadada.

'My apologies, Shrimant! Circumstances went beyond my control. I would never neglect your orders.'

'Circumstances went beyond your control?' Raghobadada frowned. 'Do you mean to say the work was not done?'

Gulabrao grinned. 'How is that possible, Shrimant? An invitation from the royal house is enough to make even the most arrogant poor person come knocking! Yes, Radhi was being a bit more arrogant than others. But she was cowed after I reprimanded her.'

Raghobadada's face turned ashen. 'Shh! Don't talk so loudly. Even the walls have ears.'

Now it was Gulabrao's turn to feel embarrassed. He whispered, 'But, Shrimant, she is asking for a bit more than ...'

'That is not a worry. Just bring her when I ask you to. You may go now!'

'Ji, Sarkar,' said Gulabrao, as he left, bowing in a mujra before Raghobadada.

Raghobadada turned pink with joy. He reclined on his bolster and pulled the silver platter of betel leaves towards himself.

At that moment, Anandibai entered the room. 'Gulabrao has left already, has he?'

'Yes,' answered Raghobadada. 'He was here for some work related to the office.' Gauging her good mood, Raghobadada continued, 'I forgot to ask you something.'

'Yes?'

'You wanted one more maid, didn't you? I have arranged for it today.'

Anandibai's face turned red with rage and she snapped, 'Oh! Is that why Gulabrao had come? As if we were indeed falling short of maids. Do whatever pleases you. Who am I to say anything?'

As Anandibai strode off into her chambers in a huff, Raghobadada made a big show of calling after her. Seeing that his wife was in no mood to listen, Dada reclined on the bolster again, the smile on his face was akin to that of a cat who has got all the cream.

∞

Madhavrao stirred in his sleep. A lantern glowed in one corner of the palace, but everything else was cloaked in darkness and silence. He woke up, glanced out of the window and sat up in bed, drawing his blanket closer for warmth. He couldn't fathom what had caused him to rouse from sleep so early. As Madhavrao sat pondering, he heard the dulcet tones of a song. Who was singing so beautifully, and at such an early hour? He wrapped a shawl around himself and made his way out of the bedroom. Soon, he came to the main door of the palace. Shripati, the guard, was dozing there. Seeing Madhavrao looming over him, Shripati fumbled to his feet and hurriedly saluted.

'Shripati, who is singing?'

'Sarkar?' Shripati asked in confusion.

'Who else is awake?'

'Only a few people at Aaisaheb's palace must be awake at this time,' replied the guard.

The palace and its spacious corridors and verandahs glowed in the soft light of the brass lanterns. Madhavrao walked in the direction of the melodious voice. It was just 3 a.m. They arrived at the main staircase that led to the courtyard. Shripati took a big lantern and led Madhavrao down the staircase into the courtyard. The voice was coming from the Ganesha Mahal.

Guards napping in the way were startled to see Madhavrao at this hour. They jumped to their feet to salute, but Madhavrao paid no attention. He was drawn to the source of the music.

'Bol naa laagi papiha …'

Madhavrao was deeply moved by the melodious voice. It seemed to come from the soul. A cool breeze blew through the peaceful surroundings, making the voice sound even more magical. Madhavrao walked rapidly towards the main entrance of the palace. He looked around as he entered. Seeing a door open, he peeped inside.

The throne in the Ganesha Mahal was glowing in the light of freshly lit brass lanterns. The idol of Lord Ganesha was bathed in radiance. The royal bard sat in front of the throne, his tanpura in hand. The entire palace reverberated with his soulful voice.

Madhavrao stood at the door, keenly observing the bard as he now switched to a rapid-paced melody.

'*Baajo re baajo, mandarwaa …*'

The bard was swaying, even the most difficult notes emanated from his throat with the utmost ease.

After a long time, the bard snapped out of his trance. He lifted his tanpura and rose. Bowing low in reverence before the idol of Lord Ganesha, he turned to leave. He was surprised to see Madhavrao smiling at him. The bard walked forward and fell at Madhavrao's feet.

'What are you doing? Stand up,' ordered Madhavrao.

'Shrimant, please forgive me.'

'For what?'

'I came here too early … started humming … and then, before I knew it, slipped into singing. I come here to sing the bhoopali, but today … Shrimant, I did not intend to wake you.'

'What were you singing?'

'Shuddha-kalyan,' the bard replied, quoting the raga he was singing.

'You sing the bhoopali every day?'

'Yes, Shrimant.'

'Do you study music?'

'Yes, Shrimant,' croaked the bard in fear. Where was this conversation going?

'Don't be afraid,' Madhavrao said, smiling. 'Keep training in music. Do not leave it midway. You have a beautiful voice. It does not matter that you did not start with a bhoopali. Who is to say that God is stirred only by a particular raga? It is emotions that stir the Lord, not notes. We never studied music, but we know one thing for sure: in addition to knowledge of music, your voice has been blessed with rare emotions. No wonder a man who was sleeping soundly was stirred enough to rouse from sleep and drawn all the way here! From today, you are no longer bound to sing only the bhoopali. Sing what you feel like. Unshackle your voice from all compulsions. Sing freely. Sing from your heart. Sing such that the Lord himself smiles upon you. We will be very happy with that. What is your name?'

'Moreshwar.'

'Moreshwar, be sure to meet the manager tomorrow. He will compensate you for your services. We shall talk to him today.'

Moreshwar bowed low in salutation to Madhavrao.

He looked in awe at Madhavrao's receding figure as he exited the palace. He could not believe what had just happened.

※

Madhavrao finished his exercise, daily ablutions and his rituals by sunrise. He returned to his private chambers to find Ramabai waiting for him with his tunic in hand. She cast a glance at her husband's muscular frame and offered the tunic to him.

Madhavrao asked, 'Has Matoshree finished her puja?'

'Long back! She has been waiting for you, wondering what has caused your delay today.'

'Yes, we were a bit delayed.' Madhavrao sat down, and Ramabai promptly picked up a tumbler of milk kept on a rosewood tripod nearby and handed it to him.

'Sasubai was saying we are going to Theur ...'

'We are. All arrangements have been made. We have also informed Matoshree accordingly.'

'Yes, but ... Sasubai was saying, "Double-check with Madhava. He is known to alter plans at the last minute."'

Madhavrao burst out laughing at the imitation of Matoshree, but Ramabai was perplexed at his reaction.

Madhavrao explained, 'I was laughing at the fact that Matoshree thinks I am so unpredictable! Do not worry. All arrangements are in place. Your palanquins will go ahead. I shall follow and reach Theur by 2 p.m.'

'Can I take Ramjikaka along?' asked Ramabai.

'Of course, why not? I will tell the concerned officers to make arrangements for him too. Now, shall we go visit Matoshree?'

They set off for Gopikabai's palace. Ramabai trailed behind Madhavrao with the pallu of her saree held firmly over her shoulders.

On reaching the palace, they were asked by Gopikabai, 'Both of you are leaving for Theur today, aren't you?'

Madhavrao answered, 'No, Matoshree. Ramabai will leave earlier; I shall follow after a while.'

'That means you are sending this young girl alone, Madhava?'

'No, Matoshree. Tryambakmama, Shastribuva and some others are going along with Ramabai.'

'And who is accompanying you?'

'Gopalrao, Ghorpade and a couple more will be coming with me. We will conduct the abhishek tomorrow and be back by evening.'

'Have a safe journey, children!' Gopikabai blessed them.

Madhavrao took his mother's leave. Shaniwarwada bustled with activity. Servants rushed about their daily tasks. Most of the royalty seemed to have finished their daily rituals and were settling down to their work of the day. Instead of going to his palace, Madhavrao walked towards the courtyard used by the troops. Servants bowed in salutation as he passed by. Madhavrao noticed the golden pennon swaying with pride over the stone-hewn tower. Glancing upwards, he saw the official royal saffron flag swaying over the palace's main gateway. Suddenly, he heard a rustle behind him. Moroba and Nana were standing there.

They both folded their hands in respect. Madhavrao reciprocated the gesture and asked, 'What happened, Nana?'

Moroba answered, 'Shrimant, Ramshastri, Gopalrao Patwardhan and Tryambakrao have all come to the court.'

'Fine, I'll be there in a moment.'

Madhavrao entered the court to find everyone waiting for him. They bowed in mujra. Madhavrao asked Ramshastri, 'Shastribuva, when did you come?'

'We were here as you requested, Shrimant.'

'My puja went on for longer than usual today.'

'That's fine, Shrimant. But don't we have to leave for Theur today?'

'Yes, of course! Nana, have all arrangements been made?'

'Shrimant, our people went to Theur yesterday. They have sent messages accordingly. We are waiting for the arrangements to be made here …'

'Shastribuva, Nana, Mama and you should go ahead with Ramabai. I will follow, along with Ghorpade and Gopalrao, after the sun goes down.'

'As you please, Shrimant,' said Ramshastri.

⊗

The sun was rising. Madhavrao stood in the balcony of his chambers. He could see the guards standing at their guard-post near the Ganesha Darwaza. A beautifully decorated palanquin was right in front of the gate. Its silver-gold embroidery shone in the bright sunlight. Another simpler palanquin was placed beside it. Palanquin-bearers wearing thick turbans, breeches and tight trousers stood near them. Outside the Ganesha Mahal, several bullock carts waited. From the balcony, Madhavrao saw Ramjikaka walking briskly towards the palanquins. The guards parted to make way for Ramabai, who had stepped out of Gopikabai's palace with a retinue of maidservants walking in front of and behind her. Apart from the maidservants, Madhavrao could also see five or six other women walking towards the palanquins. They were followed by Tryambakrao Pethe, who hurried while he held his pugree in one hand.

Ramabai sat in her ornate palanquin. Immediately, the drapes were dropped. A portly woman dressed in a Paithani saree sat in the simpler palanquin.

'Who is she, Shripati?' asked Madhavrao, unable to recognise the lady from afar.

'Mamisaheb, Shrimant.'

'Rastemami?'

'Yes, Shrimant.'

Tryambakmama signalled to the palanquin-bearers, who came forward instantly and hoisted the palanquins on their shoulders. Shastribuva and Nana sat in the bullock carts. A few horsemen hoisted themselves onto their horses, and the procession started to leave Shaniwarwada.

Madhavrao kept waiting on the balcony till the sounds of the horses' hooves and the bells woven around the bullocks' necks grew feeble. Then, he went inside.

⚭

Madhavrao went to the court mid-morning. Gopalrao Patwardhan and Ghorpade were waiting for him. The emeralds in the aigrette of Madhavrao's pugree shone brightly. He had worn a rich muslin pleated tunic with tight trousers. The pearl-studded neckpiece was breathtaking. As Madhavrao began to step out of the court, a servant rushed to get his embroidered footwear. He walked towards the Dilli Darwaza, with Ghorpade and Patwardhan following, and found Malharrao Raste there.

Madhavrao exclaimed, 'Mama! I didn't think you would be joining us!'

'How could I not? Yesterday itself Taisaheb instructed us to accompany you.'

'Yes, I am aware. Mamisaheb has gone ahead. Should we, too, leave now?' asked Madhavrao.

'As you please, Shrimant.'

'Let's leave, then.'

Twenty-five horsemen were standing at Madhavrao's service, with the reins of their regal horses firmly in hand. As Madhavrao descended the steps of the Dilli Darwaza, a servant brought his thoroughbred horse forward. On his back was a velvet saddle. Madhavrao mounted his horse and the others followed suit. The Peshwa raised his head to glance at the royal flag fluttering proudly over the palace gateway. He gave his horse a gentle nudge, the others following behind. As they entered the busy lanes of Pune city, Madhavrao and his entourage slowed down. People bowed in salutation, seeing him riding in their midst. Soon, the city was left behind and the road to Theur reverberated with the sound of the horses' hooves.

⚭

It was evening by the time this cavalcade broke off the main road to branch into a smaller one that led to Theur. Soon, the village grew visible in the distance. On seeing the crest of the main temple of Theur, Madhavrao slowed down and folded his hands in reverence to the Lord. The village of Theur was located on a small hillock surrounded by emerald greenery. A glance at the upper floors of the mansion there brought a smile to Madhavrao's lips. He sped his horse towards Theur with the others following behind. The village got to know about the Peshwa's arrival due to the galloping sound of hooves. People thronged the entrance of the village to greet their ruler. When Madhavrao arrived at the gates of the mansion, a servant promptly walked ahead and took charge of his horse. Madhavrao alighted as ceremonial drums played in his honour. Nana, Ramshastri and the others were waiting to welcome the Peshwa inside.

'Nana, good to see you. When did you all arrive?' said Madhavrao.

'We reached before noon, Shrimant.'

'That's good!' Madhavrao glanced behind Nana to see Ramji standing there, fidgeting with the small pouch he carried around.

'Ramji, where is everybody?'

'They have gone to the temple, Shrimant.'

Madhavrao turned to the others and said, 'Well then, let us all go to the temple too. We can pay homage to the Lord and then settle down for the day.'

The main entrance of the temple was ably guarded by sentries standing in rapt attention. Leaving his footwear outside the temple, Madhavrao stepped inside the cool precincts. As he entered the sanctum sanctorum, he was pleased to see the beautiful, self-manifested idol of Shri Chintamani in its divine glory. The idol was in a sitting position and hardly two feet tall. But it radiated divinity, especially as the mild flames of the brass lanterns lit beside it cast their golden glow on it. Madhavrao admired the idol for a long time. Shri Chintamani's power enthralled Madhavrao every single time. He folded his hands and closed his eyes in deep reverence. Everyone else followed suit. When Madhavrao opened his eyes, the priest came forward and placed fresh flowers in his palms. Madhavrao offered them to the idol and stepped outside, on to the porch. He stopped where he could see the Lord's idol in the sanctum sanctorum. Madhavrao sat on the cold floor there.

He turned to Ramshastri. 'Shastribuva, I am a little confused … How are we going to fulfil the responsibility that Lord Ganesha has shouldered us with?'

'What do you mean, Shrimant?'

'I am young, immature, really. Inexperienced in the complex matters of administration. And, add to that, our kingdom is besieged with many problems. At one point, our Maratha warriors had laid claim to the vast kingdoms spread between Thanjavur and Attock. But now, the state of the Maratha empire is deplorable, to say the least. And enemies like Nizam and Hyder are waiting in the shadows to take their revenge. Utter chaos prevails among our people in the north; generals and commanders are fighting amongst themselves. The state treasury is burdened with heavy debts, and there are no able elders alive to guide us through these difficult times. My mind gets very disturbed at the thought of salvaging these issues. How am I going to become capable enough to take on this responsibility? I cannot sleep a wink at night, Shastribuva. All these thoughts weigh heavily on my mind.'

'Shrimant, the one who has given these responsibilities to you will also take you through them. Don't worry so much. You chant the Ganesha Stotra religiously. You know that those chants are capable of calming even the most disturbed minds. Lord Ganesha is the destroyer of all evil, remover of all obstacles. His blessings are with you. Why do you then fear?'

'There is no doubt about that, Shastribuva. But my age and experience fall short ...'

'Shrimant, capabilities are not decided by age. If age was the criterion, Chhatrapati Shivaji Maharaj would never have been able to capture Fort Torna and establish the Maratha empire at the young age of sixteen!'

Madhavrao was not fully convinced. 'That is true, Shastribuva, but you forget ... Chhatrapati was a divine soul, an embodiment of the Lord himself. We are mere mortals. Chhatrapati Shivaji Maharaj was blessed to have Jijabai as his mother, shrewd advisers like Dadoji Konddev, and loyal officers like Tanaji-Yesaji to support him. One man's brain and brawn are inadequate to run a kingdom, Shastribuva. One requires a wholesome support system for that.'

Hearing this, Gopalrao Patwardhan interjected. 'Where are you lacking in terms of an able support system, Shrimant? You also have excellent advisers like Nana and Shastribuva, and bravehearts like Ghorpade, Vinchurkar and Darekar are willing to support and help you in every way possible. Together, we can set everything right once again.'

'We hope that such a blessed day arrives soon!' exclaimed Madhavaro. 'I am relying on the help and advice of experienced seniors like all of you. It is because you are there with us that I derive the strength to shoulder this huge responsibility. That is why I have got you all here.'

The men kept talking, unaware of the time. It was only when the sun set and the temple courtyard lit up with flambeaus that Madhavrao realised how late it had become. 'We should leave now. Dusk has settled. Have all the arrangements for tomorrow's abhishek been done, Nana?

Make sure we are on time tomorrow. We have to leave for Pune immediately after and cannot be late.'

Everyone walked towards the imposing mansion. The sentries at the main gate saluted Madhavrao and the officers as they entered the living room which was beautifully decorated and lit up with brass lanterns and lamps. A glittering chandelier hung from the tall ceiling, its tiny pendants clinking together melodiously with every gust of wind. Rich carpets were laid out all over the floor. In the centre of the room was a cot that was covered with beautiful tapestried covers and velvet bolsters.

Madhavrao reclined on the cot, supported by a bolster. Soon, the room came alive with memories and anecdotes of the past, with the talks continuing till dinner was announced.

❈

After dinner, Madhavrao came back to the living room. Moonlight streamed in through its arched windows. He walked to the windows and observed the vast tract of land that stretched all the way to the river. There was pin-drop silence.

Suddenly, a rustle of the curtains made Madhavrao turn on his heels. Ramabai was standing at the rear door of the living room with a platter of paan in her hand.

As Madhavrao welcomed his wife, someone came to the main door of the mansion.

'Who is it?' Madhavrao called out.

'It is me, Shrimant ... Vithi.'

'Vithi? Come in. Why are you here at this hour?'

'Shrimant, Mamisaheb has called ...'

'Called whom? Us?'

His question caused Ramabai to burst into peals of laughter, which immediately made Madhavrao go pale.

Vithi suppressed her giggles and answered, 'Shrimant, she has called Ramabaisaheb. She asked me to tell her that it is getting late and we need to wake up early tomorrow.'

'Oh, fine!' Madhavrao exclaimed and turned to Ramabai, saying, 'Please go and sleep.'

As soon as the two women left the mansion, Madhavrao called out loudly, 'Is anyone there?' Instantly, Shripati walked inside and saluted.

Madhavrao asked him, 'Are any of the officers still awake?'

'Yes, Shrimant, they are.'

'Then send them in and you stand guard at the door. Ensure that no one else comes in.'

Soon, Ramshastri, Nana, Ghorpade, Patwardhan, Raste and Dhere arrived.

It was only after midnight that everyone filed out of the living room.

The mansion was filled with complete silence again.

⚙

Madhavrao woke at the crack of dawn. After finishing his bath and his daily worship, he returned to his private chambers. Ramabai was already waiting for him. Seeing Madhavrao dressed in a pleated tunic and tight trousers, with a pugree on his head, Ramabai was taken by surprise. He also sported a dab of musk beneath the vermilion powder stripes that he regularly sported on his forehead.

'What is it?' asked Madhavrao.

'Do you plan to go out somewhere?' asked Rama.

'Yes. We are going to pay homage to Shri Chintamani. Would you like to accompany us?'

She nodded, saying, 'Give me a moment …' She left the room but returned almost instantly with Ramji in tow.

Ramji asked Madhavrao, 'Shrimant, who else should I take along with us?'

'No one, Ramji. It's just a short distance from here.'

The trio started off towards the temple. On reaching there, Ramji stood at the door of the temple while Ramabai and Madhavrao went inside. The priest handed them fresh flowers, which they offered to the Lord with reverence.

Coming outside, they stood in the large assembly hall, admiring the serenity of the temple. Madhavrao said to Ramabai, 'You like this place very much, don't you?'

'Yes, but this is hardly the first time I have come here!'

'Today we are going to conduct the abhishek and then leave for Pune immediately. If we had more time, I would have taken you for a stroll on the riverbank. You would have loved it there. We shall definitely go there the next time we come to Theur …' Madhavrao kept talking, as if in a trance. 'It is a beautiful place. The river is nestled amidst an extensive mountain range. You can see the river snaking its way through the pitch-black rocks of the range, like a silvery, glistening serpent. The wind blows over that expanse, creating ripples on the surface of the water. The river is surrounded by emerald greenery, which creates a stunning contrast to the azure blue sky above. It is truly incredible!'

Ramabai kept looking at Madhavrao's entranced visage as he continued: 'Days seem to fly by, don't they? Do you remember, Rama? We had come here along with Matoshree. You were a child back then. We had played here, right in this temple's courtyard. I had hit you in some silly fight and you went crying to Matoshree, complaining. I was worried about what Matoshree would say ...' Madhavrao laughed at the memory. 'But then, when you had finished complaining, Matoshree and her maidservants laughed at your naivety. Matoshree had even rebuked you lightly, saying, "Silly girl! Are you supposed to tell everyone when your husband hits you? But don't worry, I shall talk to Madhava."'

Ramabai exclaimed, 'Oh! You remember all this? I thought you must have forgotten these silly things ...'

'Rama, how can I forget those sweet memories? They remain with us all our lives as companions, as reminiscences of the beautiful phases we have all lived through. That is also a prime reason I love this place. It brings back such wonderful memories that our heart, burdened with a multitude of worries, gets solace, even if for a brief period. I have come here with my revered father many times. I used to play by the banks of the river. At times, I would bring out a horse from the stables in Pune, take a cavalier along and come riding like the wind to Theur. This place has never failed to rejuvenate me. I feel the presence of God in the real sense at Theur.'

'May I ask you something?' interjected Ramabai.

'Sure. Please go ahead.'

'Yesterday when I arrived, I heard that flowers for the abhishek had to be brought from Pune because there are no flower shrubs here. The priest was saying that even if they plant flowers, due to lack of water, they dry up in the intense summers. I wish there was a garden full of flowers here, so that the Lord can get offerings of fresh flowers all through the year.'

Madhavrao was pleased to hear Ramabai's suggestion. 'That is a wonderful idea! I will get it done. Shall we leave now? We have to return to complete the abhishek.'

⚛

As soon as dusk set in, Madhavrao stepped out of the mansion. He went to the temple, paid homage to Shri Chintamani and returned to take leave of the village administrators, who had come to see him off.

Addressing the patil of the village, Madhavrao said, 'Patil, we have heard that fresh flowers are not available for the daily worship of Shri Chintamani. That is not right. Please make sure that during this monsoon, you get flower shrubs sanctioned by the royal treasury. Also, employ a few people to bring water from the river daily to help those shrubs grow properly. When we return, we should see a nicely curated garden in front of the temple and our mansion too.'

'Yes, Shrimant. It will be done,' replied the patil.

All the officers were ready with their horses in front of the mansion. Seeing Madhavrao, Gopalrao said, 'We need to move soon, Shrimant, or we won't be able to reach Pune before midnight.'

'Yes, Gopalrao, but God knows why I never feel like leaving Theur. This place enchants me like nothing else.' By then, the cavalcade had reached the village limits. A beautiful, serpentine road stretched before them amidst the fields. Dusk was just settling in. Mountain ranges stood majestically tall, bathed in the blues of the evening and dotted with trees. Madhavrao cast one last wistful glance at the scenery and then set his steed in motion.

⚗

The guards on morning duty were at their posts near the Dilli Darwaza. People and servants rushed in and out. After a while, a palanquin was seen approaching Shaniwarwada from the main road. A guard hurriedly went inside to announce the arrival of the guest. Soon after, the pugree-sporting, wiry figure of Nana Phadnis rushed towards the main door. The palanquin was set down and from it emerged Ramshastri.

'Will I be able to meet Shrimant today, at least?' Ramshastri asked Nana.

'Buva, Gopalrao Patwardhan arrived long before you. He, too, is waiting. But Shrimant has not yet emerged from the shrine.'

'Looks like Shrimant is overzealous about his daily worship,' commented Ramshastri.

'Irrespective of what happens, Shrimant never starts any work before completing his daily worship.'

Ramshastri entered the Diwan-e-khaas to find Ghorpade, Patwardhan and a few other dignitaries sitting around, cracking jokes. Seeing Ramshastri enter, they all fell silent. Gopalrao Patwardhan greeted him with folded hands.

'Gopalrao, aren't you due to leave today?' Ramshastri asked him.

'I am, but how can I leave without meeting Shrimant?'

Ghorpade chimed in, 'That's the reason even I have been stuck in Pune for the last two days!'

Hearing this, Gangoba Tatya, who was sitting in one corner of the hall, let out a chuckle. Everyone turned to him.

Gangoba Tatya was an old attendee of the palace. An elderly dignitary, he was known to be especially close to Raghobadada.

'What happened, Tatya? Why the sudden laughter?' one of the dignitaries asked him.

'Isn't it obvious? What a silly state of affairs it has come to! If Lord Shankar is present, his Nandi is absent!'

Ghorpade interjected, 'What do you mean, Tatya? I don't understand.'

'What is not to understand, Ghorpade? Here, we need to take permission from not one, but two people. If Dadasaheb is present, Raosaheb is absent … and thus the permissions and their associated tasks keep piling up.'

The others joined in the laughter, except for Ramshastri, who suddenly got up, dusting lint off his tunic. Everyone fell silent. Ramshastri's ears had turned red with rage. His forehead, smeared with vermilion powder, quivered in irritation. He narrowed his eyes at Gangoba Tatya and said, 'Tatya, good to know what you think of our royalty. Now, be so kind as to clarify, who do you think is Lord Shankar here, and who is Nandi?'

Tatya was flustered. 'I mean ... you're mistaken ... I just wanted to say ...'

'Enough!' thundered Ramshastri. 'Tatya, this sort of behaviour is not expected of a senior like you! This is not the sort of example that you should be setting for the others. You, of all people, should know better than to speak so loosely about our masters. Beware, such talk can get you in deep trouble. Keep your tongue at bay.' Ramshastri walked off in a huff, appalled at Gangoba Tatya's uncouth behaviour.

He had barely taken four steps outside when he happened to encounter Nana Phadnis. Nana asked him, 'You are leaving already?'

Ramshastri looked up at the sun, which was almost overhead, and replied, 'Already? Nana, I'm not at liberty like Shrimant to come and go as I please. I am bound by office timings. I have been here for too long already. If I do not leave now, my day's work shall remain pending.'

'But Shrimant will come any time now ...' ventured Nana.

'Who am I to insist on that? I have been coming here for two days, trying to get an audience with him before I return to my office. But it is simply impossible to meet him before noon. Sorry, but I can't wait that long. Even if I come in the evening, Shrimant is busy reading the holy scriptures and singing hymns. Just inform Shrimant that I came once again. Whenever he deems it important to meet me, I shall come.' Ramshastri started walking off in a rage.

Nana followed him. He was well aware of the intensity of Shastribuva's anger. Suddenly, Nana noticed Shripati walking up to him.

'Nana, I was coming to call you,' Shripati said. 'Shrimant Sarkar has arrived at the durbar and is looking for you.'

Nana turned to Ramshastri. 'Shastribuva! Please wait. Shrimant has arrived in his chambers. Please don't go. I will tell him that you have come.'

Ramshastri nodded, while Nana went upstairs, along with Shripati. Soon, Shripati came down and requested Ramshastri to come along with him.

Madhavrao was sitting on a chaise lounge in his chambers. Seeing Shastribuva enter, he got up and folded his hands reverentially.

'Come, Shastribuva. Nana was telling us that you have been coming for the last two days to meet me ...'

'That is true, Shrimant.'

'I'm sorry, but it takes time to get done with my daily rituals of puja and reading the scriptures. If these things are not done properly, I feel disturbed, as though something is missing from my day. But what was so urgent that you have been seeking an audience with me for the last two days?'

'Nothing really, Shrimant ...' said Ramshastri. He waited for a few moments and then continued, 'It's just that I now feel that the time has come for me to relinquish the post of judge that was bestowed on me so honourably. I wish to retire from the service now, Shrimant, and was trying to meet you to express this wish.'

Madhavrao listened, mouth agape. He could not believe his ears. For Nana, too, this was an unpredictable turn of events.

When no one said anything, Ramshastri said, 'Shrimant, the post of a judge is one of great responsibility and also of great peril. It takes a lot of time and energy to sift through cases without bias and make decisions. I hardly get any time for my daily worship and chanting. So, I thought, looking at my age, I should now retire and devote myself to God.'

'Shastribuva, why this sudden decision to retire? I do not understand. You know we hold you in very high esteem. And with the way things are in disarray, the kingdom and this court need you now more than ever. If we lose the guidance of father figures like you, how will we be able to function efficiently?' Madhavrao said in a heavy voice.

'I agree, Shrimant. But then, whom do I look to for support?'

'Why? Am I not there for you?' Madhavrao asked in a puzzled voice.

Ramshastri cleared his throat, adjusted the shawl he was carrying and said, 'Shrimant, please don't mind me speaking frankly. I apologise in advance for what I am going to say, but I think it needs to be said. You are a Brahmin by caste. Worshipping the gods, chanting mantras and hymns, and reading holy scriptures are all duties assigned to you by the Almighty Himself. I feel immensely happy to see you do these duties so sincerely and religiously. However, Shrimant, you must not forget that even though your caste by birth is Brahmin, your caste by choice is Kshatriya. You are a statesman. You are meant to handle the affairs of the state. You are a ruler. Thousands of people look to you with hope in their eyes. However, you hardly make time for these duties! Whenever I seek an audience with you, you are busy reading holy scriptures or praying. There is indeed nothing wrong with that, but then, tell me, how and when will matters of administration be looked into? How will the kingdom function when we officers have to wait for days on end to speak to you, leave alone getting your sanction on our decisions?'

Shocked, Madhavrao didn't know how to react to this tirade. He finally stammered, 'But ... but ... Shastribuva ... I thought that at least you ...'

'Me what, Shrimant? Please speak frankly. You thought that at least I would praise you for being so religious, isn't it? Well, like I said earlier, I indeed feel happy to see you so connected to the Divine at such a young age. There is nothing holier than worshipping God and reading holy scriptures. But ...'

'But what, Buva?!'

'But these things are not meant to be done while gracing the royal throne of a kingdom! I shall speak even more frankly, Shrimant. I feel if your religious duties are disallowing you from doing justice to your duties as a king or a statesman, then Shrimant ... you must relinquish the throne. Trust me, I shall support you in your pursuance of the Divine. We both shall leave for the holy river of Ganga and spend our lives serving God.'

Madhavrao was stunned.

Ramshastri continued, 'Shrimant, have you ever given a thought to the fact that your officers and courtiers have to wait for hours on end for just one meeting with you? That highly placed officials have to run around to source tulsi leaves and flowers for your worship instead of doing their routine administrative work? This grand palace called Shaniwarwada has seen fiery discussions about how the

Marathas can conquer Attock and beyond! It is in this palace that Bhausaheb took the pledge of slaying Qutbshah. This palace has reverberated with the beats of ceremonial drums after so many victorious expeditions. And today? Today this palace sees flames and smoke from religious offerings rising overhead every day! Shrimant, this palace has been fortunate to see many political mind games being devised and played. Alas, today, the only record the palace keeps is how many mantras were chanted how many times and by whom! Please tell me, in such a scenario, how can an officer like me hope to execute decisions? How can any official work ever get done?'

Madhavrao was still silent, but Nana Phadnis had become extremely nervous. He was well versed with the potency of Madhavrao's wrath and did not wish for that volcano to burst. No one had ever dared talk to Madhavrao like this—that, too, to his face.

In a bid to pacify Madhavrao, Nana interjected, 'Ramshastri! Have you lost all sense of who you are talking to?'

Before Shastribuva could reply, Madhavrao raised his hand to silence Nana and said, 'Wait, Nana. Let him speak. Even though it is bitter, it is the truth. I have indeed erred. We must listen to Buva.'

Ramshastri said, 'No, Shrimant, I didn't mean to sermonise you. I just meant to say that if the king himself becomes so lax, then that attitude does not take time to percolate downwards. And I would not like to serve at a place where people are not true to their jobs. Thus, I thought it was prudent to leave before things started going downhill before my eyes.'

'I agree, Buva. I have erred. I promise you that, henceforth, things will not remain the same. You may come to visit me any time. I shall see you immediately. In fact, you shall see me eagerly looking forward to your visit. I hope you are no longer angry with me.'

Ramshastri smiled and replied, 'Angry? Which servant can afford such a luxury when it comes to his master? I'm not angry with you. May I leave now?'

Madhavrao halted him and asked, 'Shastribuva, why had you come today? Or had you only come to rebuke me?'

'No, Shrimant, nothing of that sort. I have people waiting for me in my office. It is already late and now I must go tend to them. By the way, as per your command, I have levied the rule of not employing daily-wage labourers. But a certain section of people are not going to be very happy with this change.'

'No problem. We shall see what to do. You may leave now.'

Ramshastri bowed low and left.

Nana Phadnis said to Madhavrao, 'Patwardhan, Ghorpade and the rest have been waiting for you downstairs for a long time ...'

'Please send them up immediately, Nana,' ordered Madhavrao.

Nana went downstairs, but Madhavrao stood rooted to the spot. Holy chants were reverberating in the air. From the window, Madhavrao saw the smoke from the anushthaan ritual rising up over Shaniwarwada.

He could take it no more. He turned on his heels, just in time to see Ghorpade and Patwardhan standing there. They both bowed low in salute.

'Please come in,' said Madhavrao, waving his hand. 'Gopalrao, will you be leaving today?'

'Yes, Shrimant,' he replied.

'Did you meet Aaisaheb?'

'I did.'

'Ghorpade, will you, too, be going today?'

'Yes, Shrimant. I have been thinking of shifting base for the last two days. I have been here since the treaty of Urali was signed. It has been a long stay indeed. Now, please allow us to leave.'

'I understand, Ghorpade,' said Madhavrao, 'but when experienced officers like you and Patwardhan are with me here, I feel more secure and confident about running the kingdom. I wish you would stay here permanently.'

'I shall be back at your service whenever you need us, Shrimant.'

'I am sure. All right, you may leave today. Gopalrao, please convey our regards to Govind Hari. Do keep us informed of the well-being of everyone there. Ghorpade, please convey my regards and salutations to your respected Matoshree. Whenever I come down south, I shall surely visit her.'

Patwardhan and Ghorpade once again offered their mujras to take the Peshwa's leave.

Soon, Shripati came in and announced, 'Sarkar, Mama has come.'

'Send him in.'

Tryambakmama came in. He seemed to be in a good mood.

'Shrimant, as per your order, we have brought twelve Arab horses to be purchased for the royal stable.'

'Are they good?' quizzed Madhavrao.

'Good? Shrimant, your eyes will pop out seeing them! It would be great if you could inspect them yourself.'

'Sure,' replied Madhavrao. 'How I wish we had heard this earlier …'

'Why? What happened, Shrimant?'

'Ghorpade left just a moment ago. He has a good eye for inspecting horses. Mama, send someone to call Ghorpade and Nana before they leave. I shall change my clothes and join you soon.'

'As you wish, Shrimant.'

⚘

All the important officers and administrators had gathered in Madhavrao's private chambers. Tryambakrao Pethe, Raste, Vinchurkar and Sakharambapu were congregated around Madhavrao, who was sitting reclined on a bolster, his face creased in pensiveness. News of the Nizam's troops running amok in the Maratha empire had reached Madhavrao. The Nizam had recently captured one of the Peshwa's important posts, Naldurga, after ruthlessly plundering the district of Akkalkot. Now his sights were set on Solapur, and he was fast making inroads to lay his claim on that region. Slighted by the insulting defeat in Udgir, the Nizam had started taking his revenge, realising that the Maratha empire had become vulnerable after the death of Nanasaheb Peshwa. He had aggressively desecrated temples and conquered Maratha territories, with his sights set firmly on Pune. Madhavrao listened to the disturbing developments with a dazed mind.

Tryambakmama finished reading the dispatches and stood up. Nobody said anything for a while.

Finally, letting out a heavy sigh, Madhavrao turned to Tryambakrao and asked, 'Mama, what shall we do now?'

'Shrimant, we need to stop the Nizam in his tracks as soon as we can, or he will soon reach Pune.'

Madhavrao roared, 'Does he think Pune is up for grabs? I am going to tackle the Nizam myself. Send urgent dispatches to Patwardhan, Ghorpade, Nimbalkar and Holkar. And where is Nana? Shripati, too, hasn't come yet …'

Tryambakrao replied, 'Let me check …'

As he turned to leave, Raosaheb interjected, 'Wait, Mama. They should be here any moment. They have been sent messages already.'

In a moment, Nana was at the door.

Seeing him, Madhavrao bellowed, 'Nana, how long do we wait for you? Did you not receive our message?'

Nana was silent for a while. 'Shrimant, I apologise for the delay, but the reason is a bit personal. Will you kindly grant me a private audience?'

'Why a private audience? Whatever the matter is, speak up here!'

'I'm sorry, Shrimant. If it were not a personal and delicate matter, I would not have hesitated to tell you here.'

Madhavrao and Nana walked out of the chambers.

'Aaisaheb has summoned you to her chambers immediately,' Nana said.

'Right now?'

'Yes, Shrimant. She specifically asked me to tell you to come as you are …'

'What is it about?' asked Madhavrao.

'I had received your message, but I was at Aaisaheb's palace at that time. Dadasaheb has come there.'

'Who? Kaka?'

'Yes. And he is indignant. He had ordered for a sacrificial ritual to be done at the palace. But when I told him that you have banned all such rituals, he threw a fit and complained to Aaisaheb.'

'Let's see what Kaka has to say.' Madhavrao started walking towards his mother's palace.

'Shrimant!'

'What is it, Nana?'

'Please be careful. Time is not on our side.'

'Is that so? Come along, Nana. When the time is wrong, even the planets go against us.'

Wordlessly, Nana followed Madhavrao, who rushed as he crossed one chamber after another, only to slow down on reaching Gopikabai's palace.

Gopikabai was reclined on a bolster. Raghobadada stood at the far end of the rich carpet laid out in Gopikabai's lounge.

Madhavrao bowed in mujra to both the elders, but Raghobadada did not pay attention to his salutations. Instead, he turned to Gopikabai and said, 'Please ask your favourite son …'

'What happened?' queried Madhavrao.

Gopikabai took a deep breath and looked at Madhavrao. 'Is it true that you have banned all holy rituals in Shaniwarwada?'

'Of course not, Matoshree! All the daily rituals are going on as prescribed. I personally look into them.'

'What are you saying, Madhava?' interjected Raghobadada in an incredulous tone. 'If all rituals are going on as earlier, then how did Nana have the courage to stop the sacrificial ritual ordained by me? He would never have dared do such a thing had it not been on your orders!'

'Well, it is true that I have ordered a halt to that particular ritual ...'

Raghobadada jumped like a scalded cat and, turning to Gopikabai, said, 'Did you hear that, Vahinisaheb? Do you trust me now, at least? But why am I surprised? Madhavrao is the Peshwa now! Why would he feel the need to consult me for administrative matters? I swallowed that insult like a bitter pill. But now it seems that he is hell-bent on erasing whatever little respect I have in Shaniwarwada.'

'Kaka! Who said you have no respect in Shaniwarwada? What have I done that has made you think so? Be particular, please! Which command of yours have I disrespected, pray tell?' Madhavarao's voice was now becoming sharp with rage.

In a bid to protect himself, Raghobadada yelled, 'Now the Peshwa has grown so big that he counter-questions me! He wants me to give clarifications. Oh, Lord, what has this world come to?'

Disturbed at the scene unfolding in front of her, Gopikabai turned to Madhavrao. 'Madhava, why did you order the sacrificial ritual to be halted?'

Madhavrao calmly replied, 'Matoshree, the ritual was not halted. It was simply shifted to a better place. There are so many temples and other serene places around the city. We only decreed that henceforth, all sacrificial rituals are to be held at those places instead.'

Raghobadada again jumped into the fray and shouted, 'See! Just look at the audacity of this young man! Of course, what else should I expect? When he does not fear God any more, why will he fear a mere mortal like me?'

'Kaka! I definitely do not fear God! Nor do I fear you!' retorted Madhavrao, his eyes blazing with fury.

'Madhava! What are you saying?' demanded Gopikabai.

'We are telling the truth, Matoshree. Why should we fear God? God is meant to be loved, revered … And, Kaka, fear is an emotion best suited for enemies, not for loved ones like you.'

'Oh, so you mean to say that you deemed it right to contravene my orders on the basis of your love for me—is that so, Madhava?'

'You are twisting our words, Kaka. This is Shaniwarwada. A much-revered seat of power. The centre of administration from where numerous provinces are controlled. This is a place where warriors come to rest and where many political battles have been won. Continuously having sacrificial rituals that come with preconditions of purity, impurity and hierarchy of caste can create a serious dent in the day-to-day affairs of the palace. Just as we have a Patwardhan coming here, so do we a Ghorpade. In such a scenario, how can a ruler abide by caste hierarchy? For a king, all his subjects are equal. He has to treat them all on a par. That was not possible due to holy rituals being conducted in the palace. I thus shifted the venue for such rituals to temples. I have not banned any personal worship from happening in the palace. We all have our own private shrines within the palace precincts. No one has objected to you conducting your daily worship there!

The only change is that, henceforth, no large-scale holy ritual shall be conducted here. Shaniwarwada is the seat of politics, not a shrine! I believe that if we are successful in protecting our subjects and the royal treasury, that in itself is the biggest offering to the Lord.'

Raghobadada asked sarcastically, 'Oh, really? Where did you learn all this nonsense, Madhava?'

Madhavrao narrowed his eyes at Raghobadada. 'From the Nizam! Kaka, the Nizam has been conducting his own sacrificial ritual out there—he is merrily sacrificing Maharashtra's material and religious wealth. Our temples are being horribly desecrated. His courage has grown to such an extent that he is now talking of conquering Pune. The ruthless man has vowed to desecrate Sri Gajanan of Toka in Ahmednagar. The Nizam has already conquered Akkalkot and reached Solapur. But, instead of getting agitated about these disturbing developments, you, a senior of the family, are fuming about misunderstandings related to holy rituals? I had sent a message to you through Bapu. All the officers were waiting for you. But you did not come! The Peshwai is heavily debt-ridden. There is utter chaos at all levels. No one knows what is going to happen next. Our generals are fighting amongst themselves. A trusted general like Jadhav comes with a five-thousand-strong troop to conquer Pune, and here you are, still throwing tantrums like a child! What do we say to this? If you still think my command was wrong, you are free to break it. You are our senior; you have that leeway. I will not lose hope, though. Till my last breath, with whatever little troop-strength I have, I shall try to keep the Nizam at bay. You need not worry; please look into the completion of your sacrificial rituals. I suppose that is more important, isn't it?'

Raghobadada was listening to this tirade silently. Suddenly, he called out, 'Stop, Madhava! Please stop it.' His eyes shone with tears. 'Madhava, this uncle of yours has fought valiantly all the way to Attock. At Udgir, he has made the Nizam cough up a territory worth fourteen lakhs. Do you think this uncle of yours has turned into a mendicant? Who all have assembled in the durbar?'

'Raaste, Vinchurkar and Chavan have come.'

'Nana, send messengers to Bhosale, Holkar and Patwardhan today itself. Tell them to come to Pune at the earliest.'

'Yes, Sarkar,' said Nana, bowing low.

'And, Nana … be sure to tell them that they should waste no time waiting for an auspicious time to start for Pune. Come on, Madhava, let us go to the durbar.'

As Raghobadada and Madhavrao turned to go to the durbar, Gopikabai called out to them.

'Please wait,' she said, summoning Vithi to the chambers. 'Vithi, go get some saffron milk for all of us.'

As Vithi rushed out to get the milk, Gopikabai said with a smile, 'Please do not leave on a bitter note. Have something sweet and leave together, putting all negative thoughts behind you.'

❈

Ramabai was sitting in the private chambers of her palace. Her trusted maid, Maina, was standing beside her.

'Maina, has Sasubai come back from Parvati?'

'No, madam. But she should be back soon.'

'Sasubai wanted me to go with her ...'

'Then why didn't you go, madam?'

'I didn't feel like going ...'

'Oh! I know the reason behind that feeling! I know that you have taken a pledge to not visit Parvati until Sarkar returns from his campaign.'

'Shut up, Maina! You are true to your name—twittering like a bird every time you open your mouth. Who told you all this?' reprimanded Ramabai.

'I heard from Vithi.'

Ramabai exclaimed irately, 'Oh, Vithi and her tongue! I had to tell her about my pledge because Sasubai was so insistent that I accompany her. In order to pacify her, I had to confess my pledge to Vithi otherwise Sasubai would have been hurt.'

'Do you know what Aaisaheb said on hearing about your pledge? "The girl has become a woman."'

Suddenly, they heard someone clear their throat. They turned and Maina squealed, 'Oh, Kakisaheb!'

Ramabai hurriedly got up to welcome Anandibai, who was now entering the chambers. Ramabai bowed at her feet with reverence. Anandibai blessed Ramabai and, holding her close, asked, 'Rama, how come you did not go to Parvati? I met Ramji on the way. He told me that you did not go with Vahinisaheb. I hadn't seen you for the last four days, so I decided to visit you.'

'Please be seated,' Ramabai requested Anandibai. Anandibai sat on a chaise lounge surrounded by bolsters, even as Ramabai sat on the carpeted floor.

Anandibai examined Ramabai's chambers with a keen eye.

The walls were painted a mild blue; a bed covered with clean white sheets was set up against one wall. The walls bore frames with paintings of Lord Rama and Sita, and Nala and Damayanti.

Ramabai could not help noticing a beautiful tanmani neckpiece that adorned Anandibai's neck.

Noticing Ramabai's interest in it, Anandibai commented, 'Do you like it?'

'It's beautiful.'

'What do I tell you, Rama? He is so generous that the moment I evince even the slightest interest in something, he gets it for me! Sometimes I curse myself for not being able to control my emotions! Madhava hasn't given one to you, it seems. Tell Nana—he shall get it for you from the royal treasury.'

'No. I'm not that fond of it,' answered Ramabai quickly. She called out to her maid, 'Maina! Come here.'

When the girl appeared, Ramabai pointed to a small treasure chest kept below the cot. 'Bring that here.'

Seeing the numerous gold and pearl-studded ornaments kept in it, Anandibai's face turned ashen.

Ramabai said to her in a calm voice, 'Sasubai gave these to me.'

'Is that so? Well, they are very beautiful indeed … your ornaments!' exclaimed Anandibai in a patronising manner.

'Maina, bring some sherbet for Kakisaheb,' ordered Ramabai.

'No, no. I don't want it. I had ordered the pantry to make motichoor laddoos. As it is, celebrations were in order after the Nizam's menace ended. So I said, let me get something sweet made. I had some laddoos already ...'

'The menace has ended?' Ramabai asked incredulously.

'Of course! Don't you know? Madhava made life impossible for the Nizam. The evil Nizam desecrated our temples and idols. Who would spare a demon like him? He made the Nizam fall at his feet at Chambhargonda. The Nizam was begging for mercy.'

'Really? And then?' Ramabai asked, her eyes as big as saucers.

'You know he is so soft at heart. Even though he had a glorious chance of finishing off the enemy and winning laurels, he decided to let the Nizam off lightly by merely signing a treaty. But, of course, the treaty is favourable to us. So the Nizam won't dare cast an evil eye on us.'

'So that means the battle is over?' Ramabai asked innocently.

'Oh, no! Do battles ever end so easily? I heard that they are headed to Karnataka now. The formal announcement should come in the next two days. But, really, Madhava should not have done this ...'

Ramabai kept silent, even as Anandibai continued, 'Miraj was under your father's administration. Madhava snatched it from him and gave it to Patwardhan. Is it good to fight with your own father-in-law? Tsk, tsk ... Very bad behaviour on Madhava's part! I'm sure you must have got this news already?'

Ramabai shook her head. 'I do not understand a thing about politics. I only know that Baba is all right. It is not my place to ponder or ask about what decisions have been taken by them.'

'Spoken like a really wonderful wife. I'm proud of you, my child,' Anandibai said in a syrupy voice, changing tack in an instant. She happened to look up as she spoke and was taken aback to see Vithi standing in the doorway.

'When did you come, Vithi? Has Jaubai arrived?'

'Yes. I had come to convey that.'

Hearing this, Anandibai got up and said to Ramabai, 'Rama, I shall take your leave. Take care of yourself.'

Ramabai bowed low at her aunt's feet and Anandibai left the palace in a hurry.

When Ramabai stood up again, her eyes were filled with tears. She looked at Vithi and said, 'Tell Sasubai that I shall come to visit her in some time. My head is aching badly right now. I shall rest and then go to Sasubai's chambers.'

Vithi left to convey the message to Gopikabai.

Ramabai went to her bedroom. On her way, she told Maina, 'Don't let anyone come in. I wish to sleep.'

Saying this, she went to her bedroom and flung herself on her bed, tears streaming down her lovely face.

Some time later, Ramabai felt a palm on her forehead. She brushed it off, saying, 'Maina, I told you not to disturb me! Go away!'

'Daughter ...'

It was Gopikabai.

Hearing her mother-in-law's genteel voice, Ramabai instantly looked up. Seeing her standing near her bed, draped in a red shawl, Ramabai fumbled. She wiped her reddened eyes and hurried to get out of bed.

Gopikabai put a hand on her shoulder. 'No need to get up, dear ... Lie down. You need to rest.'

Gopikabai's gentle demeanour and loving touch were enough to open the floodgates of Rama's heart. Leaving all formalities aside, she rushed into Gopikabai's embrace and cried her heart out. Gopikabai let her, patting her ever so lightly on her back.

'Rama, today you proved yourself a true daughter-in-law of the Peshwas! Vithi told me everything that had transpired here. Rama, I know Madhava inside out. He will never do anything inappropriate. He must have had some pressing reasons to do what he did. Rulers do not have wishes—they only have duties, which they are bound to perform, whether they like it or not. Trust me, dear. Now get some rest and then come downstairs. We shall have lunch together.'

❧

Maina ran through the corridors of Shaniwarwada, leaving the chambers behind, along with the servants and maids peeping out. She stopped only at Ramabai's chambers.

Ramabai was reclining on one of the sofas, while Ramjikaka stood near her.

Seeing Maina out of breath, Ramabai asked, 'Why have you come running like the wind?'

Maina's face was shining like the moon as she conveyed to Ramabai, 'Dadasaheb Maharaj has arrived!'

Ramjikaka scolded her. 'Maina! Never bring any news without confirming it.'

Maina's face fell. She looked at Ramjikaka with startled eyes. Ramji was standing in a thoughtful pose, scratching the white sideburns that were peeking out of his turban.

The swoops of his white moustache on his cheeks were quivering. The wrinkles on his face seemed deeper due to the frown lines on his forehead.

No one said anything. Ramjikaka was quiet, as was Ramabai, who was drawing aimless doodles with her fingertip on her starched white bedspread.

Maina was confused. When she had heard that Raghobadada had returned from the campaign, she had rushed to tell Ramabai. But it seemed as though something was amiss.

Unable to bear the silence, Maina finally quipped, 'What happened, Kaka?'

'Nothing, Maina. Dadasaheb has come back, but Raosaheb hasn't. He went directly to Karnataka. He should return in a few days.'

Maina didn't know what to say. She left, bowing in mujra.

As she approached Gopikabai's palace, she saw Vithi standing at the door. Through the doorway, Maina saw a lot of people assembled in Gopikabai's living room.

Raghobadada stood beside Gopikabai. He wore a pugree decorated with a shiny aigrette; his chest was bedecked with a heavy neckpiece and in the folds of his cummerbund was a sword, tucked in with pride. He was clutching the hilt of his sword—a beautiful piece of emerald-coloured velvet covered with lace and embroidery.

Raghobadada had an air of nonchalance about him. The onlookers were bewildered by his attitude. Till then, nobody had seen Raghobadada behaving so carelessly in front of his elder sister-in-law.

After some time, Gopikabai asked Raghobadada, 'So, it seems you have come here alone …'

'Yes!' The force of Raghobadada's reply caused many of the courtiers to look up, startled. Raghobadada paid no attention to this reaction and, instead, continued in the same demeanour. 'Madhava does not seem to need us any more. He is free to do as he pleases. Why should I become a thorn in his side? Thinking so, I returned.'

'Leaving Madhava alone?' queried Gopikabai, a distinct edge to her voice.

'He is not alone, Vahinisaheb! He has his trusted lieutenants with him. Tryambakrao, Gopalrao Patwardhan—they are all with him. You needn't worry about him at all.'

'Madhava is still young …'

'Young? Pardon me, Vahinisaheb, but that is the mother in you speaking! If you look with a dispassionate eye, you shall realise that Madhava has not remained as young or rather, immature, as you think. A person who can lock horns with his own father-in-law, wrangle a province like Miraj from him and bestow it on Patwardhan—how can he be called immature? Madhava has started treating strangers like they are his family members, whereas actual family members are being shown the door. I found it difficult to retain my honour, and so I thought it prudent to return before I got told off. Vahinisaheb, you get all messages regularly, so what more do I need to add? I got tired of all the disingenuity there. Somebody pretends to hit, somebody pretends to cry … I got tired of all the drama.'

'Bhauji! How dare you say all this? And before whom? Have you forgotten where you are and what you are saying?'

Gopikabai thundered, her impassive demeanour gave way to immense fury.

Seeing Gopikabai's eyes blazing, Raghobadada fumbled and said, 'No, Vahinisaheb … You are mistaken. What I meant was …'

Gopikabai was in no mood to listen to his pleas. She barrelled on, saying, 'Bhauji, you better be careful before casting any allegations and aspersions on my son. I'm a widow fighting alone on all fronts. Madhava has been saddled with a huge responsibility at such a young age. In such times, family members become a person's biggest strength. But here, the picture seems to be very different. You are behaving in a manner that greatly displeases me. Why so? What is the reason? Madhava treats you with immense respect. He listens to everything you say. He was not in favour of entering into a treaty with a devil like the Nizam, who desecrated our holy idol at Toka. But after I conveyed your wish to him, he agreed to do as you said.'

'Vahinisaheb,' Raghobadada butted in, trying to plead his case, 'I try to do something with good intentions, but it gets distorted to such an extent that my actions are always seen with a jaundiced eye. After entering into the treaty with the Nizam, I have become the butt of all jokes in my own family. What do you take the Nizam for? Is he some rag doll we can toss away at whim? No, Vahinisaheb. He is a snake. An evil serpent. If we had not signed the treaty, he would have waged a war, and, heaven knows, that's the last thing we can afford now. And if, during the war, something unfortunate had happened to Madhava? Then tell me, Vahinisaheb, what face would I have shown you? If I were the king, I would have waged the war, unmindful of the results. But you have placed the tender responsibility of caring for Madhava on these shoulders of mine. Isn't it my responsibility to protect him at all costs? How can I throw him in front of a poisonous snake? You do not understand my heart's anguish on taking this stand.'

Hearing this, Gopikabai seemed a bit placated. 'I let you know what people are saying. It is not necessarily my view or Madhava's. I just wanted to tell you that Madhava needs you a lot at this juncture. If you leave him alone, what will that young lad do?'

'I have not left him alone, Vahinisaheb! He is like a son to me. If that were not the case, would I have so readily relinquished my right to the throne and allowed Madhava to become the Peshwa? That, too, when Tarau herself wanted me to become the Peshwa. I was the one who told her that even though Madhava is young, he is mine. I take full responsibility for the affairs of the land. You also know this, Vahinisaheb.

'I have not left him alone. But when I can plainly see that he does not need me, why should I become a stumbling block in his way? As it is, I'm finding it increasingly difficult to handle these campaigns and the strenuous responsibilities that come along with them. Raosaheb is young blood. He has the physical energy and mental agility to handle these tasks deftly. And he is also capable. I would be happy to leave everything in his able hands and retire to spend the rest of my life on the banks of the Ganga!' exhaled Raghobadada.

'Dadasaheb, don't say that. If you leave the palace, what will I do here? Even I will accompany you to the banks of

the Ganga, but please wait till Madhava comes back. Once
he returns, we shall all discuss this in detail and take the best
possible decision. I shall write to him today itself.'

'Your wish is my command, Vahinisaheb! But for now,
please allow me to take your leave. I'm yet to take my bath.
All these other people, too, need to rest.'

'Yes, all of you please take rest.'

After everybody filed out, Maina came in. 'Madam has
sent me to check if you are free to meet her.'

'I am now. Send her here,' said Gopikabai. She mumbled
to herself, 'Now what do I tell this girl?'

Summers were blazing in the heart of Maharashtra. Pune
sizzled in the heat of April and May. One particular afternoon,
Shaniwarwada was enveloped in unusual quietude, owing to
the searing heat. The only sign of life came from the royal
kitchen, which was busy preparing meals for the household.
All four entrance doors of the palace were being guarded
by sepoys, looking listlessly ahead at the dry, parched roads.

In his private chambers, Raghobadada was lying on his
ornate bed, sweating profusely due to the heat. The khus
curtains hanging from every window of the room did little
to alleviate the discomfort, though they did bring some
respite from the bright light of the sun. Raghobadada's
special maids, Yamuna and Kesri, were massaging his legs.
Another maid, Swarupa, was fanning him. In spite of all this,
Dada could not get any sleep.

'Shyama has not come today, has she?' he asked Swarupa.

Swarupa was true to her name—'good-looking'. The tall, voluptuous maid was one of Dada's favourites. She replied, 'Shyama has come, but she is with Baisaheb.'

'Who sent here there?' asked Raghobadada.

'I did, Sarkar. When you left for the campaign, I sent Shyama to serve Baisaheb.'

'You act really oversmart sometimes, don't you, Swarupa?' chided Dada. 'Get her back here.'

'Yes, Sarkar, I shall tell Baisaheb to release her today itself.'

'And don't go and chirrup in front of your madam. Use your tact so that Shyama comes here in the next two or three days.'

'As you wish, Sarkar,' said Swarupa, adding in a sugary voice, 'His Majesty does not appreciate those who are close to him. He keeps yearning for those who have gone away. My bad luck, I guess.'

Raghobadada grinned, snatched the peacock-feathered fan from Swarupa's hand and pulled her closer. Turning to Yamuna and Kesri, he said, 'You may go now. I wish to sleep.'

They both got up to leave and Swarupa joined them.

'Not you, Swarupa. You wait here.'

Yamuna, who had reached the door, suddenly turned.

'What is it?' asked Dada.

'Bapu has come,' she announced.

'Well, well, trust Bapu to pop in at an inopportune moment,' Raghobadada grumbled as he sat up. 'Go and send in some sherbet, Swarupa. And open up one curtain on your way out.'

The light that suddenly filtered in through the window caused Raghobadada to shut his eyes. When he opened them again, Sakharambapu was standing before him.

'Welcome, Bapu. What made you come in this unsparing heat?'

Bapu did not reply. He settled himself on a carpet laid out nearby. Just then, Raghobadada heard footsteps outside the door. It was Gangoba Tatya.

'Wah, wah, Tatya! Come in. Bapu didn't tell me you too were here.'

Gangoba Tatya bowed low in mujra to Dada and sat down beside Bapu on the carpet. Of the few trusted members of Dada's coterie among the Holkars, Gangoba Tatya was an important one.

'How are you, Bapu? Tatya?' asked Raghobadada.

'What will Tatya say?' retorted Bapu, adding, 'Shrimant Malharrao Holkar has shifted his base camp from Waafgaon and camped ahead, as per your invitation.'

'Hmm … Well, Tatya, I hope you have briefed Malharrao on our discussion. What did he have to say?' asked Ragobadada.

'We are all at our wits' end. Looking at the way Madhavrao is behaving with you, we really do not know who or what to trust any more.'

'Is that what Malharrao said?' asked Dada.

'No, these are my words.'

'Well, we have to face what comes our way,' said Dada in an enigmatic tone.

'That's precisely what I am saying,' chimed in Gangoba Tatya. 'A few messages have already gone from Matoshree Aaisaheb to Madhavrao.'

'Tatya! You don't say a word!' said Bapu, butting in. 'Our Dadasaheb is such a trusting soul that sometimes I don't know whether to be angry with him or to take pity on him. He may well be going to the gallows any day now, but does he trust us? No! I have been warning Dadasaheb for over a month now, but he does what he pleases ...'

'What do you say I do, Bapu?' asked Raghobadada, running his hand over his stomach absent-mindedly.

'I'm your servant. I will do as you command. That's all I can do. But yes, Raosaheb shall return from the campaign any day now—our plan should be ready by then.'

'What plan?' Raghobadada asked in a sharp voice.

Bapu sneaked a glance at Tatya. Tatya replied, 'Dadasaheb, Bapu is right. Times are tough. By God's grace, if everything turns out fine, we will be thrilled. But, God forbid, what if something unexpected were to happen?'

'Then what?' retorted Dada. 'At the most, Madhava will ask us to retire from our royal duties. So what? I will be pleased to see my nephew becoming capable enough to not need my counsel any more.'

Bapu turned to Tatya agitatedly and exclaimed, 'See! Just listen to this. And you say I should talk to Dada ... How is it possible?'

Recognising the delicate turn that the conversation had taken, Gangoba Tatya quipped, 'Dadasaheb, very few people are as large-hearted as you are. But let me tell you frankly, it is not good to be so innocent and large-hearted in politics. I would not have said a word if this were a personal matter between you and your nephew. But this concerns the larger interests of our state. Raosaheb has given free rein to the people of Satara. After Tarau, now there are talks of a treaty going to be signed with Jijau. The adverse results of all these decisions will have to be borne by us subjects! Raosaheb is young. His closeness with Patwardhan will be seen as a childish move. So no one will blame him for it. You will be made a scapegoat, though. You will be questioned as to why you allowed such a thing to happen.'

Raghobadada looked at Tatya pointedly and said, 'Tatya, do you think I'm not aware of what is happening? I have already spoken to Vahinisaheb. We are only waiting for Madhava to return.'

'Raosaheb should be back in the next few days,' interjected Bapu.

'Whenever he comes, things are going to be sorted out,' said Dada, adding, 'Tatya, don't think I have no support.'

'Oh, no, Dadasaheb,' said Gangoba Tatya. 'Whoever said that? If you step out, all the Maratha troops shall stand by your side. Do we not know the tales of your valour? Nanasaheb never dared to speak to you in a raised voice. Don't we know the stature you hold in Peshweshahi?'

Not picking up on the sarcasm in Tatya's words, Raghobadada gave a full-throated laugh. Bapu and Tatya joined in.

A servant came in, bearing tall glasses of cool sherbet for the guests. As the trio sat sipping the refreshing drink, Raghobadada said, 'Tatya, we are going to Parvati this evening. You must come.'

'As you wish, Shrimant. After a long spell, today I finally feel as though I have indeed come to the Peshwa's palace.'

'Why so?'

'Who serves anything to us in the palace any more, Dadasaheb? I still remember the lavish spreads that Shaniwarwada used to see during Nanasaheb's reign. All festive occasions would be celebrated with musical performances and dances. Thousands of people would enjoy the delicious food prepared in the royal kitchens. The palace would be filled with the fragrance of fresh flowers ... Gone are those days! I doubt they will ever come back.'

'They will, Tatya, they will. Just wait and watch,' said Bapu.

Raghobadada listened silently, twirling his moustache absent-mindedly.

⚛

Ramabai had worn a beautiful green Paithani saree. The crescent-shaped red bindi on her forehead added to the beauty of her fair, oval face

She entered Madhavrao's chambers. The floor of the main courtroom, daubed in cow dung, looked bare without the ornate carpets that were usually laid over it.

Ramjikaka came in with the censer. The frankincense burning in it gave out a heady fragrance.

'Kaka, where are Gopal, Vishnu and the others?' Ramabai asked him. 'The carpets have not been laid out. Why so? Dusk is settling in already. What if His Majesty arrives early? What will they say?'

'Akkasaab, don't worry. All preparations are under way. I have sent Vishnu and Gopal to polish all the candelabras and lanterns. I'm taking care of the courtroom myself. Come back a little later to see how beautiful this room will look.'

Ramabai left the courtroom, but something was amiss. She didn't know the reason for her restlessness. She wandered over to the fountain in front of Gopikabai's chambers.

'Daughter!' Gopikabai was standing at the window of her palace. Ramabai went up to greet her.

'Daughter, are all the preparations in place?' asked Gopikabai as soon as Rama entered.

'Yes.'

'Good. Today feels special, doesn't it? It is rightly said that a home without its lord and master is nothing but a hollow shell. You are too young to understand the gravity of this truth right now, but in due course, you will.

'You will not understand the relief and joy a woman feels when her husband returns safely from a campaign. We women live strange lives! Who do we express our woes to? When our husbands are away fighting the enemy, the days seem to pass at a snail's pace. Every moment is rife with inauspicious thoughts. It disturbs us to no end. Applying the red vermilion on one's forehead becomes an exercise in doubt. Is the master of that red mark still on this earth? Every woman asks herself this question when her husband is on the battlefield. There cannot be a more tormenting thought for any married woman. Food becomes one's enemy; it is torturous to swallow a single morsel. Is it any wonder, then, that when I see them come through the Dilli Darwaza, my heart bursts with the joy and relief that has been withheld for all those months? You are yet to go through that experience. But when you do, you shall remember my words.'

Gopikabai stopped talking. Maybe she realised it was not appropriate to say such things to a young girl. The maids brought in the lanterns and diyas as dusk fell.

Ramabai got up and bent at her mother-in-law's feet. Gopikabai blessed her, saying, 'Run along, daughter. Ensure that all preparations are in place. If needed, take Vithi along with you.'

Maina, who was standing outside the main door, rushed along with Ramabai and Vithi towards Madhavrao's palace.

※

The air in Madhavarao's palace was heavy with frankincense. Diyas were throwing their soft glow all around. A deep-blue velvet carpet covered the floor. Candelabras and lanterns made of brass were placed artistically all around the sprawling living room. The huge rosewood bed was covered with a spotless white satin cover. Richly embroidered bolsters and pillows made the room look even more regal. Ramabai smiled with satisfaction. It was past dinner time, but there was no sign of Madhavrao yet. Seeing Ramabai dozing off, Gopikabai said, 'Daughter, it's quite late. Go to sleep now.'

Ramabai went to her room and fell into a deep slumber the moment she lay down. When she awoke in the morning, the mansion was as quiet as a child lulled to sleep. Ramabai called out to Maina, who instantly came running.

'Yes, Akkasaab?'

Ramabai stretched languidly. 'I had a nice dream ...'

'What was it?'

'I dreamt that he had come home.'

'Well, it is said that early-morning dreams always come true.'

'Oh, come on, Maina. Stop pulling my leg.'

'Why would I do that, Akkasaab? Sarkar came back late last night itself.'

Ramabai sat up in an instant. 'Is that true?'

'Yes, madam! Why would I lie to you? That, too, in this auspicious hour of the morning!'

'How mean of you, Maina! Why didn't you wake me then?'

'Sarkar asked me not to …' replied Maina.

'And you agreed? How very clever of you! Come now, don't keep staring at my face. Draw my bath. Has Sasubai woken up?'

'A long time ago.'

'Oh my God, I'm late!' exclaimed Ramabai as she rushed into the bathroom.

⚭

By the time Ramabai got dressed and came into the main chambers, it was daylight. She called out, 'Maina, run along and see if he is free, will you?'

Madhavrao's palace wore an air of quietude. Shripati was standing in the main doorway. Seeing him, Maina blushed. She moved to enter, but Shripati pressed a finger to his lips and said, 'Sarkar is sleeping.'

'Till such late hours? Why so? Is he not well?'

'He has a fever. He met Aaisaheb when he returned, and then went off to sleep.'

'What about any medicine?'

'What medicine? He has been feverish for the last eight days, but who cares? Despite being the king, he gets such shabby treatment! It is a sorry state of affairs indeed,' muttered Shripati forlornly.

Ramabai was waiting for Maina eagerly. Finally seeing her, she asked, 'Well?'

'Sarkar is sleeping,' Maina replied.

Ramabai grew concerned. 'How come he is still sleeping at this hour? It is not his habit. What could be wrong today?'

'It seems he has a fever.'

'Who said so?' Ramabai asked, incredulous.

'Shripati said Sarkar has been ill with fever for the whole of last week. He hasn't been given any medicines. He is just resting. But, Akkasaab, please don't tell anyone that you know about Sarkar's illness.'

'Why not?'

'Apparently Sarkar has given instructions not to.'

'Well! Come along, let me see how he is.'

Ramabai made a beeline for Madhavrao's private chambers. Seeing her, Madhavrao sat up in bed and asked, 'So, how is Her Majesty doing?'

Ramabai did not answer. She stared at Madhavrao with wide eyes. Suddenly, they filled with tears.

'Rama, what is it?' Madhavrao asked, flustered.

'I'm sorry. I was in a deep slumber. Nobody came to wake me ...'

'That's it?' chuckled Madhavrao.

'Why didn't you wake me up?' asked Ramabai, tears still streaming from her eyes.

'Rama, it was quite late at night by the time I reached. I didn't find it proper to disturb your sleep,' replied Madhavrao, even as a bout of cough racked his body.

'Are you not feeling well?' Ramabai asked pensively.

'It's just the campaign that has worn me out, that's all,' replied Madhavrao. He called out to Shripati to get his bath ready.

'Are you going to take a bath? With this fever?' asked his wife.

Before Madhavrao could answer, Maina came rushing in and announced, 'Dadasaheb Maharaj is coming.'

Immediately, Ramabai covered her shoulders with her pallu and stood to the side of the bed. Madhavrao got up to welcome his uncle, bowing in obeisance.

'Let it be, Madhava ... I heard that you have been ill with fever?' he asked.

'No, Kakasaheb. Nothing of that sort. The campaign has tired me out a bit, that's it. The change of water probably took a bit of a toll on me ... but otherwise, I'm fine.'

'Are you sure? I heard you have been quite ill, so I rushed to see you. Have you not had your bath yet? Get done with your ablutions and we shall talk at leisure.' Raghobadada swiftly left the chambers.

⚙

As much as Madhavrao tried pretending that he was well, his fever started getting the better of him. Doctors made regular rounds at Shaniwarwada, which was attacked by incessant rainfall on the outside and torrents of devious political machinations within. Raghobadada's palace saw officials like Sakharambapu, Gangoba Tatya, Vitthal Shivdev and Bapuji Naik hatch Machiavellian schemes, even as Gopikabai's palace hosted Nana, Tryambakrao and Gopalrao. The grey clouds of doubt and suspicion cast a forlorn veil over Shaniwarwada. The air hung thick with suspense. Malharrao Holkar had stationed himself in Pune to help these two parties build a bridge between themselves. He was incessantly going back and forth between the palaces of Gopikabai and Raghobadada. Madhavrao was keeping track of these happenings from bed. Finally, when he regained a bit of strength to participate in the discussions, the flame of treachery started making the rounds of Shaniwarwada.

It was evening. Malharrao Holkar had come to meet Madhavrao. Nana and Tryambakrao had accompanied him. Madhavrao sat on his throne, wearing a shawl over his shrunken shoulders. His face looked considerably thinner.

Malharba said to Madhavrao, 'Raosaheb, I don't think Raghobadada will agree to any sort of compromise. I see the signs of dissension in the air.'

Confused, Madhavrao said, 'I don't get this. On the one hand, Kaka comes here and asks after my health with such concern, and on the other, I hear that he is fanning the fires of discord. Why so? Why doesn't he tell me what's on his mind? When have I ever gone against his wishes?'

'Madhava, you are still young. You won't understand the nitty-gritty of these happenings. Be aware, though; still waters run deep. Raghobadada's attitude has changed. He is not satisfied with getting a slice of the administration and privy purses. He wants to run the Peshwai!'

Madhavrao found it difficult to believe what he had just heard. 'Malharba, I think you are making a mistake in judging our uncle. We revere him as much as we revere you. And Kaka's heart is as pure as the holy water of the Ganga.'

'You may be right, Madhava,' said Malharba in a cautious voice, 'but the problem with pure water is that it takes on the colour that is mixed in it; right now, the water looks muddy ...'

At this juncture, Tryambakmama interjected. 'But where exactly has Raosaheb faltered for Dadasaheb to change his attitude so much? I haven't seen any such reason so far. I have always seen Raosaheb follow Dadasaheb's advice and instructions. After the campaign at Miraj, Dadasaheb simply turned around and returned to Pune. You were not there, but I saw how much Raosaheb begged Dadasaheb to stay. But he did not listen.'

'That's exactly where you all went wrong!' replied Malharba. 'Shrimant gave Miraj to the Patwardhans. He signed a treaty with the Kolhapurkars. He gave the throne to the Satarkars. And all this happened against Dadasaheb's express wishes. And even after that, when Dadasaheb turned back to come home, you continued ahead.'

Madhavrao could no longer hold in his anger. 'Baba, you are senior to us in age as well as experience. But do you know the gravity of the ground realities here? We are knee-deep in loans. How do we run the affairs of such a large palace and state without money? How can we maintain the staff and the army? That is why we had to go to Karnataka. We managed to get some revenue from there. Who owns the throne of Maharashtra? Us? Who will believe that? It was our duty to help the chhatrapati of the Satarkars get released from captivity. We do not regret that decision. If we were to fight the chhatrapati, would you have supported us?'

Malharba replied in a quivering voice, 'Shrimant, Malharba's sword has not lost its integrity yet! Nobody is blaming you. In fact, even those who do not dare say it up front before Raghobadada are praising you behind his back.'

'I didn't do all this to get praise,' said Madhavrao quietly. 'It was my duty and I stayed true to it. Kaka swore enmity with Mama, while Bapu washed his hands off the administration. Mama also started talking about retirement. I felt alone ...'

Hearing this, Tryambakmama interjected, 'Shrimant, don't misunderstand me. Irrespective of who it was due to, Dadasaheb started showing his displeasure. Your age is tender. People would accuse me of trying to create strife between you two. Raosaheb does not trust Bapu Naik. How, then, could I have entrusted you in his hands? I was in a difficult position from all sides. Finally, I decided that, come what may, I will continue along with you to Karnataka, even after Dadasaheb turned back.'

'You made the right decision. Who would dare blame you for that? But Dadasaheb is definitely irked with you,' said Malharba.

'It is in your hands to absolve me of his rage,' replied Tryambakmama.

Madhavrao nodded, saying, 'Malharba, I am too junior to say anything to Kakasaheb in this regard. You are senior. Your words hold value.'

'Shall I tell you the truth, Raosaheb?' said Malharrao. 'It is true that Raghobadada does not cross my words, but that does not mean that he always heeds my advice. He has a coterie of people within the house whom he listens to more than me. As it is, I'm an outsider. There is a limit to how much I can advise on family matters. It is up to you and Aaisaheb to reconcile these differences with tact. In fact, it will be better to have as little or no interference from outsiders in this matter as possible, to prevent a distortion of reality.'

'Why so?' said Tryambakmama. 'If I'm the reason behind the forest fire, it is apt that I take the effort to extinguish it. I shall meet Dadasaheb tomorrow. Let me see what he has to say.'

'Please tread carefully.'

'Malharba, I don't need to be told how to behave with my masters!'

Malharba smiled and said, turning to Madhavrao, 'Shrimant, did you see why I said earlier that this situation is not as easy as it seems? A simple statement is seen in such an embittered way that it has become difficult to open one's mouth. I don't blame you, Mama. Times are such that everyone is looking at each other with a jaundiced eye. But tough times don't last, tough people do. Now it is Shrimant's time to become tough.'

'Malharba, Shaniwarwada has withstood the cruel wounds left by the battle of Panipat. Its stone walls are not so weak as to crumble under the weight of momentous family quarrels,' asserted Madhavrao.

'Well said! Nana, this is what I like best about Shrimant—his valiant and steadfast nature. I shall take your leave now, Raosaheb.'

Nana escorted him to the door. Now it was only Madhavrao and Mama in the palace.

Madhavrao said, 'Mama, I am feeling a bit weak. Can I please take your leave and rest for a while?'

'Please do, Shrimant.' Mama bowed low in mujra and left the palace.

Madhavrao was finally alone. He wiped the beads of sweat off his forehead and let out a deep sigh.

Just then, Shripati entered, carrying a candelabra. He placed it on a settee. Madhavrao folded his hands before the flame and said to Shripati, 'Close that window. The wind is getting too cold to bear.'

Madhavrao wrapped a shawl around himself and lay down with his head on a bolster. The rain had become ferocious. It was slamming against the palace roof relentlessly. Madhavrao listened to the onslaught till sleep claimed him.

※

Raghobadada paced up and down the private courtyard of the Badami Bungalow. Sakharambapu and Gangoba Tatya looked at him wordlessly.

Finally, Bapu mustered up the courage and said, 'Tryambakmama should have arrived by now, isn't it?'

'For what?' asked Raghobadada.

'It was decided so in yesterday's meeting …'

'What meeting?'

'Dadasaheb … Sarkar had gone to visit Shrimant yesterday. Nana and Mama were also there. After meeting you, Sarkar went directly to Shrimant. He was saying …'

'What was Malharba saying? Don't beat around the bush!'

'He told Shrimant that if needed, we will fight ten battles, but that he will not be party to creating dissent in the family.'

Raghoba said, 'He said the right thing.'

'That's when Mamasaheb got up and said that he shall speak to Dadasaheb and resolve this matter once and for all.'

'Oh, is that so?! It that how bold Mamasaheb has become? That he thinks he can teach me?' roared Raghoba.

Gangoba Tatya giggled. 'What a joke! Mamasaheb thinks he can "teach" our Dadasaheb? That is like a fox trying to teach a lion to hunt! Ridiculous!'

'Gangoba Tatya, it is not Mamasaheb's fault,' said Raghobadada. 'When an elephant gets stuck in a swamp, foxes feel emboldened enough to advise him. It is our mistake that we took on this responsibility—at the cost of falling into a swamp!'

'Gangoba Tatya, look who's arriving,' Bapu suddenly announced.

They all peeked outside the window to see Tryambakrao approaching Dadasaheb's palace through the Hazari Karanja chowk. Seeing him, Gangoba Tatya got up to leave, saying, 'Well, Bapu's calculations can never go wrong, can they? Dadasaheb, allow me to leave now.'

'Why do you need to leave, Gangoba Tatya? Just because Mama is coming? Not necessary. Please wait here,' said Raghobadada.

'No, Dadasaheb. I'm well aware of your gentle rage. I would not like Mamasaheb to feel restricted in our presence. I shall wait in the courtyard.'

Gangoba Tatya left, and Raghobadada signalled Sakharambapu to follow him to the inner chambers. They both went inside.

Gangoba Tatya bumped into Tryambakmama just as he was about to enter Dadasaheb's palace.

Mama greeted Gangoba Tatya. 'So, Tatya, how are things?'

'Same old, same old. I had just come to visit Dadasaheb,' replied Gangoba Tatya, adding, 'How is Raosaheb's health now?'

'He's fine. Is Raghobadada inside?'

'Yes, yes. Please go.'

'Who else is with him?'

'Who else will it be? Sakharambapu, of course.'

A servant came outside to announce that Dadasaheb had invited Mama inside.

The moment he stepped into the private chambers, Raghoba exclaimed, 'Tryambakmama? What a pleasant surprise!'

'Surprise? How is that?' asked Mama, cocking a brow even as he bowed low in mujra.

'It's a surprise that your blessed feet have touched our humble abode,' replied Raghoba, his voice dripping with sugar.

'Please don't say that, Dadasaheb. I never miss visiting you regularly. I couldn't come for the last eight days due to Shrimant's delicate health.'

'True. And add to that the responsibility of the state's administration being on your shoulders, isn't it? How would you find time for us?' Raghoba said with a sly smile.

'Well, even if the masters shirk their responsibility, we cannot. We are bound by the moral laws of servitude.'

'Why are you beating around the bush, Mama? Do we not understand your jibes? Don't worry, we are leaving now. So you can all breathe a sigh of relief.'

'Dadasaheb, even I understand your jibes. My hair has turned white in the domains of politics and administration. I'm not the sort to think that a master should leave and a servant should rule!'

'How can that be, Mama? That's the way time has turned on us,' Raghoba said dramatically.

'I don't understand, Dadasaheb. In fact, I have come here to request you to stay. I do not know who has poisoned your ears against me, and for what. Anyway, whatever their evil designs might be, at this stage, I shall not be able to withstand the shock of any dissent arising between you and Shrimant due to me,' revealed Tryambakmama.

'Khamosh!' roared Raghobadada. 'I'm telling you once and for all, Tryambakrao. You and I can no longer coexist. Matters have gone beyond the limit of my endurance. Madhava will have to choose—either you or me!'

Realising that the last embers of his hope had been put out by Raghobadada, Tryambakmama let out a deep sigh and got up. 'All right, Dadasaheb. Whichever way it may be, if the dissent in this family subsides due to me, I'll be the happiest man. I would have got sweet fruit in return for all the service that I have provided till now. Please allow me to take your leave for ever and go on a pilgrimage.'

Raghobadada fumbled on hearing this. He didn't know what to say. Finally, he said curtly, 'That is for your Shrimant to decide, not me.'

'Dadasaheb, I don't know about you, but I have never seen any difference between you and Shrimant. For me, both of you are my masters. Anyway, before I leave, I would like to say a few things that have been weighing on me. If I have your permission ...'

'Speak up,' said Raghoba, absent-mindedly playing with the pendant around his neck.

'Dadasaheb, you returned halfway through the campaign to Karnataka, leaving a young Raosaheb in my hands. I tried to take on that huge responsibility to the best of my abilities and brought the son of this family back to you. In spite of being a ruler, you never once bothered to understand what happened after you left. And now, you are coolly letting me go. I will not disrespect your wishes. You are my master and I'm your servant. But what do I tell the world? Why was I asked to leave so unceremoniously and without any explanation at this ripe old age of mine? What fault was it of mine? Have I faltered in my duties? Have I caused any loss to the Peshwai?'

Raghobadada fumbled for a plausible explanation for Mama's rational questions. 'Mama, you are not a small child who needs to have everything spelt out to you. Instead of asking me, you should ask yourself!'

Tryambakmama raised his head high, looked straight into Raghobadada's eyes, and said in a resolute voice, 'Enough of this nonsense, Dadasaheb! I no longer care what you do to me after this, but I will not keep quiet on hearing your unfair tirade. I came here to tell you a few things that would benefit you, but you are trying to be very smart, placing the blame on me. I know there are people pulling your puppet strings

to make you talk, and you are going along with it! Isn't it?
You are telling me to ask myself? Well, I did that for a long
time, and when I could not find any answers, I came to see
you. But you are playing some very evil tunes, Dadasaheb. I
ask you—did you ever bother asking yourself about what is
going wrong?!'

Seeing Mama's direct attack, Sakharambapu trembled in
his shoes, while Raghobadada's face puffed up with rage. He
screamed, 'Tryambakrao! How dare you speak to me like
that? Whom do you think you are speaking to?'

'To you, Dadasaheb! Only to you!' replied Tryambakmama
firmly. But his voice began to quiver and tears pooled in his
eyes as he said, 'After Nanasaheb's demise, you are a father
figure to Shrimant. He is a young boy shouldered with a
responsibility too huge for his age. In such a difficult time,
instead of helping him carry this burden, you are sparking
dangerous revolts against that child. You have forsaken
your own family in favour of selfish outsiders. Not just
that, you even find the Mughals closer to you than your
own kin. Do we not know this? But, Dadasaheb, you are
forgetting—tomorrow, if this Maratha empire collapses,
the blame will rest squarely on your shoulders. Are you
capable enough to withstand that? Ask yourself, or, better
still, ask those evil people who are poisoning your mind for
their short-term gains.'

Raghobadada was stunned. He cleared his throat and
said, 'Mama, do you think we like doing all this? But I
believe that a man's life is worth living only if he can live
with pride.'

'True, Dadasaheb. I'm saying just that! But you seem to have forgotten that your pride lies in being the Peshwa's uncle, not in being a lieutenant in the enemy's camp. If you set your priorities right, I can assure you that not just me but even Shrimant will not cross your path. You can rule without any obstruction.'

'You are talking beyond your limits!' roared Raghoba. 'You better accept that I love Madhava, probably even more than you do. Yes, I do get momentarily swayed by multiple people whispering multiple things in my ears, but then, that's where people like you should come in to contain us, isn't it? I swear to Sri Gajanan, I have no doubt about you in my mind. Please go and tell Madhava. In fact, help him handle this kingdom, this treasury, everything. I will happily spend the rest of my days in the service of God.'

'Dadasaheb, why are you saying all this? Who would want you to leave us and go away? In fact, your presence gives us so much solace and confidence. But the Peshwa is a mere child yet. He requires a helping hand right now. Maybe two to four years down the line, he will be capable of handling affairs on his own. Then you and I can both go on to serve the Lord. But right now, please wait.'

'No, Mama. It's all in vain now. Madhava has no respect left for us,' replied Raghoba.

'How badly have you misunderstood Madhavrao, Dadasaheb? Even while talking about you in your absence, he compares you to the Ganga! Please don't talk like this about him. If you don't believe me, you can ask Malharba. In fact, wait. Stay here, Dadasaheb. I shall convince you right now.' Mama rushed outside.

Stunned by what had transpired, Sakharambapu stared at Raghobadada. When he could no longer keep sitting, Bapu went to the chambers' window to inhale some fresh air.

As he was looking outside, he saw Tryambakmama walking towards Dadasaheb's palace with none other than Shrimant Peshwa in tow.

Seeing Madhavrao enter his palace, Raghobadada stood up in surprise and asked, 'Mama, why did you bring Madhava here? His health is still delicate ...'

Without saying a word, Madhavrao came to stand in front of Raghobadada. He bowed low in mujra and then, folding his hands before his uncle, said, 'Kaka, you are very senior to us. We look up to you. We'll never go against your word. Your wish shall always remain our command.'

Seeing Madhavrao in this position, Raghobadada's eyes filled with tears. He took Madhavrao's hands in his own and said to him, 'Madhava, have I become such a stranger to you that you have to talk to me so formally? Come here, my son ...'

Raghoba embraced Madhavrao and, patting him on his back, said, 'Madhava, I hold no doubt in my mind. I'll be glad to see you ruling this land with Mama's help. Wherever I find the need to give you some guidance, I shall do so from the sidelines. I shall also see to it that Aba, Nana and Sakharam create no interference in your affairs. My men will stay with me alone.'

Madhavrao interjected to ask, 'But, Kaka, what if we still face interference from your men?'

'Well, then, they shall face the consequences of their mistakes. Who can help that?' assured Raghoba.

Hearing this, Sakharambapu looked at Raghobadada with fright. At that moment, a servant came in to announce the arrival of Malharrao Holkar.

'That's good. Malharba has come at an opportune moment. Come, let's all go to welcome him,' said Raghobadada.

Malharba had reached the inner courtyard when he saw Raghoba, Madhavrao and Mama walking outside together. Everyone had broad smiles on their faces—except Gangoba Tatya, who, on seeing them all, wore a confounded expression.

Raghobadada called out to Malharrao and announced, 'Malharba, the eclipse has passed! From today, Madhava is the ruler and Mama his mentor. Everyone, including me, will consult only Madhava for all decisions.'

'Dadasaheb! I haven't heard such good news in months! I'm thrilled!' exclaimed Malharrao.

However, Gangoba Tatya was not as pleased as Malharba. In fact, he was quite perturbed on seeing this unexpected bonding. He asked Raghoba with unease, 'But what about these two factions that have been formed?'

Raghoba looked at him with distaste and said, 'Two factions? Have you lost your mind? Don't talk nonsense. Come on, let us all go to Vahinisaheb's palace.'

❁

Early the next day, Madhavrao finished his bath and pooja and entered the durbar. Tryambakrao Pethe, Nana Phadnis, Ramshastri and a few other important officials had already arrived and were waiting for Madhavrao. Everyone wore a glow of happiness and contentment.

'Shastribuva, we hope you heard the news?' Madhavrao asked.

'Yes, Shrimant, I did. I'm very happy to hear about this development. The goodwill left behind by Thorle Peshwa is still intact.'

'What can we say, Shastribuva? Our mind was being tossed on embers, but finally, God has showed us the way,' said Madhavrao.

Shastribuva interjected, 'But Dadasaheb should have thought about this …'

'Shastribuva, you may not know Kaka as well as I do. He is too sensitive and emotional a man to be in politics. That is as much his weakness as his strength. Anyway, where has Malharba remained today? He was supposed to come.'

Nana Phadnis replied, 'Malharba has sent a message that he shall come later in the day.'

'We are going to Parvati in the evening. We shall take Malharba with us. Shastribuva, you also come along.'

'As you say, Shrimant.'

'Come on, let us all go visit Kaka. Nana, please see if Kaka has finished his pooja and convey our wish to meet him if it is convenient for him.'

When Nana returned, Sakharambapu had also tagged along. Seeing him, Madhavrao asked, 'Bapu, are you still angry with us?'

'Oh, no, no, Shrimant! How can I be angry with you?'

'Bapu, we also need your advice. Please forget the past and let us start on a clean slate, together. We consider you our own,' said Madhavrao.

'I feel blessed to hear that. Come along, Dadasaheb is waiting for you.'

'Please go ahead. We shall follow you,' replied Madhavrao, getting up to leave for his uncle's palace.

※

By noon, the rain had subsided. Shripati was standing guard outside Madhavrao's palace. Suddenly, he saw Maina leaving the palace. He beckoned to her to come closer.

'Is Sarkar sleeping?' asked Maina as she walked towards Shripati.

'Why are you questioning me like a police officer?' asked Shripati, poking fun at Maina.

'Are you going to tell me or not?!'

Shripati laughed. 'Shrimant is awake.'

'Okay, I'm leaving now,' replied Maina.

'Will you also be coming along?'

Understanding that Shripati was talking about the excursion to Parvati, Maina giggled and said, 'No, I'm not. Why should I?'

Saying this, she ran off to Ramabai's palace.

Some time later, Ramabai went to Madhavrao's palace. Madhavrao was sitting at his desk, writing something. Seeing his wife, he said, 'I am glad you came. I was going to request you to come here.'

'Why aren't you resting today?' Ramabai asked.

'I feel very fresh today. It seems as if a burden has been lifted from my shoulders. Please come and sit here,' requested Madhavrao as he kept his pen away. 'This evening we are going to Parvati.'

'Oh! May I come along?' asked Ramabai.

'Sorry, but today I am not going alone. Ramshastri, Nana and Mama are accompanying me. We shall go some other time, okay?' Seeing Ramabai in a huff, he continued, 'And as it is, it would not have been possible for you to come along today.'

'Why not?'

'We have planned a celebratory dinner tonight. I have already informed Kaka about it. Malharba will also stay back. The kitchens have been told too. Please keep an eye on the preparations.'

'I know about it. Sasubai is overlooking the rations herself.'

'Then why are you here?' asked Madhavrao.

'Sasubai herself asked me to check if you were feeling well. So I came. And now I'm leaving.' She walked away before Madhavrao could stop her.

※

Bapu, Nana, Gangoba Tatya and Tryambakrao waited for Madhavrao that evening.

Madhavrao and Malharba finally came out of the palace, laughing and talking.

As soon as Madhavrao stepped outside the Dilli Darwaza, the garrison troops stationed there bowed low in mujra. Malharrao Holkar's fifty horsemen followed suit. Looking at Shastribuva, Madhavrao commented, 'Buva, just look at Malharba's style! A simple meeting with us is also accompanied by fifty horsemen!'

Malharba replied, 'Shrimant, it is all due to you. If you have made us this capable, why should we play it down?'

'Well said, Malharba,' agreed Buva. 'A kingdom's worth is best measured by how comfortable its subjects are.'

'Malharba, you will not be able to leave for Wanowrie after visiting Parvati. I request you to stay behind for a celebratory dinner we have planned,' said Madhavrao.

'Sure, Shrimant. But it would have been better if we could have stayed the night at the cantonment. Gangoba Tatya!' Malharrao called out. 'Take the horsemen along with you and move ahead to the cantonment. Stay the night there. In the morning, send a few horsemen back for us. We shall come to the cantonment tomorrow.'

'Why? What's the need to send the horsemen back for a single night? Food and lodging arrangements for a mere fifty horsemen are not going to create a dent in the Shaniwarwada treasury, are they?' said Madhavrao. Everyone laughed.

'As you say, Shrimant. Gangoba Tatya, you go ahead alone. Let the horsemen stay here.' Gangoba Tatya went to convey the message to the horsemen.

A few horses were brought in for the dignitaries. All climbed astride the steeds, except Sakharambapu.

'What happened, Bapu?' asked Madhavrao. 'Are you not coming along?'

'Sorry, Shrimant. It would be very helpful if you allowed me to stay back.'

Shastribuva interjected, 'Apparently, Bapu is not keeping too well.'

'Please see the royal physician and get some medicine from him, Bapu. We shall return late evening,' said Madhavrao as he commanded his horse to move.

As soon as all the horses were out of sight, Gangoba Tatya and Bapu turned to rush towards Raghobadada's palace.

Raghobadada was preparing a paan for himself in his chambers. 'Gangoba Tatya, good that both of you came,' he said. 'Have a paan and let's play a game of chess.'

'Sarkar has gone to Parvati, Shrimant.'

'And ... how come you didn't go along, then?' quizzed Raghoba.

'Sarkar asked me to depart for the cantonment. I don't understand what's going on. Sarkar himself is going to stay the night here.'

'Well, Madhava is hosting a celebratory dinner. He must have insisted on Malharrao joining.'

'But ...' faltered Gangoba Tatya.

'But what? Speak clearly!'

'He has retained the horsemen here as well,' revealed Gangoba Tatya.

Hearing this, Raghoba looked at Gangoba Tatya pointedly, but didn't say a word.

Gangoba Tatya got up, bowed in mujra, and said, 'Allow me to take your leave, Shrimant. I have strict instructions not to move from the cantonment.'

Gangoba Tatya exited before Raghoba, who was lost in thought, could say anything.

Swarupa entered Raghoba's chambers. Seeing her, he snapped back to reality and asked, 'Swarupa, what have you got?'

'The chessboard.'

'Who the hell told you to bring this? Go and throw it all in the garbage! Are *you* also habituated to eavesdropping? Get out of here!'

Swarupa turned to scamper off. Raghoba roared, 'And send Bapu in immediately! Let such a mistake not happen ever again!'

❈

Dusk fell. Bapu knocked on the door.

'Bapu, where were you?' asked Raghobadada.

'I had gone home.'

'Has Madhava not returned yet?'

'No, Shrimant.'

'Hmm … How come you didn't go along?'

'I would have if I had been ordered to. I have come to place a request at Dadasaheb's lotus feet.'

'What request?'

'I wish to leave Pune today.'

'Why?'

'Will you please come to the balcony with me for a moment?'

Raghoba followed Bapu to the balcony. Malharba's sepoys were standing opposite the Dilli Darwaza. Bapu pointed them out to Raghoba, who replied with put-on carelessness, 'So what?'

'Sarkar, the fact that Nana, Shastri and Malharba have accompanied Shrimant to Parvati … Shrimant has just recovered from a serious bout of illness—what compelled

him to go to Parvati so soon? And what about this growing
control around Shaniwarwada? I tell you, Dadasaheb, I don't
find these signs very encouraging.'

'What are you trying to say, Bapu? That Madhava will put
us under house arrest?'

'I knew you would say this. This is why I came to take
your leave.'

'So you will leave us alone and go?'

'Sarkar, what will I do staying here? In case some
connivance happens against you, I shall also be pulled into
the web. If I stay away from here, maybe I will be able to
help you.'

Raghobadada's fists had curled up in intense fury.
Trembling with rage, he roared, 'Oh, come on, Bapu! This
Raghobharari was not born to rot in some cage. Let's go
downstairs.'

⁂

The Rangmahal looked like a starlit sky, owing to the
candelabras and chandeliers that cast their glow around the
room. Silver plates were arranged in a geometric pattern
on both sides of the dining table. Every plate was encased
within a beautiful nine-coloured rangoli pattern. Alongside
each plate were kept five bowls, a glass and water container,
all made of silver. Salt, lemon wedges, papads, pickles and
chutneys were already carefully served on the plates.

A few revered shastri-purohits chanted the Trisuparna
mantra in chorus. A hundred incense sticks burnt in the

censer, right in the middle of the room. The heady fragrance lent a dreamy haze to the already wonderful atmosphere.

One by one, the guests arrived and began taking their assigned seats in the hall. Waknis respectfully guided each guest to his seat. After it was announced that all the invited guests had arrived and were seated, Madhavrao made a regal entry, along with Narayanrao. Everyone stood to pay their respects to the Peshwa.

Madhavrao cast a glance across the dining hall. 'Has Kaka not arrived yet?'

'Nana has gone to call him,' said Mama.

At that moment, Nana entered the hall—alone.

'What happened? Where is Kaka?' asked Madhavrao.

'Dadasaheb is not feeling too well. He is sleeping. He has asked you to continue with the feast.'

Madhavrao grew thoughtful. Malharrao Holkar said, 'He has also gone through a lot of mental agony. That must have tired him out.'

'We shall go visit him in the morning,' said Madhavrao, sitting down.

Everyone else followed suit. Narayanrao sat to Madhavrao's left. The seat to his right remained empty.

Soon, servers started appearing before the guests with the numerous delicacies that had been prepared for the feast.

The khus and pampas curtains covering the doorways started moving, suggesting the presence of the womenfolk behind them. A separate feast was being served there.

Before starting his dinner, Madhavrao washed his hands in the salver brought to him by a servant. Waknis drew a symbol on Madhavrao's forehead with red vermilion.

Before the Trisuparna ended, everyone's forehead bore the same mark.

The chief priest requested Madhavrao to release the samantrak udak. Soon, the dining hall reverberated with laughter and gaiety.

Only one person did not seem happy. However much he tried not to, Madhavrao's gaze kept getting drawn to the empty seat beside him.

※

In the morning, after Madhavrao's bath and pooja, Vithi came to see him.

'Aaisaheb has requested you to come,' she said.

'Right now?'

'Yes. Kakusaheb Maharaj has come.'

Madhavrao put on his coat and began walking to his mother's palace. When he reached Gopikabai's chambers, the scene that unfolded before him left Madhavrao befuddled. Anandibai was crying loudly; Gopikabai was patting her back, making a vain attempt to pacify her.

Forgetting to even offer a mujra, Madhavrao asked, 'What happened?'

Anandibai looked at him, her face tear-streaked, unable to answer.

Gopikaibai answered, 'Madhava, fate is indeed against us! Your kaka is gone ...'

'Gone? Gone where?' Ripples of shock cast a shadow of fear on his visage.

'No one knows. He left early in the morning.'

'Without telling anyone? Why? Why would he go away like that?'

Anandibai interjected, 'Madhava, only my ill fortune is to blame for all this.'

'He will come back. Where will he go?'

'No, Madhava ... It is not so simple. He said he will not be stepping into Shaniwarwada again!'

'But where has he gone?'

'To Vadgaon,' said Anandibai.

'With Bapu?'

'I have no clue, Madhava. Please, now only you can help me. My honour is in your hands!' Anandibai begged, gulping back her tears.

'Don't worry, Kaku. I'll find out what exactly transpired.'

Madhavrao's fears were confirmed—Raghobadada had indeed gone to Vadgaon, along with Aba Purandare.

After a few days, even Bapu left for Vadgaon.

⚯

News filtering in from Vadgaon disturbed Madhavrao to no end. Malharrao, Nana, Bapuji Naik and Gopalrao Patwardhan had all gone to pacify Raghoba and get him back, but to no avail.

Even Madhavrao himself, who went to get his uncle, was sent back by Raghobadada with vacuous answers.

The last resort that remained was Gopikabai. But she came back with the news that Raghobadada had left Vadgaon and gone to Paashan.

'Aaisaheb, this behaviour of Kaka's shows signs of impending doom ...' said Madhavrao to his mother.

'No, no, Madhava. Your kaka swore on his wife that he would return directly to Pune from Paashan.'

'Well, we hope to God that this comes true,' sighed Madhavrao.

However, it wasn't to be. Raghobadada sent back all the men who had accompanied him and, taking along a single horse, left Paashan to go to the banks of the Narmada. Every day brought news of disturbing developments in relation to Raghoba. Mahipatrao Chitnis, Aba Purandare, Ramchandra Jadhav and other officials met Raghobadada. But he was not in the mood to listen to anybody.

Raghoba's wife, Anandibai, was most affected by his absence. She requested Madhavrao to let her go and meet her husband. 'Let me try, Madhava. Maybe he shall listen to me,' she pleaded.

'No, Kaku, we don't think he is ready to listen. The journey just to see him is arduous. You will face numerous difficulties for no reason.'

'I don't care!' cried out Anandibai. 'It is better I die during that perilous expedition than live like a corpse here! I want to go. Make preparations for my journey, please.'

⚭

Even though Anandaibai seemed convinced, no one else had any hope that Raghoba would return on her request. Many days passed. There was no news from Raghoba or Anandibai. Everyone began bracing themselves for a war. Madhavrao called for Malharrao Holkar, Tryambakrao, Gopalrao, Anandrao Raste, Piraji Naik and Nimbalkar. Making them swear allegiance to the throne, he commanded them to start arranging for batches of soldiers. The city of Pune began to resemble a war camp as the generals started pouring in with their soldiers. News filtered in that Raghoba had joined hands with the Nizam and was bringing along Murad Khan and Vitthal Sundar to launch an attack on Pune.

And another piece of unsettling news—Raghoba had plundered Paithan in order to finance his troops. All the generals and officials at Shaniwarwada grew uneasy upon hearing this. Madhavrao's fury knew no bounds.

'Kaka has broken all limits of morality and good sense. He didn't think even once before joining hands with a Muslim ruler and, that too, to fight his own kin! Why? For what? What insecurity has compelled him to become so myopic?

'Gopalrao, why are our troops not ready even now? I had given orders long ago. Why have they not been followed?'

'Even I do not understand the cause for this delay, Shrimant. I had sent a letter to my father. His reply has come. I think the troops should be reaching here soon.'

'You *think*?! We are not in the mood to hear unsure things like 'think' and 'might'. We are going to war expeditiously.'

Gopalrao replied in a halting voice, 'Father has replied that your present planetary position is not too encouraging. The moon is eclipsed in Kartik. Your main star sign is afflicted by the coalition of four malefic planets. The astrologer has said that your victory is assured only if you go to war after Margashirsha.'

Madhavrao guffawed loudly. 'Gopalrao, what more havoc can the planets in the sky wreak after the malefic planets within this house? We don't care what happens to us, but if the Nizam enters Pune, matters will get out of hand. We are going to charge with whatever troops we have at our disposal. Tryambakrao!'

'Yes, Shrimant,' said Tryambakrao.

'Tell those generals who have not yet reached to meet us on the way. Next Friday, we set out on this campaign. Make the formal announcement.'

⊗

Friday morning saw Madhavrao inspecting the final arrangements made for the campaign. Shripati had packed all of Madhavrao's essentials in a chest and sent it ahead to the camp. Madhavrao wore a pugree adorned with a diamond aigrette. He held one end of a green shawl in his hand while Shripati held the other. Madhavrao deftly began wrapping the shawl around his waist like a cummerbund, circling it around himself. Then, Shripati offered the Peshwa's prized sword to him. Madhavrao bowed to the sword and tucked it into the shawl. When he looked up, he saw a forlorn Ramabai standing at the door.

'Please come in, Rama.'

Seeing her face fraught with worry, Madhavrao tried to make her smile. 'When a husband is going to war, it is the wife's duty to see him off with a smile.'

Ramabai finally smiled. Madhavrao commented, 'Good! Even you have mastered the art of fake smiles, like I have! Rama, till date, I have never felt sad before going for any campaign. In fact, I would be excited to charge at the enemy. But look what times have befallen us! The same Dilli

Darwaza that saw Thorle Peshwa leave for the campaign to Attock, that saw Bhausaheb leave to conquer the throne of Delhi, that saw the troops leave for the campaign to Panipat ... will now see us leave to wage war against whom? Our own uncle! Our blood! What upheaval must be going through the heart of the Darwaza now.'

Madhavrao stopped talking as a tremendous wave of fury crashed through his body. His fists were balled up in rage. His body trembled with indignation.

'Aaisaheb is waiting for you,' Ramabai said.

Madhavrao snapped out of his trance and accompanied Ramabai to Gopikabai's palace.

Soon after they entered, Ramabai performed the ceremonial aarti for him. Nobody was in the mood to talk. Madhavrao got up and bowed low at Gopikabai's feet. In a tremulous voice, Gopikabai bade him farewell, saying, 'Madhava, be careful ...'

'Matoshree, please don't worry. And please, don't cry. We promise you, come what may, we shall never do anything that will blacken the face of our family and the kingdom. We have fallen into a situation graver than the one described in the Mahabharata. But with your blessings and father's goodwill, we shall sail through it.'

∞

On hearing that Raghobadada was advancing with his troops from Nagar, Madhavrao set out in that direction. When Raghobadada set up camp at Chaarolya, Madhavrao set up his camp thirty miles from his uncle's. Gopalrao

Patwardhan, Tryambakrao Pethe and Malharrao Holkar stood strong behind Madhavrao.

Tryambakrao and Malharrao approached the Peshwa, who was in his tent, immersed in thought.

'Shrimant, the Ghod river is our main strength. We should attack before Dadasaheb comes towards it,' said Tryambakrao.

'We are thinking along the same lines,' said Madhavrao.

Malharrao asked haltingly, 'So then … do we attack tomorrow?'

'That's what we have come here for, isn't it? Let it happen then! Let us resolve this matter once and for all!'

⚘

The war conches were blown early in the morning, and Madhavrao set out with his troops to confront Raghobadada. Both the troops met on the banks of the Ghod river. Raghoba was standing with the Mughal troops where the river descended.

The battle began. Both sides began shooting arrows at each other. In spite of the Ghod river flowing with water, Madhavrao ordered his cavalry to surge ahead through it. This unexpected move caught Raghoba by surprise. Cannonballs were fired by both parties, leading to utter chaos. Both troops retreated and reached their base camps. The battle stopped when dusk fell; that marked the end of the first day of war. Both parties suffered losses—on Madhavrao's side, Nilkanthrao Patwardhan was seriously wounded.

At night, the base camp was abuzz with agitation. The turn of events had perturbed everyone, from Madhavrao to the soldiers. Sitting in their tents, the generals racked their brains—how would they put a stop to this mayhem?

Madhavrao was most disturbed at having seen his uncle face-to-face, standing as an enemy before him. He called out for Malharrao and said, 'Malharba, even though we won today, I do not feel certain about our side. Do you understand what agony it is for me to rain blows on my own uncle?'

'Shrimant, of course I understand this. But times are such … We do not have any option but to face the situation. If you allow me, I can try talking to Dadasaheb again. Maybe he will change his mind?'

'I don't mind you trying. But I'm sure that if Kaka realises that we have come to talk about compromise, he will not shy away from placing irrational demands before us. And if we agree to those demands, what face shall we show to those who have supported us with so much trust?'

'Shrimant, compromise shall happen only if the terms are fair. We shall not agree to any unfounded demands.'

Madhavrao's base camp was being guarded by alert sentries. The flames of the lit flambeaus flickered in the wind. Apart from the movement of the sentries, everything was silent. An air of forlornness seemed to have engulfed everyone. Even the moon seemed to wear a tired look.

Sometime after midnight, Malharrao was seen coming out of Shrimant Peshwa's tent.

After that began Malharrao's incessant rounds between both the camps. People at Madhavrao's base camp seemed to heave a sigh of relief at the signs of an impending compromise.

One day, Malharrao came with a message that said: 'Let Madhavrao shift his base camp and only then shall we commence the discussions for a treaty.'

'Shrimant, please do not give in to this demand,' advised Gopalrao.

'Why not?'

'Dadasaheb has deliberately put this condition across to see how soon you will falter. Rather than give in to such insulting conditions, it is better to die the death of a hero on the battlefield. Don't worry, you are not alone. We are all with you.'

'I understand what you are trying to tell me, Gopalrao. Kaka has become emboldened due to the support of the Mughals. If we persist and do not give in to Kaka's demand, the mass murder that will ensue will happen due to my stubbornness. Make preparations to shift our base camp to Aalegaon.'

'But, Shrimant ...' Gopalrao tried persisting.

'This is my command!'

'As you say,' Gopalrao said as he left the tent.

※

Madhavrao was waiting for Malharrao's message at his new base camp at Aalegaon. He was anticipating the treaty to happen any day now. People in Madhavrao's camp were more relaxed at the prospect of the treaty. Daily work was being carried on as usual. Horses were being taken to be washed at the Bheema river. Soldiers and sepoys relaxed in the waters of the Bheema. Tents were being cleaned daily. And winter was slowly making its presence felt.

One day, Madhavrao was standing in the doorway of his tent, taking in the sun. Shripati was standing beside him. They heard the sound of a horse's hooves coming their way. Madhavrao turned to confirm: a horseman was coming towards his tent at great speed. It was Gopalrao.

He halted his horse near Madhavrao's tent. He held an unsheathed sword in his hand and, leaping from the horse and running towards Madhavrao, cried, 'Shrimant! We have been tricked! You did not listen to me, and now, it has taken a toll on us …' His face dripped with sweat.

'What has happened?!' asked Madhavrao.

'Dadasaheb is advancing towards us with his troops!' Madhavrao's face drained of all colour. 'What? What are you saying, Gopalrao?'

'It's true, Shrimant. Our spy has just brought this terrible news. Dadasaheb will get here any moment now.'

Madhavrao couldn't believe his ears. He stood rooted to the spot in shock. Gopalrao shook him by the shoulders and said, 'Shrimant, don't wait here. We are not prepared. There is no time to combat Dadasaheb. You go along with Shripati and hide somewhere. I will think of some way to halt Dadasaheb in his tracks.'

'Gopalrao, what are you suggesting? We should leave you to fend for yourself while we hide like cowards? No way. As it is, our life has not remained that valuable that it must be saved at any cost. Please go ahead and gather as many soldiers as you can. We shall get ready for combat. Let fate decide its course!'

'But Shrimant ...'

'Go, Gopalrao. We don't have much time!'

The camp suddenly came alive with fear and urgency. Drums were beaten to call back the soldiers who had gone to the river. Conches and horns were blown to announce the latest development. Horses were saddled in a rush. The cooks, who had just started preparing the day's meal, left their vessels on the burning stoves and rushed for their lives. People ran helter-skelter. Gopalrao had a tough time getting the soldiers equipped for battle and ensuring discipline around the chaos.

Madhavrao was getting ready in his tent. As he wrapped his cummerbund around his waist, Shripati handed over the Peshwa's prized sword to him. Suddenly, they heard roars of 'Har, Har Mahadev' right outside the tent. Madhavrao clenched his sword. 'Come along, Shripati!'

Both men got on their respective horses. Seeing Madhavrao's horse flying like the wind across the camp, the previously fearful soldiers felt a surge of encouragement. Soon, a thousand horsemen were following Madhavrao. Gopalrao Patwardhan met Madhavrao just outside the base camp, right as Raghobadada's troops came crashing down upon their battalion like a huge wave. Raghobadada's troops worked their way through Madhavrao's army relentlessly and without any holds barred. The onslaught was too cruel and forceful for Madhavrao's troops to bear. The Aalegaon camp was razed to the ground within minutes. Piercing screams and the clanking of swords filled the air. People were crushed under the hooves of horses running amok. Such utter chaos ensued that no one knew who was fighting whom. Somehow, amid all this confusion, Madhavrao managed to gather a sliver of his troops and rushed to combat his uncle.

The war grew fiercer with every passing hour; they didn't even realise when dusk fell. Madhavrao gathered as many soldiers as he could and waded across the Bheema to set up camp there. Soon, gravely wounded soldiers started entering the camp. Madhavrao began tending to them himself.

The tired, weary Peshwa finally sat in front of his tent. Dewdrops were forming. Everyone was hungry. A huge campfire had been started to keep everyone warm. Madhavrao looked forlornly at the flames reaching the sky. All the generals stood before Madhavrao with their heads bowed low. Finally, Gopalrao came ahead and called out to the king.

Madhavrao looked at him. Seeing the helpless expression on Madhavrao's young face, Gopalrao could no longer control himself. He covered his face with his palms and began to weep like a child.

Madhavrao let out a deep sigh. 'Gopalrao, all of you fought valiantly. We could only do so much. Finally, winning and losing is in the hands of fate, not ours. I am aware of everything. Tomorrow, I shall go and surrender myself before Kaka.'

'I shall also come,' said Gopalrao.

'No. I shall go alone.'

Madhavrao got dressed in silence. He wore a white tunic and salwar. A pugree adorned with a pearl aigrette sat on his head. He didn't place his sword into the cummerbund around his waist but held it in his left hand. He tucked a small dagger into the cummerbund, put one end of the shawl on his left hand and said, 'Come on, Shripati.'

Two hundred horsemen were waiting outside his tent. Generals were also waiting for Madhavrao, teary-eyed. As soon as Madhavrao stepped out, everyone bowed low in mujra to him. Graciously accepting their greetings, Madhavrao beckoned a man standing with the reins of a white horse in his hands.

Tryambakmama came forward and said, 'Shrimant, I shall also come with you.'

'For what? Don't take the trouble, Mama. We are not going to discuss any terms. We are simply going to surrender to Kaka. Please look after the base camp. Those who wish to leave should be allowed to do so.'

Madhavrao mounted his horse and commanded it to start trotting. Shripati and the two hundred horsemen began following him at a slow pace.

❀

Raghobadada was sitting in his huge tent, reclined on a bolster. Pampas curtains hung from the four doors of the tent to prevent the hot air from coming inside. Ruffled fringes in red adorned the side walls of the tent, as did plush carpets laid out on its floor. The settees were also adorned with rich tapestried throws. Raghobadada sat grinning as Purandare, Bapu and other trusted officials of his looked on.

'So, Bapu, how was yesterday?' asked Raghobadada, referring to the sudden attack that had been launched on the Peshwa.

'Oh, what do I tell you, Sarkar? Purandare was saying they were stunned, as if tasered, by the sudden attack. No one could make any sense of what was happening. They all started running around like ants!' Bapu cackled in mirth.

Purandare joined in, adding, 'Bapu, I have never seen such a frightened army before! Children would have reacted more bravely than these so-called warriors!'

Raghobadada couldn't control his joy. Patting his thigh with satisfaction, he announced, 'We shall wait till evening; else, we shall exert our last option.'

'Oh, no, Dadasaheb. I don't think we will even have to think of that option. They'll hardly have any strength left to fight another war. After such a shameful loss, I doubt Gopalrao and Mama have waited with Madhavrao. What a fool! He thinks he can win a war against a giant by using hired help! Hah!' exclaimed Bapu.

Gangoba Tatya came running into Raghoba's tent.

'Shrimant! If I had wings, I would have come flying to reach here faster! Shrimant Madhavrao Peshwa is coming to visit the victorious Raghunathrao Peshwa with his head bowed low!'

'What?!' exclaimed Raghoba. 'Are you sure? Did you see him?'

'Why don't you see for yourself, Shrimant! The whole camp is watching their master's unbridled success with stars in their eyes!'

Raghoba walked out of the tent. Indeed, Madhavrao was riding towards his tent via a hillock to the right. Even though there seemed to be a couple of hundred horsemen with him, they were walking in such silence that their hooves made almost no sound.

Raghobadada twirled his moustache and exclaimed, 'See, Bapu? How I have reduced this lad to a pile of nothingness in just one attack! Now that's the difference between a veteran and an amateur.'

Bapu reacted cautiously. 'Shrimant is inexperienced. He is quite young. He has done a wise thing by surrendering to you, Dadasaheb. Please tread carefully.'

Madhavrao Peshwa entered Raghoba's base camp. His head was held high, his gaze steady and fearless. The sepoys and soldiers looked at him with a mixture of awe and curiosity. As if on cue, they were bowing low in mujra to the Peshwa as he made his way to meet his uncle. Madhavrao kept moving ahead, graciously accepting those greetings.

As he approached Raghobadada's tent, he raised his hand, signalling his horsemen to halt. He dismounted and, sword in hand, looked around with a piercing gaze as he made his way to his uncle's tent.

Except for the squeaking of Madhavrao's shiny footwear, there was not a single sound to be heard. Seeing Madhavrao walking to his tent, Raghobadada went inside and reclined on his bed regally.

Gangoba Tatya stood outside the tent. When Madhavrao reached the tent's entrance, he looked at Gangoba Tatya pointedly; Gangoba Tatya did not dare raise his head to look into the Peshwa's eyes. Bapu had fled a long time back.

Inside, Raghobadada stood with his back to the door. When he heard Madhavrao enter, he turned and exclaimed, 'Oh my God! Who do I see here? The great Shrimant Madhavrao Peshwa! Tell us, what is your command, my lord?'

'Command? No, Kaka … I'm surrendering before you. What command would I give?' replied Madhavrao, his voice unwavering.

'You are surrendering?' Raghobadada cackled. 'You came with a huge army to fix us, and now you are talking about surrender? Do you think that sounds believable, Madhava?'

'Kaka …'

'Stop it, Madhava! Or should I say, Shrimant. Our relationship as uncle and nephew ended the moment you decided to wage war on me.'

'That is your view, Kaka, not mine. If you hadn't left from Pune the way you did, none of this would have happened in the first place.'

'You're right. How would it have happened when, instead, you would have imprisoned us?'

'Kaka, you will never believe what I tell you. You are just not in that frame of mind, and this is also not the time to discuss these things.'

'Good, you understood this, at least, now. So, tell me, what conditions do you have in mind to place before us?'

'I have no conditions, Kaka. Believe it or not, I have come here purely to surrender before you. Whatever you command will be followed by me without question.'

Raghobadada could not believe what he was hearing. He searched his nephew's face for signs of betrayal or treachery. But he found none. Suddenly, his heart surged with intense love and guilt. He said in an overwhelmed voice, 'I cannot believe this, Madhava ...'

Madhavrao's lips quivered. He glanced at Raghobadada's seat, removed his pugree and placed it on the centre of the carpet that covered the floor. Then he took Raghobadada's shoes in his hands and, holding them close to his chest, said, 'Kaka, this pugree symbolises the Peshwai. Hence, I have kept it on the carpet; otherwise I would have kept it at your feet. But I have held your footwear close to my chest to show you the love and respect I still hold for you.'

Raghoba was stunned. 'What are you doing, Madhava? Put my shoes down.'

'Why, Kaka? I feel no shame in carrying your footwear. You are my own uncle. I have never seen any difference between you and my father. What's the shame in carrying the footwear of one's own uncle—nay, father—in one's hands or even on one's head? Kaka, please rule the Peshwai as you wish; accord me any punishment you feel right. But, I beg of you, do not allow the Nizam to take advantage of silly family disputes and enter the fray! I have come here only to make this one request. The rest is up to you.'

Seeing his nephew—the true ruler—standing before him without his pugree, footwear in hand, Raghobadada could no longer hold back his tears. He rushed forward, snatched the shoes from Madhavrao's hands, flung them away and held his nephew in a tight embrace. Raghobadada's tears fell on Madhavrao's uncovered head.

'Madhava, now don't say anything. Just go back to your base camp and rest. I shall come to you in the evening, and we shall talk in depth. Go, son; don't think about anything now.'

Madhavrao bowed low in mujra and turned to go away. Realising Madhava had forgotten his pugree, Raghobadada called out to him.

'I did not forget it, Kaka. I left it there deliberately,' replied Madhavrao.

'Wait!' Raghobadada placed the pugree on Madhavrao's head. His attention was caught by a few mud stains on Madhavrao's tunic. As he attempted to wipe them off, Madhava said, 'Let it be, Kaka. Those stains are not going to be wiped off so easily.' He stepped outside the tent.

※

The turn of events had left Raghobadada feeling quite uneasy. As he sat ruminating on his chair, Sakharambapu came inside.

'Dadasaheb, I heard everything. I was standing right outside the tent.'

'What do I do, Bapu? Madhava reminds me so much of Nana. I couldn't help but forget everything and hold him close to my chest.'

'Sarkar, God has gifted you with a loving nature. It is indeed a good thing, but in politics, such a nature becomes a bane rather than a boon. If you start behaving so emotionally, what will happen to us? We will end up as nothing but villains in this game of family politics.'

'You would have done the same thing had you been in my place, Bapu.'

'Maybe, Sarkar. But the consequences would have been different. Your intention of conquering Pune remains hanging in the air. I'm just reminding you ... Please don't mind.'

'You think that still remains, is it? Madhava has himself placed the pugree of the Peshwai at my feet. I can wear it on my head any time I wish. Do you disagree?'

'No, but I do think it will be a big mistake if you were to do that!'

'Why? Who is going to prevent us from donning the crown of the Peshwai?'

'Dadasaheb, even though time may be on your side, the "right time" has not yet come. The subjects still hold immense respect for Shrimant Madhavrao. They have still not forgotten Shrimant Nanasaheb Peshwa. The generals supporting Madhavrao stand firmly by his side, and we are yet to get confirmed support from the Holkars and Shindes.

'Make Madhavrao your puppet! Let him stay on the throne as the Peshwa but only as a figurehead. Make him say what you want him to say, do what you want him to do. By becoming a puppeteer operating from behind the scenes, all the blame will fall on Madhavrao's shoulders and your path to becoming a Peshwa will get cleared of all thorns. Not to mention, you will be elevated in the eyes of the subjects for letting Madhavrao retain the title of Peshwa despite defeating him in war.'

Raghobadada smiled slyly. 'I definitely have an eye for selecting the right people. It is not for nothing that I have retained people like you in my camp, Bapu! Go on, make arrangements to move our base camp to Paargaon.'

❈

The next day, Madhavrao and Raghobadada set up their base camps at Paargaon together.

Despondent that Madhavrao had unconditionally surrendered before Raghobadada, Gopalrao and Tryambakrao had returned to Pune, as per Madhavrao's command. Madhavrao had decided to fend for himself in this situation.

Discussions between the officials ensued in Raghobadada's tent.

'So, Dadasaheb, what happens now?' said Malharba, starting talks.

'Malharba, Madhava is not our enemy, is he? He is like a son to me. He is young, inexperienced. Whatever mistakes he makes have to be borne by me. My duty is to make him mature and capable enough to handle the kingdom and the finances ably,' said Raghobadada.

'True!' said Bapu. 'Dadasaheb will get the most happiness and peace managing the affairs of the kingdom by holding Shrimant Peshwa by the hand.'

'We want Madhava to henceforth act only according to our advice. Sakharambapu will oversee the administrative work. We hold no anger towards Madhava, but those selfish, opportunistic people who tried to sway Madhava will not be spared from our wrath. We are being very clear!' bellowed Raghobadada.

'But, Kaka, if I take decisions on someone else's say, then—'

'Keep quiet, Madhava! Do not forget that you have surrendered to us! And the one who surrenders has no say or opinion,' snapped Raghobadada, shutting the Peshwa up instantly.

Raghoba continued, 'It is because of these opportunistic home-wreckers that I had to join hands with the Nizam in the first place. Thankfully, the Nizam came running for my help. We will now need to pacify him and send him back with due honour. Since the land for which all this drama ensued is being ruled by Madhava, he will have to agree to this compromise.'

Madhavrao looked at his uncle with a steady gaze. 'As you command,' he said.

'Bapu!' Raghobadada called out. 'Convey to Murad Khan and Vitthal Sundar that Madhava and I have reached a compromise. Request them to come to our base camp. Madhava will meet them there.'

Malharba interjected, saying, 'It is good that you have taken the reins in your hands. I'm sure that Shrimant will perform well under your guidance. Now, both of you please proceed together to Pune and allow me to take your leave.'

'No, Malharba, you will not be able to leave like this. We are going to send a message to the Gwaliorkars. We will return to Pune only after ironing out the creases formed on our kingdom's administration. You may go only after we have taken the Nizam's leave,' said Raghoba.

He then turned to Sakharambapu. 'Bapu, Murad Khan shall arrive tomorrow. See that he is given a royal welcome.'

The next day, Murad Khan and the Nizam arrived at Raghoba's base camp. Discussions took place. Dadasaheb handed over the territory won in the battle of Udgeer and the Daulatabad Fort to the Nizam.

These developments proved excruciating for Madhavrao. He fell ill again and spent most his time lying in his tent with a burning fever.

⚙

Madhavrao sat at the table in his tent. Diyas glowed around him. Quills, ink and a sheaf of writing papers lay before him. Seeing these writing accessories, he was reminded of Gopikabai. He had sat down many times to write a letter to his mother, but had always abandoned the exercise midway, unsure of what exactly he would write. But this time, he sat resolutely to finish writing.

> 'Respectful greetings, Aaisaheb. I hear that you have been agonised by the events that have transpired here. Please don't be. All times are not the same, as you very well know. What has to happen, will happen. I request you not to show any pain, sadness or agony on your face. I am as troubled as you are, but I am taking care not to express it overtly. It will not bode well to do so in public. I also hear that you are planning to go someplace for a few days. Please do not leave for now. It will not go down well with Kaka. Sakharambapu behaves well with me but is quite busy.'

Madhavrao paused to wipe the beads of sweat forming on his forehead. As he lifted his quill to write, Shripati came bursting into the tent. Gasping for breath, he announced, 'Sarkar! We have been betrayed! Gardis have surrounded us from all sides.'

Madhavrao looked at Shripati, who had his sword in his hand. The Peshwa smiled wryly. 'Shripati, first keep that sword in its sheath and stand guard at the door. Whatever happens, never raise your sword. That is my command.'

Shripati reluctantly sheathed his sword and went to stand outside the door, confused. The Gardis were setting up their checkposts all around Madhavrao's tent. The commotion was heard by Madhavrao, who silently picked up his pen again and began to finish his letter:

> 'Officials are looking into repairing the finances. We probably failed to manage the affairs well. Maybe that was responsible for the deplorable state of our kingdom. People we trusted went against us. Our word holds no importance any more. The enemy is getting stronger by the day. If we had enough money, we could have still fought these problems. But in such conditions, it is getting impossible to foster the troops. No money, no troops; and no troops, no money. Too many of these small and big problems are leading to a collective descent. Anyway, I have laid my faith at God's feet. He shall see us through all this, as will father's goodwill.'

After he had finished writing, Madhavrao sprinkled some sand on the letter to help the ink dry faster. Then, brushing off the sand, he rolled the letter carefully and kept it away. He called out to Shripati and said, 'Why are you getting so perturbed by the presence of these Gardis? How many are there?'

'Sarkar, please come out and see for yourself. There are easily more than a thousand of them.'

'So what? It is a sign of how important we are,' said Madhavrao, wrapping a blanket around himself. 'And how will one single Shripati be able to tackle a thousand Gardis? Go to sleep and stop worrying.'

As the night advanced, the camp fell silent, except for the rustle of the Gardis. Madhavrao kept tossing and turning in bed, his mental agony increasing alongside his fever.

⁂

Aalegaon had morphed from a battlefield into the seat of politics. After Madhavrao's defeat, Gopalrao and Tryambakrao had returned to Pune. Only those generals and officials belonging to Raghoba's camp remained, along with the Gardis. Madhavrao was being kept under strict vigilance. Even though he was still the ruling Peshwa, everyone knew that his strings were being pulled by Raghobadada. Madhavrao had also sent Nana Phadnis back to Gopikabai. Now he was all alone, surrounded by the covert and overt enemies.

Days passed. The Nizam's and the Peshwa's base camps showed no signs of moving. Raghobadada and Vitthal Sundar were meeting up on a daily basis. Holkar, Gaikwad and Janoji Bhosale were playing mediators. Feasts were being held every day. Raghoba's victory was celebrated in both camps for days on end.

One evening, Raghobadada went to Madhavrao's tent. Madhavrao was sitting on a low settee. Seeing him, Raghobadada asked, 'How is your health, Madhava?'

'I'm okay, Kaka. There has been no fever for the last four days.'

'I thought as much. Come on, buck up now. We have to go for a shikaar tomorrow. Nizamalli has sent a special invitation.'

'Kaka, is it okay if I do not come? Please?'

'Have you decided to disobey everything I say?' bellowed Raghobadada. 'I have already promised Nizamalli that you will be coming.'

'But, Kaka—'

'Madhava, I'm not requesting you. It's an order! Be ready tomorrow morning. I will summon you after getting word from the Nizam, all right?'

'Yes, Kaka,' said Madhavrao as Raghobadada stormed out of the tent.

Shripati came in with Madhavrao's shawl in hand.

'You heard, didn't you?' asked Madhavrao.

Shripati nodded.

'Keep my outfit ready for tomorrow. I shouldn't be late; I don't want to be disgraced in front of strangers.'

'Which weapons will you take along, Sarkar?'

Madhavrao laughed. 'Only decorative ones. You forget, we are not supposed to carry any real weapons now!'

※

The base camp of Aalegaon was mired in bone-chilling cold. The dense curtain of fog was slowly lifting due to the rising sun's rays. Madhavrao finished his pooja and came out of his tent. There was a smattering of Gardi soldiers around his tent. However, most of them were sleeping. Seeing Madhavrao standing at the door of his tent, the few Gardis who were awake looked at him keenly. Madhavrao paid no attention to them. He inspected the various groups of tents in the base camp, each with a different flag waving over it. He spotted the Asafshahi tent a long distance away.

It had been almost six months since Madhavrao had surrendered at Aalegaon. Many things had changed in this duration. As soon as he got the power in his hands, Raghobadada had started taking drastic revenge. It seemed as if he had vowed to turn Madhavrao's entire administration topsy-turvy. Accountancy handled by the Bhanus for generations on end was taken away from them and handed over to Chinto Vitthal. Tryambakrao was removed from the post of manager, and the responsibilities had been handed over to Sakharambapu. In spite of Gopikabai being in Sinhagad, Raghobadada had turned a deaf ear to Madhavrao's pleas and handed over the administration of Sinhagad to Sakharambapu. Purandar, one of the Peshwas' special forts, was handed over to Nilkanth Abaji Purandare. Tryambakrao and Gopalrao had gone back to their respective villages, waiting to see what was going to happen. But the greatest agony Madhavrao faced was that of Raghoba carelessly signing away Daulatabad Fort and a territory worth sixty lakh rupees to the Nizam, simply in a bid to foster the friendship. Add to that, in order to cut the roots of the very chhatrapati from whom the Peshwai derived strength, Raghobadada was now on a zealous mission to remove Chhatrapati Ramraja and instal Janoji Bhosale in his place. Janoji's right hand, Devajipant, the Nizam's Vitthal Sundar and Raghoba's Sakharambapu were all plotting vigorously to make this plan a success. Madhavrao had no option but to witness this mutely.

Finally satisfied that all his planning had fallen into place, Raghobadada moved his base camp out of Aalegaon. Fired by the idea of taking revenge against Madhavrao's trusted lieutenant, Gopalrao Patwardhan, Raghoba made a beeline for Miraj.

After hearing that Dadasaheb was fast advancing towards Miraj, Gopalrao and his father, Govind Hari, started making preparations to build their camp in Miraj. On the other side, Tryambakrao made preparations to confront Dadasaheb, in case he reached Baramati.

Raghoba had other plans, though. First, he went to Satara, where Bhavanrao was the representative of the Peshwas. He dismissed Bhavanrao and nominated his son as the representative. Then, he went on to Miraj. Raghoba did not have an easy time conquering Miraj—Govind Hari put up a tough fight for two months. However, Govind Hari finally accepted defeat and surrendered. Gopalrao Patwardhan was made to join hands with the Nizam.

Being witness to the pitiable state that Raghobadada had reduced Gopalrao to, Madhavrao was furious. It was for Gopalrao's friendship that Madhavrao had defeated his own father-in-law and handed Miraj over to the Patwardhans. Now, Raghoba had driven Gopalrao away from Miraj and made him the Nizam's dependent.

Raghobadada had become drunk with power. His victories had intoxicated him beyond belief. It was in the fog of this intoxicated state that Raghoba began eliminating all the good people that Madhavrao had gathered around him.

However, Raghobadada could not enjoy this elevated state of mind for too long. While planning to go on to Karnataka after Miraj, he started hearing rumours, some true. The Nizam and Janoji Bhosale had signed a 60:40 treaty. Hungry for the post of a chhatrapati, Bhosale did not think too much before signing this treaty. He only thought about the chhatrapati's own territory located on the south of the Bheema river, happily flinging away the rest to the mercy of the Nizam. The Nizam set up operations on the banks of the Bheema, accompanied by his forty-five-thousand-strong battalion, along with the thirty-thousand-strong battalion of the Bhosales, ten thousand Gardis and a hundred and fifty cannons. This news was enough for Raghobadada to start losing sleep.

✂

Raghobadada was pacing up and down in his tent. Madhavrao sat peacefully reclined on a bolster. Sakharambapu stood on one side with his head bowed low. The Nizam had sent a letter to Raghoba in which he had demanded that Raghoba return all the forts he had taken from the Nizam, and henceforth, carry on all the affairs of the kingdom according to the Nizam's and Bhosale's advice.

Raghoba was burning with fury. Waving the letter in his hand, he yelled at Sakharambapu, 'Bapu, what do we do now? Tell me! Why is your chattering tongue not letting loose today?!'

Not knowing what to do, Bapu kept quiet. This angered Raghobadada even more. 'Is this what you compelled us to leave our home for? This nonsense? How do we face the Nizam now? Tell us! I'm warning you, if we do not escape from this situation unscathed, all the blame shall rest on your head!'

'We are not prepared to fight the Nizam. The Nizam has tied the Bhosales, Gopalrao, Jadhav and many others with him. That has increased his strength tenfold ...' stammered Bapu.

'Don't you dare teach me what I already know, Bapu!' roared Raghoba. 'Tell me what to do in this case!'

'Umm ... reconciliation ... that's the only way ...'

'Wow! Look at that, Madhava. See our manager's brilliance! He wants us to reconcile. What do you think should be done?'

'What can I say, Kaka? What is in my hands?' Madhavrao replied in a soft voice.

'You must be very happy, isn't it?' remarked Raghobadada.

'About what?'

'About the fact that the Nizam is out to ruin us!'

'Kaka, I have never been in favour of thinking that the kingdom should fall prey to enemies and be ruined so that one can settle one's personal scores. That is as foolish as burning the house so as to rid it of bedbugs.'

'Then why aren't you saying anything?' pleaded Raghoba.

'I'm nothing but your prisoner. I have also promised you that I shall do as you ask me to; so far, I have abided by this promise completely. It is your greatness that you even asked me my opinion, but I don't think I'm in a position to give it.'

'No, Shrimant,' Bapu interjected. 'Dadasaheb is asking for your opinion with a genuine heart. The enemy is at the doorstep. Why are you talking like an outsider in times of such distress?'

'Oh! Bapu? Is this actually you?' asked Madhavrao, his voice as sharp as a sword and his gaze burning into Sakharambapu. 'You were the one to poison Kaka's ears and refrain him from joining in the celebratory feast. You were responsible for making Kaka attack us unawares when we set up camp at Aalegaon as per your word. Once you gained power, you behaved with a despicably vengeful attitude and alienated all the trusted, loyal officials the Peshwas had handpicked. Gopalrao, one of our most loyal officials ... you drove him out of his home and right into the treacherous hands of the Mughals. Thanks to your evil schemes, today the Nizam's power has grown exponentially. He can attack us any time. But you know what? If the Nizam attacks and we are defeated, no one will blame you. The blame will fall squarely on Kaka!'

'That it will. You are right, Madhava ... That is exactly what will happen,' sighed a gloomy Raghobadada.

'Kaka, what had to happen, has happened. But what *will* happen is still in our hands.'

'What do you mean, Madhava?'

'Kaka, who will believe that you are the same Raghobharari whose shamsher blinded everyone all the way to Attock? Look at you today! A mere Nizam is proving enough to make you breakout in a cold sweat. This Bapu here used to be counted among the clever gems of the Peshwai. Today, he is advising us to reconcile. What a sorry state you have reduced us all to! Kaka, there is a vast difference between brandishing your sword in a fit of vengeance and running the affairs of a kingdom properly!'

'What is the point of talking about things that have passed?' asked Raghobadada irksomely. 'Why don't you suggest what can be done next?'

'Bapu, write a letter to Holkar,' suggested Madhavrao.

'I have written a stack of letters already, but Gangoba Tatya is acting too pricey! I started writing letters to him when I saw that the Nizam tightening his noose, but Gangoba Tatya has put forth too many conditions. We have reached the limit on the number of requests we can make to them.'

'Requests? And Malharba? An unlikely combination. But honestly, I don't blame them. Once the rot sets in, even the best of apples can't help but fall. Our generals have become used to thinking that a catastrophe befalling the kingdom is a ripe time for them to make a quick buck. Write a detailed letter to Malharba again. Tell him that I, Madhavrao, am overseeing this campaign. Raghoba and I have joined hands again. And yes, Bapu, start packing to leave Miraj as soon as possible. This campaign cannot happen staying in one place.'

'The Nizam is going to go to Pune. We should reach there before he does,' cautioned Raghoba.

'If we do that, the Nizam's target will get fulfilled very easily. And we shall be razed to the ground!' replied Madhavrao.

'Shrimant is right. We cannot confront the Nizam right now. We have no money to keep the troops functional.'

'Don't worry about that,' said Madhavrao. 'Kaka, let us charge on Aurangabad.'

'What are you saying, Madhava?' Raghobadada asked in surprise.

'Kaka, the Nizam is eager to meet us, but there is no point going face-to-face with him. It will destroy us. Instead, let us follow Chhatrapati Shivaji Maharaj's tactic. We will start plundering the Nizam's territory. Before the Nizam can react, Malharba will also come and join us. Even Gopalrao will not decline our request for help. We will keep the Nizam guessing till our battalion becomes strong enough. Once he gets to know about our progress, he shall immediately turn around to protect Aurangabad. But by then he shall be completely exhausted. It will be very easy to hammer him to defeat!'

'What about the expenses?' asked Bapu.

'Levy the generals with the chauthai cha hukum, the rule of one-fourth. Tell them that they will stay alive only if we do. Thus, there is no scope for discussion. They have to pay up. Come on, get going.'

Bapu rushed off to do Madhavrao's bidding. Raghobadada fixed his gaze on Madhavrao.

'What happened, Kaka?' asked Madhavrao.

'Nothing. I just remembered how during the battle of Udgeer, Nana would also issue such swift commands with immense confidence and authority. Your demeanour reminded me of him. Go on, Madhava. Get some rest. From tomorrow, you will not get a second to lie down.'

Madhavrao bowed low in mujra and left for his tent. After many weeks, he finally smiled.

The base camp was moved from Miraj within the next two days, and they all set out for Aurangabad. Madhavrao plundered and burnt the Nizam's territory on the way. Malharrao Holkar joined him in Aurangabad. After looting the surrounding provinces, the Peshwas let cannonballs loose on Aurangabad. The entire Nizamshahi was left shaken to its roots by this sudden vicious attack by the Peshwas.

Madhavrao was sitting in his tent set up at the base camp outside Aurangabad. Malharrao Holkar stood before him, shaking with fury. He said, 'Shrimant, you are young. That is why we came to help you during these trying times. And what did we get in return? A forced contribution of one-fourth of the funds! I think there has been some mistake in this command.'

'Malharba, you are senior to me and very experienced. What do I tell you? Why don't you go and join the Mughals as Patwardhan has done? That way, the Maratha Empire shall be destroyed; you will become a highly ranked general in the Mughal army, and then, you will not have to adhere to the chauthai cha hukum.'

'What are you saying, Madhavrao?'

'Surely nothing inappropriate. You are one of the protectors of the Maratha Empire. The entire province equates Shinde-Holkar with the Maratha Empire. If you do not lend a helping hand to the empire when it is in trouble, everyone else shall also shy away from performing their duties. But remember, Malharba, you will remain only as long as the empire remains. Will you get the honour and respect you are now getting if all of this were to collapse?'

'Well, if you wish for us—'

Madhavrao cut him off. 'Not my wish, Malharba! My wish, if you want to know, is that you should pay one-fourth of the expense of your own accord. You are a senior; once you pay, others will follow suit. In fact, it is your duty to establish these norms among the others.'

'As you command, Shrimant!'

Sakharambapu stepped into the tent.

'What happened, Bapu? How come you have come so early in the morning?' asked Madhavrao.

Bapu looked forlorn. 'I have come bearing grave news, Shrimant …'

Madhavrao's heart skipped a beat. 'What news?'

'Just now, a messenger came riding from Anandvalli to bear the unfortunate news of the untimely death of Raghobadada's son Bhaskar in an accident.'

A stunned silence hung in the air. Bhaskar was Raghoba's younger son. He had been made the representative instead of Madhavrao.

Finally, Madhavrao spoke up, 'Does Kaka know?'

'Yes …'

'Oh no! He should not have had to bear such a huge loss at this age. Come on, Malharba. Let us go and meet Kaka.'

Raghobadada sat desolate on a settee, head in hand. Seeing Madhavrao, Raghobadada cried out, 'Madhava! My Bhaskar, my sunlight, has gone, Madhava! There is only darkness in my life now!'

Madhavrao ran ahead and held his uncle close. 'Kaka, while I'm alive, please don't consider your Bhaskar gone. Imagine that Madhava has gone. Look at me as your Bhaskar—your Bhaskar is standing before you right now!

Please, Kaka, I beg of you—do not let any more tears flow from your eyes.'

Raghobadada thumped Madhavrao on his shoulder. 'I will not cry, Madhava. Why should I cry when a son like you is alive, hale and hearty?'

Madhavrao turned to Bapu and commanded, 'Do not start the entrenchment at Aurangabad today. Let us wait for two days and then do the needful.'

'Why?' interjected Raghoba. 'There is a battle going on. We have no time to mourn here. Bapu, start the entrenchment as planned. I shall join you soon. We have to conquer Aurangabad today, come what may. Madhava, you and Malharba go to the north; I shall look after the west.'

Seeing Raghoba standing firm despite the terrible tragedy that had befallen him, Madhavrao felt a surge of immense pride for his uncle. He touched Raghoba's feet, stepped out of the tent and said to Malharrao, 'Seeing Kaka in this valiant avatar, I feel as if a spring of courage has risen within me.'

❈

It was evening. After planning the strategy for the next day, Raghobadada stepped out of Madhavrao's tent. Twilight had enveloped the base camp in a soft glow. The cool breeze was a welcome change after the relentlessly hot day. The camp was filled with the sounds of cooking, talking, even singing. Raghobadada walked towards his tent, casting glances at the activity going on around him. A few armed guards walked behind him.

Suddenly, someone ran like a flash right in front of Raghoba. Before anyone realised what had happened, an armed man stood before Raghoba. The sharp blade of his sword glistened in the twilight. Though Dada swiftly moved aside as soon as he realised the man was about to attack, the blade still managed to slice through his shoulder. Dadasaheb was taken aback; he stumbled. The armed guards rushed to help their master. Before the attacker could flee, the guards caught him. One of the guards raised his sword.

Raghobadada cried out, 'No, wait! Don't kill him.'

The guard lowered his sword. The attacker stood quaking in his boots. Raghobadada stood up, blood dripping from his shoulder. He looked into the eyes of the man and said to his guards, 'See that no harm befalls him. No one should discuss what happened. Bring this man before me tomorrow morning.'

In his tent, Dadasaheb's wound was examined by the royal physician. It was not too deep—medicine was applied and it was dressed.

Soon, dusk set in. Madhavrao came to Raghobadada's tent. He looked at his uncle's wound and said, 'Kaka, it is indeed by God's grace that you were spared.'

Raghobadada laughed and said, 'My dear nephew, God has not saved me through all the battles I have fought only to have me die at the hands of such a lowly insect. He has saved me because my responsibilities towards the kingdom and the family are not over yet.'

'That is true, Kaka,' said Madhavrao, looking at the royal physician meaningfully. Taking the hint, the physician left the tent.

'Has the identity of the attacker been revealed?' asked Madhavrao.

'No. Let us deal with him in the morning.'

'Kaka, times are tough. One night is a long time to waste, given the circumstances. Why wait till morning? Let us call him now.'

Raghobadada agreed, and a servant was sent to bring in the attacker.

'Who do you think is behind this?' Madhavrao asked his uncle.

'I cannot say anything for sure, Madhava. These days, everyone is going against us. It has become difficult to ascertain who is loyal and who is disloyal.'

The guards brought in the attacker. He trembled with fear. He had no courage to look into Madhavrao's eyes.

Suddenly, he prostrated himself before Madhavrao and stuttered, 'Forgive me, my lord ... I only carried out my master's instructions ... What was I to do?'

'Who is your master? Which group do you belong to?' Madhavrao growled.

The attacker kept mum. Madhavrao's face reddened with fury. 'All right! Let's see how long you can keep your mouth shut!'

Madhavrao charged at the attacker, who cried out, 'Forgive me, Sarkar. I will speak. I was sent by the Jadhavs.'

Raghobadada's lips trembled with rage. 'Madhava, our riches have been infested with rot! When will this end? I do not understand—why is the Lord so angry with us?'

'No, Kaka. The Lord is not angry with us. In fact, He is still showering us with His blessings,' replied Madhavrao.

'What do you mean?'

'Enemies are bound to come. The best part is we caught the enemy by his forelocks before he could hurt us. Isn't that the mercy of God Himself?'

'True, Madhava. And God has also stated the punishment for such a huge offence ...'

When Madhavrao finally came out of Raghobadada's tent, his face had hardened like stone. The frown lines on his forehead were prominent in the glow of the flambeaus.

⚘

The next morning, clouds had gathered in the sky. The base camp was idle.

Suddenly, conches started blaring. Recognising the summons, the soldiers started getting ready as fast as they could.

No one knew what had prompted these sudden summons, but the suspense didn't last too long.

In the next few hours, led by Naro Shankar and Bapuji Naik, the Peshwa's troops charged towards the Jadhav camp.

The Jadhav camp was utterly taken aback by this sudden attack. They didn't get any time to think, let alone act. Jadhav himself didn't get any time to even raise his sword. Naro Shankar stood before him, death incarnate. Jadhav was soon bound and taken to the Peshwa's camp.

Madhavrao was sitting in Raghobadada's tent when word came that Jadhav had been brought in captive. Madhavrao frowned deeply, as Raghobadada roared, 'We have no wish to see the blackened face of a traitor! Tell the generals to stone this despicable man to death and then throw his body out in the fields for scavengers to feed on!'

The servant turned to leave with Raghoba's command, but Madhavrao called out, 'Wait!'

Raghoba looked at Madhavrao questioningly. Madhavrao continued, 'Tell Naroba to keep Jadhav under surveillance in Daulatabad Fort till he receives further orders from us.'

'Madhava!' cried out Raghoba.

'Kaka, some things have to be dealt with coolly. Look at it in the long-term perspective. All said and done, Jadhav is a Marathi man. He will come to our aid in times of distress. At least, that's what we hope …'

Raghobadada did not say anything, but the deep creases on his forehead conveyed his displeasure with Madhavrao's decision.

The servant waited for his orders. Finally, Madhavrao told him, 'Go and convey what we have said.'

'Yes, Sarkar,' said the servant, rushing off. Just then, Sakharambapu entered the tent.

Seeing his crestfallen face, Madhavrao asked him, 'What happened, Bapu? Has any message come?'

'No, Shrimant …'

'Hmm, we understand. It is so sad that in this land where Chhatrapati Shivaji Maharaj established a glorious swarajya, today we have such short-sighted individuals who, in spite of their experience, do not want to help when the Maratha Empire is in a dire state. How do we rule? How do we carry on the affairs of such a large kingdom when people do not step up when we need them?' said Madhavrao in anguish.

Bapu said falteringly, 'Shrimant, they are asking for a province of ten lakhs.'

'Exactly!' said Madhavrao. 'Why is everyone thinking with such a narrow perspective? Whom does all this wealth belong to? Us? Whom are we fighting for? How tormented will the soul of Chhatrapati Shivaji Maharaj feel on seeing such a narrow-minded attitude? Anyway, Bapu, this is not the time for discussions. The enemy is at our doorstep. If we let him loose for even a few days more, he will become too overpowering to rein in. We need to take action. Kaka, there is no point in waiting any further.'

'That's exactly what I feel, Madhava,' agreed Raghoba. 'We don't need to talk any more. The tails of such disloyal dogs are forever crooked. Madhava, send a message to all our generals. Tell Malharba to sit twiddling his thumbs ... One day, all these people will be back at our feet, begging for mercy. They should remember that!'

'That's true, Kaka, but we also have to think realistically. Today, our condition is very critical. We cannot just go and wage a war on such a huge force.'

'Then? What do you suggest?' asked Raghoba.

'Just as Chhatrapati Shivaji Maharaj brought the powerful Aurangzeb to his knees using guerrilla warfare, we also need to do the same here. That is especially why we feel the need for the Holkars to be here.'

'Oh! Is that so? Then go on, fall at his feet!' Raghobadada roared in anger.

'Kaka, there are times when even God needs to bend down in front of humans. We, then, are mere mortals. Sometimes an intelligent compromise, keeping aside one's ego, is the only way to success. Why should we deny it?' said Madhavrao, adding, 'We are going to Chandwad today.'

Saying this, Madhavrao exited Raghobadada's tent.

※

When Madhavrao came back the next day, his face was beaming with satisfaction. He went directly to Raghobadada's tent and called for Naro Shankar, Bapuji Naik, Baburao Hari and Ramchandra Ganesh. After they all congregated, Madhavrao announced, 'A few days from now, Holkar will be joining our troops.'

Everyone was thrilled to hear the news. Raghobadada added, 'Janoji Bhosale is daydreaming about becoming the chhatrapati. We need to snap him out of those dreams. We shall move early tomorrow; Holkar will join us midway.'

That night, the troops were divided into three groups. One troop was led by Raghobadada and Madhavrao, the second by Bapuji Naik, Baburao Hari and Ramchandra Ganesh, and the third by Naro Shankar. Malharrao Holkar was meant to meet this third group.

As dawn broke, the troops started charging towards Varhaad. They kept looting and plundering enemy territories on the way, especially the Nizam's. Malharrao met them at the decided location. From there on, the troops, now further strengthened, reached Varhaad. The province of Varhaad, which belonged to Janoji Bhosale, was looted in mere minutes. When Madhavrao got news of Bhosale's troops coming towards Varhaad, he fanned the rumours of an imminent war. The Nizam's troops entered Varhaad prepared to put up a tough fight. But by then, Madhavrao's troops had long withdrawn from Varhaad. When Bhosale reached the plundered province of Varhaad, he could do nothing but wring his hands in despair.

On the other hand, after hoodwinking the Nizam, the Peshwas charged straight on to Hyderabad. They kept the Nizam guessing and swatting in vain, even as they looted Paithan, Naldurg, Udgeer, Medak and then Hyderabad again. When Madhavrao realised that the Nizam was not coming to Hyderabad, he ordered for the camp to be set up there.

⚹

One evening, while Madhavrao, Raghobadada and Holkar were planning the next move of the troops, Mahipatrao Chitnis entered their tent. He bowed low in mujra to all of them and presented a letter to Madhavrao.

'What's this, Mahipatrao?'

'This letter has come from Pune, Shrimant.'

'Well, read it aloud.'

'Today, the Nizam's troops entered Pune and created a tremendous ruckus. They looted the ordinance of whatever they could find. There are some traitors who showed the Nizam the way to the most important areas. We suspect some of the rich people in Pune of having joined the Nizam in this shameless act. Even after being promised a huge compensation, these people have not stayed loyal to us. The Nizam has desecrated the idols of Lord Vishnu, Mahadev and Goddess Parvati. He has cut off and taken away the pinnacle of the temple of Lord Devdeveshwar. He has not spared a single

God's idol from desecration. He has burnt down the Sarkar's
mansion and seven other mansions in Somwar-Mangalwar
Peth. He has looted everything in sight. Of course, how could
you have helped it? It is all God's will.'

Mahipatrao stopped reading. Madhavrao's face had gone
red with fury. He got up from his seat, as did Raghobadada,
who shook with rage.

Raghoba roared, 'How dare he?! Malharpant, direct all
the troops to Pune. We shall go and cut off the filthy hands
of that Nizam who dared touch our gods!'

'Kaka, this is definitely the Nizam's cunning. He wants us
to come to Pune. If we react by going to Pune just now, he
will easily conquer us.'

'What are you saying, Madhava? We let the Nizam do
as he pleases? What will Bhau say? The Nizam was begging
for his life in front of us during the battle of Udgeer. Today,
he is shamelessly looting Pune. No, Madhava … Bhau will
laugh at us.'

'Yes, they will laugh, but at our thoughtlessness. For
falling prey to the Nizam's plot.'

'What do you mean?'

'Kaka, please understand. The Nizam is looting Pune,
desecrating our idols, not because he has anything against
our religion or to amass more wealth. Malicious politics
is behind this move, and the puppeteers of these ideas are
none other than clever and experienced generals like Janoji
and Vitthal Sundar. These people know that touching Pune
is like touching our heart. They know that if any hazard
befalls Pune, we shall come running to save it. And that's

exactly what they want! So that we fall like a rabbit in a hole before the Nizam, who will devour us alive.'

'Shrimant is right,' affirmed Malharrao. 'The Nizam would not have dared charge on Pune by himself. There is definitely dirty politics behind this ploy. If we fall prey to it, we stand to lose everything.'

'Be patient, Kaka. The Nizam will soon get entangled in his own web.'

Dadasaheb did not say anything; he sat in a pensive mood.

Malharrao and Madhavrao left Raghoba's tent. As Madhavrao reached his tent, Malharrao took his leave. But Madhavrao halted, saying, 'Malharba, please wait. I wish to talk to you.' The two men walked into Madhavrao's tent.

'Malharba, the situation is indeed tricky. We need to find a way out of it soon,' continued Madhavrao.

'Please do not worry, Shrimant. If you allow it, we shall charge on the Nizam today itself. Then let him see the dance of fury this sword can perform!'

'I trust you, Malharba. But we also need to think about the situation from a larger perspective. The Nizam is depending on Janoji Bhosale and representatives like Gamaji Yamaji and Naik-Nimbalkar.'

'Yes, that's true.'

'I am wondering if it is possible to get all these generals to enter into a compromise and break them away from the Nizam. The Nizam will fall weak in no time, and then we can overpower him easily. I entrust you with this responsibility, Malharba. Use all the weight you can; keep the generals from getting into a war.'

'Okay, Shrimant, I shall try my best,' said Malharrao.

'You have been my experienced and valued general from the days of my father's regime. You can bear this responsibility very well. Try all the arguments you can. Do not forget that this wealth is yours.'

'No, Shrimant. If at all I had continued thinking like this, I would not have come back to serve you, would I? I shall take your leave now; it is getting late.'

Malharrao went to his tent. Madhavrao kept thinking for a long time after he left. The night was going to be a long one.

❈

Holkar was doing everything in his capacity to get the generals to compromise. The monsoon was about to set in. Madhavrao was wondering whether to take the next step or not. The troops had been away from their homes and families for many months now; understandably, they were weary. While there was confirmed news that the Nizam was going to set up camp at Bedar, he was not doing anything proactively. Rumour had it that he had also sent a part of his troops back. Madhavrao was also thinking of sending some of his troops back. Malharrao's efforts were gaining fruition. He knew Bhosale's weak points. First of all, he tried breaking off Janoji's brother, Madhoji. That idea was successful. Naturally, Janoji was getting anxious. In recent times, the Nizam had also started behaving brusquely with him. After plundering Pune, the Nizam had not sought Janoji's advice again. Janoji was feeling resentful. He was left with no option but to compromise with Madhavrao. Unbeknownst to him, the Nizam was getting slowly hollowed out from within.

One day, the Bhosales sent a letter to Madhavrao. Seeing the contents of the letter, Madhavrao immediately went to see Raghobadada and called for Malharrao too. As soon as Malharrao arrived, Madhavrao announced the arrival of the letter and said, 'The Nizam is getting ready to cross the Godavari river and reach Aurangabad. He has to be intercepted immediately. Bhosale has kept his troops ten to twelve miles away from the Nizam's. Other generals are also on our side. The day that we have waited for has finally arrived! Malharba, now there should be no delay from our side; otherwise, we will have to repent our whole lives. Bhosale has taken your advice and made the Nizam change his plans; that is why he is setting up camp at Aurangabad.'

'This is great news, Shrimant! There shall be no delay from our side. We cannot afford to lose a single second. We have to move our camp today itself. I shall take your leave,' said Malharrao, before he stepped outside with fervour.

Raghobadada was thrilled with the development. He was working with renewed vigour at the thought of the Nizam finally being trapped. Madhavrao had issued commands to all the generals and senior officials. The troops were explained the strategy of the attack. In spite of their increased strength, it was not going to be easy for the Peshwas to attack the Nizam headlong. They had to entrap him from all sides and get him to his knees.

The rain had become relentless. However, that had not stopped the Peshwas from tailing the Nizam. The Godavari was flooded. The Peshwas aimed to catch the Nizam there because they knew that the Nizam would maintain his camp at the banks of the Godavari till the floods subsided.

The Peshwas had set up their base camp at Mohi. There, all the news about the Nizam duly reached them. The Nizam was not waiting for the floods to abate. He was trying his best to cross the flooded Godavari in whatever small boats he could manage to wrangle. Vitthal Sundar was waiting on the other side with ten thousand troops. The Nizam was crossing towards that side with some of his troops. Madhavrao was sure that if they wasted more time, he was bound to take the remaining troops across too. He also knew that the Nizam was dependent on Vitthal Sundar to achieve this aim; thus, it was necessary to intercept Vitthal Sundar in time. On the eve of Ashadh Amavasya, the Peshwas left Mohi under the cover of darkness and charged towards Rakshasbhuvan.

They reached Rakshasbhuvan next morning. Vitthal Sundar was shocked by the sudden attack but managed to launch a counterattack. However, the Peshwas' ace generals, Aba Purandare and Vitthal Shivdev, managed to stand strong against Vitthal Sundar's cannon attacks and defeated him. At a crucial juncture, Raghobadada entered the battlefield and drove Vitthal Sundar to greater despair.

Madhavrao observed the ongoing battle while perched on his horse. He had saved a thousand-strong army for himself. The Mughal army was accepting defeat, but then suddenly … Vitthal Sundar himself came ahead to fight! He let loose all his remaining force into the battlefield. Stunned by this unpredictable move, the Peshwa troops started skittering backwards. The battle changed colour in minutes.

The Mughals seemed to be on a winning streak. The elephant on which Raghobadada was sitting was surrounded from all sides by enemy soldiers, and they started leading Raghobadada and his elephant to the enemy fold. The Peshwa troops were nowhere to be seen. Raghobadada had still not lost his fervour, but the scene unfolding before them all was reminiscent of the battle of Panipat.

Madhavrao watched this ... and then, in an instant, turned to his troops and roared, 'Har har Mahadev!'

Hearing this war cry, the soldiers charged at the enemy like wild dogs. Madhavrao kept encouraging the troops that were trying to go back.

Grey clouds had given way to rays of sunlight. Madhavrao's face dripped with sweat. His throat had gone hoarse from shouting, but he still pressed on furiously. After some time, Malharrao moved towards Madhavrao with a portion of the wounded soldiers tagging behind him.

Malharrao said to Madhavrao, 'My child, please go back. We are not seeing any victory today.'

'And Kaka?' asked Madhavrao.

Malharrao answered cryptically, 'If there had been any hope, would I have turned back?'

'Malharba, I grew up hearing that during the battle of Panipat, you left Bhausaheb to fend for himself on the turf and returned alone. I never believed it ... until today. You have left me with no choice but to believe it. You move on to the base camp ...'

'And you?'

'If I come back leaving Kaka alone in Vitthal Sundar's captivity, I shall not even find place in hell. If I return, it will be with Kaka. Else, consider this our last meeting.'

Madhavrao's sharp words tore a hole into Malharrao's heart. He stammered, 'No, Shrimant ... I was worried about your victory. I have lived my life. Henceforth, whether I live or die does not make much of a difference. Please ignore any prejudices you have about me. I shall come along with you. See your Malharba's loyalty for yourself.'

Saying this, Malharba turned his horse around. Seeing him re-entering the battlefield, the troops who were loitering behind also charged into action. The war cry of 'Har Har Mahadev' reverberated through the battlefield again. Malharrao started swiping his sword mercilessly and eliminated the soldiers who had surrounded Raghobadada. Seeing that circle broken, the Peshwa troops charged inside like a wave. In a matter of minutes, Raghobadada's elephant came out from his captors' ring.

Then, Malharrao focused his attention on Vitthal Sundar's houdah. Amidst the seven houdah-carrying elephants belonging to the Mughals, the one in the centre carried Vitthal Sundar. He was trying his best to keep fighting the enemy. In this commotion, Mahadaji Shitole appeared before Madhavrao, bowed low to him in mujra and said, 'Sarkar, I'm going to aim directly for Vitthal Sundar. If I'm successful, please give me an inaam.'

Madhavrao smiled; Mahadaji let his horse loose. He held a spear in one hand and ordered his horse to charge directly at Vitthal Sundar's elephant. The horse ran like the wind. Mahadaji was mercilessly spearing any Mughal who came in his way. He was only focused on Vitthal Sundar, who was still fighting from his perch on the houdah. Before Vitthal Sundar knew what was happening, Mahadaji's spear came swinging through the air and directly pierced his heart. He collapsed, clutching his chest, as the spear in his hand fell to the battleground helplessly. Seeing Vitthal Sundar dead, the Mughal soldiers started running helter-skelter for their lives. Utter chaos ensued. But the soldiers got caught between the rising waters of the Godavari on the one side and the merciless Peshwa troops on the other. A few soldiers jumped into the torrential waters in a vain attempt to save themselves.

Meanwhile, Vitthal Sundar's head was impaled on a spear to be put on display before the joyous Peshwa troops.

Madhavrao watched with immense pride. His heart was filled with joy at their well-deserved victory. Soon, Mahadaji Shitole came to Madhavrao.

Madhavrao said, 'Mahadaji, I am extremely happy with the valour you have displayed today. It is due to bravehearts like you that the Maratha Empire bounces back every time people think it is collapsing. I hope you shall continue to serve the Maratha Empire with your loyalty and valour. I give you the province of Maanjri as inaam, along with the title of Sardar.'

Mahadaji bowed low in mujra.

⚒

The next morning, when Madhavrao came out of his tent, his gaze turned towards the opposite bank of the Godavari.

He was surprised to see that the area that held the Nizam's base camp till last night was completely empty. Madhavrao rushed to get his binoculars to inspect the area closely. There was not a single person. Apart from a couple of abandoned cannons that lay around, it seemed as if the entire camp had been wrapped up in a hurry, leaving behind whatever could not be taken along.

Malharrao's voice broke the silence. 'What are you looking at, Shrimant?'

'Look at that, Malharba,' said Madhavrao, handing over his binoculars to the general. 'It seems that the Nizam has run away.'

'Shrimant, how can we be sure that this is not a ploy to make us cross the banks and overpower us?'

'He does not have the strength left for that. His façade diminished the moment he saw Vitthal Sundar collapse. He will not dare wage a guerrilla war on us. But yes, we need to be alert. The Nizam will not stop playing the cat-and-mouse game with us. We have to eliminate him before he becomes a looming monster again.'

'That is true, Shrimant,' agreed Malharba. 'But today, this river is not allowing us to search for and kill that despicable Nizam! Had the waters abated by now, we would have pulled the Nizam out of his hiding place and eliminated him in a swipe.'

'Malharba, the river is a mother. Whatever she does is to help her children. By not abating, she is showing us another road to take.'

'You mean we should turn back?' Malharrao asked in a confused tone.

Madhavrao laughed. 'Who turns back after such a victory? I said the river is asking us to change our route. Move the base camp. If the Godavari is not giving us way from this side, let us search for an area where she is giving us passage from.'

Just then, Sakharambapu walked up to them. 'Shrimant, the Bhosales have sent a message.'

'What do they say?'

'They wish to meet you, Shrimant.'

'All right. Tell them they can come whenever they want to.'

⚇

Soon, evening approached. Clouds had gathered in the sky. The base camp was almost completely packed up and ready to move.

Sakharambapu asked Madhavrao, 'Shrimant, we move tomorrow, isn't it?' When Madhavrao nodded, he continued, 'If you go charging on Aurangabad from here, the Nizam is bound to get completely demolished.'

'That's what we want. Don't you want that as well?'

Sakharambapu only looked away in response.

The evening wind had turned chilly. Madhavrao turned to go into his tent, when, from the corner of his eye, he saw a horseman riding towards him. In an instant, Madhavrao's guards unsheathed their swords and rushed to counter the stranger.

However, on coming closer, the stranger announced, 'Huzur, refuge ... refuge ...'

He dismounted from his horse. Madhavrao's guards surrounded him and took away all his weapons. Then they brought him to the Peshwa. The stranger collapsed to his knees before the Peshwa, who asked him, 'Who are you?'

'Huzur, this humble man's name is Meer Musa Khan. I'm the Nazeem-e-harkar of the Nizam's army.'

Madhavrao stood looking at the Nizam's spy coldly. 'What is the reason for coming to us?'

'Huzur, the battle has left our army in tatters. Everyone has run for their lives. Somehow, I remained behind. It became difficult to stay in hiding any longer. Thus, I thought, instead of getting killed by some random person, it is better I surrender to you. Please, grant me refuge, Sarkar ...'

'Get up, Meer Musa Khan. We offer you refuge!' said Madhavrao.

Tears started streaming down Meer Musa Khan's face as he held Madhavrao's tunic in his hands and kissed it.

Bapu came up to Madhavrao and whispered, 'But Shrimant ...'

Without taking his gaze off Meer Musa Khan, Madhavrao replied, 'Bapu, during our father's reign, Sherjung voluntarily came to join us after he got tired of the Nizam's demonic regime. Take Meer Musa Khan to him. We are sure this man will prove to be an asset for the Peshwas.'

As Meer Musa Khan was taken away, Bapu asked Madhavrao, 'Shrimant, do you know this man?'

'No, Bapu, but we know about his fame. This man is a capable gem. He is weary of the Nizam.'

'Why?'

'Why? Well, why did Sherjung come to seek refuge with the Peshwas? The Nizam is a Sunni, while Sherjung and Meer Musa Khan are Shias. However loyally they serve the Nizam, their efforts will never receive due respect and recognition.'

'But what will be the consequence of this decision?' asked a doubtful Bapu.

'I am not psychic, Bapu. Let us see ... Come on, don't worry so much.'

The base camp moved out early the next morning. They walked along the riverbank and reached Paithan. From there, they crossed the Godavari to reach Aurangabad. Soon, Aurangabad was besieged by the Peshwas. The Nizam had lost a political gem like Vitthal Sundar. He had also lost thousands of soldiers in the battle of Rakshasbhuvan. Now, the Peshwas besieging Aurangabad was too big a blow for the Nizam to bear.

※

Madhavrao was resting in his tent. Bapu and Malharrao stood beside him respectfully.

A servant came running in with a message for Madhavrao. 'Shrimant, Dadasaheb Sarkar has called.'

'Okay. Who else is with him?' asked Madhavrao.

'He is alone, Sarkar.'

Madhavrao walked to Raghobadada's tent with Bapu trailing behind. Accepting the mujras of the guards at the door, Madhavrao went in.

'Kaka, did you call me?'

'Yes, I did.' Raghoba said so in a furious tone.

Madhavrao could not understand the reason behind Raghobadada's rage. He waited for his uncle to explain.

Grinding his teeth in fury, Raghobadada asked Madhavrao, 'Did you grant the title of Sardar to Jadhav?'

'Yes, but I did not think it was inappropriate .'

'Oh, yes, absolutely! You did not! Your hands have touched the sky now, right, Madhava? You cannot see what lies beneath your feet? You have kept a poisonous snake beneath your feet and are carrying on without any care. Such a childish, impulsive attitude will take you and your kingdom down the drain! Be warned, Madhava!'

'But, Kaka, what exactly have I done wrong?'

'Great! Even now you need to ask me this question? Had you asked me this earlier, I would have warned you in time. This is the same Jadhav who drew his sword against Bhau in the battle of Udgeer. He is the same devil who did not think twice before plundering a holy place like Pandharpur. You actually forgave such a devil? This Jadhav did not stop at Pandharpur either. He tried killing us at Aurangabad. I told you then to eliminate him, but you went against my wishes and simply imprisoned him. You thought your uncle was the bigger enemy than Jadhav, that I wanted to snatch the Peshwai for myself. Madhava, you are not listening to me. This childish act of yours will endanger our reign in the Deccan at any moment. Consider yourself warned!'

Hearing Raghoba's tirade, Madhavrao replied, 'Kaka, the Deccan is not so weak any more. And I have also seen Jadhav's valour. You conveniently forget that, initially, you had got him close. In the battle of the Ghod river, it was this Jadhav who had brought the Nizam's younger brother, Meer Mughal, to you. Today, the Nizam has no option but to sign a treaty with us. Vitthal Sundar is no more; Sherjung and Meer Musa Khan have joined us. The Nizam trusts Jadhav. That is why we have accorded him the Sardarki. We need someone capable to keep an eye on the Nizam at our borders. Who better than Jadhav for that? I, at least, do not see a better man than him at this moment. Everyone makes mistakes, Kaka. The problem begins when those mistakes are not rectified in time. Everyone should keep this dictum in mind, and you are no exception to this rule, Kaka.'

Saying this, Madhavrao walked out.

Stung by Madhavrao's words, Raghobadada looked at his retreating figure for a long time.

⌘

Though the Nizam had begun talks for a treaty, he had grown restless with the conditions put forth by Madhavrao. Madhavrao had asked for the province worth eight-five lakh rupees that had gone to the Nizam in the treaty of Udgeer. He had asked for Sherjung to be given back his jagir. The Peshwa had also put forth the condition that the Nizam should come to the Peshwas' aid whenever the need arose. He had also threatened that if the Nizam did not agree to these conditions, he would be replaced by Salabatjung on the throne.

The Nizam had no option but to agree to all the conditions.

Madhavrao and the Nizam had a formal meeting. The treaty was formalised.

'We hope you will not contravene the agreement of this treaty.' Said Madhavrao.

'Pandit Pantpradhan, I stay true to my word,' replied Nizamalli.

'I have one more request.'

'Please go on,' the Nizam replied humbly.

'I request you to make your Nazeem-e-harkar, Meer Musa Khan, your chief minister. He should be made the Madar-ul-maham.'

The Nizam was taken aback. He coldly said, 'Pandit Pantpradhan, whom we appoint as our chief minister is entirely our prerogative. You have no business speaking on this matter.'

Madhavrao steadied his grey eyes on the Nizam and replied in a firm voice, 'Bandagaane Ali Aala Hazrat should take cognisance of the delicate situation he is in. Meer Musa Khan shall be your chief minister. You shall not go beyond his advice. Is that clear?'

The Nizam swallowed his words. He called for the ceremonial robe and made Meer Musa Khan his chief minister. Musa Khan was given the title of Rakna-ud-doula.

After signing the treaty with the Nizam, Madhavrao left Aurangabad for Pune. Raghobadada refused to come along and, instead, went ahead to Anandavalli.

2

Madhavrao had returned victorious from Rakshasbhuvan, but the constant pressure on his mind and body during the war had taken a toll on his health. He kept contracting fevers but would slowly recover with the help of the royal physician.

One morning, after his bath and pooja, Madhavrao was sitting on a settee in his palace in Hirkani Chowk. He was in a good mood and gazed adoringly at Ramabai, who sat before him.

Suddenly, a gust of wind shut the window. When Ramabai went to bolt it, she spotted Sakharambapu walking hurriedly towards the Dilli Darwaza.

'Oh, where is Bapu rushing off to?' she exclaimed.

'When did Bapu come?' asked Madhavrao, going to look outside the window.

Bapu was followed by Nana and Moroba. Madhavrao called out to a sentry. 'Vinayak, go and see what is happening outside the Dilli Darwaza.'

'Sarkar, when I came, a few people had gathered outside the gate.'

'Which people?'

'I don't know, Sarkar. I came straightaway to report to my duty here.'

'Send Bapu here immediately.'

When Bapu came in, Madhavrao asked him what was happening outside the Dilli Darwaza.

'Nothing important, Shrimant. People are coming with hopes and demands ...'

'Who are they, though?' asked Madhavrao.

'Our own subjects. Punekars. The ones whose homes and shops were razed by the Nizam. They have been coming to meet you. But please, don't worry about such small matters. I will tell them not to keep bothering you; your health is not good.'

'And the people will listen to this?' asked Madhavrao in surprise.

'Why won't they? What option do they have?' said Bapu.

'Who told you to say this to our subjects?' Madhavrao's voice was sharp and his grey eyes cold.

Seeing Madhavrao's changed demeanour, Bapu fumbled and replied, 'No ... no ... Shrimant, your health ...'

'Our subjects are coming here to meet us and you are turning them away?! What will they think of us? They must have tried to meet us for so many days, and God knows what you have been telling them to send them back. This is terrible! Surely, their needs must be urgent if they are taking the time to come here every day. Go down immediately and tell the people that I am coming down to meet them,' said Madhavrao.

Sakharambapu rushed off. Madhavrao crossed Hirkani Chowk and went straight towards the Dilli Darwaza, where he came face-to-face with Bapu, Nana and Moroba.

The Dilli Darwaza was thrown open. Armed Gardis stood on both sides of the doorway. There seemed to be more than a hundred people gathering on the grounds outside. Madhavrao stood on the threshold of the Dilli Darwaza. Seeing him, pin-drop silence ensued. When the Peshwa took a step forward, many of his subjects came running up to him.

Nana, Moroba, Bapu and the armed guards ran behind Madhavrao. But he was oblivious to everything, including the searing heat of the sun, except for what his subjects were telling him. Seeing their ruler listening attentively to them, the people grew bolder and crowded around him.

But Madhavrao's gaze fell on a very old woman who stood to the side of the jostling group. When she saw Madhavrao looking at her, the old woman came forward with measured steps.

'Who is this lady?' Madhavrao asked Nana.

'I think this is Nimbalkar's wife, Jiu.'

'Who does she live with?'

'No one. She is alone. Her home in Budhwar Peth was plundered. Her husband was a courtier during Thorle Shrimant's time. He and both their sons were martyred on the battlefield.'

By then, the woman had reached Madhavrao. In spite of being in her eighties, she stood tall and straight. As she came closer, she looked at Nana, Moroba and Bapu, and asked, 'Who is Madhavrao Peshwa among you all?'

Madhavrao smiled. Without the royal insignia on his person, the old woman had failed to recognise him. 'Matoshree, it's me,' he said.

'You?!' exclaimed the woman, looking at the young Peshwa in surprise.

'Yes, Matoshree. It's me,' affirmed Madhavrao.

'Good you finally met me, son. I was almost ready to give up and go home. I'm sorry I did not recognise you. Albeit, how could I when I have never seen you? I have hardly ever left my house and ventured outside.'

'Why have you come today, Matoshree?' asked Madhavrao.

The old woman stretched out her arm and uncurled her fingers. On her wrinkled palm was a small yellow idol of Lord Ganesha.

Madhavrao folded his hands before the idol in deep respect, and asked the woman, 'What's this, Matoshree?'

'This is an idol from our temple at home, son. Years ago, my husband had gone on a campaign to the north with your grandfather. While coming back, he got this idol for our temple. Now my husband is gone and so are both my sons. After their death, I was living alone in the house, but now even that has been razed to the ground. Somehow, this small idol survived the plunder. I wanted to hand it over to you.'

The old woman's story gave Madhavrao goosebumps. He stepped back and asked, 'Why give this to me, Matoshree? Why not keep it?'

'Son, what kind of God would give me nothing but pain? Either you take this idol, or I shall simply throw it into the river. What kind of God is He who would snatch away my husband, my two young sons, and now even my house?'

In an instant, Madhavrao stepped forward, held the old woman's hands in his own and said in a gruff voice, 'Matoshree, why are you so helpless when you have a son like me? Please don't be angry with Lord Ganesha. Today, I shall come to your house and take care of all your troubles. Bapu, call for a palanquin and take Matoshree back to her home.'

Then, Madhavrao turned to Bapu. 'Tell the subjects that I shall go around the city myself. I want everyone to come forward with their problems. I shall resolve all of them. But no one should give me any gifts; no one should hold any elaborate welcome rituals.'

※

As he toured Pune, Madhavao realised that most of the two-storey houses in the city had been plundered. Mansions that had stood for generations had been mercilessly demolished. Even worse was the condition of the temples. They had all been ransacked, their idols smashed to pieces. Madhavrao's eyes filled with tears as he took in these sights.

Madhavrao was instantly sanctioning funds to those affected, according to the gravity of their loss. He also issued instructions for the money to be disbursed on an immediate basis. Those who had agricultural land were offered advances to carry out the next harvest.

Madhavrao covered almost every road in the city. As dusk fell, a few flambeau-bearers joined the entourage. The Peshwa's officers took down every command so as to make the disbursements properly. Many hours passed, but Madhavrao kept marching on.

However, as they entered Budhwar Peth, Sakharambapu couldn't help but say, 'Shrimant, it is true that the people have suffered a great loss. But we have to be mindful of our treasury. If we keep sanctioning funds like this, what will remain for the Peshwa's and the palace's own expenses?'

'Bapu, what I am doing now is repentance for my mistake,' replied Madhavrao.

'Your mistake?'

'Yes. The subjects always live under the canopy of their ruler. In spite of knowing everything, I could not save my people from the Nizam's savagery. A king who cannot protect his subjects has no right to sit on the throne. If I could not save them from the Nizam, the least I can do now is compensate them for their losses. Otherwise, the people will lose trust in me. The money that I have taken from the Nizam is being used to compensate the subjects. If the funds still do not suffice, I shall sell the jewellery held in the royal treasury and fulfil my word. As it is, in the condition my subjects are in, I have no interest in roaming around with diamond and pearl aigrettes on my pugree.'

A crowd had gathered in front of Jiubai Nimbalkar's wada. Madhavrao asked, 'Why have all these people gathered here?'

'This is Jiubai's house, Sarkar.'

Madhavrao dismounted from his horse and started climbing up the steps of the house. As soon as she saw Madhavrao coming, Jiubai beckoned to a few women to wash the Peshwa's feet. Then, Jiubai carried out a ritual to ward off the evil eye. Madhavrao observed Jiubai's house while these rituals were on. One door had been entirely ousted from its place. The other door bore axe marks on it. Madhavrao went inside. A simple carpet had been laid on the floor.

'Matoshree, I have come as promised. Now, tell me, what all have you lost? I shall compensate you for everything.' said Madhavrao.

'What do I tell you, my son?' said Jiubai. 'Such a vexing situation this is! The one who looted is our own, and the one who is compensating is also our own. What do people like us say?'

Madhavrao looked at Jiubai, befuddled. 'What do you mean, Matoshree? Who did this?'

Jiubai answered fearlessly, 'It is true that the plunderers were Mughals. But who showed them the way? Do you know?'

'Who?'

'Ask your mama!'

'Lady, what are you saying?' Nana interjected.

Madhavrao stopped Nana in his tracks and beckoned to Jiubai to go on. 'Matoshree, don't be afraid. Tell us whatever you know. Are you referring to Raste Mama?' When Jiubai nodded, Madhavrao continued, 'Are you sure he was with the Nizam?'

'Yes, absolutely. Everyone here is quiet because they fear your anger. But it was Raste who showed the Nizam the way. If you don't believe me, go straight ahead from here. You will see the Raste mansion. Not a brick of that mansion has been moved out of place. How is that possible? Was the home empty that the plunderers did not find anything to loot?'

Madhavrao stood up with a determined expression on his face and said to Jiubai, 'Matoshree, don't worry at all.

Tomorrow, Nana shall come here and inspect your house properly. You shall get an even bigger and better mansion than you had. We shall take your leave now.'

Madhavrao stepped outside and mounted his horse. Then, he turned to Nana and commanded, 'Tomorrow morning, I want Malharrao Raste to be summoned before me.'

⚛

The next morning, Shripati came in and announced, 'Raste Saheb has arrived.'

'Send him in,' said Madhavrao.

Raste came in and greeted the Peshwa.

Madhavrao said, 'Come, Raste. You are a general of the Peshwas. You are also related to the Peshwas by blood. Yet, in all these weeks since we have returned from Rakshasbhuvan, you haven't come to see me even once? I sent messages for you to come see me. Those were also ignored. What is my mistake that you are so angry with me?'

'No, Shrimant … my health …' stammered Raste.

'Oh, was it not good? It doesn't seem so!' replied Madhavrao, cutting Raste short.

'It was nothing serious …'

Madhavrao roared, 'Raste! Do not forget that you are talking in front of the Peshwa! You ignored all the commands issued to you. And now I have come to know *you* were one of the shameless few who helped the Nizam plunder Pune! My own uncle, my mother's brother! A general! Do you disagree with any of this?'

Raste was quiet, trembling in his shoes. Madhavrao turned to Nana in fury and exclaimed, 'See, Nana? These are my family members, and this is how they behave! I'm ashamed. If this is the loyalty and discipline within the family, what example are we setting for our subjects?'

Raste wiped the sweat off his forehead with his shawl and, in a tremulous voice, pleaded, 'I made a mistake, Shrimant. Please forgive me.'

'Forgive you? How dare you even expect such a thing from me? Raste, your mistake—nay, your crime—is so big that even if I tried, I would not be able to find it in my heart to forgive you. How ironic that when the enemy was plundering our city and desecrating our temples, my own relative was lending him a helping hand. I can probably forgive the Nizam for his atrocities, for he is but an enemy—but you? You were my own.

'Malharrao, since this is your first mistake, I am letting you off. I am levying a fine of five thousand rupees on you. If you do not pay this fine in the next three days, I shall confiscate your property in lieu of the fine. Shastri, Nana, it is your responsibility to see that my orders are carried out properly.'

Everyone sat in stunned silence. Malharrao Raste now trembled in rage, rooted to the spot.

Raste was senior in age and honour. He could not withstand this insult. He bowed in mujra to Madhavrao and walked out of his palace to go straight to his sister, Gopikabai.

Gopikabai was shocked to hear about the fine levied on her brother.

'What mistake did you make for Madhava to issue such a harsh order?' she asked Malharrao.

'Well, sister, my only mistake was that when the Nizam came to loot Pune, in order to reduce the gravity of the attack, I pleaded and prostrated before the Nizam to save whatever I could. I got a good "reward" for my services.'

'I shall talk to Madhava. He will not go against my word,' said Gopikabai.

'That is up to you. But if I have to pay this fine, I shall not return to Shaniwarwada ever again, that's for sure!' With that, Malharrao walked away in a huff.

Gopikabai was furious. She sent a messenger to call Madhavrao to her palace.

Madhavrao came and bowed low in mujra before his mother. Not paying any attention to his greeting, Gopikabai snapped, 'Raosaheb, what is this I hear?'

Knowing what his mother was referring to, Madhavrao answered, 'What you have heard is correct, Matoshree.'

'Oh, is it? Why then, pray tell, have you levied this fine on your own uncle?'

Madhavrao had never seen Gopikabai so angry before. He replied, 'Well, when the Nizam came to loot Pune, Mama joined hands with him. He showed the Nizam which houses and temples to plunder. All this openly took place on the streets of our city. Do you wish to say that this act is forgivable?'

'Why not?' countered Gopikabai, adding, 'Gopalrao Patwardhan had also gone to the Nizam's side—you gave him the province of Miraj. Not just that, you also bestowed a generalship on Jadhav. On the parameters of what loyalty was that done?'

'Matoshree, when the mind is biased, everything seems to be coloured in a different hue. Gopalrao and Ramchandrarao are not our relatives—they joined the Mughals because of the injustice meted out to them by us. That is why I had to balance out matters later by doing what I did. But in Malharrao's case, while you were at Sinhagad and I was busy with the campaign, my trust was reposed in him. But he bit the hand that fed him. The crime he has committed is too huge to be let off with just a fine, but I didn't forget his relationship to me. Had it been someone else in his place, I would have had him hanged.'

Gopikabai was stunned with Madhavrao's demeanour. She had never expected her son to behave like this. But she also knew how stubborn he could be. She changed tack and said to him, 'Madhava, please think about my honour too. If you insist on the fine, I shall have no face to show to my family.'

'Matoshree, do you think I am happy to do what I did? He is your brother, but he is also my uncle, isn't it?'

'Then you will remit the fine, right?' Gopikabai asked in a hopeful voice.

'Malharrao should have come and met me after I arrived from Rakshasbhuvan. Or he should have met you, at least. Maybe something would have been possible then ...'

'So you mean to say there is nothing you can do?'

'There is,' said Madhavrao. 'If you allow it, I will be happy to pay the fine from my personal finances.'

'I very well understand your jibes, Madhava! Thankfully, the Rastes have not become so impoverished that they cannot pay a paltry fine! No need for the Peshwa to be so generous!

But you better remember one thing, Madhava. If this fine is taken from my brother, I shall not stay in Shaniwarwada to even have a drop of water!' warned Gopikabai.

Madhavrao's eyes filled up at the thought of what Gopikabai was proposing. But soon, he composed himself and said, 'Unfortunately, if you decide to do that, there shall not be a worse pain for me. You also know that. But I am bound by my duties. Politics does not run on emotions. I have no right to tell you what to do and what not to do. You are free to make your own decisions.'

Saying this, Madhavrao did a hasty mujra and walked out of his mother's palace, while Gopikabai looked at her retreating son confoundedly.

※

In the days that followed, Madhavrao visited his mother every day, but noticed that Gopikabai was getting increasingly curt with him.

One day, Madhavrao was sitting in his palace when Nana Phadnis came to him.

'Shrimant, as per your command, the fine was recovered from Malharrao Raste today.'

'Did you have to take orders for confiscation?' asked Madhavrao.

'No, Shrimant. He paid the fine on his own. I have come to ask where we should deposit this fine.'

'Give the amount to some charitable institution, Nana. As it is, the desecrated temples are going to be rebuilt. This amount will be helpful for that,' said Madhavrao.

He muttered, 'This amount is going to prove very costly for me …'

Nana overheard him. 'What do you mean, Shrimant?'

'You shall come to know in due course.'

The next day, when Madhavrao entered his palace after his bath and pooja, he saw Ramabai waiting for him.

'Are you angry with me? You seem upset,' said Madhavrao when he saw how quiet Ramabai was.

'Sasubai says she is leaving today. Is it true?' asked Ramabai.

'Yes,' Madhavrao affirmed with a deep sigh.

Instantly, Ramabai's eyes filled with tears. 'Isn't there any way we can stop her from going?'

Madhavrao smiled sadly. 'Once your mother-in-law decides something, even God cannot make her change her mind. Rama, I know you are feeling sad, so imagine what condition my mind is in. You may not understand what I'm about to say, but some day you will realise that in the events that happened, neither Matoshree nor I was wrong. But some things are bound to happen. Come on, wipe your tears. Let us go to bid farewell to her.'

Madhavrao started walking towards his mother's palace, followed by Ramabai, wiping her eyes.

❈

No one spoke for some time at Gopikabai's palace.

Finally, Gopikabai broke the silence by asking her son, 'Raosaheb, are all the preparations for my travel in place?'

'Yes, Matoshree,' replied Madhavrao. 'I do have one request, though. I have no support apart from you. Even if you are going to Gangapur, I request you to keep guiding me from there. And please convey to me whatever you need while you're there. Whenever you command, I shall be there to see you.'

'I'm not angry with you, my son. And even if I'm not here, Parvati Kaku will be here to look after you. Rama is also not that young now. She is mature enough to handle the affairs here. Even you have grown up well. So it's better for me to get detached from these ties that bind me here.'

Hearing this, a sob escaped Ramabai's lips. Gopikabai hugged her while Ramabai sobbed like a child. Patting her back, Gopikabai said, 'No, daughter. Don't cry. You have grown up here, so you are bound to feel my absence. But remember, this is not just your husband's home—it is yours. If ever you miss me, go see Parvatibai. I have already told her. Look after your home and hearth. Take care of your husband. If you feel like meeting me, come to Gangapur. Madhava, take care of this daughter of mine. Come on now, Rama. Wipe those tears. I have to leave.'

⚘

One afternoon, Madhavrao came into the special courtroom after a short siesta. Sakharambapu, Pethe and Nana were also present. Madhavrao was in a good mood. Much talking and laughter ensued.

Then, Bapu asked, 'Shrimant, did you get to know about Shastribuva's new feat? A few foreign delegates came to Shastribuva with a complaint. They alleged that Visajipant

Lele had plundered their ships. Shastribuva summoned Visaji to the court, but he did not come.'

'Was the complaint nullified?' asked Madhavrao.

'No! Instead, the matter reached quite another end. Shastribuva asked for Visaji to be arrested and brought to the court. So he had no option but to come. He created quite a ruckus, but Shastribuva held his ground. He ordered Lele to compensate the foreign delegates within three days, specifying that if he failed to do so, his properties would be confiscated and the payment made through them.'

Nana Phadnis interjected, 'But, Sarkar, I think whatever happened was inappropriate ...'

'Why so? Were the ships not plundered?' asked Madhavrao.

'No, no. They were indeed. But to summon a prominent man like Visaji Lele to the court like this ...'

'Nana! I'm surprised you are saying this! You are well aware what prompted Matoshree to leave Shaniwarwada and go to Gangapur,' snapped Madhavrao.

'Shrimant, if someone like Visaji can be pulled to court, then tomorrow who will spare us?' said Bapu.

'If such a situation arises in your case, you will not be spared from the judiciary. In fact, why just you? I will also not be spared!'

'But how will Visaji tolerate this? He will definitely not feel good about being insulted in front of other officials and generals,' continued Bapu.

'So what do you propose, Bapu?' asked Madhavrao.

Looking visibly relaxed, Bapu answered, 'Umm, Shrimant ... Visaji has come to meet you. He is waiting downstairs. Please do tell him off, but kindly see that he is not subjected to such a harsh punishment.'

Madhavrao began to laugh. 'Bapu, I am quite junior to you in age and experience. However, when you started recommending Visaji and even Nana added his two bits, I recognised that Visaji must have come to see me.'

Embarrassed. Bapu asked, 'Shall I bring him in to see you?'

'Sure. If Visaji is bold enough to face me, please do bring him in. I shall carry out due inspection.'

Bapu rushed off to get Visaji just as Narayanrao stepped inside. Seeing him, Madhavrao asked, 'Narayana, did you not sleep this afternoon?'

'No, Dada. Vahini has asked if she can go to Parvati today.'

'Who else is going?'

'Parvati Kaku.'

'Since you are taking your Vahini along and Parvati Kaku is also there, I have no objection,' said Madhavrao. He then turned to Tryambakrao and said, 'Mama, please make arrangements for their visit. If possible, please accompany them.'

After Narayanrao left, Bapu returned with Visaji Lele. Visaji was dressed in a spotless white tunic and salwar. He wore a green cummerbund and perched on his head was a pink turban with decorative aigrettes. He bowed in mujra before the Peshwa and then said, 'You must have understood why I have come.'

'Yes, Bapu briefed me.'

'If this is the kind of treatment that will be meted out to me, it will be difficult for me to serve you, Shrimant.'

'I understand,' said the Peshwa, prompting everyone to heave a sigh of relief.

Emboldened by Madhavrao's reply, Visaji continued, 'Shastribuva holds some prejudices against me.'

'Is that so?'

'Yes. And honestly, Shrimant, there should be a limit to certain things. He didn't think twice before berating you in the courtroom too.'

'Berating me? How?'

'When he summoned me to the court, I made it amply clear to him that I serve you.'

'Then?'

'Then Ramshastri said, "Madhavrao may be a Peshwa in his home. His recommendation won't work in my court!"'

'Is that what Ramshastri said?'

'Yes, Shrimant. You can ask anyone. The court was filled to the brim.'

'This is not a small matter. I shall definitely speak to Ramshastri about this ... but that does not absolve you of your crime,' Madhavrao said coolly.

'What?' exclaimed Visaji.

'You did plunder those ships, didn't you?' asked Madhavrao.

'Sometimes, one is required to do such things,' Visaji replied haughtily.

'Accepted. Was the loot deposited into the royal treasury, then? Nana? Bapu? Do you know anything about this?'

Nobody spoke. Visaji Lele stood rooted to the spot.

'Speak up, Lele! Was the loot deposited into the royal treasury?' Madhavrao asked again.

'No.'

'No?' Madhavrao roared. 'And you dare come to me with a complaint against Shastribuva? Do you think the Peshwas are easy accomplices for plunderers like you? We may plunder but not for personal gains.'

With folded hands, Lele said, 'Shrimant, I made a mistake. But if you decide to, you can tell Shastribuva to reduce my punishment.'

'Lele, I cannot change Shastribuva's decree,' Madhavrao declared plainly.

Visaji Lele's ego raised its head. 'Shrimant, may I ask you one question? Who is the real ruler here? You or Shastribuva? Once I know that, it will be clear who I am serving.'

Hearing this brazen question, Bapu yelled, 'Visajipant!'

But Madhavrao interjected, saying, 'Wait, Bapu. He asked a question—I shall answer it. Visaji, I may be the ruler here, but that does not mean I am above the judiciary. The judiciary has another ruler.'

'And who is that?' asked Visaji.

'The Lord above!'

'So that means my properties here in Pune will be confiscated after all?'

'I suggest you pay the fine immediately and safeguard your properties.'

'If this is the protection I get in lieu of my services, why should I serve you at all?' asked Visaji.

'Lele, you are crossing your limits!' roared Madhavrao. 'You have already received one punishment, but I can sentence you for your insult too! You had no business taking my name in court or mentioning the fact that you serve me when you had clearly committed a crime. I am forgiving you this once, but if you repeat this behaviour, I shall take serious cognisance of it. Now go and immediately pay the fine levied on you. Do not dare come to me before you have paid that!'

After Lele left, Madhavrao asked for Ramshastri to be brought to him.

Around dusk, Ramshastri came to meet Madhavrao.

'Come, Buva. I was waiting for you,' said Madhavrao.

'Greetings, Shrimant. Why did you summon me so urgently?' asked Shastribuva.

'You were so harsh on our Lele.'

'Oh! So news of that episode has finally reached your ears, Shrimant.'

'I know he has erred, but he is also one of our top generals. The armoury is in his care. To levy a fine on him means ...'

'So, Shrimant, you are ordering me to cancel the fine?' asked Ramshastri.

'Not ordering, requesting,' Madhavrao corrected.

'Shrimant should only order, not request. It is also your right as the Peshwa. But then I will no longer stay on. Lele is in the wrong. I honestly believe that the punishment meted out to him is fair.'

'And I heard you also insulted me in court?'

'No, Shrimant, I did not insult you. When Lele started throwing your name around in court to defend himself, I pulled his ears.'

'What did you say? I wish to hear.'

'Shrimant, I told him that he may be a decorated and favoured general of the Peshwa, but that those things have no relation to his crime or to the fact that he has been summoned. In this case, even if the Peshwas were to intervene, their word would not prove heavier than the word of law.'

Madhavrao's face shone with happiness. Tears welled up in his eyes as he said, 'Shastribuva, I am immensely pleased with what you said. I expected nothing less of you. I am very happy with your sense of duty.'

Saying this, Madhavrao removed his pearl-encrusted necklace and offered it to Shastribuva, saying, 'Buva, this is not a prize. I am giving you this to wear close to your heart every day, so that you and I are always reminded of this occasion.'

'Shrimant …' said an overwhelmed Shastribuva, unable to say any more.

'Do not say anything, Buva. Please wear it.'

As Shastribuva fastened the necklace, Madhavrao said to him, 'Buva, rest assured we shall never interfere in your judicial processes. Even if the Peshwas were to stand in front of you on any occasion, do not let that impact your judicial process. May your tongue never falter in pronouncing only the apt and fair judgement for anyone.'

'Shrimant, I'm very fortunate to be serving under a ruler like you, who believes in the transparency of the law. If more rulers become like you, there will be fifty more Ramshastris standing up to serve the Goddess of Justice impartially.'

⚔

In the afternoon, Madhavrao set out for Badami Bangla from the Gauricha Mahal, without giving anyone a chance to inform Raghobadada. By the time Raghoba got to know that Madhavrao was coming to meet him, his nephew had already entered his chambers. Madhavrao bowed low in mujra before Raghobadada.

'Madhava, what a pleasant surprise! How did you find time to come here at this hour?'

'Kaka, I have been wanting to meet you for many days now, but I just couldn't find the time. So I decided to come here as soon as I finished my lunch. All arrangements have been made for Hyder's campaign. When shall we leave?'

'Who, me?' laughed Raghoba, adding, 'Please don't insist on my coming. I won't be able to.'

'Kaka, it would be very helpful to have you with us,' requested Madhavrao.

'I know, Madhava. But I'm really not feeling up to it. And if at all you feel the need for my help, send a message and I shall join you immediately. But I'm sure such a time won't come at all. You will easily defeat Hyder.'

'Alright, Kaka. As long as I have your blessings, nothing shall go wrong. I shall keep conveying updates to you.'

'Take care of your health, Madhava. Don't overexert under any circumstances. And, whatever happens, do not mix in a crowd,' advised Raghoba.

When Madhavrao turned to leave, Raghoba called out to him. 'By the way, I'm going to Nasik soon. Make arrangements for my travel.'

'Yes, Kaka.'

❈

Madhavrao started for the campaign against Hyder. He first went to Satara, met the Satarkar Chhatrapati, paid obeisance at the Shambhu Mahadev temple and went on to Kolhapur from there. As per Matoshree Jijabai's command, he conquered the provinces of Chikodi-Manoli at Kolhapur and handed them over to Jijabai.

The Peshwas set up camp outside the boundary of Kolhapur. One by one, generals like Gopalrao Patwardhan, Murarrao Ghorpade, Vinchurkar and Naro Shankar began arriving and setting up their own camps near the Peshwa's. Since the Peshwas were not yet tasked with any heavy-duty work apart from conquering and extorting money from provinces like Chikodi and Manoli, there was an air of happiness and excitement in the camps.

※

It was early morning. Madhavrao stood outside his tent. Around fifty horsemen from the Huzarati cavalry waited in front of the Peshwa.

Madhavrao turned to Sakharambapu, who was standing beside him, and asked, 'Bapu, how come there's no message from Aaisaheb yet? Patwardhan should have returned by now.'

Hardly had Madhavrao uttered these words when Bapu saw Gopalrao Patwardhan in the distance.

'Patwardhan shall live for a hundred years!' exclaimed Bapu. 'Here he comes.'

Gopalrao Patwardhan soon reached Madhavrao, a small troop of horsemen trotting behind him. He told Madhavrao, 'Aaisaheb Maharaj is waiting for you.'

'Let's go.' Madhavrao turned to Bapu. 'Where is Narayanrao? Tell him I have called him.'

Narayanrao soon came to Madhavrao's tent. They mounted their horses and reached Jijabai's chambers.

Jijabai was sitting on a settee, Ghorpade and Daphle stood beside her reverentially. As Madhavrao entered, Ghorpade and Daphle bowed low in mujra thrice. Madhavrao glanced at Narayanrao, who immediately prostrated before Jijabai.

'This is my younger brother, Narayanrao,' said Madhava.

Resting her piercing gaze on Madhavrao, Jijabai said, 'So? Have the Peshwas got tired of our Kolhapur so soon? Patwardhan was telling me that you are planning to move your camp.'

'Where can we, your humble servants, go? But we have heard that Hyder is spreading his reach in the south. If he is not arrested in time, it will prove costly for our kingdom. Hence, the hurry.'

'Don't worry, I spoke in jest,' said Jijabai. 'You will come to see me after the campaign, won't you?'

'Yes.'

'And then, while going back, you will be taking a pit stop at Satara too, won't you?' Jijabai's voice dripped with sarcasm.

Madhavrao understood the hidden context behind this seemingly simple question. 'I consider Kolhapur and Satara to be two provinces of the same master.'

'Yes, but Satara is closer to Pune,' said Jijabai.

Madhavrao decided to tread carefully. 'Aaisaheb! Maharashtra has two prime deities—Shambhu Mahadev and Bhavani Aai. I go to Satara to pay obeisance to Shambhu Mahadev and then come to Kolhapur to meet you.'

'Madhavrao, you very well know the condition of the kingdom. You are aware that the Satarkars consider us lowly. I have no objection to all the help you are extending to the Satarkars, but, looking at the enormity of it all, sometimes I do worry about the kingdom.'

'Aaisaheb, I understand the reason behind your worry—it is quite justified. But I can only request you to forget what happened in the past. Neither one of us is responsible for what happened during Taraau's regime. I had promised to conquer and hand over the provinces of Chikodi, Manoli and Kagal to you, and I have been working towards it. But regarding what you said about Satara … if I have your permission to speak candidly, I would like to do so.'

Jijabai smiled. 'Please do. In politics, it is always better to do away with formal discussions in favour of a free dialogue. It resolves a lot of misunderstandings.'

'I realise you do not like the fondness I hold for Satara. But I hold equal respect for you and your throne. The chhatrapati's throne is like a banyan tree. In the past, it grew to encompass the entire wealth of the Deccan. Its roots and branches grew to bring so many provinces and people under its shade. However, in doing so, the trunk of that banyan tree got ravaged badly. Nevertheless, it is still standing, protecting not just the people and the provinces that are under its shade but also the roots and branches that have stemmed from it. Tomorrow, if this trunk were to give way, we all shall be razed to the ground. If the chhatrapati is no more, how will this Maharashtra live on? Protecting the chhatrapati and his throne is as much my duty as yours.'

'I am not refusing that at all! But when everyone starts going against me, it is but natural for me to start worrying about my kingdom, isn't it?'

'True,' agreed Madhavrao, 'but forgive me for talking so brazenly—who started this circle of enmity? Taraau Aaisaheb was the one to imprison Satarkar Chhatrapati. Can you tell us the reason behind it? Today, the condition is such that if, by God's grace, I sustain physically and mentally, then only you shall be protected. The thrones of Kolhapur and Satara are both on their way to extinction. Add to that, the Bhosales have signed a treaty with the Nizam, according to which they are trying their best to wipe out Kolhapur and Satara and become the chhatrapati themselves. If we do not maintain unity among ourselves, how can we ever face these challenges singlehandedly?'

Jijabai was silent for a long time. Finally, she said, 'I do trust you.'

'If you allow it, I would like to install an advocate from our side at your palace. If there's any need for my assistance, I shall get to know of it instantly.'

Jijabai looked at Madhavrao with a piercing gaze. 'Shrimant, you are the Peshwa, the prime minister of the chhatrapati. It would be suitable if one of my advocates was installed in your office, instead of the other way round. I won't allow your advocate in my court.'

Madhavrao got up. 'I shall take your leave, Aaisaheb. If you still hold any prejudice about me in your mind, I shall

not insist on changing that. Please be assured that I am
always at your service.'

Madhavrao left Jijabai's palace. The sun was scorching.
Madhavrao and the rest of the group immediately started
riding towards the base camp. As soon as they reached, orders
were issued to move the camp. Vinchurkar went with his
troops to Kagal, while Gopalrao went to conquer Chikodi,
Manoli and Hukkeri. Madhavrao himself went to Jat with
the aim of setting up his base camp there. Once Gopalrao
and Vinchurkar returned, the Peshwas started moving
towards Dharwad. Their aim was to conquer Dharwad and
some surrounding territories, extort around thirty to forty
lakh rupees from Hyder and then return after Dussehra for
another campaign.

⁂

Madhavrao's troops were advancing step by step. The Peshwa
had entered Karnataka with a troop of around sixty thousand
men. All the generals were getting daily updates and messages.
Madhavrao had around fifteen thousand horsemen from the
Huzarati cavalry. He also had fifteen hundred Gardis and
twenty cannons, as well as a few thousand Arabs and Maval
Hetkaris with him. As soon as they heard that Madhavrao
had come to help them, Nabab of Savanur and Murarrao
Ghorpade came to join forces with the Peshwa. Madhavrao
was determined to raze Hyder to dust.

Seeing that the Maratha troops were advancing upon
him, Hyder started his own preparations. Just as he had
given indemnity to the Nabab of Savanur, Madhavrao had

extended his protection to the Desais of Sondhe. Hyder sent his general Meer Faizulla to conquer Sondhe. Hyder's troops also conquered Shiveshwar, Sadashivgadh and Ankola.

Understanding Hyder's ploy, Madhavrao issued due instructions to his armoury.

Accordingly, Sayajirao Dhulpa took three hundred canoes and conquered Honavar Fort, the harbour and a few provinces surrounding it. In a matter of weeks, Hyder's hold over the area loosened and Meer Faizulla retreated to go to Savanur.

By then, Hyder had understood that Madhavrao was not going to be pacified easily. Dharwad was an important and big province in Hyder's captivity. Instead of wasting time on Dharwad, Madhavrao began conquering Hubli, Kundgol, Gadag, Navalgund, Behatti, Mulgund and Jalihaal. He had set up his base camp at Savanur.

Hyder's base camp was at Rattehalli. Madhavrao decided to take him headlong there. Hyder got excited and agitated in equal measure on seeing the troops sent ahead by Vinchurkar and Patwardhan. He prepared to raze them to the ground, not realising that it was exactly what Madhavrao wanted.

Madhavrao had expected that Hyder would come out of his base camp to diminish the advancing troops, thus making it easier for Madhavrao to attack him. His idea worked— when Hyder came out of his base camp, he found himself surrounded by Maratha troops from all sides. They cracked down heavily on Hyder.

Winds were blowing at a rapid pace. Clouds of dust floated in front of their eyes. No one could see anything. With visibility affected so badly, chaos ensued among the troops.

Hyder used this to his advantage and escaped. Agitated, Madhavrao returned to his base camp.

The next day, Hyder lifted his base camp and went into hiding in the jungle of Anwadi.

Madhavrao came back to his tent after taking a tour of the base camp. Narayanrao was waiting for his elder brother.

'Dada, Hyder was made a fool of, wasn't he?' Narayanrao asked.

'Yes, Narayana. Too bad he escaped due to the unpredictability of nature.'

'Awesome! I am going to tell Vahini all these fun stories. She will enjoy hearing them. And if I tell her these stories, only then shall I be able to accompany you for the following campaigns.'

Narayanrao kept talking about his plans. He looked at Madhavrao expectantly and saw his brother lying down with his eyes closed.

'Dada? When do we return?'

Madhavrao sat up. 'Narayana, I have accepted the responsibility of the kingdom. It does not suit a ruler to talk or even think of going home when the enemy is playing right in his courtyard. You should know better than to ask me such a question.'

'No, Dada … I only asked because … because I was excited at the thought of narrating all this to Vahini,' Narayanrao said falteringly.

Madhavrao fell silent. He went to Narayanrao and patted him on the back. 'Come on, go to sleep. It is quite late.'

Madhavrao had finished his morning rituals and was waiting for Sakharambapu in his tent.

When Bapu arrived and took his seat, Madhavrao said, 'Bapu, yesterday we lost Hyder by a nick. Today, I have been informed that he is hiding in the jungles. I don't think he will come out easily now.'

'What do we do now, Shrimant? How long do we wait? The monsoons are due to arrive any moment now. We have barely sixty thousand soldiers with us. Expenses are mounting by the day. Animals are not getting adequate food. In such a scenario, isn't it better to sign a treaty?' ventured Bapu.

'Bapu, don't be silly. If we leave this wounded snake in the open, we will be causing another catastrophe to the Maratha Empire. And, tell us, have we not signed any treaties with Hyder till now? Nana had made a treaty. I had made a treaty during the last campaign. But he is not the sort to live up to his promises.'

'Then what do we do?'

'We should launch a full-fledged, no-holds-barred attack. Eliminating Hyder should be the only agenda of this attack. God willing, we shall carry out this agenda properly.

'We will have to spend this monsoon here. Hyder knows our pattern—we tend to fall back on the eve of the monsoons. But this time, we shall not do so. We shall stay on. Hyder will keep playing cat and mouse with us till the monsoons arrive. The jungle of Anwadi is new terrain for us, but for him, it is his usual playground. He is bound to use that fact to his advantage. But yesterday, Murarrao Ghorpade joined us. With such experienced people on our side, we need not fear anything,' explained Madhavrao.

'And what about the younger Shrimant?' asked Bapu.

'I am sending him back to Pune.'

Hearing this, Narayanrao, who was sitting nearby, leapt up and announced, 'I am not going anywhere. I shall return to Pune only with Dada.'

Madhavrao felt proud but made sure not to show it. Instead, he turned to his brother and said, 'Narayana, you will get bored here in the monsoons. Initially, you may find it exciting, but as the days go on, you will have nothing to do.'

'No, Dada. I shall not get bored when you are here with me,' insisted Narayanrao.

Madhavrao smiled. 'Bapu, tell all the generals to be present for a durbar this evening.'

A few hours later, all the generals congregated in Madhavrao's tent: Narsingrao Dhaigude, Anandrao Gopal, Malharrao Raste, Ramchandra Ganesh Kanade, Murarrao Ghorpade and Shahaji Bhaapkar. Madhavrao reclined against a bolster, flanked by Narayanrao and Bapu. Everyone was waiting for the durbar to begin, but Madhavrao's gaze kept flickering towards the entrance.

Understanding who Madhavrao was waiting for, Bapu exclaimed, 'Strange! How come Gopalrao hasn't come yet?'

'He will come. He won't be late without reason,' said Madhavrao.

Just then, everyone heard a horse neighing outside the tent. Instantly, Gopalrao entered.

'Apologies, Shrimant. Please forgive me for coming late. I had just set out when I received a message from Purandar.'

'Anything special?' asked Madhavrao.

'Yes, Shrimant. The people of Purandar have staged a protest against Aba Purandare.'

'But why?'

'Purandare removed the old fishermen and employed new ones. The old ones, who are now jobless, have staged a protest for their rights. I had already told Purandare ...'

'Gopalrao, there is no point in talking about what happened in the past. Let us see how we can improve things for the future.'

'Yes, Shrimant,' said Gopalrao, lowering his head.

'Today marks three months since we came on this campaign, but our aim remains unfulfilled. I am not blaming you all for this. If Hyder had not escaped that day, he would have been dead by now. You fought like heroes, but fate decided to side with Hyder that day. Who do we blame?'

Raste interjected, 'Shrimant, may I suggest something? Why don't we go after Hyder with a small batch of troops? If we do that, Hyder will start running helter-skelter and will eventually come out to the plateau.'

Murarrao Ghorpade sat up determinedly, his eyes shining. 'Shrimant, my troops shall do this job. I assure you that Hyder will definitely come out.'

'All right, Murarrao,' said Madhavrao. 'But don't forget that Hyder is not a weak or foolish enemy. He may be in hiding, but from there, he is definitely plotting our defeat.'

Soon, the durbar ended. Madhavrao and Narayanrao sat together to read their holy texts. After some time, Shripati entered and handed a letter to Madhavrao. As Madhavrao began reading the letter, the frown on his forehead grew deeper. Narayanrao observed the changing expressions on his brother's face.

'Call Bapu here immediately!' Madhavrao ordered Shripati.

As soon as Bapu arrived, Madhavrao showed him the letter and said, 'The Savanurkars have sent a letter.'

'Saying what?'

'The Nabab of Savanur is getting agitated by the repeated attacks by Hyder. Apparently, Hyder's troops are creating a ruckus in Savanur.'

'Shrimant, we need to fix this Hyder once and for all.'

'What do we do when fate favours him all the time, Bapu? We are doing everything we can. I need to make immediate arrangements to protect the Nabab. If I falter, it will be a black mark against my name. I had planned to go to Mudgal from here, but plans should be changed now.'

'Shrimant, I can think of only one person capable of protecting the Nabab in these circumstances. Gopalrao Patwardhan. He is a general who can fearlessly face the biggest of troubles.'

⁂

The next morning, Gopalrao's face shone with joy as he came out of Madhavrao's tent.

In the evening, when Bapu came to meet Madhavrao, he got to know that Gopalrao had already left for Savanur.

'That is a great development. Gopalrao Patwardhan can take on this responsibility.'

'Gopalrao belongs to a family that has been loyally serving the Maratha Empire for generations. Such families have the blessings of the higher power to discharge their duties successfully,' said Madhavrao.

'Has Gopalrao gone alone?' asked Bapu.

'No. Nilkanthrao, Narayanrao, Kanherrao and Parshurambhau have also gone along with him.'

'But, Shrimant, don't you wish to leave?'

'No, I have cancelled that plan for now. For the next fortnight, Gopalrao has to look after Savanur. After that, another batch of troops will be sent ahead. Then we shall plan our next move.'

Madhavrao was eagerly waiting for some good news from the Savanur front, but Hyder's general was giving Gopalrao a tough time.

Days passed.

Madhavrao was sitting in his tent, wondering what could be done about Hyder, when Bapu came in bearing two letters.

'Shrimant, Shinde has written that some person, who is Bhau's impostor, is advancing towards the south with a large batch of troops.'

'And what does the other letter say?'

'It's from Nana. He says Dadasaheb has been conducting meetings with generals and other senior officers in Nasik.'

'I'm stunned to hear about this impostor, Bapu,' said Madhavrao.

'Shrimant, we should arrest this impostor before he becomes a menace. If we manage to do that, then what is the cause for worry?'

'If the man does not turn out to be an impostor, I will be happy. But if he is a rogue and arrives when we are off to Karnataka, that will definitely be a problem. Do one thing, send letters to the Holkars and Shindes asking them to ascertain who the impostor is. If he is Bhau, tell them to send him here with due respect and pomp. But if he is an impostor, ask them to imprison him immediately. Either way, they have to be alert about the movements of this man.'

'Yes, Shrimant.'

'As for Kaka, I shall reply to that letter myself.'

'As you say, Shrimant.'

'Bapu, there is no news of Gopalrao. When problems come, they come advancing from all sides. I suppose that's life,' said Madhavrao with a sigh.

Just then, Mahadev Shivram entered and handed a letter to Madhavrao.

'Gopalrao's spy is here. He says Gopalrao has defeated Hyder and emerged victorious!' he said.

'What? Is this true? What fabulous news!' Madhavrao exclaimed in utter joy.

However, Bapu was not as happy with this news. For he had an ulterior motive in sending Gopalrao to fight with Hyder. He had been sure that Gopalrao would not be able to defeat Hyder and, thus, would fall from the coveted position in Madhavrao's durbar.

Madhavrao handed the letter to Bapu and told him to read it aloud.

'We went to Hyder's base camp with a small batch of troops. It was a terrible battle. We had the towering fort of Bankapur in front of us. We also had a lot of luggage with us. But, without getting intimidated by all this, we kept moving ahead. Finally, we defeated Hyder. God was with us. Seven

horses and four men from Hyder's side were killed. We lost one horse. Ten soldiers have been wounded. Our Raut was circling Hyder constantly. He brought the news that Hyder had gone to Hangal ...'

Gopalrao went on to narrate the account of the final tussle with Hyder. Gopalrao had managed to outwit Hyder, who was waiting for them at Bankapur Fort. Finally, as the next batch of troops reached, Hyder had retreated.

'Bapu, now we need to plan the next move and arrange for funds. Call Gopalrao directly to Dharwad,' said Madhavrao.

'But what about Savanur?'

'Send Raste for that.'

The troops started moving towards Dharwad in batches. The infantry went ahead. The base camp was packed up. Madhavrao and Narayanrao were sitting in a houdah on an elephant.

'When do we halt?' Narayanrao asked his brother.

'After travelling another fifteen to twenty miles.'

'And then?'

'Then to Dharwad,' answered Madhavrao as he observed the surrounding topography. As far as the eye could see, the soil was black. Bare hillocks stood at a distance. Babul trees, their yellow flowers in bloom, created a sharp contrast with this landscape.

Narayanrao chatted away, but Madhavrao barely paid any attention to him. His mind was engaged in serious matters.

Soon, they reached their halting spot. Madhavrao's mind remained restless. He ignored the tents being set up for the night and the soldiers rushing around to make arrangements.

Finally, unable to keep silent any further, Madhavrao said to Bapu, 'I am feeling very uneasy.'

'About what?' asked Bapu, not understanding where this conversation was headed. 'I have received some disturbing news from Nasik. Kaka is plotting against me.'

Bapu didn't respond; he looked at Madhavrao silently.

'Bapu, I think we should call Kaka here to join us in the campaign.'

'Yes, why not?' agreed Bapu.

'But what if he refuses to come?' asked Madhavrao.

'Why would he? If you broach the topic in a careful manner, he will definitely come.'

'I hope so, Bapu. We are just about regaining our lost wealth. I do not wish for it to start getting squandered again.'

'Shrimant, instead of Dadasaheb trying to loot your wealth by joining hands with the Nizam, it is better that you resolve your personal misunderstandings and bury the hatchet. What difference does it make whether the wealth is with you or with Dadasaheb, as long as it is in the family? It is better to take control of things, so that Dadasaheb doesn't blow this money on strangers. He must have been angry with you about Purandar. That's the way he thinks. He is blaming you ...'

'Yes, I know. That's the way fate is playing with me,' sighed Madhavrao.

Madhavrao could see that Raghobadada's short-sighted actions were bound to cost them all dearly. He knew that if Raghobadada was allowed to operate on his own for too long, the Nizam would again rear his head against them.

But another thought gnawed at Madhavrao's mind: What if Raghoba had joined hands with Hyder?

※

Madhavrao had not given up on Hyder. Irrespective of the problems that came his way, he followed Hyder incessantly. Madhavrao and Hyder had stationed their troops on opposite banks of the Wardha river. Hyder had assumed that the Marathas would retreat during the monsoons, but Madhavrao had stayed put.

Madhavrao captured the province of Haveri by sacrificing many able soldiers from his retinue. He captured the fort of Dharwad, thus making Hyder even more helpless. He conquered many territories standing before the Tungabhadra river, which were previously under Hyder's command. Only Bankapur remained to be conquered.

During his stay at Mishrakoti, Hyder started sending out feelers for a treaty; Madhavrao did not pay heed. He thought of first capturing Bankapur, but Murarrao and Shinde suggested launching a surprise attack on Hyder. Accordingly, the Maratha troops followed Hyder to Anwadi and set up their base camp a few miles away from Wardha.

Madhavrao was sitting on a rock, observing the dense forest in front of him.

'Shrimant …'

Hearing Bapu's voice, Madhavrao broke out of his reverie.

'Everyone is waiting for you,' said Bapu.

Patwardhan, Vinchurkar, Naro Shankar, Raste and Bhosale were all waiting for Madhavrao outside his tent.

Madhavrao's horse was called for. As the Peshwa mounted his horse, the generals followed suit.

The horses galloped towards the Wardha river. When they reached the base of a hillock, everyone dismounted and began climbing up the hillock. From its peak, they could see Hyder's base camp on the banks of the river.

'Bapu, do you see that?' Madhavrao said.

'Yes, Shrimant. This seems to be the perfect place to attack from. But we have to keep in mind that Hyder's troops are well acquainted with the jungle.'

'Yes, I am aware of that. Before launching an attack from here, someone should go with a thousand soldiers and stand guard at the periphery of the forest. That way, Hyder will be caught in a trap.'

Later that evening, the Peshwa's side pushed cannons up the hillock. The generals searched for vantage points to place the cannons. Murarrao, Patwardhan and Vinchurkar chose the best of their horsemen. Preparations went on late into the night.

As dawn broke, Murarrao and Raste took a few chosen horsemen along and, taking due advantage of the dim light, stationed themselves on the periphery of the forest.

Madhavrao had already reached the peak of the hillock and was waiting for the sun to rise properly. When it did, Hyder's base camp came into view. Madhavrao gave the signal.

Immediately, a cannon was fired. Before the sound from the blast died down, the troops began firing more in quick succession. People in Hyder's base camp were caught unprepared—they began running helter-skelter. Hyder took a few of his expert horsemen and fled deeper into the jungle. However, he was intercepted by Murarrao and his men on the periphery. But this time, Hyder had started firing cannonballs at the Maratha troops. The troops started backtracking. Murarrao tried to encourage them, but the troops were petrified. Thankfully, Gopalrao and Vinchurkar reached to combat Hyder.

When Madhavrao got news of what was happening below, he unleashed his sword, climbed on his horse and cried out, 'Har Har Mahadev!'

Hearing this war cry, the horsemen behind him also got animated.

Soon, the jungle began echoing with cries of 'Har Har Mahadev'. Madhavrao caught Hyder's Gardis by their forelocks and entered the deadly maze. The air reverberated with the sounds of clashing swords and screaming soldiers.

Finally, the clashing of swords stopped. The only sound that could be heard was of the wounded soldiers moaning. All the generals were returning to the base camp one by one. Murarrao was the last to reach.

As he dismounted from his horse and bowed in mujra to the Peshwa, Murarrao exclaimed, 'Shrimant, if we had even a little bit of plain ground, Hyder could not have escaped today!'

But Madhavrao's attention was caught by the blood seeping from Murarrao's shoulder.

Murarrao smiled and said, 'Shrimant, do not worry about this small wound. Hyder's escape is a much bigger wound to my heart than this.'

Madhavrao removed his cummerbund and, ignoring Murarrao's protests, tied it to around the wound. Then he said, 'Murarrao, I am not worried about anything. While I have brave generals like you with me, I can defeat ten Hyders. But this wound requires medical attention. Be sure to show it to the physician.'

The rest of the day went in tending to the wounded soldiers and gathering whatever loot had fallen into their hands. A cool breeze started blowing in the evening. The tired soldiers rested in their tents. Madhavrao also sat in his tent, thinking. He knew that Hyder had faced tough opposition after many years; he would not dare mess with the Marathas anytime soon. But Madhavrao also knew that Hyder was not the sort to keep quiet eternally. Some day in the distant future, he was bound to avenge today's defeat.

Bapu entered the tent.

Madhavrao said, 'Bapu, take a pen.'

'Yes, Shrimant. Who are we writing to? Matoshree?'

'No.'

'Then? Shastribuva?'

'No. We are writing to the Nizam.' Bapu looked at him in shock, mouth agape.

'Bapu, start writing. Inform the Nizam about whatever happened today.'

Bapu began penning down the incidents of the day.

❈

Every night, Madhavrao would sit in his tent and have discussions with his generals. Hyder had somehow managed to keep outwitting them. It had been a year since they had left Pune for this campaign. The troops were anxious to go home. Madhavrao knew that there was no point stretching their patience too far. But he also didn't want to go back without trapping Hyder first.

Madhavrao had lost sleep. When he shut his eyes, he only saw Hyder's face. His fever would keep coming back due to the stress, but Madhavrao would ignore it. Narayanrao was getting homesick, but he did not dare say a word in front of Madhavrao.

Night had fallen. The diyas in Madhavrao's tent were burning brightly. Shripati stood guard outside. From his position, he could hear snatches of the conversation going on inside, and they made him uneasy.

Patwardhan was saying to Madhavrao, 'Shrimant, what if we stop the rations coming to Hyder from Bidnur?'

Murarrao interjected, 'Patwardhan, your idea is good on paper, but it won't be practically feasible. The jungle has so many covert and overt entries and exits. How do we block them all?'

'It will be difficult, yes, but not impossible. Someone will have to give up their life for it.'

Vinchurkar said, 'But who is ready to stake his life here?'

'Shut up!' bellowed Madhavrao. 'Please think before you speak. All the people who are here have not come so that they can put their tail between their legs and run away.'

Vinchurkar was flustered at being yelled at by Madhavrao. He apologised for his mistake.

For the next few moments, everyone was silent. Finally, Madhavrao said, 'Patwardhan, your suggestion is worth a serious thought. When a snake is holed up in his burrow, there is no point beating around the entrance of the burrow.

That would simply be a waste of precious energy and time. We have to put our hand inside the burrow and pull the snake out.'

'Yes, Shrimant,' said Murarrao. 'Even if we have to spend one or two months in this exercise, it will be worth it when Hyder finally crawls out and lands in our hands. Dadasaheb will also come and join us, so we shall have additional troop strength. It will not take much time to defeat Hyder then.'

Hyder, who was hiding in the jungle of Anwadi, was soon surrounded by Maratha troops on all sides. The troops were engaged in breaking down all the exits and entries that Hyder depended on. Day and night, the sound of trees being felled rang through the air. Rations coming in from Bidnur had been successfully halted. Hyder had been badly trapped in the jungle.

One night, Hyder's Gardis tried to break the circle formed by the Maratha troops at the jungle's periphery. However, their attempt was utterly foiled because the Marathas beat them black and blue. They were left with no option but to run back into the jungle.

For eight to ten days after that incident, nothing happened.

Then one night, chaos ensued in the jungle near Bidnur. As soon as they got wind of something happening, the Maratha troops began running in that direction. However, Hyder had managed to escape under the cover of darkness. The generals and the soldiers were crestfallen. All these months of planning and working hard had finally yielded no results. There was also no point in pursuing Hyder, since he had already sought asylum with the Bidnurkars. The fact that Hyder had escaped from their hands yet again left everyone sleepless. A deathly silence pervaded the Maratha base camp that night.

Two days later, the soldiers learnt that an attack on the Bidnurkars was being planned. They were informed that Raghobadada was arriving with his troops. That news sent a ripple of excitement through the camp.

Soon after, ten horses came galloping towards Madhavrao's tent one evening. As the troops watched intently, Govind Shivram dismounted from his horse.

Madhavrao came out of his tent and, accepting Govind Shivram's mujra, invited him in.

'Has Kaka not come?' Madhavrao asked.

'Yes, Shrimant. He has come too,' replied Govind Shivram.

'Then where is he?'

'He has set up camp at the previous station.'

Madhavrao looked at Govind Shivram with confusion. Shivram handed a letter to Madhavrao.

Madhavrao hurriedly read the letter.

'Kaka still does not trust me!'

'Shrimant, I don't understand …' said Shivram.

'Govindrao, Kaka is still behaving like a stranger with me. He wants me to hand over the reins of this battle entirely to him. I have no qualms doing that. But why did he need to ask this in such a formal manner, sending us a letter dotted with conditions? Would I have refused him if he had asked me directly?'

'No, Shrimant, it's not like that …' Shivram said, trying to appease him.

'Kaka is like a father to me. Mistakes are made by everyone. The problem arises if and when they are not rectified in time. Govindrao, please go back to Kaka and tell him that everything belongs to him, not me. This wealth, this power, it is all his. He can come here without any doubt in his mind.'

That night, all the generals walked out of Madhavrao's tent after a long discussion, and the next morning, all the soldiers were ordered to stay prepared.

In the evening, Dadasaheb came along with his troops to Madhavrao's base camp.

'Madhava, I should have come and met you directly,' said Dadasaheb, 'but, God knows why, suddenly my mind grew uneasy. Doubts started creeping in. Whatever anybody tells me, I do not find peace till things happen according to my wish.'

The reins of the campaign were in Dadasaheb's hands. He decreed that an attack be launched on Bidnur.

Before the campaign, Dadasaheb said to Madhavrao, 'Madhava, you haven't seen your uncle's sword dancing like fire on the battlefield. Tomorrow, you will. What you people could not achieve in a year, this Raghobharari shall achieve in one day. You shall see!'

Madhavrao smiled. 'Kaka, if that happens, Nana's soul shall finally attain peace.'

Nana's memory made Raghobadada emotional. He said, 'Madhava, if Nana had been alive today, the entire Deccan province would have been under his regime. But such is life and such is fate! Anyway, let us sleep now. Tomorrow's is a very important battle.'

As Raghobadada approached his own tent, Bapu came up to him. He bowed low in mujra before Raghoba, who said, 'Bapu? How come you came to see me this late at night?'

'Dadasaheb, when it comes to his master, night and day are the same for any loyal servant.'

Raghoba instructed the guard at the entrance of the tent not to let anyone in while Bapu was there.

'So, what's been decided?' Bapu asked.

'What else? We have to catch Hyder by his forelocks. Tomorrow's battle should be such that Hyder can never dare look at us again.'

'Nasik is a good place, isn't it?'

Raghobadada was caught off-guard by this unusual question posed by Bapu. 'Yes, it is. But why do you ask?'

'Well, Sarkar, after this battle ends, you and I are destined for Nasik. So I wanted to know if the arrangements are decent enough for both of us to spend our old age there. I mean, I hope I shall also get some place there to rest my weary body.'

'What are you saying, Bapu?' Raghoba asked in an irritated manner.

'Nothing, Dadasaheb. I can only talk this frankly with you, can't I? I'm voicing my concerns about the future in a candid manner. Once this battle is over, you and I are bound to get carted off to Nasik forever!'

'Even if I hold the reins of power in my hands?' Raghoba asked incredulously.

'You are dreaming of having this power in your hands forever now. But if you would have thought clearly about the snake loitering behind these dreams, you would have been more alert. I will not be able to see you spending the rest of your life hellishly because of your emotional attitude. Hence, I'm overstepping my limits—please forgive me for that—but I will say this clearly: Open your eyes, Dadasaheb!'

Raghobadada could not believe what he was hearing. He found it hard to believe that Madhavrao could be as devious as Bapu was alleging. 'Why would Madhava have agreed to all my conditions if he had such devious plans in mind? And that, too, without a murmur of disapproval?'

'Yes, Dadasaheb, but see, that's what the problem is. I'm your faithful servant. I know that I'm not supposed to say all this, but if I do not do my duty, I shall be banished to hell after death. You have a very loving and emotional disposition. You have taken great care of us all till now. You have showered us with your benefaction. We owe our lives to you. Dadasaheb, just think. Shrimant agreed to all your conditions without a single word of disapproval. Didn't you sense anything amiss about that? I can see the stirrings of a devious scheme in this, Dadasaheb! Shrimant is being very shrewd politically.'

'Politics? Where is the politics in all this, Bapu?'

'What else is there if not politics? Shrimant is playing his cards brilliantly. He is using you to defeat Hyder. The Nizam is, as it is, a slain chicken already. Once Hyder is also defeated, there remains only one stone in his way … and that is you! Today, you are busy planning Hyder's defeat. So you do not have the time to think about all this. But once Hyder is defeated, who is going to care for you here? Shrimant? No way! I won't be able to see your pitiable state at that time, Sarkar, so I'm trying to caution you in due time. Please, I beg of you, become aware before time slips from your hands.'

Raghobadada broke into a cold sweat. Wiping the sweat from above his lips, he asked, 'Are you sure this is what Madhava will do with me?'

'Absolutely, Dadasaheb! You look at Shrimant as a son, a mere child. But if he can stand sword in hand before you at the battle of Ghod river, can't he do everything else I just described?'

'Bapu, my hair has greyed fighting innumerable battles and dealing with so many conspiracies. I am not going to fall prey to this youngster's machinations. It was because I suspected that he was planning something against me that I asked for the reins of the battle. Now, just you see what happens tomorrow ...'

Hearing this, Bapu cackled; Raghoba joined in.

༄

The next day, the Peshwa's troops made their way towards Bankapur. Raghobadada was administering every move. Just before Bankapur arrived, the opposite party's lawyer came to the Peshwa's camp to start talks of a treaty. All the generals were unhappy with what was happening.

Madhavrao was trying to make Raghobadada see sense. 'Kaka, I strongly feel we should not go ahead with this treaty. It is time to teach them a lesson via battle. That is the only way to stop this menace once and for all.'

However, Raghoba was not ready to listen. He turned to Madhavrao menacingly and said, 'Madhava, don't try to teach me what is good for our welfare and what is not. I'm not that much of an idiot, am I now? Today if we go headlong into battle and we fail, what then?'

'Is it indeed you who is talking about defeat, Kaka? Please, I beg of you, till we have the blessings of Shiv Chhatrapati on our Maharashtra, we need not even think about being defeated.'

'Yes, sure! But I am still recovering from the wounds of Panipat. I don't know when this paper tower will come crashing down!'

'Kaka, you will not be able to do this …'

Raghoba rolled his eyes. 'Is that so? Well, if you thought me to be so incompetent, what was the need to call for my help? If you think you know more than I do, then why is it that even after one year of trying to catch Hyder, you have suffered continual setbacks? Madhava, don't try to bite off more than you can chew. If you are defeated by Hyder, what face will you have to show back in Pune? You should realise that Hyder is not the same as the Nizam, whom you toppled at Rakshasbhuvan. I am telling you for the last time: You will have to listen to me, and that's final.'

Madhavrao could take it no longer. Helplessly, he screamed, 'Kaka!'

Behaving as if he hadn't heard a thing, Raghoba continued nonchalantly, 'Beyond this, if you still want to go as per your wishes, I am ready to relinquish all the powers vested in me at the feet of Shrimant Peshwa and return. If I had known I was called here to be insulted, I would not have come at all.'

Madhavrao's eyes welled up on hearing his uncle's tirade. 'Kaka …'

'Yes, Shrimant, do speak up!' said Raghoba.

'Please don't make me feel further ashamed by saying anything else. When I decided to hand over the reins to you, I also decided to follow whatever you said. But I spoke out of sheer desperation ...'

Tears started streaming down Madhavrao's face as he spoke.

Seeing this, Raghobadada held his nephew's hand and said in a soft tone, 'Madhava, who am I doing all this for? My life is as good as over. Who knows for how long I may even be alive? But if I go without ironing out all the creases that have fallen on the fabric of our kingdom, my soul will not rest in peace. I can never forget that you are Nana's son. If I do not discharge my responsibilities towards you in an able manner, what face will I show Nana once I die? Listen to me, son. We can always defeat Hyder some other day. But if we return defeated today, how will you ever be able to reign over the north? Today, Hyder is willing to return all our provinces that he has in his captivity. Plus, he will give us thirty lakh rupees and return the provinces of Murarrao Ghorpade and Nabab of Savanur. What else do you want at this moment? If Hyder goes back on his word, believe me, my sword will be the first one to slice his neck. If you still do not trust me, I swear on Nana that ...'

'No, Kaka. I do trust you. Please tell Hyder that I am ready for the treaty,' Madhavrao said wearily.

In the next three days, all the generals bade farewell to the Peshwa and to Raghobadada. Both of them also moved their base camps. The treaty with Hyder had left Madhavrao so despondent that he did not even have the energy to walk a few steps. As the days passed, Madhavrao retreated into himself, unwilling to talk to anybody. The retinue started making its way back to Pune, setting up temporary base camps and collecting dues on the way.

⚯

Madhavrao had returned to Pune after more than a year. However, he got almost no time to rest after coming back. He got pulled into looking after the balance sheets of the campaign. Then there was also the matter of the fishermen at Purandar. But what proved to be the biggest headache was the matter of Sadashivbhau's impostor. The impostor had been caught and repeatedly questioned by various generals. Madhavrao was engaged in seeing that the politics behind this impostor being planted did not harm Shaniwarwada in any way.

Ever since the impostor had been brought into Pune, Nana, Bapu, Moroba and Ramshastri had continually held discussions with Madhavrao about what to do next. How could they ascertain that he was indeed an impostor?

One day, while everyone sat pensively in Madhavrao's palace, thinking about the issue at hand, Madhavrao said, 'Bapu, you have met the impostor, haven't you?'

'Yes.'

'What is your opinion?'

'We are all sure he is an impostor. People who have seen Sadashivbhau are also sure of the same. I don't understand why you are being so cautious.'

Madhavrao smiled sadly. 'Then what should I be doing?'

'Better to declare him an impostor immediately and close this matter once and for all. The more it keeps getting dragged, the more the environment becomes murky with doubt and intrigue.'

'Bapu, if it were that easy, would I have wasted all this time? The revered Anubai has confirmed the same, as have responsible people like Kashiram Shivdev. Still ...'

'Still what, Shrimant?' asked Shastribuva.

'Shastribuva, I still cannot take a decision in spite of all these affirmations received. I am the Peshwa, the ruler of this kingdom. If I were not sitting on this throne, I would have sounded my decision a long time ago. But I am worried about how the people in the family will react to an adverse decision. I will not be able to bear any unfavourable opinions in this regard. That is, in fact, why I didn't even go to see the impostors of Jankoji and Bhau myself.'

'So, Shrimant, what do you think should be done?'

'Let the public decide. There are many old people in Pune who have seen Bhau. Make the impostor stand before the citizens and we shall go by whatever verdict they give.'

'But, Shrimant, this will cause a lot of mental agony for you ...'

'I am prepared to undergo that. Nana, present the impostor before the people tomorrow. Shastribuva, you be present there. I shall take the final decision after their verdict.'

An announcement was made all over town. Every house in Pune was abuzz with the news of the impostor. Early next morning, the impostor was made to stand near a water tank in Budhwar Peth so that people could take a good look at him. He was duly chained and accompanied by alert guards.

People who had seen Sadashivbhau inspected him and returned dejected.

At Shaniwarwada, Madhavrao sat in his palace alone. He had already sent Ramabai away to Parvati Kaku's palace. He felt uneasy. Soon, dusk fell. Parvati Kaku appeared at the doorstep. Madhavrao got up to welcome her. He folded his hands before her and said, 'If you had sent a message, I would have come to meet you. Why did you take the trouble, Kaku?'

'Me? Send a message to the Peshwa? Is that even possible?' Parvati Kaku said in a bitter tone.

'Kaku! Why are you speaking like this?' asked Madhavrao.

'Why should I not? If you considered me your own, you would not have put that man on display at Budhwar Peth. Raosaheb, I have only come to plead with you—please do not make a public spectacle of my husband's honour like this. I cannot bear it.'

'Kaku, please don't speak to me like this. I may be Raosaheb and Peshwa to many, but I will always be your Madhava. If I have made a mistake, it is your right to punish me. I shall bear any punishment you give me, but please don't talk to me like this!'

Parvati Kaku said in a soft voice, 'But, Madhava, what is this I'm hearing? Is it not true that you have made him stand for public scrutiny at Budhwar Peth?'

'I have, Kaku. But I took this step only after confirming from multiple reliable sources that the man is indeed an impostor.'

'Who are these people who claim that the man is an impostor?' argued Parvatibai.

'His paternal aunt, the revered Anusayabai Ghorpade, has confirmed this, Kaku.'

'And you believed her? Then what about the letters sent to me by Bhaskarbhat Vaze and Shivram Dikshit confirming that it is indeed Sadashivbhau who has come back? Are those letters false?'

'Yes, Kaku, sadly those letters are false. Neither of them is ready to sign a pledge confirming their claims. Kaku, please understand. Would I not have been thrilled if Kaka had been found? I respect your feelings in this matter, and that is why I had not displayed this impostor all this while when he was in our captivity. Please trust me—I'm trying my best to resolve this matter without any bias.'

'Madhava, this is a personal matter, something that concerns our family. You do your duty but not in front of prying public eyes. I cannot bear this public spectacle being made of my husband,' Parvati Kaku said, sobbing.

Seeing her in this state, Madhavrao said, 'As you command, Kaku. I shall immediately issue orders to stop the public scrutiny. Tomorrow, I shall start the investigation myself. Is that okay?'

'Yes, Madhava,' said Parvatibai.

❈

No one in Pune could discuss anything except the impostor. The next day, braving the chilly winds, people started making a beeline for Parvati. Every step and bench on the hillock was full of people, right up to the top.

Commoners were not allowed entry into the temple of Parvati. The temple had been fortified with guards and sentries on all sides. The impostors of Jankoji and Sadashivbhau were seated right in front of the Goddess's idol.

Carpets with bolsters and cushions had been laid out for the officers. Shrimant Madhavrao Peshwa sat on a special seat, flanked by Nana Phadnis, Visaji Krushna Biniwale, Moroba and Khasgiwale. Ramshastri and Ayyashastri, both esteemed judges, were also present to make expert observations on the proceedings. Ramshastri requested Madhavrao's permission to begin the proceedings.

Drums were beaten outside the temple to signify the start of the proceedings. Everyone fell silent. The judges fired questions at the impostor of Sadashivbhau. He answered everything in a placid voice, unperturbed by the fact that he was on trial. His face bore a striking resemblance to Sadashivbhau's, but Madhavrao was especially astonished by the fact that there was not a single trace of fear or uncertainty on the man's visage.

'When you were staying at Shaniwarwada, where were your residential quarters?' Shastribuva asked him.

The impostor laughed and replied, 'On the second storey of a palace near Hazari Karanja.'

'How many storeys does that building have?'

'Five.'

'How would you go from the ground storey to the second one?'

'By the staircase.'

'Well, you must have taken that staircase countless times. Can you tell me how many stairs it has?'

The man did not answer. Seeing him quiet, Shastribuva grew excited at the prospect of having caught the man. He egged him on, saying, 'Tell me. Why are you quiet now?'

The man looked at Shastribuva with a steady gaze and then counter-questioned him. 'Shastribuva, you are wearing a crystal-bead necklace. Can you tell me how many beads it contains?'

Shastribuva, his face ashen, feel silent.

Ramshastri got up. 'If you are indeed Sadashivbhau, why didn't you come straight to Pune, instead of wandering around in so many places?'

The man laughed. 'To avoid the *welcome* I am receiving today.'

'Even if we all agree to that logic, tell me one thing: How is it possible that in Pune city, where you were born and brought up, there is not one person who is ready to recognise you as Sadashivbhau? How is that possible?'

'Why is it not possible?' the impostor asked, looking fearlessly at Madhavrao. 'Who will dare say he recognises me when everyone knows that the ruler himself is against me, without any solid proof to back his claim? Who will dare speak against the ruler's wishes and wreak havoc on his peaceful life?'

Madhavrao stood up, his eyes blazing. So potent was his rage that the hitherto confident impostor shied away from meeting his gaze.

Madhavrao said, 'If I had not been judicious in thought and approach, I would have trampled you under an elephant's foot the very day you were caught. I would not have wasted so much time and energy on a fraudulent man like you. Till today, you have been swearing that you are Sadashivbhau, isn't it? Well, today, we are going to test you. I have fully recognised you—you are not Bhau. But I will arrange for some bel-bhandara to be kept in front of you. If you swear on that bel-bhandara that you are indeed Sadashivbhau, I will not ask you a single question further.'

Everyone sat silent in rapt attention. Being made to hold bel leaves and turmeric and swear in Lord Shiva's name was the ultimate test. The man started getting antsy. A fistful of bel-bhandara was kept in front of him.

Madhavrao continued, 'Before you touch the holy bel-bhandara, let your conscience think about whose name you have taken on, what his lineage is, what his greatness is, and then say what you wish to say. I am not sitting here to judge you by your face. As it is, no one has come forward to recognise you by the face, so you have lost that credibility too. But think before you speak now. If your conscience is that dead, you may again speak lies with the bel-bhandara in your hands. That's fine. I shall accept you heartily as Sadashivbhau and take you back with me with pomp. But there's one person you haven't thought of till now— Sadashivbhau's wife. That lady who refuses to believe that her valiant husband has been martyred on the battlefield. That lady who continues to dress as a married woman and not as a widow, in the hope that her husband will stand before her some day. Think! Will you be able to continue with your charade in front of that guileless, innocent woman who is only alive because of that one hope? Think of the terrible sin you will be committing if you cheat her. Come on, lift the bel-bhandara and answer!'

The impostor suddenly raised his head. His forehead was drenched in sweat, his lips had turned dry. Unable to bear it any longer, he fell to his knees and cried out, 'I'm sorry, Shrimant! I'm very, very sorry! I'm not Sadashivbhau … I'm an impostor! An impostor!'

'What is your name?' Ramshastri asked.

'I'm a Kanoji Brahmin. My name is Sukhlal. I come from a village named Tanoji in Bundelkhand. My father's name is Ramanand. My mother is Annapurna. Weary of the daily quarrels and extreme poverty back home, I left and started roaming around the country as an ascetic. The subhedar of Narvar and Ganesh Sambhaji transformed me into Sadashivraobhau. I tried protesting many times, but they did not listen to me. They made arrangements for the troops and sent me here as him. But I'm not him. I am a student of yoga, an ascetic. I have erred immensely. While I do beg mercy from you, whether or not to forgive me is entirely up to you.'

'How do we know you are speaking the truth now?' Ramshastri asked.

'You may investigate. All my family members will tell you the same thing.'

Everyone began murmuring among themselves. Seeing this impostor own up, Jankoji's impostor lost his nerve. He also confessed to his real name.

Madhavrao announced, 'Shastribuva, since this investigation was done in front of me, it is apt that I pronounce the punishment for both these deceitful cretins. Since they have confessed to their real identities from their own mouths, they are eligible for due punishments. They dared to pose as two great, valiant men and caused immense turmoil in our administration and kingdom. Many innocent people lost their lives. Thus—'

'Please! Please show some leniency to a Brahmin, Shrimant!' Sukhlal cried out.

Ignoring him, Madhavrao continued, 'Thus, I sentence both of them to life imprisonment! Put them in the dark dungeons of Nagar Fort. They shall stay there till their deaths.'

※

Madhavrao was lying on his cot when Shripati announced, 'Sarkar, Bapu has come to see you.'

He went out and soon returned with Bapu. Seeing him, Madhavrao slowly sat up. The trial against the impostors had taken a toll on him—his fever had returned.

'Bapu, where is Nana?'

'He should be here any minute,' replied Bapu.

When Nana arrived, Madhavrao said to him, 'Nana, it has been quite a long time since we returned from the campaign, but the balance sheet of the expenses is not ready. Why?'

'Shrimant, due to this matter of the impostors ...' ventured Nana.

'Khamosh! What is the relation between that matter and what goes on in the office? Nana, I want to see the letters I sent from the campaign about the funds needed, and the entries made of the funds sent accordingly. And I want to see it immediately. Is that understood?'

'Yes, Shrimant.'

'I shall be coming to the office from today on. If I see any instance of the accounts having been fudged, I shall not spare anybody!' warned Madhavrao.

Bapu and Nana looked at each other wordlessly. Madhavrao turned to Bapu and said, 'Any news from the Nagpurkars?'

'N-no, Shrimant,' Bapu stuttered.

'Oh, that's just great! That is the alertness you display! Over there, at the Bhosales' court, our advocates are threatened with dire consequences. The Shindes and the Holkars are asked for support against us. Madhosingh of Jaipur has defected to their side. Yet, this is how coolly you are responding!'

Bapu lowered his eyes in embarrassment. Madhavrao continued, 'Send a letter to Janoji Bhosale. Tell him to stop his monkey business immediately and come see me before I turn against him.'

⚞⚟

Janoji Bhosale did not come to see Madhavrao, in spite of the letter sent to him. Each transgression by the Bhosales caused Madhavrao to erupt in fury. Finally, he decided to launch an attack on them. He called for the Nizam's support for this exercise. Having been defeated in the battle of Rakshasbhuvan, the Nizam was compelled to do Madhavrao's bidding.

Seeing the troops of the Peshwa and the Nizam come together, Janoji Bhosale lost all his machismo. Madhavrao easily conquered the province of Varhaad. He extorted money from Balapur and Akola and then started advancing towards Nagpur.

Bhosale could see his dark future before his eyes. He went to Raghobadada to request his help. Raghoba intervened to get Madhavrao to sign a treaty. The Nagpurkars were sending letters begging for forgiveness. Finally, Madhavrao relented and signed a treaty. The Bhosales gave provinces worth twenty-four lakh rupees to the Peshwas. From that, Madhavrao gave provinces worth fifteen lakh rupees to the Nizam, thus further cementing their friendship.

In the north, the Shindes and the Holkars were busy solving the problems that had arisen there. The British had their sights set on the Badshahi in Delhi. Madhavrao sent Raghobadada with some troops to the north while he returned home from Nagpur, as his health had taken a beating.

Madhavrao and the Nizam had grown quite close during the Nagpur campaign, but they could not meet freely in the presence of Raghobadada. After Raghoba went to the north, the Nizam asked to meet Madhavrao, since Sakharambapu was also not around.

Madhavrao decided to take this opportunity and accepted Nizamalli's invitation to meet. Dhondiram Vakil and Krushnarao Balla from the Peshwa's side were to mediate this meeting. Sherjung and Rakna-ud-doula were doing the same for the Nizam. It was decided that Madhavrao and the Nizam would meet at Kurumkhed.

It was winter. The days were crisp and the atmosphere pleasant. Madhavrao arrived at the Nizam's base camp. The latter stepped forward to greet the Peshwa. 'I am so glad you accepted my invitation. Please, come inside.' They stepped inside the Nizam's shamiana.

'Pandit Pantpradhan, is your health better now?' asked the Nizam.

Madhavrao reclined on a bolster and replied, 'Yes, it is better. All thanks to the greetings and blessings of well-wishers like you. I pray for your good health too.'

Rakna-ud-doula clapped his hands. Instantly, a few servants came forth bearing platters covered in velvet cloth. Madhavrao touched the platters, signifying his acceptance of the same. They were uncovered to reveal a gold rose studded with precious stones, rich embroidered textiles, perfumes and carved gold leaves.

Madhavrao smiled and said to the Nizam, 'Generally, the gifts exchanged during such visits comprise studded swords or such other weaponry. The precedence that you have set through the gift of this beautiful rose has no parallel.'

The Nizam and the Peshwa started meeting daily. More gifts were exchanged between the two.

A fortnight went by. Soon, it was the last day of Madhavrao's stay.

The Nizam said to Madhavrao, 'Our friendship has gone from strength to strength in the last fifteen days, but my heart is still not satisfied.'

'Why so?' asked Madhavrao.

'You came to my help when I was in trouble. But I could not do anything substantial for you. You are not fond of hunting or dance performances or even lavish meals. I just kept talking with a wide-open mouth.'

'Well, Nababsaheb, we may have spoken with a wide-open mouth, but it is because of these conversations that I am returning with a heart full of good memories.'

'Wah, that's true. But still, I have a request …'

'Please tell me,' said Madhavrao.

'I wish that you would tell me at least one wish of yours. I would be eager and glad to fulfil it.'

Hearing this, Madhavrao's eyes sparkled. 'When we were returning from the campaign at Nagpur, we diverted our route and went to Verul. It is a spot hidden in dense jungles and quite inaccessible to most. Please don't think that I am saying this with a religious bias, but the sculptures I saw there were so magnificent that words will fall short to describe their beauty. I have no doubt that our relationship will only grow from here, but in case, unfortunate circumstances compel this friendship to fall apart, I request that those sculptures are never desecrated—not by you or by us. If you give me this one promise, the happiness I will get will be unparalleled.'

Nizamalli stepped forward and embraced Madhavrao. 'Wah, Pandit Pantpradhan, wah! I salute your love for beauty and promise you that whatever happens in the future, those sculptures at Verul will not be touched by me. Ever.'

⚔

After his stay at Kurumkhed, Madhavrao halted at Toka during the eclipse. He was happy with the way his meetings with the Nizam had gone. More than that, he was glad that they had cemented a bond of friendship.

One afternoon, Madhavrao woke from his slumber with a start. Since it was summertime, his face and neck were drenched in sweat. Gusts of wind were causing the cloth tent to flap loudly. Madhavarao called out to Shripati. He came inside immediately, holding a bowl of cold water. As Madhavrao washed his face, Shripati announced the arrival of Bapu and went off to fetch him.

'When did you come, Bapu?' Madhavrao asked when Bapu entered the tent.

'Not too long ago, Shrimant.'

'So, what's new in Pune?'

'Everything is fine, Shrimant.'

'How come you came to see me here then?' asked Madhavrao.

'Well, Shrimant ... Dadasaheb has gone to the north with all his troops, and we have got news that Hyder has again raised his head in the south. I thought it prudent to tell you about this development.'

'I had already received this news from Nana. As soon as I reach Pune, I am going to start preparations for a campaign to Karnataka. The treaty signed between the British and Hyder is not so inconsequential, it seems ...' Madhavrao said thoughtfully.

Bapu mustered up his courage and said, 'Shirmant, I heard you met with the Nizam at Kurumkhed. Who was with you?'

'Why did I need anybody along with me? It was a private meeting between me and Nizamalli. We only had some interpreters with us to overcome the language barrier. Are you surprised?'

'Well, not really, but I feel that such a critical meeting should have taken place amidst more security and care. If Shrimant permits, may I ask what the terms of the treaty that was signed were?'

'There was no treaty signed, Bapu. I offered some provinces to the Nizam as a token of my friendship and goodwill.'

Bapu was shocked. 'What? No treaty?'

'No. We just spoke openly. That's it.'

'Shrimant, you went to meet the Nizam alone … at a faraway spot … without informing anybody. I'm wondering what the reason was.'

Madhavrao laughed. 'Bapu, did you really not understand my motive, or are you waiting to hear it from me? You have been in politics since before I was born! I am sure you know the reason.'

'Shrimant, you recognised the prime dangers to the kingdom and made this move. The kingdom is endangered by three elements. The Nizam, the Bhosales and …'

'Yes, Bapu. Go on,' said Madhavrao.

'Dadasaheb. You realised that if Dadasaheb or the Bhosales were to attack you, they would only do it with the help of the Nizam. They would not dare charge on you alone. That is why you made the clever move of befriending the Nizam.'

Madhavrao was pleased. 'Wah, Bapu! Your intelligence and ability to read between the lines have always amazed me. When you came to meet me today, I instantly understood the purpose behind your visit. Do you like this unique "treaty" that has been signed?'

'Shrimant, please don't think I'm trying to curry favour with you, but this is probably the best move you have made in your whole career.'

⚜

From Toka, Madhavrao returned to Pune and instantly plunged himself into preparations for the battle against Hyder.

Since Shinde, Holkar, Naro Shankar and Vitthal Shivdev had gone with Raghobadada, the responsibility of the battle with Hyder had fallen on Patwardhan and Ghorpade. Madhavrao sent Patwardhan ahead and then, after finishing the Dussehra celebrations, started for the campaign.

After establishing his control over Panchmahal, Madhavrao moved to Srirangapattinam. Hyder began to back off. But the Peshwa was well aware of the problem that lay in front of them. He requested the Nizam for help. The Nizam set out with his son and his troops to help his friend.

Madhavrao captured Shira and the territories up to Kolar.

Only Srirangapattinam and Bidnur remained in Hyder's custody. Hyder found out that the Nizam was advancing towards him on the request of the Peshwa. That was the last straw for him. He sent his advocates Appajiram and Karimkhan to initiate a dialogue with the Marathas.

The monsoons were due any day. Madhavrao was engrossed in planning his next move.

One day, Gopalrao came to see Madhavrao.

'Yes, Gopalrao? What does Hyder say?'

'Shrimant, he will agree to any condition you put forth now. I think we should conquer Srirangapattinam and Bidnur and bring Hyder to his knees, once and for all.'

Madhavrao laughed. 'Gopalrao, even though Hyder is our enemy, it will not be right to undermine his courage. He is not so weak to give in easily. And it is not easy to conquer Bidnur either. Add to that the arrival of the monsoons. Our men will not be happy fighting in the rains.'

'What do you suggest, Shrimant? Do we sign a treaty?'

'Hmm, that seems to be the only good option now. As it is, we have got back all our provinces and also collected a good sum of money.'

'But why the sudden rush, Shrimant?'

'Due to the worrisome letters arriving from Pune, Gopalrao! Kaka has returned from his campaign in the north. A lot of mix-ups and problems have occurred. The Kolhapurkars have signed a treaty with the British. You are well aware of my uncle's nature. And Bapu is by his side as an adviser. I am not keeping well, but I need to be in Pune as soon as possible for the kingdom's benefit.'

Madhavrao's health had again deteriorated. He had a fever and respiratory troubles, and was low on energy.

Yet, he persisted and called all his generals to tell them about his plan. Except for Murarrao Ghorpade and Gopalrao, everyone agreed to the idea.

Madhavrao accepted the treaty put forth by Hyder. According to it, Hyder agreed to give back all the territories of the Marathas that he had with him. He also agreed to give thirty-three lakh rupees as ransom money.

The Nizam, who had come with his troops to assist Madhavrao, was utterly displeased with news of the treaty. He sent Rakna-ud-doula to talk to Madhavrao.

'Meer Musa Khan, I think your Nizambahadur has forgotten about what transpired at Rakshasbhuvan,' Madhavrao said to him. 'I fully understand when to go for a treaty. I do not undermine the fact that the Nizam bore a lot of trouble, coming all the way here for us. I will arrange for Hyder to give a substantial amount of money to the Nizam too. Once he gets that, you can return.'

At the onset of the monsoons, Madhavrao returned to Pune. Myriad official matters awaited him. Many generals who had gone to the north asked to meet Madhavrao. Raghobadada had returned in defeat and carrying debts from the north. He was quick to blame it all on Madhavrao.

'Madhava, you are responsible for this humiliating defeat I have encountered. I kept telling you to send more troops, but you turned a deaf ear to my demands. How did you ever expect us to win such a big battle with a handful of troops? If you had sent more men, you would have seen your uncle's miracle then!'

Madhavrao snorted. 'You are absolutely right, Kaka. I gave you a large portion of our troop strength and fought a vile enemy like Hyder with the handful of remaining troops. I returned victorious, got our provinces back and secured a huge sum of thirty-three lakh rupees. And you?'

'Why did you stop, Madhava? Say it. I brought a debt of twenty-five lakh rupees, isn't it?' yelled Raghoba.

'Kaka!'

'That's it, Madhava. I do not wish to hear more pearls of wisdom from you. You think I'm burdening you with my debts. Fine. Give me my share and I shall see how to repay these debts on my own.'

'Share?' asked Madhavrao, looking at Raghoba with a piercing gaze. 'Share of what?'

'Of the kingdom.'

Hearing his uncle's reply, Madhavrao flew off the handle. His face flaming red in rage, Madhavrao roared, 'Kaka! Whose kingdom? Tell me, whose kingdom is this? Yours? Mine? Kaka, you saw what happened after the chhatrapati divided his kingdom into two. But he is the master. He can do what he pleases with his kingdom. We are Peshwas. We are not masters; we are just the custodians of this kingdom. It seems you are forgetting this. I have never refused you from taking the title of Peshwa. In fact, I have offered it to you, time and again. But do not talk about splitting up the kingdom.'

Madhavrao started coughing violently. His body trembled as he choked. Seeing his worrisome state, Raghobadada rushed to hold him, but Madhavrao spurned him with disdain and walked out of Raghoba's palace. Raghoba stood near the window and watched as Madhavrao, coughing and spluttering, walked towards his palace, swaying. His left hand was clasped to his chest. The guards in the courtyard looked at him in surprise.

When Raghoba turned around, he found Gulabrao standing before him.

'Gulab, when did you come?' asked Raghoba.

Gulabrao bowed low in mujra and replied, 'I came a while back.'

'And ...?'

'And three lovelies have also come along from Jaipur,' Gulabrao said with a wink.

'Where are they?'

'I have kept them at Anandvalli.'

'Very well,' said Raghoba, his mood transforming instantly. 'We shall leave for Anandvalli tomorrow.'

❈

Madhavrao woke up to see that the sun had already risen. Ramabai was looking down at him. Seeing his wife, Madhavrao smiled. He sat up, folded his hands before the pictures of Lord Ganesha and Shahu Chhatrapati and got up from the bed. Ramabai brought him a bowl of cold water.

'I won't need this today, Rama. I am feeling better. I will bathe properly in the bathroom. Why are you dressed so early?'

'Mamanji left early, that's why.'

'Kaka left? For where?' asked Madhavrao.

'For Anandvalli.'

Hearing this, Madhavrao sprung into action, forgetting all lethargy. 'Please tell Shripati to send Bapu here immediately. I shall quickly get dressed by then.'

When Madhavrao came back to the palace after his bath and pooja, Ramabai handed him his pills and milk.

'If you hadn't been in my life, it would have been impossible for me to have these medicines. Who wants to have pills twice a day at the age of twenty-one?' He looked at his wife as he downed the milk.

'Why are you looking at me like that?'

'I cannot begin to describe to you the solace I get from looking at you, Rama.'

Ramabai came closer to her husband and played with the buttons of his white tunic. Madhavrao pulled his wife into a loving embrace. Ramabai nestled her head against Madhavrao's broad shoulders, but soon pulled away, saying, 'Oh no, what are we doing? What if someone comes in?'

'Who will come?' Madhavrao asked lovingly.

Shripati happened to come in at that moment. 'Sarkar, Nana and Bapu are waiting for you downstairs. Shall I send them up?'

'No, I shall go down.'

'Please wait!' Ramabai called out to Madhavrao as he turned to leave. 'I will get a new tunic for you.'

'Why? What's wrong with this one?' asked Madhavrao.

She came closer and pointed out the stain of kumkum that had fallen on Madhavrao's tunic. Trying to wipe it away with her hand, Ramabai said, 'This stain ... what if someone sees it? It will be so embarrassing.'

Madhavrao laughed. 'You are worried about this? Don't be!'

'Please, listen to me. I beg of you. What will Nana and Bapu say?' Ramabai pleaded, trying her best to wipe off the stain.

Madhavrao suddenly turned serious and, looking at her, said, 'Let it be, Rama. I already bear so many stains that I should be ashamed of. I cannot wipe those off. This is one stain that brings a smile to my face. Let it remain there.'

Nana saw Madhavrao approaching. He straightened his pugree, and he and Bapu stood up to greet him.

'Bapu, did you know Kaka had left?' Madhavrao said.

'Yes, I just came to know from Nana.'

'You did not know earlier?'

'No, Shrimant. Dadasaheb has been quite displeased with me ever since he returned from the north. If you don't believe me, you can ask Nana here.'

'No, that won't be necessary. I trust you,' said Madhavrao, adding, 'Kaka has asked for his share of the kingdom.'

Bapu and Nana fell silent.

Madhavrao continued, 'Bapu, go to Anandvalli and try to make Kaka see sense.'

'Shrimant, you consider me to be a favoured person in Dadasaheb's posse, but the truth is that ever since I have come to work for you, Dadasaheb does not trust me like he did earlier. After he came from the north, I tried reasoning with him several times, but you know how stubborn he can be. This is a very delicate matter. Please do not make me take on more than I can chew at this old age.'

'But, Bapu, somebody has to talk to Kaka, and soon. His abrupt departure is not a good sign.'

'Shrimant, I think you should ask Govind Shivram to talk to Dadasaheb. Dadasaheb trusts him quite a lot.'

'Then tell Govind Shivram that I have summoned him.'

⚘

As soon as he reached Anandvalli, Raghobadada started gathering various generals together.

Madhavrao summoned Patwardhan urgently and set out to confront his uncle, hoping that he would be ready for a compromise—if not, war was inevitable. Govind Shivram and Chinto Anant met Madhavrao at Rahuri, bringing Dadasaheb's invitation to meet up.

They met at Kurudgaon, on the banks of the Godavari. From there, Madhavrao went along with Raghobadada to Anandvalli. Diplomats and advisers from both sides were also present.

One afternoon, everyone congregated at Raghoba's palace in Anandvalli.

'So what have you decided?' Raghoba asked Madhavrao, broaching the topic directly.

'Kaka, I have never gone against your wish and command. Dirty linen should not be washed in public. Family matters are best resolved in the privacy of one's home.'

'I don't disagree, Madhava. But this situation has arisen because I have been debt-ridden.'

'Who am I to tell you how much to spend?' said Madhavrao.

'Did you see that, Bapu? If I speak frankly, this is the kind of reply I get. Isn't it better to give me my share and get rid of me, once and for all?' Raghoba replied, irked by Madhavrao's snide comment.

'Kaka, division is out of the question. This kingdom is not my own. If you wish, you can handle all the affairs by becoming the Peshwa; I will happily relinquish my title to you. Else, sit tight with whatever provinces you have under your command. You will have to pick from these two options. You always create a ruckus and make irrational demands by listening to people beneath you. You never give a thought to the upheavals you cause in your family and the people dependent on you by behaving in such a juvenile manner. But now, I have had enough. This cannot go on. I am giving you a final choice: If you are willing to resolve this matter amicably, it's fine ... or else ...'

'Else what?' Raghobadada growled.

'Else, I will be compelled to resolve this question on the battlefield. With so many problems pertaining to the kingdom hovering in my mind, I have no time to take part in this nonsensical family politics.'

Madhavrao's emphatic pronouncement left everybody stunned. Raghoba turned into a mewling cat from the tiger he had been before.

'Madhava, please don't go to such extremes. I'm badly hit by this debt and by the worry about how I am going to repay it. Please, help me this time around and I shall never interfere in your matters again. As it is, I am sick of this politics. I wish to spend the rest of my life peacefully, in the service of God.'

Madhavrao finally agreed to repay Raghoba's loan. In exchange, he confiscated all the forts under Raghoba's command and made his uncle pledge not to interfere in any matters henceforth.

❈

It was late afternoon. Madhavrao set out from his Chowk Mahal in the direction of the main courtyard. Nana, Dhere and a few others were sitting in the courtroom, chatting.

When they saw Madhavrao approaching, they all stood up to greet him.

'Iccharampant, when did you come?' Madhavrao asked.

'A long time ago.'

'Then why didn't you come inside? This room is not meant for family members.'

Just then, Bapu came to the courtroom.

'Shrimant, the British advocates will be arriving in Pune tomorrow to meet you.

'The Nizam's and Hyder's advocates have already arrived. When the people from Delhi arrive, we will have the full quorum. It will be safe to say that everyone has agreed to Maratha dominance.'

Madhavrao did not comment. Bapu continued, 'It is not a common thing for the British advocates to be coming here. Those people rule the world. We need to be in their good books.'

'Yes, yes,' said Vishnubhat. 'They are the reincarnation of Lord Hanuman. It is said they also have a small tail that they hide in their trousers.'

Madhavrao snapped at Vishnubhat, 'Vishnu, this is a courtroom, not a temple in which you are giving some kirtan. Why have you come?'

'Shrimant, tomorrow is the last day of the abhishek … I had just come to tell you that …' stammered Vishnu.

'Okay. Understood. You may go now!' Madhavrao commanded.

Stunned by Madhavrao's rage, Vishnu scampered off like a frightened rabbit.

'Nana, Bapu, Moroba, I am tasking you three with the responsibility of looking after the British advocates. See that they are not left wanting for anything,' said the Peshwa.

※

The next evening, Bapu came to Madhavrao to announce the arrival of Mr Mostin.

'Shrimant, he is very eager to meet you. He is a nice man. Very talkative and pleasant. Will it be possible for you to meet him tomorrow?'

'No, Bapu. It won't be prudent to meet him so soon. Let him stay here for the next week. Keep stalling him on the pretext of my health. Station a few of our trusted people around him. It is important to know his motive for meeting me, as well as his line of thought.'

Two days later, Nana came to Madhavrao with the news that the British had sent an advocate named Braun to Raghobadada.

'Just as we thought,' said Madhavrao. 'Nana, be very careful and alert. I need to know everything that is going on. Also, one more thing: When I finally meet the advocate, the durbar should be opulently decorated. He should go back duly impressed with our power and pomp.'

Mostin met with Nana, Sakharambapu and the king of Bidnur, who was under Madhavrao's refuge. Madhavrao was being duly briefed about all these meetings. Finally, he decided to meet Mostin.

On the day of the meeting, palanquins started arriving at the Dilli Darwaza, one behind the other. Ramshastri and

Moroba stood at the gate to welcome the guests. Some of the finest horses from the Peshwa's cavalry were lined up on both sides of the Dilli Darwaza. The horsemen atop them wore bright yellow turbans. Gardis wearing red pugrees were also stationed. Seeing this regalia, the generals understood the importance of the durbar.

Mostin arrived. Shastri and Bapu stepped forward to greet him. He was dressed in a coat, slim trousers and a white hat.

As he entered the main courtyard, hat in hand, Mostin noticed the fluttering flags of the Peshwa's kingdom. The fountains in Chimnebaug danced merrily. Bapu and Shastri guided Mostin to the chowk of the Ganesha Mahal.

Madhavrao stood on the terrace and examined Mostin's reaction. He smiled, noticing how awed the British officer looked. He turned and walked away to his palace.

It was hardly any surprise that Mostin was awestruck by what he saw. The Ganpati Mahal was decorated to the hilt. Its carved rosewood canopies gleamed. The durbar room was bedecked with low settees with bolsters and cushions arranged tastefully on them. Every settee had a plush Persian carpet laid out in front of it. Frankincense accorded a heady atmosphere to the room. The canopy over the idol of Lord Ganesha was bedecked with precious stones that shone like stars. The throne was covered with a richly embroidered cloth, and two green velvet bolsters were set on the throne for the Peshwa to recline on.

On the right side of the throne, a special settee was arranged for Mostin. He sat there, admiring the durbar. He asked Bapu, 'When will Madhavrao Peshwa arrive?'

'The durbar will commence at exactly 4 p.m., as decided,' replied Bapu.

'Is the Peshwa that much of a stickler for time?'

'You shall see for yourself, sir.'

Just then, trumpets were blown and drums were beaten.

'*Ba Adab, Baa-Mulahija, Hoshiyaar ...*'

The entire durbar got up to pay salutations to Madhavrao Peshwa, who entered, following a retinue of sentries and guards. Ramshastri tied a garland of flowers on Madhavrao's wrist and then Madhavrao walked towards his throne. Mostin keenly observed everything.

Madhavrao's pugree had a beautiful diamond aigrette and plumes. He wore a spotless white tunic-salwar and a pearl necklace, and a sword rested in his cummerbund. Madhavrao accepted the mujras of the audience as he walked to the throne.

The durbar commenced after a perfunctory dance performance. Bapu introduced Mostin to Madhavrao. Interpreters from both sides came forward. Madhavrao accepted the gifts offered by Mostin. He also made small talk with Mostin.

Then, Hyder's advocate, who was present in court, also greeted Madhavrao in the same way.

Madhavrao spoke to Mostin through the interpreters and then commenced the work of the durbar.

Before the durbar ended, Madhavrao extended an invitation for Mostin to meet him.

Four days later, Mostin went to meet Madhavrao at Shaniwarwada.

Very few people were present during this meeting. Apart from the interpreters from both sides, only Bapu, Nana, Govind Shivram, Moroba Phadnis and Madhavrao's physician, Hakim Mohammed Ali Khan, were present.

'So, what does your government want?' Madhavrao asked.

'I have come with the Company Sarkar's message. They want the relations between us to always remain cordial and friendly.'

'Tell the Company Sarkar that I also wish the same,' said Madhavrao.

As the interpreter said this to Mostin, the Englishman's face eased into a smile. He said to Madhavrao, 'We wish to have some concessions from you.'

'Go ahead.'

'We want permission for our ships to be let through the ports of Malvan and Rayri.'

Madhavrao's forehead creased deeply. 'What for?'

'That route will be convenient for us to carry our arms and ammunition to defeat Hyder.'

'Are you waging a war on Hyder?' Madhavrao asked in surprise.

'Yes, it is all fixed now. Shrimant, if you sign a treaty with us, we shall help you in all your wars in future. We value nothing more than friendship. To cement our friendship, you give us Vasai and Saashti, and, in return, we shall win Soundh and Bidnur for you.'

Madhavrao looked at Mostin, amused. 'Sahib, who is my enemy? The Nizam? The Badshah sitting in the north? Hyder sitting in the south? The fact remains that if any of these are victorious against us, they are still our own people.

They are Indian. How can we take the help of foreigners like you to fight against our own kin? Look at you … You came in as merchants but have been so quick to trade your scales for swords!'

'Shrimant, our motive is not bad. We only wish for our friendship to get strengthened.'

'Is that so?' Madhavrao said, his voice growing sterner. 'If that's the case, then what discussion is your Mr Braun having with my uncle in Nasik? Friendly talks? What kind of treaty did you sign with the Nizam? One of friendship? Why did you meet the king of Bidnur, who is under our refuge? Do you think we do not know about these things? Sahib, your friendship is a dangerous proposition. One day, it is going to cost our country dearly.'

Mostin began sweating profusely. He realised that his dreams of getting Saashti and Vasai were evaporating into thin air. The meeting had unexpectedly taken a deeply unpleasant turn.

He stuttered and said, 'Shrimant, you misunderstand me. We want Vasai only for mercantile purposes.'

'Compromises and treaties are never one-sided, Mostin Sahib! We shall give you Vasai, but only if you agree to our terms and conditions.'

'Yes, yes, why not!' exulted Mostin, seeing the possibility of things turning in his favour again. The Company had asked him to get Vasai and Saashti at any cost.

Madhavrao carefully chose his words. 'Mostin Sahib, I shall be glad to give you Vasai and Saashti if that strengthens our friendship. But in lieu of that, you also have to give me something to make me happy …'

'Yes, of course, Shrimant. Please tell me what you want. We will be more than glad to fulfil it.'

'Sahib, I will give you Saashti and Vasai if you give me two such places in your country where I can build forts, maintain my troops and conduct business from.'

Mostin's dreams came crashing down in an instant. 'I ... I shall ... tell the Company about your condition ... and come back to you with their reply.'

'Absolutely. I shall wait to hear from you,' Madhavrao said coolly.

※

Even though they faced disappointment at Madhavrao's court, the Englishmen did not lose heart. Mostin and Braun went back to Raghobadada. By then, the Bhosales had openly sided with Raghobadada. The Holkars' generals, Gangoba Tatya and Chinto Vitthal, had stationed themselves as Raghoba's advisers. Madhavrao got the news that Raghoba had started assembling his army at Nasik. He called for an urgent meeting with Nana, Moroba, Bapu, Shastri and Iccharampant.

'Shrimant, Dadasaheb has started gathering his troops,' Moroba said. 'Gangoba Tatya and Chinto Vitthal are helping him with their own troops. Apart from that, the Nagpurkars and the Gaekwads are also with Dadasaheb. This is the situation as it stands today.'

'So it seems Kaka has decided to wage war,' said Madhavrao. 'He is determined to add fuel to the fire of this domestic quarrel, instead of resolving it amicably.

Fine. I want all of you to give me unbiased advice, without considering the fact that I am up against my own Kaka.'

Patwardhan said, 'Shrimant, I have my troops with me. If you permit, I can immediately charge on Dadasaheb for committing treason. But, considering this is a family matter, it will be best resolved amicably between the both of you.'

Madhavrao smiled sadly and said, 'Gopalrao, don't I realise that? Do you think I am happy waging a war on my uncle? But there's a limit to forbearance. You are aware of what chaos Kaka has created in the north. In spite of that, I paid off his huge debt of twenty-five lakh rupees. Still Kaka is back to square one. Today, I really miss one person.'

'Who, Shrimant?'

'Malharba! He was a big support to me. His death has created a big void in my life. I don't think there will be anyone good enough to replace him. He used to get angry with me, tease me, everything ... But he never held me ransom. If he were alive today, this situation would never have arisen in the first place.' Madhavrao sighed. 'Bapu—'

'No, Shrimant. Dadasaheb will not listen to me,' Bapu stated emphatically.

'So what should we do?' Madhavrao asked.

'Shrimant, I do hold affection for Dadasaheb, but I am at your service. I think it is best to start this campaign before Dadasaheb joins hands with the British or the Mughals, because if that happens, we cannot be assured of success.'

'I agree with your opinion, Bapu,' said Madhavrao.

'But, Shrimant, we are still falling short of troops. It is better to embark on the campaign when we have sufficient troop strength. Else, we will be overpowered by Dadasaheb's troops,' Bapu said cautiously.

'Bapu, I do not have time to think so much,' replied Madhavrao, adding, 'Nana, start preparations to embark on the campaign with whatever troops we have. Send an order to the north to meet us midway. Patwardhan, Raste, Dhaigude and Biniwale are with us, so let us start without wasting further time. We should set up our base camp in the next two days.'

Horsemen were leaving from Pune. The generals immersed themselves in preparing for the campaign. Horsemen began leaving from Pune. Soon, Madhavrao, too, was ready to leave. He took the offering of a coconut that Shastribuva gave him in the temple and set out for the base camp. The drums started beating at the Dilli Darwaza, signalling to the Punekars that the Peshwa was beginning his campaign.

∞

It did not take much time for news of Madhavrao's preparations to reach Raghobadada. At the last moment, the Holkars refused to get involved in what was clearly a family argument. So Raghoba started off to tackle Madhavrao with the troops he received from the Gaekwads. Janoji Bhosale retained his support for Dadasaheb. He came all the way to Tuljapur, plundering villages and collecting ransom money on the way. He had joined hands with the British for their support. Dadasaheb assembled his troops at the confluence of the Warna and the Godavari rivers.

He reached Chandwad, but realising that Madhavrao had a bigger army, refrained from launching an attack. Instead, he sought temporary refuge in the village of Ghodpe. But Madhavrao was close on his heels. He managed to catch up with and confront Dadasaheb near Ghodpe. A dismayed Raghoba had no option but to rise to the occasion with the twenty-five-thousand-strong army he had.

The battle began in the afternoon, and it became evident early on that Madhavrao was winning. Raghoba's trusted lieutenant, Chinto Vitthal, got wounded. His brother, Moro Vitthal, was slain. Dadasaheb's troops began retreating in fear. Chaos ensued.

Crazed by the victory, Madhavrao's soldiers plundered Raghobadada's base camp. They took twenty elephants, all the arms and ammunition, five hundred horses and eight hundred camels. Raghobadada was stunned. He took refuge in the fort of Ghodpe. Madhavrao ordered Patwardhan, Ramchandra Ganesh and Visajipant Krishna to hold the fort captive from all sides.

The next day, Madhavrao inspected the siege and started towards the main checkpost located on the road to the fort's entrance. That post was being overlooked by Patwardhan.

It was a sweltering day. Ignoring the blazing sun overhead, Madhavrao rode up to Patwardhan and told him, 'Go up to the fort and tell Kaka that if he does not come down in the next two and a half hours, we will be left with no choice but to fire cannonballs at the fort. The responsibility of that attack shall remain not on us but on Kaka.'

Gopalrao and a few horsemen galloped like the wind to carry out Madhavrao's instructions. Seeing the rivulets of sweat trickling down Madhavrao's young face, Visajipant said to him, 'Shrimant, please rest a bit in the shade till Patwardhan comes down.'

But Madhavrao refused, saying, 'No, Visajipant. I will not be able to rest till I resolve this issue, once and for all. Tell the ordnance to be prepared to fire the cannons.'

He turned to Moroba Phadnis and said, 'Call for the Huzarati horsemen, along with our elephant.'

The sun was beating down mercilessly, but Madhavrao stood his ground with fierce determination. Straddled on his horse, he looked towards the fort to see what message would be coming forth. After about an hour, Gopalrao came down with his horsemen. 'Shrimant, Dadasaheb is coming down from the fort to surrender to you!' he exclaimed.

'Thank God! The Lord has saved us from further embarrassment,' said Madhavrao.

Raghobadada walked towards the Peshwa with his head bowed. He wore a white tunic, salwar and a cummerbund with a small dagger. Beyond that, he had nothing on his person. No necklace, no aigrette in the pugree, nothing.

Madhavrao stepped forward and prostrated at his uncle's feet. 'Kaka!'

Raghobadada was astounded with this gesture. He had not expected this treatment.

'Madhava, I have been defeated. I stand before you in utter surrender.'

'Kaka, the heat is relentless. Please, let us go to our base camp and rest a bit.'

Raghoba raised his head to look at Madhavrao, who was pointing towards an elephant bedecked with a silver houdah. The mahout made the elephant sit down and rested a stepladder against his back. Wordlessly, Raghobadada climbed up. Just as Madhavrao began taking his first step, he heard the sound of galloping horses.

A subhedar who had stood duty at the siege came up to him. 'Sarkar, he was trying to escape by disguising himself.'

Gangoba Tatya had been brought to him in chains. Tatya looked at Raghobadada sitting on the elephant and instantly fell at Madhavrao's feet, crying, 'Shrimant, mercy, Shrimant …'

Madhavrao did not even look at him. He said to the subhedar, 'Bring him to Pune and make him stand before me in chains. That is your responsibility.'

Then he turned to Visajipant Biniwale and commanded, 'Take your troops and set up camp at Nasik. Come back to Pune only after you have recovered all the provinces that were under Kaka's jagir.'

❀

When the procession reached the Dilli Darwaza, Shrimant Peshwa alighted from the houdah. He looked at Raghoba and said, 'Kaka, please come.'

Raghobadada started walking alongside Madhavrao, his head lowered. As they reached Hirkani Chowk, they saw Bapu and Nana standing there to welcome them. When Bapu looked at Raghobadada, his eyes welled up.

Ramabai and Narayanrao's wife, Gangabai, came forward and bowed low at Raghobadada's feet. He blessed them both and walked slowly to his palace. Madhavrao looked at his retreating figure sadly.

Along with Raghobadada, all his companions had also been arrested. Sakharambapu tried his best to get them released, but his efforts proved futile.

Late one evening, Madhavrao and Ramshastri were talking in his palace when Nana Phadnis came in.

'Dadasaheb Maharaj has sent for Shrimant,' he announced.

'Why? What happened?'

'Last night, after the main gates of the wada were closed, Raghobadada's refugee Vinayakbhat started leaving from the wada. He was prevented from doing so. This matter reached Dadasaheb's ears and he is now fuming about it.'

'Who else is there?'

'Bapu was there but he left just before I came here.'

Madhavrao looked at Shastribuva. 'Did you see that, Buva? This is what happens. I do something to protect Kaka and it is always taken in the wrong sense.'

'Go on and meet Dadasaheb, Shrimant. I shall take your leave.'

Madhavrao and Nana went to Raghobadada's palace. Madhavrao saw his uncle pacing up and down his chambers like a wounded tiger.

Seeing them, Raghobadada yelled, 'Oh! Did you hear about what transpired?'

'What, Kaka?' Madhavrao asked coolly.

Pointing to Nana, Raghobadada barrelled on, saying, 'This ... this stupid clerk of yours dared insult me to my face! I wanted to send Vinayakbhat out for some work, but he was disallowed from exiting the wada. If my commands don't hold even this much value, why should I stay here at all? No! I shall not stay here. I shall go to Anandvalli. I do not wish to stay here for a moment longer! Why are you looking at me like this? You think I'm joking?'

Madhavrao simply laughed. This caused Raghoba to get even more incensed. He asked Madhavrao, 'What's so funny? Why are you laughing? Is it because I'm leaving?'

'No, Kaka. I am not laughing at you. I am laughing at my fate. I am forced to do just what I never wished to. Kaka, have you forgotten so early that you surrendered yourself to me completely at Ghodpe?'

The last sentence was enough to stun Raghoba. He composed himself and said, 'If imprisoning me was your aim, why do it with false pomp and celebration in my honour? Why bring me to Pune in a procession?'

'Kaka, it is indeed my bad luck that I need to spell out the reasons for you. I had to do it to protect our family's honour. Had I brought you to Pune like a normal prisoner, people would have laughed at us. I brought you back in pomp to protect the family name, but, unfortunately, you took it as something else.'

'Oh! So, Shrimant Peshwa, I am your prisoner then, is it?' Raghobadada asked sarcastically.

A nerve on Madhavrao's forehead started twitching. Unable to control himself any longer, he bellowed, 'It's good you yourself accepted and proclaimed that title. Remember that title the next time you talk to me like this. And why should you not be imprisoned, tell me? Give me one good reason!'

'Now you dare raise your voice, Madhava? I have done nothing but take care of you, help you, protect you ... and this is how you repay me?' screamed Raghoba.

'Khamosh! Do you really not know what you have done for me and this kingdom in the last ten years? Are you that deluded? If you are, let me tell you what you have done. My father passed away and I became the Peshwa at the tender age of sixteen. Your duty was to guide me, help me. Instead, you chose to simply walk away from the campaign at Karnataka, leaving everything in my inexperienced hands. When I returned victorious, instead of patting me on the back, you joined hands with the Nizam and Bhosale, and stood as an enemy against me. You wreaked sudden havoc on me at Ghod river. I embraced your shoes to my heart and asked you to take the Peshwai in your hands—still you did not trust me. You cemented your friendship with the Nizam by giving away the provinces that I had won in battle. It was my good fortune that the Nizam betrayed you and plundered Pune. I defeated the Nizam at Rakshasbhuvan, and, without me willing to, the responsibility of the entire kingdom came to rest on my shoulders …'

Madhavrao's voice was getting sharper with every sentence he uttered. Raghobadada trembled with impotent rage.

Madhavrao continued, 'I still forgave you. Without holding any grudges, I called you for the next campaign to Karnataka. I put all the power in your hands because you stubbornly asked for it. And how did you use that power? By signing a treaty with Hyder! That too, when Hyder was on the verge of being defeated! Opportunities like that come knocking only once, but thanks to your actions, I lost that golden opportunity too. Hyder escaped right from under my nose.'

'Madhava, if you were so angry—' Raghoba tried interjecting.

But Madhavrao cut him short. 'Kaka, don't interrupt me. I am not interested in hearing anything. You never placed any premium on blood ties, and I never let go of them. That is why all this has happened. In spite of losing to Hyder, I consoled myself with the knowledge that I had got my uncle back. I was happy with the fact that our relationship had improved. That is why I sent you to the north. But everybody knows what great things you have achieved there! Nana, that is what Kaka is known best for—running away from every battlefield at the crux ...'

'Madhava!' Raghoba said with a trembling voice. 'Who are you saying this to? To this Raghobharari?'

Madhavrao smiled wanly. 'Kaka, tell these tall tales to people under your patronage. Maybe they will believe it. Don't tell me. You had gone up to Attock. But at the most important point, you returned, giving the false excuse of your father's letter having summoned you.'

'Madhava, what do I tell you ... What do I tell you about the efforts I took during the campaign to the north?' Raghoba said, trying to salvage his pride.

'You don't need to tell me anything, Kaka. Everything is crystal clear. If a campaign goes well, one at least returns with some ransom. You knew that I am under heavy debt. Yet, instead of bringing in some money, what you brought back was just more debt. Not just that—you also brought back the disrepute of torturing a modest lady like Ahilyabai. When I read the letter written to me by that motherly figure, I couldn't meet my own eyes in the mirror. The Holkars have always supported the Peshwas—but you? You went ahead and tortured their widow for money! Your actions are despicable, to say the least!'

'Madhava, you are daring to say all this because I'm your prisoner, isn't it? At least be aware that you are saying all this to a Brahmin.'

'Why are you even uttering that word, Kaka? Do you even know the duties of a Brahmin? It is not as easy as running a theatrical troupe like you do! And a Brahmin who plundered a holy place like Paithan should really think twice before calling himself that!'

Raghobadada lowered his gaze in shame.

'Kaka, I still forgave you, but you continued to act like a new bride, huffing and puffing at us. You went to the extent of asking for your share of the kingdom. I went all the way to Anandvalli to make you see sense. I tried to cajole you. I even paid off your debt. But you went behind my back to start talks with the British. Kaka, today you are feeling insulted because I have imprisoned you. Have you ever given any thought to what I felt when you stationed two thousand Gardis and imprisoned me at Aalegaon?'

Turning to Nana, Madhavrao continued, 'Nana, from today, Kaka will be under formal imprisonment. Put up checkpoints around here. No business shall be done here without my permission. Make a list of people under Kaka's patronage. I shall choose whom to retain and whom to be let go of. Make arrangements to see that Kaka gets all the things he requires, but only what he truly needs; I shall permit no luxuries. Anyone who dares to transgress our orders shall be sentenced to death.'

Madhavrao stomped out of Raghobadada's palace without turning back to look at him.

❈

Shaniwarwada wore a completely different look after these orders given by Madhavrao.

Raghobadada was kept under strict vigilance.

Gaekwad, who used to help Raghobadada, escaped Madhavrao's wrath because he died an untimely death, but other helpers of Raghoba, like the Nagpurkar Bhosales, were not so lucky. Madhavrao levied a fine of thirty lakh rupees on Gangoba Tatya, but seeing that the money was not forthcoming, he summoned Tatya before him in the court.

'Tatya, you are an eminent general of the Holkars,' said Madhavrao in the courtroom. 'I had expected so much loyalty from you. But you were never true to those expectations. I never show any relent towards anyone who dares to be disloyal to the Peshwai. But looking at your age and position, I decided to just levy a fine on you. However, you have still not deposited that fine in our treasury. Do you have anything to say about this?'

Gangoba Tatya and his son, who had accompanied him, looked at Madhavrao with blazing eyes. Somehow, Tatya composed himself and said, 'Shrimant, you have levied this fine on me because you got an upper hand in the battle. If you really think this fine is justified, may I ask how much fine you have levied on Raghobadada, on whose instructions I fought against you?'

Madhavrao smiled. 'Gangoba Tatya, you forget ... Raghobadada is my relative. Not just that, he has gone all the way to Attock for the Maratha Empire. By God's grace, he has that one redeeming point. Tatya, you tell me one thing you have achieved for the Maratha Empire. If you can, I shall reduce your fine. Ramshastri is also present here. If I am saying something wrong, he shall correct me. As the judicial head of our kingdom, his advice shall be heeded.'

In his heart, Gangoba Tatya knew he was defenceless, yet he tried to salvage his pride. 'Shrimant, what is the relation between your family disputes and what I have done for the Maratha Empire? The two matters are completely unrelated. But I don't blame you. You are too young to understand these intricacies. That's the lament of the kingdom right now. Maturity has gone for a toss and children are running matters of the kingdom. How can I even expect to get justice in such a scenario? Thirty lakh rupees is not a small amount for a simple man like me. And it is not even fair to expect me to pay such a big amount, just because the Peshwa's treasury lacks funds. This is nothing but another form of extortion. And I don't understand one thing: Why is the Peshwa nourishing a live snake in his own house and then trying to kill a rope by labelling it a snake?'

Madhavrao stood up, trembling with rage, and bellowed, 'Wah, wah, Tatya! I don't know what to say to you! You dare to call the man who patronised you a snake? How can I ever expect you to say anything even remotely good about me? Tell me once and for all—are you going to pay the fine?'

'Fine? What fine?' screamed Gangoba Tatya. 'Has the Peshwa started thinking of himself as a king, to levy such fines? That right rests with the Chhatrapati, not with the Peshwa. In such matters, the Peshwas have only as many rights as the Holkars do. Don't you think you are overstepping your boundaries?'

Madhavrao roared at the guards nearby, 'What are you waiting for? Handcuff these two! Whip them into sense till their arrogant tongues find their way back to the right place.'

The guards ran forward and handcuffed the duo, but no one dared raise a whip. Madhavrao stepped down from his throne, snatched a whip from one of the guards and started lashing Tatya. Tatya's helpless screams filled the courtroom. He fell at Madhavrao's feet, grovelling for mercy.

Ramshastri came forward and held Madhavrao's hand. 'Shrimant, please control your rage. It does not befit a Peshwa like you to punish a lowly person like Gangoba Tatya yourself.'

Madhavrao composed himself and went back to his throne. A bloodied Gangoba Tatya lay on the floor, writhing in pain. Madhavrao looked at him with distaste. 'Pick this man up and make him stand before the Dilli Darwaza. Let people understand what punishment they are in for if they dare to be disloyal to the kingdom. Don't let this father and son go before they pay up. Until they pay, they'll be spending their time in the dark dungeons of Nagar Fort.'

Gangoba Tatya and his son were whisked away. Madhavrao turned to Bapu and said, 'Bapu, I always turn to you when I need advice. And today, I am in need of some advice. I like the fact that you give unbiased advice. So tell me, how do I stay alert and careful while taking care of the kingdom when these family disputes keep coming up? How can I rule with a carefree mind?'

'Shrimant, I realise what you are trying to say. My unbiased advice is to retire all people like me. That's when you will be able to rule peacefully.'

Bapu's candid answer made Madhavrao smile. 'Bapu! Thank you for giving me such clear advice. You never let me down.

'Moroba, from now on, keep an eye on Bapu's house. Just as I have kept Kaka under strict vigilance, ensure that the same is applied to Bapu. There should be no laxity in this. Bapu, I hope you are not angry, are you?'

Bapu smiled and replied, 'Shrimant, as long as I enjoy your patronage, an officer's post is as good as being under house arrest. Your wish is my command.' Saying this, Bapu stormed off in rage.

After that day, nobody dared go against the Peshwa's word. Sakharambapu was kept under strict house arrest. Nobody could meet him without Madhavrao's permission.

But two enemies constantly pricked at Madhavrao's heart: Hyder and the British. After having lost to Hyder thrice, Madhavrao was growing increasingly anxious to bring him to his knees.

Janoji Bhosale was trying to create trouble for the Peshwa. During the battle at Ghodpe, Janoji had tried to help Raghoba, but his plans got foiled by Madhavrao's strategic moves. Now Janoji was trying to get Raghoba out of imprisonment. Raghoba had planned an escape from the prison with the help of Janoji, but the plan was revealed before it could be executed. The people who had attempted to help Dadasaheb were arrested. Madhavrao decided to choke the very power that was at the root of all these plans—Janoji Bhosale.

Thus, he decided to battle Janoji with the help of the Nizam. He got news that Janoji had joined hands with the British and was preparing for the battle. Immediately, Madhavrao started gathering his troops.

The Nizam sent around eight thousand soldiers. Piraji Naik Nimbalkar also came to help Madhavrao. Together, they charged on the Bhosales' provinces. Bhosale tried using guerrilla tactics, but in vain. Soon, Madhavrao took away all the provinces that Bhosale had received as prizes or as payment for his services. He plundered Nagpur and seized Bhuikot Fort.

Bhosale was left with nowhere to go. He finally started talking about signing a treaty. Devajipant was accorded the power to make the treaty on Janoji's behalf. Since the Peshwas had lost time due to this campaign on Janoji and couldn't go north, they agreed to the treaty.

❀

Madhavrao had ignored his fever all through the campaign, but it violently raised its head after his return to Pune. After finishing his course of medicines, Madhavrao got back to work. Hyder was again getting active in the south. He had started conquering the Peshwa's territories. Madhavrao was more worried about the south than the north. It was getting increasingly necessary to stop Hyder before he became too huge a problem to control. Madhavrao ordered all his generals to assemble in Pune with their troops. He set them up for continuous campaigns, one after the other. Even though it was getting tiring for all of them, no one dared speak a word against Madhavrao's orders.

The only general who hadn't come to Pune was Bhosale. Bhosale's advocate, Devajipant, however, happened to be in Pune. Madhavrao summoned him and asked, 'What's the matter? Why is Bhosale not here?'

Devajipant looked embarrassed. 'It's a long distance. And there are so many soldiers travelling with him. Raje has already left from Nagpur. He should arrive in the next eight days.'

Hearing this, Madhavrao's anger was slightly abated. Devajipant took this opportunity to put in a request.

'I wish to meet Bapu, Shrimant.'

'Why?' Madhavrao asked with a glint in his eyes.

Devajipant stammered, 'No special reason, Shrimant. Just that we have had an affectionate relationship for so many years, and it has been a long time since I met him. So ...'

After pondering for a moment, Madhavrao said, 'Why not? Please go ahead and meet him.'

Madhavrao called out for Shripati and said to him, 'Shripati, go to the office and get Keshav here.'

Shripati brought back the clerk Keshav with him. Keshav was one of the few trusted members in Madhavrao's administration.

'Keshav, this is Devajipant,' said Madhavrao. 'Take him to meet Bapu. Convey to the guards that I have allowed this meeting.'

The next morning, Keshav came to meet Madhavrao, who was inspecting his horses in the royal stable.

'Did the two meet?' Madhavrao asked.

'Yes, Shrimant.'

'Did anything happen?'

'No, Shrimant. When we got there, Bapu was playing chess with two of his servants. They both exchanged greetings; Devajipant told Bapu that Raje was coming from Nagpur soon, to which Bapu replied with a simple "all right". That's it.'

'Neither of them said anything else?' Madhavrao asked in surprise.

'No, Shrimant,' said Keshav, and then added, 'except for one thing … Bapu asked one servant to make a peculiar move on the chessboard.'

'What was that?'

'He said, "Take the king two steps back."'

Madhavrao looked at Keshav with a smile and said, 'Go to the office and write down this incident with today's date. Also, if Nana has come, send him here.'

As soon as Nana arrived, Madhavrao said to him, 'Nana, from today onwards, I need to know every single thing that goes on with the Nagpurkar Bhosales. Make arrangements accordingly.'

'Yes, Shrimant. I shall arrange to send messengers today itself. From day after, we shall get all the news.'

Two days later, Nana came to Madhavrao with the news that the Bhosales had arrived at a place some distance away from Pune but had retreated from there instead of coming to Pune.

'Just as I thought. Nana, call Devajipant,' said Madhavrao.

When Devajipant came, Madhavrao asked him, 'Pant, there is still no news from your Raje. What happened?'

'Shrimant, Raje has already set out. He should be here in the next two to four days.'

'On whose behest? Mine or yours? I have already got wind of the fact that the Bhosales had come forward and then gone back. You found Bapu's advice better heeded than my command, is it?'

'Shrimant … me … I …' fumbled Devajipant.

'Shut up! Devajipant, I am sparing you only because you are Bhosale's advocate. Otherwise, I would have had you trampled to death under an elephant's feet for playing such games with me. Before you think I am incapable of doing that, think about the fact that the one who gave you this advice is sitting under house arrest, playing chess with his servants. Now, without any delay, convey my message to your Raje. Tell him that if he doesn't arrive in Pune in the next eight days, he shall have to retreat a hundred steps back. If he doesn't arrive as per my instructions, the troops gathered here for the campaign to Karnataka shall first charge on Nagpur. Is that clear?'

Devajipant scampered away in fear to convey the message to Bhosale.

Madhavrao called for Nana. He handed him a special chess set made of ivory and said, 'Give this to Bapu. Tell him I am impressed with his skills in chess.'

3

Everyone in Raghoba's camp was frightened on seeing the strict and merciless demeanour adopted by Madhavrao. Madhavrao was looking into all official matters himself— at the cost of his health. Khasgiwale was giving him daily reports of the plans being etched out with Devajipant.

One evening, Madhavrao was sitting in his office, flanked by Nana and Moroba. 'I am going to Parvati. I heard that the refurbishing of the temple is near completion. Will you come along?' Madhava asked Nana.

'Yes, Shrimant.'

The trio left the office and walked towards the Dilli Darwaza, where a retinue of Gardis was waiting for him. They bowed low in mujra and Madhavrao mounted his horse. Nana, Moroba, Paage, Dhulap and Shripati also mounted their horses. As Madhavrao trotted ahead, the others followed at a respectable distance. The Gardis walked behind this small procession.

Soon, they reached the peak of Parvati. Khasgiwale was already present there, waiting for Madhavrao to arrive.

Madhavrao paid obeisance at the temple of Goddess Parvati and then sat at one of his favourite spots on the hillock. From there, he could see the entire city of Pune spread out before him. Soon, the sun began to set and Nana requested Madhavrao's permission for everyone to return to Shaniwarwada.

They all began trotting downwards at a slow pace, chatting on the way.

Suddenly, Ramsingh Gardi steered his horse ahead with speed. He managed to veer away from Nana's horse, bumped into Shripati's and got close to Madhavrao. Seeing the blade of a sword glistening in Ramsingh's hand, Shripati screamed at the top of his voice, 'Sarkar! Deceit!'

Madhavrao wheeled around just as Ramsingh's sword came slashing down on Madhavrao.

Madhavrao pulled the reins of his horse hard, and the sword plunged into the Peshwa's shoulder, instead of into his heart. Madhavrao yelled out in pain as blood gushed from the wound. Scared by its master's screams, the horse began wildly bucking. Unable to control it with both hands, Madhavrao's feet lost grip of the stirrups and he came crashing down.

Seeing Madhavrao on the ground, Ramsingh tried to escape. A fuming Shripati instantly steered his horse in Ramsingh's way. He lifted his sword and it clashed against Ramsingh's. During the clash that ensued, Ramsingh tumbled off his horse. Instantly, Shripati jumped to his feet and was about to stab him in the heart, when Madhavrao called out, 'Wait, Shripati! Don't kill him.'

Madhavrao tried to get up. Shripati cast off his sword, removed his cummerbund and used it to tie together

Ramsingh's hands. The Huzarati horsemen crowded around the Gardis on all sides. Nana, Moroba, Dhulap and Paage looked stunned, but helped Madhavrao to his feet.

Dhulap removed his cummerbund, tore it in two and wrapped one piece of it around Madhavrao's wound. Moroba wiped the sweat off Madhavrao's forehead. The Peshwa's face displayed no pain but his eyes were bloodshot.

Shripati kicked Ramsingh with fury and, pulling him by the hair, made him sit up.

Ramsingh stumbled to his feet and started grovelling before Madhavrao. Between sobs, he said, 'Huzur, please forgive me. I know I'm not worthy of being forgiven, but please find it in your heart to forgive me. I did not do this on my own. I was made to.'

Madhavrao's eyes were blazing by then. He called out to Shripati, 'What are you waiting for? Tie this despicable man up!'

Turning to Nana, he said, 'Take him back to the fort and throw him into a dungeon. No one should be allowed to meet him or speak to him. Keep him under strict vigilance. I shall investigate this matter myself.'

'Yes, Shrimant,' said Nana, adding, 'let me call for a palanquin for you.'

'No, Nana. That won't be necessary. I will go on my own. As it is, if you call for a palanquin, this incident will get publicised, and I don't want anyone to know about this.'

Nana and Moroba helped Madhavrao wear his tunic. As Nana adjusted the pugree on Madhavrao's head, tears started streaming down Nana's face. Everyone else was equally overwhelmed. Madhavrao patted Nana's shoulder and said softly, 'Nana, these things happen. Lord Ganesha saved me from being dishonoured today. Why should I worry when I have a protector and saviour like Him? Come on, let's go back.'

Darkness was descending on the hillock. Madhavrao saw a retinue of flambeau-bearers climbing upwards.

'Go ahead and stop them on the way. Let them walk in front of us as we go down,' Madhava said to Nana.

Madhavrao mounted his horse with Dhulap's help. Except for the bloodstains on his tunic, there was no visible sign of the attack. When they reached Shaniwarwada, Madhavrao entered through the Ganesha Darwaza instead of the Dilli Darwaza. The guards were surprised to see the Peshwa coming through. They bowed low in mujra, but Madhavrao did not dismount from his horse there. Instead, he rode through and dismounted in the main courtyard.

He walked till he reached the beautiful garden in front of the Gauri Mahal. From there he could see Dadasaheb's palace, and Dadasaheb himself standing on the terrace of the second storey. Seeing his uncle, Madhavrao changed his mind and started walking towards his own palace, but someone called out to him from behind—it was Vinayak, one of Raghobadada's trusted servants.

'Yes, what is it?' Madhavrao said with a frown.

'Shrimant, Dadasaheb Maharaj has sent for you.'

Madhavrao sighed and started walking back to his uncle's palace. Raghobadada was waiting for Madhavrao at the door. Seeing Madhavrao, he asked, 'Madhava, is it true? What I heard ...'

'What?'

Raghoba's gaze rested on Madhavrao's bloodied shoulder. 'That the Gardi attacked you?'

'Yes.'

'Is it a deep wound?'

'No. It's a flesh wound.'

'Thank God! So ... what about that Gardi?' Raghoba asked haltingly.

'He is alive. We have caught him.'

'So ... did he say anything?' stuttered Raghoba.

'No, Kaka. Before he could say anything, I had him arrested and thrown into a dungeon.'

'You should have made him speak, Madhava. Why be lenient in such important matters?'

'Kaka, why would he have attacked us unless he was instructed to do so by someone? Had I got to know the name of that loathsome person who ordered this attack, I would have been left with no choice but to punish him with a death sentence. But don't worry, Kaka. I have no strength left in me to find out who that person is!'

Saying this, Madhavrao walked out of Raghoba's palace.

※

Madhavrao's condition was not good. He went to Siddhatek for a change in ambience, but those two months did little to improve his health. He had constant fever and was taking medicines from Cunningham but was still getting weaker by the day. Mood swings became a regular occurrence. Madhavrao's officers and generals were not in favour of Cunningham's treatment. They believed it was causing an adverse effect. After he returned to Pune, Madhavrao did not even have the strength to sit upright for a long time.

One morning, Madhavrao was moodily looking at the clouds drifting by in the sky, when Shripati came in and announced, 'Bapu has come.'

Madhavrao got up from his bed and sat on the carpet. Bapu came in, folded his hands and sat in front of Madhavrao.

'Bapu, how come you arrived early today?'

'Shrimant, I heard that you fell very ill last night. Is that true?'

'That has become a common problem. Don't worry about it. I heard that you are also not keeping well, Bapu?'

'Yes, my knees ache a lot and my feet get numb. The vagaries of advancing age, what else? That's why I came to take your permission.'

'For what?' asked Madhavrao.

'I wish to try the medicines that the foreign doctor gives you. May I?'

'Sure,' Madhavrao said with a laugh. 'Why do you need to ask me that?'

'Why not, Shrimant? After all, I'm under arrest by you. How can I do anything without asking you?'

'Bapu, you will also agree that this arrest is namesake. Apart from those related to political matters, there are no restrictions on you. In fact, I start missing you if I don't see you for a couple of days. Does that show you my anger or my love?'

'So shall I take medicines from Cunnigham?'

'Of course. Is the pain that bad, Bapu?' Madhavrao asked with concern.

'Don't even remind me about it, Shrimant. Once the pain starts shooting through my knees, it becomes impossible to sit or stand up. Unbearable!'

Madhavrao smiled. Seeing that, Bapu asked, 'What happened, Shrimant? Do you think I'm exaggerating?'

'No, Bapu. I smiled because I thought of how I do not believe in heaven or hell after death. I believe that every person has to iron out his or her checks and balances in this birth itself. Whatever bad things we do in this life come back to haunt us in the form of illnesses and pain. There is no respite but to bear them till our karmas are evened out.'

Bapu did not answer.

'What happened, Bapu? Do you disagree?'

'No, Shrimant, but is it okay if I speak frankly?'

'Yes, absolutely. I will not hold it against you.'

'I'm sorry, Shrimant, but in that case, what I don't understand is why someone like me would get away with arthritis, whereas you have been ...'

'Afflicted with a deadly disease like tuberculosis, isn't it?' interjected Madhavrao, adding, 'This should not come as a surprise to an intelligent man like you, Bapu. See, I have many people like you working for me. Whatever you do is as per my command. So if you do something that hurts someone, the karmic blame for it rests on my head, not yours. That is why people like you escape with mere arthritis, whereas I have no choice but to live and die with tuberculosis. I am cursed to live a short life.'

Sakharambapu felt sad that his simple question had led to such a serious discussion. He looked morose. Madhavrao said to him, 'Bapu, I did not say all this in anger. Nowadays, I do not feel like getting angry with anybody.'

A servant came in to announce the arrival of Dr Cunningham.

'Bapu, you are lucky. You didn't need to wait for the doctor. He came to you,' said Madhavrao.

However, Bapu got up, saying, 'No, Shrimant. Let the doctor see you first. I shall wait for him downstairs.'

As Bapu turned to leave, Madhavrao called out to him from behind. 'Bapu, when you meet Cunningham, don't ask him for anything apart from medicine. He is a good friend of mine.'

Cunningham came in and examined Madhavrao. Ramabai stood at the door.

'So, doctor, how is my health?' Madhavrao asked in a weak voice.

'It is okay, Shrimant,' replied Cunningham.

'You mean to say it has not worsened, isn't it? May I ask you something if you don't mind?'

'Please do.'

'Everybody is advising me to return to taking medicines from Ganga Vaidya, our home-grown doctor. I was taking his medicines till I started seeing you.'

'Yes, yes, absolutely. You should do whatever you feel like. I won't have any problem,' replied Cunningham.

'But you should keep visiting me too, doctor ...' pleaded Madhavrao.

'Yes, Shrimant. I shall keep coming till you feel better, don't worry.' Cunningham squeezed Madhavrao's palm gently.

Once the doctor left, Ramabai stepped into the room.

'You are planning to stop taking Cunningham Uncle's medicines?'

'Yes. I do not feel like taking anyone's medical advice now, Rama. Everyone is saying I should go back to Ganga Vaidya. Let's see. What have you brought?' Madhavrao pointed to the glass in Ramabai's hand.

'I have got some teertha for you. Please have it,' said Ramabai, pouring a spoonful of the holy water in Madhavrao's open palm.

'Do you see, Rama? Everyone tries doing what they can to make me feel better. Don't I have to see that no one is hurt due to me? If I had refused this teertha just now, how bad would you have felt?'

'When did I ever say that you should not take Ganga Vaidya's medicines? I just want you to feel better as soon as possible, be it through medicines or through this teertha,' snapped Ramabai.

Madhavrao laughed. 'My hot-headedness has afflicted you as well. It is these difficult religious vows you keep making for me that make you so irritable. Vaidyaraj will come in some time. He will feel better on seeing me.'

❈

That night, Madhavrao lay awake in bed. Worries gnawed at him from within.

He called out to Shripati, who came running. Madhavrao pointed to a nearby casket. 'Bring that here. And get me a brazier from downstairs.'

Madhavrao took a sheaf of papers out of the casket and, using the brazier Shripati had brought him, started burning them one by one. The smoke from the burning papers made Madhavrao's cough worse, but he didn't pay any attention to it.

Just then, Bapu arrived, but he stopped at the door. He was stunned to see the billowing smoke.

'Come in, Bapu,' said Madhavrao. 'I was waiting for you.'

'What is all this, Shrimant? The doctors have asked you to rest as much as possible. Did you have to do this now?'

'Yes, Bapu. It was very important for me to do this right now,' said Madhavrao, looking at Sakharambapu with a steady gaze. 'Do you know what these papers are? These are written proofs of the treacheries conducted against me by the officers and generals I always thought were loyal to me.'

'If that is the case, why burn the proof? They will come in handy when sentencing those disloyal people to death!'

'Is it? Well, read this.' Madhavrao handed over a letter to Bapu.

As Bapu put on his spectacles and started reading the letter, his hands began trembling in fear. It was a letter written to the Nizam by Bapu himself. Its contents spoke about the amount of money that Bapu had received from the Nizam for his services.

'Tell me, what do I do with such letters, Bapu?' asked Madhavrao, adding, 'Sit down. I did not call you for this.'

Madhavrao threw the letter into the brazier, where it burnt to the last bit. He turned to Shripati and said, 'Stand guard outside. Make sure no one comes in. I have a lot to discuss with Bapu tonight.'

When Shripati left, Madhavrao sighed and said, 'Bapu, there are many such letters in this casket. The last decade has added a lot of "wealth" to this collection. Apart from the several letters speaking about your dealings with the Nizam, there are also letters written by Kaka, the Nagpurkars, the British ... There are letters about Patwardhan joining forces with the Nizam. There are letters written by the Shindes and the Holkars about me. It won't be fair on my part to start punishing everybody at this stage. These are all people who have been loyal and affectionate to me over the years. However, power and politics make such a heady concoction that such momentary lapses are but natural. It will not befit me to judge all these people negatively, keeping in mind only these interim wrongdoings. I have started burning these letters because I do not trust my health any more. It is better that I destroy this evidence before it falls into the hands of some evil person.'

'Shrimant! Why are you saying such things? Why this helplessness?' Sakharambapu cried out.

'I am just being practical. I am not going to live to see the evening of my life—tuberculosis will not allow it. How can I sit around knowing that my life may slip out of my hands at any moment? This is why I have called you ...'

'Please command this humble servant of yours,' said Bapu.

'Bapu, I know that you are attached to Kaka. When I became the Peshwa, you were his manager. Kaka was guiding me through the affairs of the kingdom at the time. Both of us could have done much more for the betterment of the kingdom, had it not been for Kaka's negative attribute of trusting the wrong people. Not to mention his wayward ways and affinity for the vacuous pleasures of life. The first attribute disallowed him from trusting anyone for a long time. The second kept him from taking on any responsibility. You got crushed in between due to these problems.'

A violent bout of cough racked Madhavrao's body. As it passed, he continued, 'I have always respected you for your intelligence. Very few people possess the level of canniness and intelligence you do. The Nizam's Vitthal Sundar, Devajipant of the Bhosales and you are the only three people who come to mind. Your political acumen is worth saluting. In the beginning, I used to be afraid of you. Later, I started finding it interesting to have a battle of wits with you. Why else would I have gifted you an ivory chess set after you gave that piece of advice to Devajipant? You advised me to make you sit at home in order to run the administration properly. But, to tell you the truth, it led to new problems cropping up for me. You are a very ambitious person. You cannot live without power in your hands.'

'Shrimant, why are you troubling yourself with these thoughts?' Bapu interjected.

'I am beyond caring about my troubles, Bapu. Don't worry about that. Don't think that I have only ever seen your faults. Not at all. I appointed Nana as a chief officer not because he had no faults. Do you think I did not know his shortcomings? His shrewdness, his penchant for keeping himself safe in every matter … But I ignored all of it in favour of his astuteness in maintaining accounts. I have never peeked into anyone's personal life. That is not my right. But when it comes to the kingdom, I go purely by the call of duty.'

'Shrimant, I salute your thoughts and the maturity behind them. Otherwise ...' Bapu said in an overwhelmed voice.

'Bapu, you are as great as you think me to be. Remember Aalegaon? I had been defeated and imprisoned. Anyone else in your place would have advised Kaka to become the Peshwa. As it is, my moony-eyed uncle lived to see that dream come true. He would have definitely become the Peshwa on my arrest. But you dissuaded him from becoming the Peshwa. I cannot begin to tell you what a great service you did to the Maratha Empire.'

Madhavrao grew emotional. His voice quivered. as he spoke. 'Bapu, I'm telling the truth. If Kaka had become the Peshwa, our Maratha Empire would have been doomed. It is easy to set up a new kingdom, but to break down an existing one and replace it with a new one is a very tough job. There's always the possibility that the subjects will not accept the new order. Thankfully, you realised that. If for nothing else, for this one benevolence of yours, I am willing to overlook a hundred such letters.

'This one decade has ravaged my body to the core. The mind wishes to do hundreds of things, but the body refuses to cooperate. The campaigns to Karnataka, battles with the Bhosales, responsibilities of the kingdom, family disputes ... how much can I handle? I have only one wish now. Before my body becomes completely useless, I wish to carry out one last campaign against Hyder. Once that campaign is successful, I will not want anything else.'

Bapu was stunned to hear this. 'Shrimant? A campaign? In this condition?'

'Yes. It is necessary. I know that Hyder will not join forces with the British, but I am not willing to take a chance. Plus, my debts are increasing. I need to rein them in. But this is not why I called you, Bapu ...' said Madhavrao.

The strain of talking at a stretch had taken its toll on Madhavrao, who fought breathlessness for the next few minutes. Then he continued, 'I am nearing the end of my life. I can see the signs of the Maratha Empire spreading from the Tungabhadra to Attock, but I may not live to see that happen. I am worried about Narayana. I had never thought death would come to claim me so soon, but it has. So I am going to leave Narayana in your care. I wish to make him the diwan, and you, his mutaliq. Both of you will handle the affairs of the kingdom very well. Narayana is young; he is inexperienced. Your experience and guidance will be of great help to him. In due time, I shall also release Kaka.'

'Shrimant, you are giving me a very big responsibility ...' said Bapu.

'I cannot think of anyone better than you to handle this responsibility. Nana is capable but, like me, he is too young. He does not have the wealth of experience that you have. Narayana will not be as safe in Nana's hands as he will be in yours. Please, Bapu, take care of my brother. He is immature. He needs a strong hand to guide him. Promise me that you will do this.'

'I'm never beyond your command, Shrimant.'

⚯

Madhavrao returned from Katora. He had participated in the Suvarna Tula ritual there, weighing himself against pure gold and donating the gold to the needy, but there was no improvement in his health. Instead, it worsened by the day. Severe chest pains and high temperatures plagued him. Sometimes, his head would ache to the point of tears. In spite of his failing health, Madhavrao would go to check on office work or meet his officers.

One morning, Madhavrao was sitting in his palace, writing letters. He sensed Ramabai's presence only when she came and stood close to him. Madhavrao felt a pit in his stomach when he looked up and saw how frail and weak his wife had become, owing to the constant fasts she was keeping for his health.

'Is it necessary to write these letters when you are burning with fever?' Ramabai asked.

'Fever? I don't have a fever now.'

Ramabai touched his burning forehead in response. 'Come on ... you need to rest.'

Madhavrao smiled weakly and lay down.

'Happy now?' he asked Ramabai.

'Yes. Can't you think of anything but work?'

'Nothing of that sort, Rama. You know I think of you the most,' said Madhavrao, holding his wife's hand.

'You're lying!'

'I'm telling the truth. Whenever I see anything beautiful, I am reminded of you. It is true that for most of our married life, I have been out on campaigns, but never has the memory of your beautiful face ever left my mind. During the campaign to Karnataka, the luminous moon and the starlit sky would make me think of running into your arms.

When I was in Verul, the sculptures there reminded me so much of you that I was overwhelmed.'

'Are those sculptures so beautiful?' asked Ramabai.

'Beautiful is too insignificant a word for them. But to tell you the truth, I don't need to see something so spectacular to be reminded of you, Rama. A tender green shoot on a tree, a cottony cloud drifting through the sky ... such pure and lovely things invoke memories of you in my heart.'

Ramabai's eyes welled up. 'I feel blessed to have a husband like you, whose love cannot be measured against anything in this world.'

'No, Rama. You are invaluable. You may not realise it, but I have been blessed to get a gem like you as my wife.'

'Have you ever imagined how lonely and helpless I feel when you leave me and go on campaigns? I cannot concentrate on anything ... When you went to Katora, I could hardly eat, I was so worried about you ...' said Ramabai.

'What worry?'

'Oh! As if you don't know about the sacrificial rituals being aggressively conducted almost every day by Mamanji!'

Madhavrao smiled sadly. 'Yes, I know about them. But I have only kept Kaka under house arrest. I cannot dictate what he should or should not do in his home.'

'Why don't you release Mamanji? You travel, but for me to see all this in front of my eyes is torture.'

'Is that why you have also started performing all the rituals that you do? As a countermeasure?'

'Who told you about those?' Ramabai asked in surprise.

'Why should anybody tell me? Look at yourself in the mirror. See how frail you have become. Rama, please understand. I do not feel happy about having imprisoned Kaka. But in the larger interest of the kingdom, it is better he stays confined. As for the rituals, you place your faith in God. He will see us through.'

'I have not lost faith in God. I have done everything possible. One crore chants of the Maha Mrityunjay mantra, feeding a one hundred thousand people, making vows to the Lord, donating to charity ... But what has been the use? What else should I do? I'm at a loss!' Ramabai exclaimed.

Madhavrao kept silent for some time. Then he turned to Ramabai and said, 'Rama, there is one thing on my mind ...'

'What's that?'

'Harihareshwar is our family deity. I have been wanting to go visit his temple for long. The deity is known for his miracles. However, I may not be able to bear the strain of travelling so far. Will you go for me? I don't know why, but I feel like if I get Lord Harihareshwar's blessings, my health may improve.'

'Of course, I will go,' said Ramabai.

'Thank you, Rama. Take Parvati Kaku along if she is ready to go. Else, if Narayana agrees, take Gangabai along.'

⌘

All three ladies were keen to visit Harihareshwar. Madhavrao had already informed Janjirenbaba and sent letters to the castellans informing them of the visit. Ramabai came to Madhavrao's palace to say goodbye to him.

'Are all the preparations in place?' he asked.

'Yes.'

'Go and return safely.'

Madhavrao was sitting reclined on a bolster. He looked frail and his voice had weakened considerably.

'I don't feel like leaving you alone in this condition. There is no one to look after you in the wada now. Will you take care of yourself?'

'I will, don't worry. In fact, I have been feeling a bit better ever since you agreed to go to Harihareshwar for me.'

'Praise be to the Lord!' exclaimed Ramabai.

'By the time you pay obeisance to Lord Hairhareshwar, I may feel so good that I may meet you halfway on your journey back.'

Tears spilt from Ramabai's eyes. Madhavrao held her hand.

'Rama, while you are journeying to Harihareshwar, look around at everything. Observe the beauty of the sea. See the waves crashing gently on the sandy beaches. You will pass from under a canopy of trees so tall that they almost touch the sky. Their fan-like leaves do not allow even the most intense sunlight to pass through. Be sure not to miss the sunset at all. In the evening, as the sun goes down, its rays look as if they are coming to touch your hands …'

Ramabai smiled. 'When did you see all this? And how do you remember it all?'

'I had once gone, before the Peshwai made me a slave to time. Rama, whatever I have learnt so far has been largely through observing the various moods and forms of nature. The sea taught me how to bear pain in love. The tall rocks in Karnataka taught me how to stand strong even in the face of the most terrible storms. The torrents leaping over the cliffs taught me about sacrifice. There are so many examples to talk about! Anyway, you should be on your way, else you will get delayed. You will receive ceremonial welcomes on the way. At Harihareshwar, the Nabab will send you gifts. I have arranged for gifts for him to be sent with you. Give them to him. You may also need to survey the armoury. Do everything without any worry or fear.'

Maina came in to call Ramabai. It was time to leave.

⚘

Ramabai returned from Harihareshwar after two months. She was hoping to see her husband in better health but was aghast to see how much his condition had worsened since she had left. Madhavrao had deliberately not allowed news of his poor health to reach Ramabai when she was at Harihareshwar.

Madhavrao set out for the fourth campaign to Karnataka, despite the doctors and physicians advising him against it. At her immense insistence, Ramabai was taken along. But Madhavrao was so weak that it became difficult to move from one place to another quickly. During their stay at Miraj, Madhavrao finally accorded the responsibility of the campaign to Tryambakrao Pethe and returned to Pune.

However, Madhavrao did not rest after coming back to Pune. Taking Dr Cunningham's advice, he went to Katora for a change of weather. Ramabai stayed behind at Shaniwarwada along with Parvatibai, Narayanrao and his wife, Gangabai.

On the other side, Raghobadada's sacrificial rituals showed no signs of abating.

⚔

'Welcome, Shastribuva,' Bapu called out when he saw Ramshastri entering the court.

Nana, Daulatrao Ghorpade, Moroba and Bapu were in the court. As Ramshastri took his seat, Daulatrao asked him, 'When did Shrimant come back from Saswad?'

'Last night,' replied Ramshastri.

'I was planning to go to Saswad to meet him. I had been waiting for long ...' remarked Daulatrao.

'For what?' Shastribuva asked him.

'He needs to re-join the campaign. Tryambakrao sent me to give him this message.'

Ramshastri sighed deeply. 'Daulatrao, medicine can work only if the body gets ample rest. If you think after returning midway from the Karnataka campaign, Shrimant has been resting peacefully, you are mistaken. He has been travelling to Nasik, Nagar, Jejuri, Saswad, Theur, Katora and Siddhatek. His mind is constantly engaged in what is happening in the administrative affairs. Shouldn't an ill man rest his mind and body a bit to recover?'

'Shastribuva, why don't you tell Shrimant? He listens to you,' someone piped in.

'Yes, that's true,' agreed Daulatrao. 'During the third campaign, Shrimant immediately moved our base camp after he received a letter from you.'

'Do you all think I do not tell him anything? But what you are saying about Shrimant listening to me is an old tale now. As his health is deteriorating, Shrimant is getting more aggressive and irritable by the day. A person who is afraid of death takes due care of his health. But Shrimant seems to harbour no such fear!'

At that moment, Madhavrao entered the court. Everyone got up to greet their Peshwa.

'I hope Murarrao is keeping well?' Madhavrao asked.

'Yes, Shrimant.'

'Good. When did you come?'

'Four days ago. I was waiting for you. Tryambakmama sent me for news of your health ...'

'No need to worry about my health. Do finish this campaign victoriously. I trust you,' said Madhavrao. He grew emotional as he continued, 'Today, I am missing Gopalrao a lot. It is very difficult to find a loyal and intelligent person like him. I never planned anything without his advice. The campaigns to Karnataka took a toll on him. His sudden demise has been a blow for the Peshwai.'

'True, Shrimant. Gopalrao's death came as a shock for the troops too,' said Daulatrao.

Madhavrao sighed. 'If we hadn't had gems like Gopalrao and Murarrao with us, it would have been impossible to have all these successful campaigns to Karnataka. There are very few people who have such extensive and minute knowledge of the Karnataka region like these two did. When Gopalrao realised that his stomach ailment was irreparable, he got his brother, Vamanrao, to help us. Such loyalty is rare.'

'Daulatrao is saying he will leave tomorrow,' Ramshastri said to Madhavrao.

'Yes, he should. He has a big responsibility on his shoulders. Daulatrao, I shall hand over a letter for Tryambakmama to you, but you also narrate to him the situation here.'

Daulatrao bowed low in mujra and exited the court.

⌘

Dawn had just broken. The sun had begun to rise when Madhavrao's palanquin was set down in front of the mansion at Theur. A handful of horsemen were following close behind. Two camels, laden with Madhavrao's luggage, ambled along slowly. The flambeau-bearers, who had run ahead of the palanquin, stood drenched in sweat. Drums were beaten from the music gallery to inform the residents of Theur of the Peshwa's arrival.

Madhavrao had decided to shift to Theur after a vermilion-stained lemon was found in the corner of his chambers in Shaniwarwada. This was a sign of black magic, and though the Peshwa did not believe that these rituals would do any harm, he was bound to the rules of the palace, which stated that Shaniwarwada was no longer safe.

No one had any idea that Madhavrao Peshwa would arrive so suddenly. Everyone rushed around. Iccharampant Dhere came riding on his horse. Seeing Madhavrao, he dismounted and bowed low in mujra.

It might have been the cool weather or the travel, but something had served well to alleviate Madhavrao's rage and unease. Two days ago, at an auspicious time, Madhavrao had set out from Shaniwarwada to stay at Bhawani Peth. Everyone back in Pune knew about Madhavrao's decision to stay at Theur, but Madhavrao was getting increasingly agitated at Bhawani Peth. His agitation increased to such an extent that he made the sudden decision to leave Pune and move to Theur. Everyone was taken aback by the sudden development, but they had no choice. Madhavrao had issued the command to move at such an irregular hour that all the usual servants were out for their nightly errands or free time. Enraged at the fact that they could not assemble immediately on his calling, Madhavrao took a handful of horsemen and two camels and set out for Theur.

As Madhavrao stood outside the mansion of Theur, Iccharampant rode to him and said, 'Shrimant, it is very cold. Shall we go inside?'

'Pant, I shall enter the mansion only after paying obeisance to Lord Ganesha. That ritual has remained unchanged over all these years.'

Madhavrao walked to the temple, followed by Iccharampant.

They stepped into the sanctum sanctorum and stood before the Lord. Madhavrao kneeled in front of the idol.

'Pant ...'

Immediately, Pant stepped forward and handed a rectangular jewellery box to Madhavrao. Madhavrao opened the box to reveal a pearl- and diamond-studded aigrette resting on the blue velvet lining. He picked up the aigrette and reverentially placed it in the salver in front of the idol. Then he bowed his head low, his eyes brimming with tears.

'Gajanana, I'm tired now. I have no strength left in me. All my hopes and ambitions are placed in front of You. With Your blessings, I could capture a large territory, stretching from the Tungabhadra to Attock, but stability eludes it all. I want just four more years—not to enjoy the royal luxuries but to bring stability to all the affairs that are in flux right now. But to give me these four years is only in Your hands. Today, I'm keeping my aigrette, the symbol of my victories, at Your feet. It is You who has given me this honour; now, I'm placing it in front of You. Whatever I have been able to achieve so far has only been due to Your blessings. Let the future, too, unfold with Your blessings and as per Your wishes.'

⚭

Late that afternoon, the royal palanquin made its way towards the women's quarters. The maidservants ran outside. The horses that had accompanied the palanquin stood waiting in the courtyard. Old Ramji came forward to welcome Ramabai as she stepped out of the palanquin. Iccharampant bowed low in mujra.

Ramabai entered Madhavrao's chamber, while Maina and the maids went to arrange Ramabai's luggage in her chambers.

Madhavrao smiled widely when he saw his wife. 'You arrived earlier than I had anticipated.'

'I could say the same about you,' replied Ramabai. 'I woke up at dawn and got to know that you had already left for Theur.'

'Are you angry that I did not inform you before leaving, Rama?'

'No, I'm habituated to that now.' She sighed. 'How is your health?'

'There's no fever today. I feel fresh. Come here and look at this ...'

Madhavrao led her to the window. From there, Ramabai saw the flowering shrubs in full bloom.

'Oh my God! These look so beautiful!' she exclaimed in wonder. 'I did not notice them while coming upstairs.'

'Do you remember, the last time we had come here for the abhishek ritual, you had asked me to make a small garden here? I had promised you that you will get fresh flowers for the Lord every time you come here. This morning, when I saw the garden in full bloom, I couldn't help but miss you intensely. Those little praajakta flowers remind me of you a lot ...'

'Why so?' asked Ramabai.

Madhavrao placed his hand lovingly on Ramabai's shoulder and said to her, 'Once, I had finished the durbar and gone to Aaisaheb's palace. You were standing there with your head covered by your pallu. Initially, I didn't realise that it was you. But the shiny embellishments on your saree were glowing brightly in the light of the sunrays coming from the window. Today, the praajakta flowers reminded me of that sight.'

⚛

Madhavrao woke up. He was startled to see bright daylight outside. Ramabai was standing at the window. Madhavrao lay in bed, looking at his wife. Soon, Maina came inside. The tinkle of her bangles made Madhavrao look up, but Maina did not realise he was awake. Ramabai pressed a finger to her lips, indicating that Maina should be quiet. She bowed low in mujra and bustled outside. Ramabai came closer to Madhavrao.

'When did you wake up?' she asked.

'A few minutes ago …'

'Why didn't you call me?'

'I was looking at you.'

'For what?'

'To see how you looked.'

'What do you mean?'

'My health is deteriorating, but you are also growing thinner by the day because of all the fasts you have been keeping for me.'

'Oh, you worry for nothing. I'm fine. Nothing's wrong with my health,' chided Ramabai.

Madhavrao smiled at his wife. She, too, smiled and realised that it was the first time in many months that she was seeing Madhavrao so fresh on waking up in the morning.

'What is it that you have in your hands?' Madhavrao asked, pointing at Ramabai's closed fist.

'Praajakta flowers! A bountiful of these were scattered in the temple precincts when I went there this morning. They were giving off such a divine fragrance. So I got some for you. Here …' Ramabai offered the flowers to her husband.

Madhavrao smelt them and exclaimed, 'Rama, I am amazed at the divine gift that your hands have been blessed with! These praajakta flowers are so delicate that they can hold on to their life only in the presence of pure love and a golden heart. See how these buds have remained fresh in your palm even in the searing heat?'

'Oh! You always praise me. Come on ...' Ramabai said, blushing coyly as she held out a hand for her husband.

However, Madhavrao got up on his own, without any support, and said, 'I really fell into a deep sleep today. Even the sound of the drums beating at dawn did not wake me.'

'Well, you were having trouble falling asleep at night. So I ordered for the drums—'

'To be kept silent, isn't it?' Madhavrao laughed. 'I hope you didn't order for Lord Ganesha's prayer and ceremonial drums to be shut down?'

'Oh, no! How could I ever do that?'

'Have Iccharampant, Nana and Mama come downstairs?'

'Yes, they have.'

'Come on. Today I am going to be late to the temple.'

Iccharampant, Moroba and other officials were waiting for Madhavrao. They bowed low in mujra as Madhavrao took his seat on the settee. He looked fresh and rested.

'I hope you got a good night's sleep, Shrimant?' Moroba asked him.

'Yes,' Madhavrao replied with a smile.

'Good to know the weather of Theur has made you feel better. Now the monsoons have also said goodbye.'

'I am feeling better not due to the weather change but because of the blessings of Lord Ganesha. I had tried medicines from every possible doctor ... even a foreign physician. But nothing worked. But, on coming to Theur, I seem to be magically feeling better. Now I have decided to keep my faith in the Lord and nothing else. Come on, let us all go to the temple.'

Madhavrao got up and walked outside to the courtyard. Two men were standing beyond the music gallery. One came forward. He wore a spotless white tunic and salwar, and a saffron pugree. He was fair, with piercing grey eyes and a well-maintained moustache. He walked forward with slow but confident steps and stood before Madhavrao.

'Who are you?' Madhavrao asked.

The man bowed low reverentially and answered, 'Huzur, I'm Moreshwar.'

'Moreshwar?' Madhavrao tried connecting the name to a face for a few moments.

Suddenly, he exclaimed, 'Oh! Moreshwar! The talented singer from the durbar! Is that really you?'

'Yes, Shrimant!' Moreshwar replied, thrilled that Madhavrao had recognised him.

'How many years has it been, Moreshwar? I remember you were singing in the palace very early in the morning. I didn't get a chance to meet you after that.'

'Yes, Shrimant. You went to Karnataka and I left Pune to go to the north. I was there till recently.'

'I'm sure you mustn't have left Pune without a compelling reason. Something unpleasant must have occurred for you to make the drastic transition. I shall not ask you about that. But I hope all is well with you now?'

'Yes, Shrimant. Thanks to your blessings, I'm doing very well. I'm now in service at the durbar of Jaipur.'

'Very good. Those people know a gem when they see one. Anyway, for what special reason have you come to see me today?'

'I got to know that you are not keeping too well and felt a strong urge to meet you. I first went to Pune. There, I was told that you had come to Theur.'

Madhavrao felt a surge of emotion coursing through him. Eyes filled to the brim, he turned to Iccharampant and said, 'Do you see this, Pant? Such are the beautiful bonds that life blesses me with. Such love is hard to come by unless ordained by karma and destiny. I am blessed to have such people in my life. This man travelled such a long way simply because he heard that I was ill.'

He turned to Moreshwar. 'Moreshwar, I do not believe in keeping any debts pending. But when I come across people like you, I realise that some debts cannot be repaid.'

'Shrimant, whatever good life I'm enjoying today is because of your benevolence,' said Moreshwar.

'Tell me, what can I do for you?' asked Madhavrao.

Moreshwar looked at Madhavrao keenly. There was no trace of the handsome young Madhavrao that Moreshwar remembered seeing in the palace. The man standing in front of him now was a mere shadow of that Madhavrao. His frail body and weathered face looked aeons away from the Madhavrao of the past. The only thing that had survived the ravages of the disease was Madhavrao's piercing, intelligent eyes. They remained the same.

'Tell me, Moreshwar. Don't hesitate. What do you want?' Madhavrao coaxed.

Moreshwar was shaken out of his reverie by Madhavrao's voice. He said, 'Shrimant, I have come all this way with only one wish in mind. I wish to sing for you once more!'

Madhavrao smiled. 'Moreshwar, you must have made immense progress in your singing abilities in the last few years. But I continue to remain as clueless about the nuances of music as I was back then.'

'But, Shrimant …'

'I am not refusing you. I would love to hear you sing. Nana …'

Nana Phadnis stepped forward.

'Nana, tomorrow the Nagpurkar Bhosales are also coming here. Arrange for Moreshwar's singing programme in front of Lord Ganesha tomorrow night. I will be present for it.'

Moreshwar prostrated before Madhavrao.

❧

Theur reverberated with the sound of horses' hooves as Tryambakmama, Raghunathrao, Shripatrao, Krushnarao Kale, Patkar and Darekar began arriving at Madhavrao's mansion, one by one.

Nana went hurriedly to tell Madhavrao about Tryambakmama's arrival.

'Shrimant, Pethe, Patankar and Patwardhan have all arrived.'

'Go on, Nana. I shall join you soon,' said Madhavrao.

As Madhavrao entered the court, everyone stood up and bowed low in mujra. They were horrified to see Madhavrao looking almost skeletally frail. But no one said anything.

'So, Mama, how did the campaign go?'

'Shrimant, what can I tell you? You should have been there during the battle of Moti Talao. Gopalrao and Nilkanthrao sacrificed their lives to get Hyder down to his knees. We indeed owe the battle's success to those two valiant warriors.'

Gopalrao's memory overwhelmed Madhavrao as he said, 'Mama, I still cannot believe that Gopalrao is no more. His demise has left a huge void in my heart and in the Peshwai. It was my duty to console Haribhau, but I had no courage left to do that. What could I say to a man whose lineage has been sacrificed for the Maratha Empire?'

'Shrimant, such things cannot be helped when it comes to administration. I soon got to know about your health. I signed a treaty with him only because of your letter. Otherwise, I would not have returned without razing him to the ground!'

'Mama, I could not be with you till the end of the campaign. But it is a matter of great joy and satisfaction for me that you all saw the campaign to its successful end. I have nothing more to ask for now. I have acquired almost as much province as there was during Shiv Chhatrapati's reign. The Maratha Empire seems stable again. What more do I need?' exclaimed Madhavrao.

'How is your health, Shrimant?' asked Mama.

'I came to Theur when I realised that my disease is not to be cured by any medicine. I am mentally prepared to accept any verdict that destiny hands me now. Karma won't allow me to die until my duties are over.

'Mama, tomorrow the Nagpurkar Bhosales are arriving. But I don't think I shall have enough energy to give them a formal reception. You, Nana and the others must take care of those formalities.'

⁂

The mansion was decorated in anticipation of the Bhosales' arrival. The floors were covered with plush carpets. The settees reserved for the special guests were draped in ornate blue velvet. Lanterns and chandeliers were polished till they were spotless.

In the evening, word came that the Bhosales were arriving. Madhavrao was already present in court to welcome Janoji Bhosale. He wore a rich tunic and salwar, with a pugree decorated with an aigrette and plumes. A pearl necklace and a nine-gem choker bedecked his neck, and beautiful bracelets were stacked on his wrists.

Tryambakrao brought Janoji into the court with fanfare. Madhavrao stood at the door to welcome him. Janoji bowed in mujra before Madhavrao, who clasped Janoji's hands in his own and led him to the special settee.

'So, tell me, Raje, what can I do for you?' Madhavrao asked Janoji.

'Shrimant, I heard that you were not keeping well. Thus, I came to meet you,' replied Janoji.

'That is indeed gracious on your part, Janoji. But I cannot help but wonder the reason behind this sudden change of heart …'

'Shrimant, this Janoji may have done a lot of things in his life, but he cannot be untrue. Whatever I have done has been done with truth and fearlessness. Had it not been for that attitude, I would never have stood against the Peshwas so many times.'

'Wah, Raje! I am really happy with this candid answer of yours. But sadly, this change in our relationship has come a tad too late. My health is not good at all, Janoji. I do not know how many days or months God has written in the diary of my life now. But I wish to tell you one thing ... I may have waged battles on you, even defeated you ... but those victories never gave me real joy. How could anyone be happy defeating their own kin, Janoji? But I had to do it. I had to answer the call of our duty towards the kingdom. Anyway, what had to happen has happened. I request you to let bygones be bygones and not harbour any ill will towards me. I have always told you that the Maratha Empire requires you. But you never believed me, owing to the influence of my uncle and Devajipant.'

'Shrimant, I heard about Dadasaheb too ... He and I go back a long way. When we met at Jejuri, you had promised to release him soon. I hope you ...'

'I remember that, Janoji,' said Madhavrao with a sigh. 'Do you think I enjoy keeping Kaka under imprisonment? It agonises me to think about it. But an administrator cannot work on the basis of emotions. Nevertheless, Kaka is no longer under my watch. I shall be releasing him as soon as I can.'

'Shrimant, even I've aged a lot now. My health also keeps see-sawing. Family matters are the same at my place as they are at yours. I'm hoping to adopt the son of my brother, Mudhoji. That might help quell the quarrels at home and bring some much-needed peace.'

'I understand and agree to your wish. I shall approve of it. But, Raje, please do not forget one thing, ever! Do not let your family break up owing to the feud for Satar's throne. It was because of this feud that Tarau imprisoned Ramraja. My father also did not give the matter as much attention as it required. Consequently, it led to the Peshwa's humiliation at Panipat. The Chhatrapati released me from imprisonment and took me to Satara. But there, too, my wish remained unfulfilled.

'I want the Chhatrapati of Satara to become great again. Please fulfil this wish of mine. You will remain unconquered only till you acquiesce to the regime of the Chhatrapati. The Chhatrapati's throne is the gem in the crown of the Maratha Empire. Don't try to remove that gem. If such an effort is made, the fates will turn against you to strip you of all your honour, power and wealth. You and the Kolhapurkars will never be able to get that throne. Power does not thrive in the marshland of emotions,' said Madhavrao.

'Shrimant, we have been talking for a long time. Please allow me to take your leave for now,' requested Janoji.

Before he bid him farewell, Madhavrao pinned a pearl aigrette to Janoji's pugree. It was a gesture beyond protocol. Janoji was suitably overwhelmed.

Madhavrao clasped Janoji's hand and said, 'Now, at least, are you convinced of my friendship and affection?'

That night, everyone got ready to go to the temple for Moreshwar's concert. Madhavrao had to take Iccharampant's and Shripati's help to even walk up to the main door, where his palanquin was waiting for him.

The temple hall was lit up with lanterns, chandeliers and rows of lamps. All the dignitaries, including Janoji Bhosale, had gathered there.

Moreshwar was sitting on the carpet laid out for him, along with his musicians. As the musicians finished tuning their instruments, Moreshwar touched Madhavrao's feet and asked, 'What do I sing for you, Shrimant?'

'Moreshwar, my health will not allow me to even sit for the entire concert. I would like you to sing anything that will help me forget this pain of mine, at least for some time. Something that will make us all introspect ...'

Moreshwar folded his hands before the idol of Lord Ganesha and started singing a soulful hymn about how all humans are minuscule before the Almighty.

⚘

It was a hot afternoon. Theur was scorching under the blaze of the merciless heat. Everything was quiet except for an occasional dog barking or a horse neighing. The base camps set up by Patwardhan, Darekar, Baramatikar and Raste went all the way up to the river, but not a murmur was heard from any of the tents. The generals and officials stood outside the mansion with worried looks on their faces. Ramshastri was due to arrive any minute; they were waiting to receive him.

Soon, Ramshastri's cavalcade came into sight. He ordered the horses to stop some distance from the mansion and started walking up. By the time he reached Nana and Pethe, Ramshastri was drenched in sweat. Wiping the rivulets of sweat streaming down his face, Ramshastri asked Nana, 'How is Shrimant's health now?'

'To be honest, it is deteriorating fast.'

'But what exactly happened for things to take such a bad turn?'

'What can I tell you, Shastribuva? A few days ago, Shrimant went to the temple for a concert. From that night on, his health has been deteriorating. His fever shows no sign of abating. He is coughing incessantly. And now, he's coughing up blood.'

'Whose medicine is he taking?'

'Nobody's! Shrimant has given up all medicines and other regulations after coming to Theur. If anyone tries to reason with him, he starts talking about the inevitability of death. Press a bit more and he flies right off the handle. Everyone is afraid of his unpredictable rage now. He won't listen to anybody. That is why we requested you to come. Shrimant holds you in high esteem. Maybe he will listen to you ...'

Followed by Nana and Mama, Ramshastri went inside to see Madhavrao. In spite of many servants bustling around, there was pin-drop silence in the corridors. As Shastribuva was about to enter the chambers, Iccharampant came outside.

Seeing him, Shastribuva asked, 'How is Shrimant's health now? Is it any better?'

'His fever has reduced a bit. He was sleeping till now. He's just woken up ...'

'Who is it?' Madhavrao called from inside.

Shastribuva went in and bowed low in mujra. Turning to Iccharampant, who had accompanied Shastribuva, Madhavrao said, 'Pant, please help me sit up.'

Iccharampant propped Madhavrao up on a bolster. Ramshastri could not bear to see this frail condition of the once-rugged Peshwa. He turned his eyes away.

'Glad to see you here, Shastribuva. I hope all is well back in Pune?' asked Madhavrao.

'Yes, Shrimant. I came to see you because I heard you were not keeping too well.'

'That's hardly news now, is it?' replied Madhavrao.

'Whose medicine have you been taking, Shrimant?' Shastribuva asked.

'The one that Lord Ganesha has prescribed!'

'Shrimant, how will you get better if you refuse medicine? Whatever the disease, proper medication can always help alleviate the pain, if not the disease itself. Nana, send for the royal physician today itself.'

'No, Shastribuva. That won't be necessary. It will not bear any results,' said Madhavrao.

'Shrimant, forgive me for talking frankly; I have no right to say anything to you, but I wish to tell you that till one is alive, one has to take care of the body properly. The scriptures also say the same thing.'

Madhavrao did not say anything.

Nana took this opportunity to duck outside and write two letters, which he dispatched on an urgent basis to Pune.

The next day, the renowned physicians, Ganga Vishnu Maheshwar, Ranchhod Naik of Terdal and Rupeshwarbuva of Satara arrived. They were followed by Dr Cunningham, whose medication Madhavrao had taken for a long time.

Dr Cunningham first examined Madhavrao. His face creased with worry on seeing Madhavrao's state.

'Doctor, everyone is advising me to restart the medication. But I want your honest opinion. Will it be worth it?'

'Sarkar, try taking medicines. If they do you good, why not?' Cunningham replied diplomatically.

The three Indian physicians were then sent inside, led by Ganga Vishnu, who was famous for being the personification of the God of medicine, Ashwinikumar. Ganga Vishnu was the one who had gone to Gangapur when Gopikabai had fallen ill. His medicine had brought immense relief to her.

Ganga Vishnu examined Madhavrao in detail. Then he pronounced, 'Shrimant, I shall be frank with you. Too many different medicines and regulations have caused more hindrance than help. It would have been helpful if you had stuck to one line of medication and regulations.'

The others present around Madhavrao were incensed to hear this stark verdict, but Madhavrao simply smiled and asked, 'Vaidyaraj, that means I do not need any more medicine now, isn't it? That's what I have been telling everyone … that no medicine is going to help me now…'

Ganga Vishnu was taken aback by Madhavrao's calm acceptance of the situation. He composed himself and said, 'No, Shrimant, nothing like that. Our duty as human beings is to keep trying till the very end.'

'Vaidyaraj, I know my disease inside out. I will take the medicine you prescribe for me, but do tell me one thing frankly. For how many more days do I have to suffer from this agony? I am ready to bear whatever you tell me, but tell me the truth. I do not fear death, but I am tired of waiting to see when death will arrive, suffering in pain till it does. And my death is not a private matter. It is going to have a multitude of repercussions on the kingdom, its administration and my subjects. For that reason, too, I need to know how much time I have. Speak fearlessly, Vaidyaraj. After God, only an expert doctor can tell his patient about the perfect state of his health.'

Madhavrao coughed as he spoke. Hari Phadke wiped off the sweat that was forming on Madhavrao's forehead.

Ganga Vishnu looked at Madhavrao intently. 'Shrimant, death cannot be foretold by anybody. Still, according to my analysis, you have around a month to live. Nana, I'll prescribe some decoctions and medicines. Be sure that Shrimant takes them on time and also follows the other regulations I will tell you.'

'Vaidyaraj, why are you taking the trouble?' Madhavrao said, interrupting Ganga Vishnu.

'As it is, death is going to come, so why prolong the wait with medicines?'

'Shrimant, these medicines are to see that whenever death comes, it comes as painlessly as possible. They may help ease your pain till the inevitable happens.'

Madhavrao was alone in his chambers. He was resting in bed. Ramabai stepped inside and sat near his feet. Madhavrao looked at her wordlessly. Ramabai covered her face with her hands and started sobbing loudly.

Madhavrao let out a deep sigh. 'Rama ...'

Ramabai's sobs intensified on hearing Madhavrao call her name.

'Rama, why are you crying? Vaidyaraj has said I will be fine in a month's time.'

'Don't lie to me! I heard everything.'

Madhavrao did not say anything in response. Ramabai wept. At one point, she fell at Madhavrao's feet and cried, 'What can I do? What shall I do?!'

Madhavrao struggled to get up. Patting his wife on the back, he tried to console her, saying, 'Rama, don't behave like this. Trust the Almighty. Who knows, by some miracle, I may even recover from this illness.'

Ramabai looked up and locked eyes with her husband. She wiped her tears determinedly. 'The Almighty? Really? Where is He? If He is indeed present, then tell me, what am I yet to do to please Him? I have done everything anybody has told me to do. What else remains to be done for you to get better? I cannot imagine how this disease came to afflict you. I hate it from the core of my heart! It has ruined the wonderful life that we could have had together!'

'Rama, how much do you detest this disease? Don't hate it so much, please. Have you realised—there cannot be a more loyal friend for a person than his disease! Whether you accept it, reject it, take care of it or ignore it, a disease will always stay with you. Please, do not hate this singular, loyal partner of your husband's …'

'You have a penchant for making light of everything,' said Ramabai, getting up to leave.

Madhavrao held her hand and asked, 'Are you angry with me?'

'No. I'm not capable of that,' replied Ramabai.

'Are you going to Pune today?' Madhavrao asked her.

The question caused Ramabai to look at her husband in panic. She answered, 'No.'

'But why? Parvati Kaku has been there alone all these days.'

Ramabai answered in a desperate tone, 'Till date, I have never asked anything of you. But today, I do ask: Please do not insist on me going to Pune. Earlier, even when your health was not good, you sent me to Gangapur. I did not refuse. You kept travelling around Pune for a year, in spite of knowing that your health could not afford it. I stayed put in Pune. Then, you came to Theur and started travelling to and fro. That caused even more deterioration to your health. Now the thought of leaving Theur scares me. I beseech you, please do not send me to Pune.'

Madhavrao felt Ramabai's hand tremble in his own. He said, 'Okay, don't go. Even I don't understand why I keep sending you to Pune, time and again. Maybe it is due to my fears about Kaka … about Narayana being too young to deal with anything unpleasant that may get thrown his way … I feel secure with someone trustworthy being around to know what is happening. And who can that be but you? I do understand your worries about my health. In fact, I also badly require you by my side when the shooting pains start in my stomach. That agony is unbearable!'

Ramabai felt Madhavrao's hand squeeze hers. His forehead was again laced with sweat.

'See, you are exerting yourself again. Please don't talk so much. Rest for a bit. Till then, I shall go to the kitchen to see if your decoctions are ready.'

'I want no decoctions, Rama!' Madhavrao cried out. 'And as for rest, I shall rest only on reaching that final destination. My life was not meant for rest. Leave all this, Rama. I am worried about Parvati Kaku being alone in Shaniwarwada. I honour her immensely. I am awed by the unshakeable faith she displays even in the face of truth. People talk nonsense about her for behaving like a married woman in spite of being widowed. But I find it extremely courageous of her to keep her faith, even when she knows it is hollow. Till date, I have done all that I could to keep her protected from cruel taunts and jibes. I did not bother about tradition and custom while trying to protect her. But now, she is alone, and I am worried for her.'

'Shall I arrange to bring Sasubai here? She is also yearning to see you,' suggested Ramabai.

'Why didn't you say this before? Who can refuse Kaku's wishes?'

'She is afraid of your temper, so …'

'Will there be no one who can really understand me? People think I am hot-tempered, a disciplinarian with an extreme affinity for justice …'

'Is it not true? During the campaign to Karnataka, when Mir Raza's camp was plundered, you ordered for the hands of the wrongdoers to be chopped off!'

'Yes, I did. But it did not please me to do so. If I had let that incident go unchecked, the tendency of plundering would have spread like wildfire across the camp, and then chaos would have ensued. Sometimes, one needs to take extreme measures to prevent a bad tendency from spreading beyond control. Rama, do not look at an incident in solitude. Try to understand my rationale behind the decisions I have taken. Remember the time Matoshree left for Gangapur? Remember when I gave a jagir to Ramchandra in spite of his mistakes? Think about how I have behaved with Kaka so far. If you think about all these things holistically, you will understand why I behaved in that manner.'

'These complex matters are beyond my understanding. Should I send for Parvati Kakusaheb?' asked Ramabai.

'Yes, please do. Her company will do you good. And, in a way, you share the same thread of grief.'

'How so?'

'She behaves like a married woman in spite of being a widow, and you behave like a widow—'

Ramabai leapt to place a hand on Madhavrao's lips and shrieked, 'What are you saying?!'

'Sorry, Rama. But listen to me. Faith is good but blind faith leads a person to nowhere but doom.'

'I shall remember that. But you also should realise one thing. You are a man. You will never understand the delicate mind and the strength of faith that a woman has. A woman's faith can move mountains. For a man to understand that he has to be born as a woman!'

Ramabai turned on her heels and walked off. Madhavrao kept looking at her, trying to understand the depth of what she had just said.

※

One afternoon, Ramshastri and Bapu went to Madhavrao's chambers, despite it being the time the Peshwa took his siesta.

'Bapu, where is Kaka?' Madhavrao asked as soon as he saw them.

'In Pune.'

'Then?' asked Madhavrao, not understanding what was so urgent.

'A letter has arrived from the north. So we had to wake you,' replied Bapu, handing the letter to Madhavrao, who accepted it with trembling hands.

'What is it?' he asked.

'It is good news. Our troops have done a marvellous job up there.'

'What?' Madhavrao exclaimed in immense joy. He started reading the letter hurriedly. His face glowed with happiness. 'I never thought I would have the good fortune of seeing this day!'

Madhavrao got up and called for his tunic and pugree. 'Come, let us go to the temple and offer our thanks to the Lord. It is all due to His blessings!'

Madhavrao held Bapu's hand and started climbing down the steps. As he reached the courtyard, all the sentries stood to attention, startled to see the Peshwa coming.

Iccharampant ran to receive Madhavrao, who charged ahead with whatever little energy he had.

It was late afternoon by the time Madhavrao returned from the temple.

Madhavrao's face did not look tired. Instead, it glowed with happiness—a rare sight after his illness had begun.

'Shrimant, can we celebrate this occasion?' Bapu asked him.

'Yes, absolutely! Not just here—we shall celebrate at Pune too. In fact, all of Maharashtra needs to celebrate this joyous occasion.'

Bapu went outside to make arrangements, and Madhavrao made his way to his room.

Just then, Madhavrao heard drums being beaten outside. He eagerly went to the window and saw a cavalcade of horses in the distance. A deafening sound filled the air. Cannonballs were being fired from near the mansion. Clarions and trumpets were being blown from the mansion's music gallery.

Madhavrao turned around with a smile, only to see Ramabai observing him from afar.

'When did you come? Sorry, I didn't realise.'

Ramabai smiled. 'I came long ago, when the drums started beating. I do not understand anything about politics, but I do understand that something has made you immensely happy. Won't you tell me what it is?'

Madhavrao held Ramabai by her shoulders and exulted, 'Rama, you are right. I am so, so happy today! Thrilled, rather. Do you know why these celebrations are going on?'

'For the victory in the north, right?' Ramabai ventured.

'It is not just for this one victory,' said Madhavrao. He pointed at a portrait of the chhatrapati on the wall. 'Shrimant Peshwa Thorle Bajirao had placed the covenants with the north, at the feet of the chhatrapati. Our Marathas had shown exemplary valour in the north; they had gone up to Attock; but suffered a humiliating defeat at Panipat. The Rohillas and the Pathans slayed the Maratha troops by the lakhs. No one thought the Marathas could ever avenge that defeat. The sting was so bad that even when the Dillipati regained the throne with the help of Shinde and Panse, it did not serve to ease the pain of that defeat. Even when the heir of Delhi's throne, Shah Alam, ascended the throne with our help, it did not make us feel satisfied enough to forget the wounds of Panipat.

'But today's news? The value of today's news cannot be described in words, Rama! The fact that our able generals, like Visaji Krushna Biniwale, Mahadaji Shinde and Tukoji Holkar, could raze the Rohillas and the Pathans to the ground has brought such an immense sense of calm to my agitated mind that I cannot describe the experience to you in words.' Madhavrao's eyes were filled with tears, but there was a beautiful smile on his face.

⚭

After the celebratory dinner that night, which saw everyone talking and laughing at length, Madhavrao retired to his bedroom. From his bed, Madhavrao could see the starlit sky. Soon, he heard the sound of drums and other instruments being played by the soldiers in the camps. Someone was singing a wonderful powada. Madhavrao went and stood near the window.

Fireworks filled the sky. Madhavrao watched them with a content heart. Just then, Ramabai came inside.

'Good, you came in time. The celebratory fireworks have just begun,' Madhavrao said.

'I have seen enough of them. You need to be in bed right this moment. Come on.'

But Madhavrao did not move. Instead, he said, 'Rama, you cannot imagine the satisfaction I am feeling today. Eleven years ago, when I was made the Peshwa, my mind was boggled by the enormity of the responsibilities that lay before me. The Peshwai was knee-deep in debt; the Maratha Empire was living in fear of my father's distinctively Brahmin style of reigning; feuds had gone from bad to worse in the chhatrapati's family; the Kolhapurkars and the Satarkars were at each other's throats; and I was so young and inexperienced. Those at home, whom we looked to for advice and help, showed us such a brutal side of themselves that I started fearing them more than the enemy outside. That moment when I had to place the aigrette representing the Peshwai on the floor and hold my uncle's footwear in my hands, just to keep the Peshwai's honour intact, caused such a searing pain in my heart and mind. But thankfully, the Lord was on my side. Today, Hyder stands defeated. The Nizam, who was the enemy of the Peshwas for generations on end, has become an ally. The Dillipati has got his throne back due to our help. The humiliating defeat at Panipat has been rightfully avenged. No dream regarding the kingdom remains unfulfilled.'

The victory in the north had charged Theur with a unique energy. The offices were buzzing with clerks running around. Letters to be dispatched to the north were being readied. They were brought to Madhavrao to be signed. Even Madhavrao was in high spirits. Except for his physical weakness, there was no sign left of the disease that had taken over his body. There was no topic being discussed in the mansion except for the victory in the north.

But one day, suddenly, Madhavrao's fever shot up. He began sweating profusely. The air of happiness in the mansion clouded over with worry. The vaidyaraj was summoned on an urgent basis. Ganga Vishnu came along with Rupeshwar and examined Madhavrao.

When he came out of Madhavrao chambers, followed by Ramshastri, Pethe and Bapu, he was unnaturally quiet.

When he did not speak for a while, Ramshastri prodded him. 'What happened, Vaidyaraj?'

'I shall give him some medicine ...' Ganga Vishnu said, without directly answering the question.

'But how did the temperature suddenly rise so much in such a short period?' Ramshastri asked.

'Suddenly?' exclaimed Rupeshwar, his eyes wide as saucers. 'Shastribuva, I'm sure all you learned people are intelligent enough to understand that this rise was not sudden. Shrimant's health was extremely delicate. He had been advised complete rest. In spite of that, he kept exerting himself, casting away all regulations with abandon. What else was going to be the outcome?'

'You are right, but who could tell Shrimant?'

'Then do not expect any miracles. Shrimant is alive purely because of his willpower. Till that willpower remains intact, we have hope,' Rupeshwar said flatly.

He handed over some medicines to Shastribuva, underlined a few regulations to be followed and left the mansion.

⋙

Madhavrao's fever showed no sign of abating. He was coughing incessantly and sweating profusely. His throat was dry. Ramabai was sitting at his bedside, wiping the sweat off his forehead, but Madhavrao was flipping like a fish out of water.

Seeing Ramabai's worried face, Madhavrao said to her, 'Don't worry, Rama. The fever will go down. I have no fear now. I wish to live.'

'Please don't speak. Vaidyaraj has asked you not to,' Ramabai pleaded.

A few moments had passed when Nana's arrival was announced.

Nana entered and bowed in mujra before the Peshwa. Madhavrao said to him, 'Nana, good you sent the letter from the north to me immediately. Does everyone back in Pune know?'

'Yes, Shrimant. We had sent a messenger all around Pune. People were thrilled to hear the news. The entire city celebrated!'

'To the chhatrapati ...?'

'As per your wishes, we sent a letter to him that very day, with Dhaakte Raosaheb's seal and signature.'

'Good. Narayanrao has a bigger responsibility on his shoulders. It is easy to win a province, but more difficult to retain and maintain one.'

'Dadasaheb Maharaj has also come along,' Nana said in an uneasy tone.

Everyone snapped to attention. Ramabai stared at Nana with fear-filled eyes, but Nana could not look at her.

'Kaka is here?' said Madhavrao. 'Then why is he standing outside? Such telepathy, I tell you … In the last two days, I must have remembered him at least a thousand times. Please bring him inside.'

As Raghobadada came in, Ramabai cursorily took his blessings and went to the inner chambers. Madhavrao folded his hands to his uncle, still lying in bed. But Raghobadada did not come up to him. He stood rooted to his spot, not willing to meet Madhavrao's eyes.

Nana swallowed hard and said, 'Shrimant, I'm helpless. Please forgive me. I know your health is not good at all. I also know that I shouldn't be telling you anything that will disturb you. But some things went beyond my control …'

'What has happened? Speak up, Nana. Don't be afraid,' said Madhavrao.

'Shrimant, we were all busy celebrating the victory in the north. Using that opportunity, Dadasaheb tried to escape his house arrest. We happened to check on him in time, or else, he would have escaped from our hold long ago. Much against our wishes, we had to arrest Dadasaheb again. We could not take a decision about this delicate matter on our own. Thus, we had to come and trouble you. We had no option but to summon Dadasaheb before you. Please forgive us all.'

There was pin-drop silence in the room. In spite of his high temperature, Madhavrao sat up. Raghobadada was standing with his head bowed low.

Madhavrao cast a glance at everyone present in the room and then said to Nana, 'Nana, send a letter to Satara immediately. I had asked them to send the ceremonial robes of the Peshwai for Narayanrao. Tell them to cancel that and, instead, send the robes for Kaka. Let me also have the good fortune of seeing Kaka become the Peshwa.'

'Madhava!' exclaimed Raghoba, taking a step forward. 'What are you saying? I have no ambition of becoming the Peshwa.'

'Enough, Kaka!' Madhavrao bellowed with whatever little strength was left in him. 'I am in no state to have any arguments or play any mind games with you. Death is hovering over me. I have tried everything to make you see sense. But I suppose that is never going to happen.'

'No, Madhava, please believe me ... I did not do all this to snatch the Peshwai for myself. Really, I do not wish to rule—'

'Stop it!' roared Madhavrao. His body was trembling, and his face was contorted with immense rage. 'You don't want to rule, but you want to revolt. You don't want responsibilities, but you want indiscipline and indulgences. I requested you to become the Peshwa thrice. But you rejected my requests. Sorry, Kaka, but I can take this no more. Did I have no other work than to keep indulging the whims and fancies of my errant uncle? Had it been someone else in your place ...'

'Then what, Madhava?' Raghoba asked in fear.

'Are you really asking me this, Kaka? Do I really need to spell it out? All right, I will tell you. If it were anyone else in your place, I would have hammered his head into pieces! Even if it had been my own son!'

The tirade caused Madhavrao to fall into a helpless coughing bout. Dhere ran up to him with a glass of water. Madhavrao sipped in silence.

Taking that opportunity, Raghobadada said, 'Madhava, you need to rest now. We shall talk later. Allow me to take your leave.'

Before Madhavrao could reply, Ramabai called out from inside, 'Wait, Mamanji!'

Everyone turned as Ramabai came into the room. She looked at Raghobadada determinedly and said, 'Speak up, Mamanji. Do not leave this discussion incomplete today. The Peshwa has no strength in him to bear it anymore.'

'Daughter!' Raghobadada cried out in anguish. 'Why are you talking like this? Am I such a sinner?'

Unable to bear the torment that his own mind was causing him, Raghobadada started crying. Madhavrao said to him, 'Kaka, don't cry. I have no strength for all this. You revolted against the Maratha Empire not once but thrice. I tried everything I could to control you, to keep your dangerous activities in check. But nothing seems to have worked. I did know that you had a fondness for the Mughal lavishes, but I didn't know you also had their traits in your blood. It is their norm that when a father lies on his deathbed, his sons stages a revolt without even waiting for him to die. It seems you are following in their footsteps …'

'Madhava, please! Please do not say that!' cried out Raghoba.

'I am not saying this in anger. I am not even saying this with sarcasm. In fact, I am requesting you to not stage another revolt. Take on the role of the Peshwa and sit on the throne. I shall be happy to see you do that while I am still alive.'

'Madhava, what do I tell you? I really never wished for the throne. I know I have erred many times. These hangers-on poison my ears for their own lowly gains, and I get carried away. But really, I am not the greedy, conniving man that you make me out to be.'

'I know that too, Kaka. But it is also true that your heart does not find solace in good company and correct advice. Finally, it is up to us whom we listen to. Anyway, there's no point in telling you all this. Narayana is young. He is hot-headed and inexperienced. I do not think he is capable of handling the overbearing responsibility of the Peshwai. It is best that you—'

'I shall not take on that responsibility, Madhava! I prefer death over snatching the throne from you or Narayana. And now, I also do not wish to go back to Pune. If you wish, sentence me to death and finish this chapter, once and for all. Or, let me stay here. It is your decision. But don't send me back, please.'

'From today onwards, you are free, Kaka. I release you. You may stay here if you wish. Bapu is also here. He will give you proper advice. Now, I wish to rest. Gajanana ...' said Madhavrao, closing his eyes, unable to bear the immense strain he had been subjected to.

Ramabai ran forward to hold Madhavrao's hand and lay him down on the bed.

⚝

Madhavrao decided to visit the Ganesha temple. But as he stepped inside, Madhavrao's condition worsened beyond belief. His fever suddenly escalated unnaturally. He started burning from the heat. His stomach twisted in pain, and he screamed like an animal being butchered.

Madhavrao's disease had made his body hollow from within. He had no strength left to bear anything. Ramshastri, Bapu, Raghobadada and Sakharampant were agonised to see Madhavrao's worsening health, but there was nothing they could do. Ramabai was staying alive only on gomutra—she had forsaken food. Her lips had gone dry from praying to all the gods possible.

As he lay contorted before the idol, Madhavrao screamed, 'Gajanana, how long are you going to test me like this? Please release me … please … I cannot take it any more!'

Iccharampant tried to hold down Madhavrao's body. Suddenly, Madhavrao screamed, 'Where is Kaka? Call him now!'

Iccharampant gestured to Shripati. He immediately ran outside to fetch Raghoba.

Raghoba was sitting with Nana, Pethe and Bapu in an adjacent room. 'Sarkar, come fast …' Shripati said.

'Why? What happened?' asked Raghoba, getting up in an instant.

'Shrimant Sarkar is in tremendous pain. He has called for you.'

Raghobadada banged the heel of his palm against his forehead and exclaimed, 'Oh no! What a fool I am! Two days ago, Madhava was screaming in pain and was asking for a dagger to kill himself. That time, I stopped him, saying that if his pain did not lessen in the next two days, I would give him the dagger myself. How can I now go before him? Shripati, I cannot ... You go ...'

Shripati went back in. Madhavrao was swooning, but as he saw Shripati coming, he asked, 'Has Kaka come?'

Shripati only bowed his head low in reply. Madhavrao smiled. 'I know why Kaka is not coming in front of me. What a coward!' He yelled as the pain went searing through his body.

Iccharampant kept wiping his sweat, and said to Madhavrao with tears in his eyes, 'Shrimant, please calm down.'

'That is what I am going to do, Iccharam,' Madhavrao said in a painful slur. 'Give me my dagger.'

Iccharampant stepped back in fright.

'Iccharam, did you not hear what I said? It is the Peshwa's order.' Iccharampant placed both his hands over his ears.

'Oh! So your daring has reached this level? Shripati, bring my whip!'

Shripati ran outside and returned with Madhavrao's whip. His face was full of fear.

'Why are you looking at my face? Whip Iccharam's back! Come on, don't waste my time,' Madhavrao commanded.

Shripati bit his lips and, with a very heavy heart, brought the whip down on Iccharampant's back.

'Once more!'

Another lashing …

'Once more!'

Another lashing …

Madhavrao kept yelling, even as Iccharampant kept taking the lashes. It was getting difficult for him to stand upright, but he bore the punishment silently.

Maina happened to enter the room. She took in the sight before her and ran outside without a word. Narayanrao was dozing off in the courtyard. He had stayed up with Madhavrao the whole night, and was resting for a while now. When Maina asked him to go inside, he was stunned to see Iccharampant sprawled on the floor, the back of his tunic wet with fresh blood.

Madhavrao turned his head to see who had come. That is when he noticed the blood-soaked Iccharampant. Understanding the magnitude of what he had done, Madhavrao's eyes filled with tears. His lips began trembling.

Iccharampant stumbled up and looked at Madhavrao. Seeing the tears in the Peshwa's eyes, he hobbled forward. Wiping Madhavrao's tears with his hands, Iccharampant said, 'Shrimant, please don't cry. Vaidyaraj has asked you to not take stress of any kind.'

Madhavrao clasped Iccharampant's hands in his own and cried out, 'Iccharam … this dastardly pain made me do what I would never have dreamt of doing! Please, forgive me!'

Then he called out to Narayanrao, 'Narayana, come here!'

As his younger brother came closer, Madhavrao put his hand in Iccharampant's hand and said, 'I am handing over the heir of the Peshwas to you. Please take good care of him. Promise me you will!'

'Shrimant! I swear with Lord Ganesha as my witness ... I shall take Dhaakte Shrimant under my wing. I shall protect him like an eagle protects its young. Please do not worry about him.'

Madhavrao shut his eyes and murmured, 'Now I have no worry about Narayana ...'

❈

Maina came running into Ramabai's chamber. Ramabai was sitting in front of an idol, chanting a mantra.

'Akkasaab! Come fast!'

Ramabai looked at her and remarked, 'What happened to you?'

'Akkasaab, Sarkar is writhing in pain. He is not listening to anyone. He ordered Shripati to give a terrible lashing to Iccharampant.'

'What?! Why?' shrieked Ramabai.

'Because ... Pant refused to give a dagger to Shrimant ...' Maina replied, her head bowed low.

Ramabai placed her prayer beads in a salver and rushed out to see Madhavrao.

Seeing Ramabai, Iccharampant lowered his head. Haripant Phadke also got up. Both of them left the room. Ramabai did not miss the blood-soaked back of Iccharampant as he walked out.

Madhavrao looked at his wife. She had become even more gaunt and frail due to her constant fasts. Her face was contorted in pain. Madhavrao could no longer meet her gaze.

Ramabai sat next to him and murmured, 'Why did you behave like this?'

'Rama! You can never imagine the pain that is searing through my body. Do you think I like behaving like this?'

'I understand, but is that any reason to mete out this injustice to a loyal man like Pant? I have been hearing this for the last four days ... You want a dagger, isn't it? Okay. I shall give you one. Why take so much trouble for one little thing?'

Madhavrao looked at Ramabai, startled. 'How do you have a dagger? Who gave it to you?' he asked.

'Don't worry. In the past, when the Nizam had plundered Pune, Sasubai and I had to go to Sinhagad. Sasubai gave it to me then, for my defence. If you wish, I can bring it to you. I have no right to tell you what you should and should not do, but I will tell you one thing. Remember that whatever you do is being witnessed by Lord Ganesha Himself.'

'I am sorry, Rama. I promise you I will not behave like this. Please don't be angry with me.'

'I have never been angry with you. You know that,' she replied.

'Rama, don't leave. When this pain starts when you are not around, it becomes impossible for me to bear it alone. Your presence gives me a lot of courage to face my pain. As it is, I don't think I will have to bear it for too many days now ...'

Madhavrao dozed off while speaking. Ramabai left and walked rapidly to the room that was given to the royal physicians for their stay in Theur.

As she entered, Ramabai saw Rupeshwarbaba busy creating some medicinal potion.

Rupeshwarbaba was shocked to see that it was the Peshwa's wife. Till date, Ramabai had never come to confront him directly like this. He averted his eyes.

'Vaidyaraj, I consider you the embodiment of the God of medicine, Ashwinikumar. I can no longer survive on false hopes. I have come here to know the truth from you.'

Vaidyaraj began trembling on hearing Ramabai's demand. Somehow, he mumbled, 'Baisaheb, Shrimant shall soon be all right ...'

'The truth, Vaidyaraj! Lord Ganesha is your witness here!' Ramabai interjected in a firm voice.

Rupeshwar did not know how to break the truth to her. But seeing the determined Ramabai in front of him, he finally revealed, 'Baisaheb, if you insist ... these hands can no longer assure you of a successful outcome. We are in the Lord's temple. Now, the final decision rests with only Him.'

As Rupeshwar raised his head to look at Ramabai, he saw that she had already gone.

⚯

Ramabai held on to her courage until she reached her room. But on seeing the idols on the little altar there, she broke down. She didn't know how long she had been sobbing till someone touched her shoulder and said, 'Daughter ...'

Ramabai turned her tear-streaked face to see Parvatibai sitting behind her. Ramabai let out a bigger sob and rushed into her embrace.

'What do I do, Sasubai? What do I do?!'

Parvatibai could not say anything. Tears began running down her face too. Finally, in a choked voice, she said, 'Have patience, my child. God will listen to your prayers.'

'No, Sasubai! He has turned a deaf ear to all my pleas. I did everything I could ... but my luck fell short.' She howled like an animal in pain.

'Rama, please don't behave like this. Look at me ... What can I do to lessen your pain? See, for a woman, nothing is more important than the symbols that proclaim her to be a married woman with her husband alive. For you and Madhava, I am even willing to do this ...'

Parvatibai took a finger to wipe off the kumkum from her own forehead and reached forward to apply it to Ramabai's clear forehead. A startled Ramabai stumbled back and cried out, 'No! Please don't!'

In an instant, Parvatibai realised where Ramabai's fear stemmed from. She consoled her, saying, 'I'm sorry, daughter. I should have realised ... At such a crucial time, a cursed symbol also evokes fear in one's heart.'

As Parvatibai bowed her head low, Ramabai realised what a dent her reaction must have caused in her mother-in-law's heart. She instantly walked forward and said, 'Till date, I have never refused anything that you have asked of me. But please forgive me today, Sasubai. I do realise the magnitude of the gift you were offering me. No woman can ever have such a large heart. But please forgive me ...'

Ramabai got up and called out to old Ramji. As he came huffing along, Ramabai said to him, 'Ramji, I have some work for you. But it needs to be kept strictly confidential. Will you do it?'

'Absolutely, Akkasaab.'

'Promise me, you will not let anybody know about it.'

'Akkasaab, do you not trust this old servant of yours? I have seen you from the time you were a child. You can trust me completely.'

'I do trust you immensely, Ramji. But it is quite a delicate task. So I want to be assured of complete secrecy.'

'I promise you, Akkasaab.'

'Okay. You do know how to ride a horse, don't you?' Ramabai asked Ramji.

'What, Akkasaab? Are you teasing me now? Of course, I do. Don't go by my age.'

'Good. Then get on a horse right now, go to Pune and get me the ceremonial garb for the ritual of sati.'

'Akkasaab!' Ramji cried out, unable to believe what he was hearing.

'Keep quiet, Ramji. Do as I have told you. I'll be waiting for you. Go on now ...'

Before the sun set that day, Ramji, along with a few horsemen, rushed to Pune.

❊

Madhavrao's health seemed beyond help. His body was swelling up. Fever and the intrinsic heat showed no signs of abating. Realising the gravity of the situation, the temple was fortified from all ends to keep out the crowds. People were banned from entering the temple's courtyard, lest Madhavrao be disturbed by their chatter. Generals came from all over and set up their camps in Theur.

One day, Madhavrao called for Raghobadada.

'Kaka, I will go any day now …' Madhavrao said.

'Madhava, don't lose heart. Trust the Lord.'

'Kaka, that's what I am saying. Let the Lord be witness to whatever happens now. Please keep my bed in front of the Lord's idol.'

The next morning, Madhavrao sent for everyone. He wore a clean tunic and salwar, a pugree on his head and a scarf over it. He sat reclined against a bolster, propping up his weak body with a lot of effort, as several Brahmins conducted the anushthaan ritual in the sanctum sanctorum. Madhavrao observed the ritual from his bed.

Nana Phadnis, Morobadada Phadnis, Haripant Phadke, Khasgiwale, Sakharambapu and Panse congregated near Madhavrao. Shastribuva had arrived before all of them. Accepting their mujras, Madhavrao requested them to sit down.

'Today, I have called you all here with a purpose. I know that I will not be alive to trouble you all for too long.'

'Shrimant!' Shastribuva said in an agonised voice.

But Madhavrao gestured for him to stop, and said, 'Let me talk, Buva. I have no worry about the kingdom now. I do not think Hyder will dare raise his head again. The victory in the north has brought immense peace to me. That victory is not mine—it is yours. You have to maintain it carefully. I have finished almost all the work the Lord ordained for me. But three things remain …'

Nana stepped forward. 'Shrimant, please do not hesitate. All your wishes shall be fulfilled. If at all they are beyond our reach, we shall tell you so. But do not keep anything in your heart now.'

Madhavrao breathed deeply. 'First, raze the Gilchis to the ground. Until that happens, I will not feel that the insult of Panipat has been avenged completely. Then, raze Hyder to the ground. I could not do that in spite of trying thrice. And third, my debts … I had to take a lot of loans to run the kingdom. I could not repay those in my lifetime. But please see to it that all the debts are settled. Till that happens, my soul will not rest in peace.'

Everyone stood in silence, their eyes filled with tears. Finally, Nana wiped his eyes and said, 'Shrimant, do not worry. We shall treat your wishes as the wishes of the Lord Himself.'

He signalled to Ramchandra Naik, who came ahead with a pile of letters that he presented to the Peshwa.

'What is this?' asked Madhavrao.

'Shrimant, we knew that you were always keen on settling these debts. Hence, we have prepared guarantees worth twenty-five lakh rupees to settle debts to that tune. The rest of the money shall be repaid accordingly.'

Madhavrao's gaunt face broke into a smile.

⌘

Ganga Vishnu and Rupeshwarbaba came the next day to check on Madhavrao. Madhavrao's body and face looked even more swollen than before.

Once they were done examining him, Madhavrao said, 'Vaidyaraj, I know that after my health started deteriorating, a lot of people began speaking ill of you. But, please, do not heed them. It is a doctor's fate to be praised when the patient gets better and heckled when he succumbs to his destiny. Death is inevitable and only in the hands of God. But God does not like to take the blame for it.'

'Shrimant, please don't lose hope. We have seen patients getting better from diseases even worse than yours,' Rupeshwar replied.

Madhavrao smiled sadly. 'What an ego, Vaidyaraj! Maybe you are saying this to pacify me. But I have just one request. I know what my condition is. When my end comes near, I don't care what else happens to my body, but please see to it that my speech remains clear to take Lord Ganesha's name.'

A commotion was heard outside the temple. Madhavrao craned his neck and asked, 'What is all this noise?'

'Madhava, people have been coming from Pune in hordes to meet you. We are having a tough time controlling them,' explained Raghoba.

'Why control them, Kaka? Let them come inside. I would also like to meet them.'

After receiving Madhavrao's permission, people started streaming in quietly to meet him. Raste was one of them.

Seeing Raste Mama, Madhavrao frowned and asked, 'Mama, who is keeping watch over Shaniwarwada when all of you trusted officials are here? I had left Shaniwarwada in your care, isn't it?'

In spite of his weak health, Madhavrao's rage was just as potent as always. Malharrao Raste shook with fear but somehow answered, 'Shrimant, please forgive me, but my condition was no different from that of other people. A messenger comes from Theur and purchases the garb of sati. What are we to glean from this? How can we hold on? The day that messenger came to Pune, everyone was on tenterhooks. Shops were closed. The city was abuzz with rumours ...'

Hearing the word 'sati', Madhavrao's rage flared up in an instant. His first thought was that someone had deliberately spread the rumour of his death for selfish gains—someone like Raghobadada.

'Kaka!' he called out.

But Raghoba folded his hands and said, 'No, Madhava. I have not done anything. Believe me.'

Madhavrao turned to Nana Phadnis and commanded, 'Find out who went to Pune and summon him before me.'

⚮

Two days went by. No one dared face Madhavrao. Nana Phadnis was very worried for Madhavrao's health. As if the fever and weakness were not enough, Madhavrao was now fuming like a raging bull.

Finally, Ramji came to Nana. 'Nana, I can bear it no more. So I have come myself,' he said.

'What are you talking about?'

'I was the one who got the sati garb. Whatever happens now ... I could no longer hold myself back from confessing.'

'Who sent you?' asked Nana.

'That I will not tell you, even if I'm sentenced to death! Take me before Sarkar.'

They both set out to meet Madhavrao.

'Ramji, good you came,' said Madhavrao. 'I hardly see you these days.'

Nana gulped and said, 'Shrimant, he is the one who went to Pune.'

Madhavrao could not believe his ears. In an instant, his weakness was replaced by a stern expression. He looked at Ramji and asked, 'Is that true?'

Ramji merely nodded in affirmation.

'Who told you to do that?' Madhavrao screamed.

Ramji refused to say a word. Madhavrao's rage escalated.

'Oh! So your daring has reached these heights, is it? Nana, chop off his hands!'

Without a word, Ramji held his hands out before Nana. His face bore no expression of fear or regret.

Suddenly, someone called out: 'Wait!'

Madhavrao turned to see Ramabai approaching them rapidly. Everyone backed away with hurried mujras as Ramabai rushed towards her husband.

'If you want to punish someone for this crime, punish me!' she cried.

'You? For what?' Madhavrao asked incredulously.

'For telling Ramji to get the sati garb for me. He went because I told him to.'

Madhavrao's face softened.

Ramabai signalled to Ramji and Nana to leave. She sat down next to Madhavrao, who said to her in a choked voice, 'Rama, may your penance get its due reward. Rama, you won't believe it, but when I was having my will prepared, for some inexplicable reason, I could not write anything for you.

I could have left the entire kingdom and its riches to you …
but somehow, my heart told me that you will not live after
I am gone.'

'What more can I ask for? This trust that you have reposed
in me is the validation of our love,' replied Ramabai, her
voice choked with emotion.

⊠

It was a Wednesday. Madhavrao was alert and completely in
his senses. He called for all his generals and special officials.

Madhavrao also called out for Bapu.

Wiping his tears, Bapu came to him. 'Shrimant, I cannot
bear to see your pain any more.'

'No, Bapu. I have gone far beyond feeling the pain in my
body. I am just very happy to see you all. But …'

'But what, Shrimant?'

'Bapu, everyone who supported me in my career is here.
But the one person who gave birth to me, who raised me …
Matoshree … I am bereft of meeting her. There is not one
day when I do not remember her. After I go, please tell her
that her son pined for her till his last breath.'

Then Madhavrao called out to Shripati and Maina. He said
to Patwardhan, 'These two have served me well. At Aalegaon,
when I was put under imprisonment with two thousand
Gardis keeping watch, only Shripati stood by me. I was keen
to see the wedding of Shripati and Maina, but now please
fulfil this wish of mine after I go. Take good care of them.'

Maina and Shripati stood near Madhavrao's feet, tears
streaming down their faces.

'Narayana … Come here …' Madhavrao called out to his brother.

When Narayanrao came close, Madhavrao said to him, 'Narayana, you are not a child any more. You have a big responsibility on your shoulders. Act according to Kaka and Sakharambapu's advice. Your temper has always been a cause of worry for me. Rein it in. A temperamental attitude looks good only on an achiever. Achieve something … Achieve a lot, my brother.'

Then he called out to Raghobadada. 'Kaka …'

Madhavrao placed Narayanrao's hand in Raghoba's and said, 'Kaka, I am leaving Narayana in your hands. He is stubborn, but please bear with him. Even though he may be the next Peshwa, I am leaving you with the responsibility of having the final say in all decisions. But please treat Narayana like your own son. I will then be free to die in peace.'

'No, no, Madhava … Don't speak like this … Narayana is my blood. He is like a son to me. I swear in front of Lord Ganesha, I shall treat him like a son.'

Madhavrao smiled sadly. 'How I wish I could believe this oath of yours, Kaka! I would have died taking your name in place of Lord Ganesha's. Anyway, now everything is in your hands. Take care.'

Turning to his generals, Madhavrao said, 'Till date, you have upheld the Maratha Empire with each other's help and mutual respect. Continue to do so. Don't harbour any negative thoughts in your mind.'

Ramabai, Parvatibai, Raghoba, Gangabai, Dhere, Bapu and Nana had all gathered at Madhavrao's bedside, sobbing. The whole courtyard was full of people.

Madhavrao called for the Brahmins.

When they came, he folded his hands and said, 'I am leaving. Please make preparations for my final journey.'

Chaos ensued on hearing this proclamation. Everyone began to wail. Madhavrao could hear nothing any more. He had gone into a trance, taking the Lord's name.

'Gajanana, Gajanana …' he kept chanting.

In the sanctum, a constant stream of holy water was being poured on the Ganesha's idol. The Brahmins were trying their best to concentrate on the mantras that they were chanting.

At one point, someone realised that the holy water being poured was almost over. He fumbled to get more water, taking a tumbler in his hand …

He got the water hurriedly and just then, Ramabai howled like a wounded animal.

The tumbler fell from the man's hand and the water lay spilt in front of Lord Ganesha.

⊠

It was afternoon, but Theur was still cold. All roads leading to Theur were crowded with people wanting to see their Peshwa one last time. Sobs and cries filled the air.

Madhavrao's corpse was kept in the courtyard of the temple. With his eyes closed and his body wrapped in a woollen shawl, it seemed as if Madhavrao was finally sleeping peacefully after months of suffering. Iccharampant Dhere and Patwardhan sat near the corpse, tears streaming down their faces.

The womenfolk could be heard in the adjacent rooms, beating their chests in grief. Crowds were coming and bustling along to see Madhavrao, but there was no commotion. It was as if everyone was taking due care not to disturb Madhavrao's sleep.

Raghobadada sat hunched on the steps of the temple, head thrust between his knees. Ramshastri and Sakharambapu were standing close by. Nana brought a broken, frightened Narayanrao before Raghobadada and called out, 'Dadasaheb ...'

Raghoba looked up and saw Narayana staring at him with solemn eyes. Instinctively, Raghoba opened his arms to embrace his nephew. Holding Narayanrao close to his chest, Raghoba cried out, 'Narayana, my Madhava has gone! He is gone forever!'

Ramshastri managed to wipe his tears and said to Raghoba, 'Dadasaheb, please control yourself. If you behave like this, who will this child look to?'

The chaos in the women's chambers suddenly stopped. Everyone turned to see what had happened. They saw Ramabai entering the courtyard.

Ramabai walked with slow, measured steps. She wore a silk saree in white. She had just taken a bath, so her hair was wet and hung loose over her back. She wore pearl- and diamond-studded earrings, coupled with a diamond choker and a ruby tanmani around her neck. Her fair arms were adorned with glass bangles. A diamond nath shone on her nose. Her forehead bore a crescent-shaped kumkum along with a green dot.

She seemed unaffected by the crying and sobbing that was going on around her. She calmly went up to Madhavrao's corpse and started fanning him with a peacock-feathered fan.

Everyone was devastated and terrified to see Ramabai in this avatar. They looked on wordlessly.

Ramshastri turned to Narayanrao and said to him, 'Shrimant, the women have already tried their best to dissuade Ramabai. I cannot think of anyone apart from you now.'

Narayanrao ran towards Ramabai and cried out, 'Vahini!'

He fell at her feet and holding them tightly, sobbed, 'Vahini, don't do this, please. I beseech you.'

Ramabai's eyes grew misty as she looked at her young brother-in-law. He had been like a son to her. He was as much hers as he was Madhavrao's. But nothing could make her change her mind.

'Narayanrao, get up. You are not a child anymore. You are the swami of this kingdom. The ruler. And it does not behove a ruler to cry and grovel like this. If the Peshwa were to see these tears just now, what would he have said?'

Narayanrao looked at her, agape.

Ramabai's face creased into a smile as she said, 'Come on. Prepare for my last journey.'

※

The news of Ramabai preparing for sati spread like wildfire.

Composing himself and answering the call of duty, Nana took charge of the preparations.

By now, it was afternoon. People were thronging to take a final glance at Madhavrao and Ramabai. Forgetting all barriers of caste and creed, people rushed to touch Ramabai's feet. Ramabai was giving away every piece of jewellery she was wearing to whomever came in front of her.

When Ramshastri and Iccharampant came forward and Ramshastri went to touch Ramabai's feet, she stopped him, saying, 'Shastribuva, I have always seen him taking your blessings. Please accord me the same honour.'

'No, Matoshree. I do not have that authority now. Today, even the gods will bow in front of you. Please, bless me.'

As Shastribuva took her blessings, Ramabai removed a diamond ring from her finger and gave it to him.

All preparations were complete. Ramabai went to the doorway of the temple. Narayanrao and Gangabai fell at her feet, sobbing. She cupped their faces in her hands and turned to Raghobadada, saying, 'He already requested you, but I shall request once more. Please take good care of these children. They are immature. Take them under your wing.'

Wordlessly, Raghobadada embraced Narayanrao. Ramabai removed her nath and handed it to Gangabai, saying, 'Be careful with this. Sasubai had given this to me.'

The procession to the riverbank began. Ramabai walked behind the palanquin.

The whole road was guarded by sentries. The Maratha generals wore white turbans; the Brahmins wore only dhotis. The riverbank was full of people. The river flowed oblivious to the storm raging in everyone's hearts.

A sandalwood pyre was erected on the bank. Ramabai completed the rituals, went around the pyre and then stood on a plank that was kept for her near the pyre.

Suddenly, Maina came running like the wind and hugged Ramabai. She could control her tears no longer.

Ramabai patted her on the back and said, 'Maina, don't cry. I wanted to see your wedding, but I am sure you and Shripati will have a happy married life. I bless you for the same.' She took off her earrings and handed them to Maina. 'Keep these as a token of my remembrance. Now, let me go.'

Ramabai was absolved of all her jewellery, except for the mangalsutra around her neck.

Ramabai folded her hands to everyone present and climbed a ladder to enter the funeral pyre. Calmly, she placed Madhavrao's head on her lap. The crowd screamed and cried, but Ramabai was oblivious to it all.

She looked up to see the silvery river her husband had once described to her. It glistened, just as he had mentioned. Ramabai kept looking at the river, etching it in her heart.

Suddenly, the scene in front of her started growing hazy. In a few moments, all she could see before her were the flames leaping up to touch the sky.

The pyre had been lit. The sandalwood logs burst apart. The flames rose higher.

The last thing everyone saw was a piece of silky white cloth fluttering in the air before the flames gulped it up.